SAINT NICHOLAS AND the HOUSE of MYRA

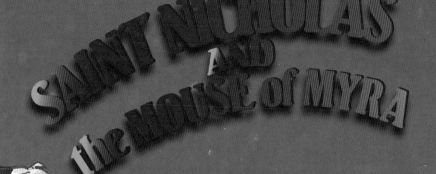

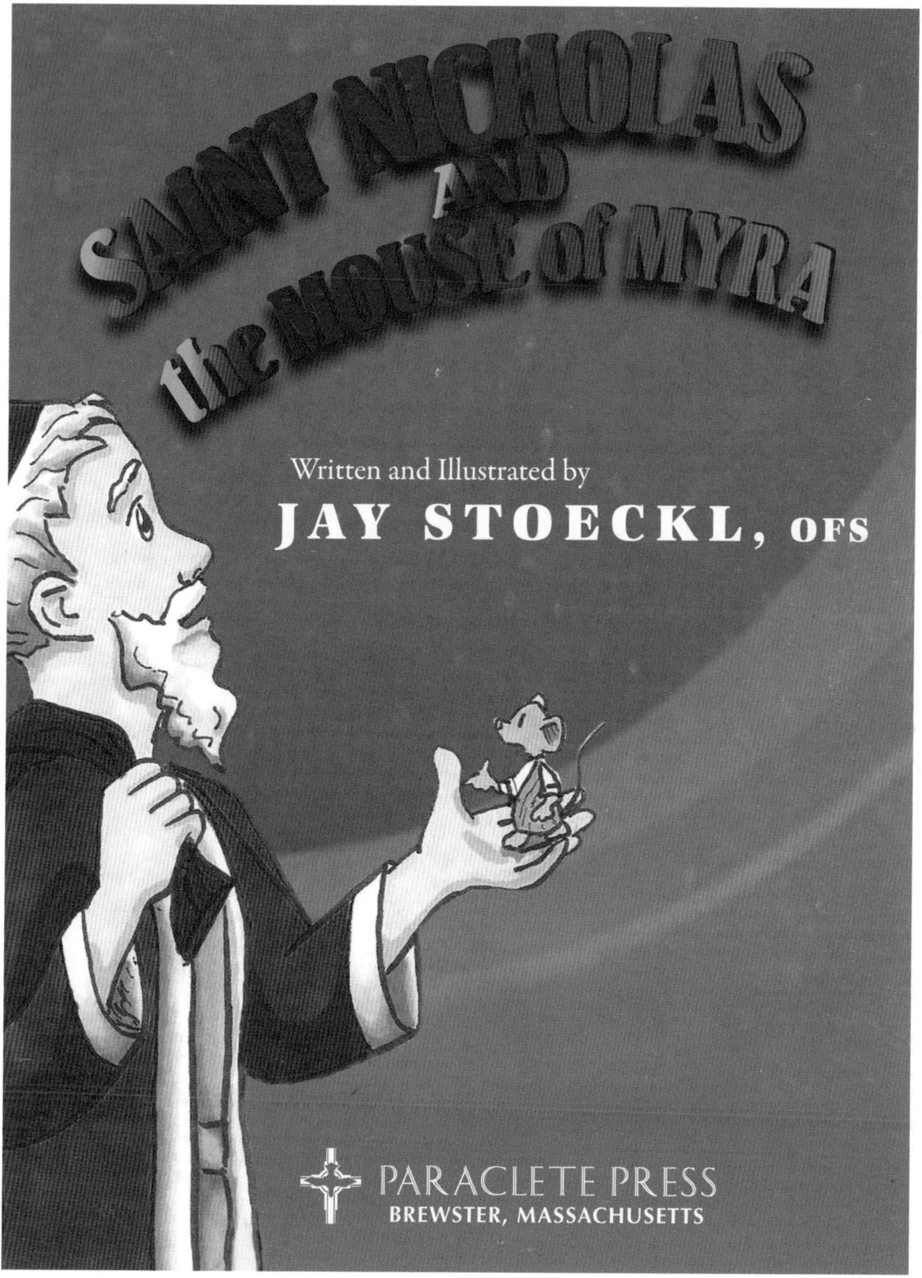

SAINT NICHOLAS AND the MOUSE of MYRA

Written and Illustrated by

JAY STOECKL, OFS

 PARACLETE PRESS
BREWSTER, MASSACHUSETTS

This book is dedicated

to my Father

Paul T. Stoeckl

who always loved Christmas

2014 First Printing

Saint Nicholas and the Mouse of Myra

Copyright © 2014 by James Raymond Stoeckl

ISBN 978-1-61261-470-0

Coloring by Jennifer L. Stoeckl and friends.

The Paraclete Press name and logo (dove on cross) are trademarks of Paraclete Press, Inc.

Library of Congress Cataloging-in-Publication Data

Stoeckl, Jay, OFS.
    Saint Nicholas and the Mouse of Myra / written and illustrated by Jay Stoeckl, OFS.
        pages cm
    ISBN 978-1-61261-470-0 (trade pbk.)
    1. Nicholas, Saint, Bishop of Myra--Juvenile literature. I. Title.
    BR1720.N46S76 2014
    270.2092--dc23   2014009444

10 9 8 7 6 5 4 3 2 1

Published by Paraclete Press
Brewster, Massachusetts
www.paracletepress.com
Printed in the United States of America

CHAPTER ONE
THE ADVENT OF NICHOLAS

I saw the Lord always before me,
for he is at my right hand so that I will not be shaken;
therefore my heart was glad, and my tongue rejoiced;
moreover, my flesh will live in hope.
For you will not abandon my soul to Hades,
or let your Holy One experience corruption.
—ACTS 2:25-28

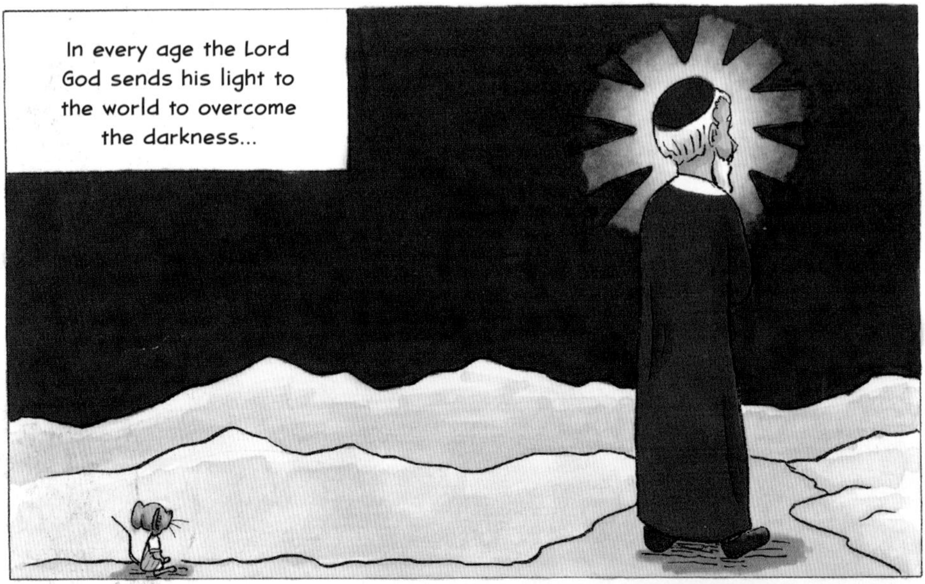
In every age the Lord God sends his light to the world to overcome the darkness...

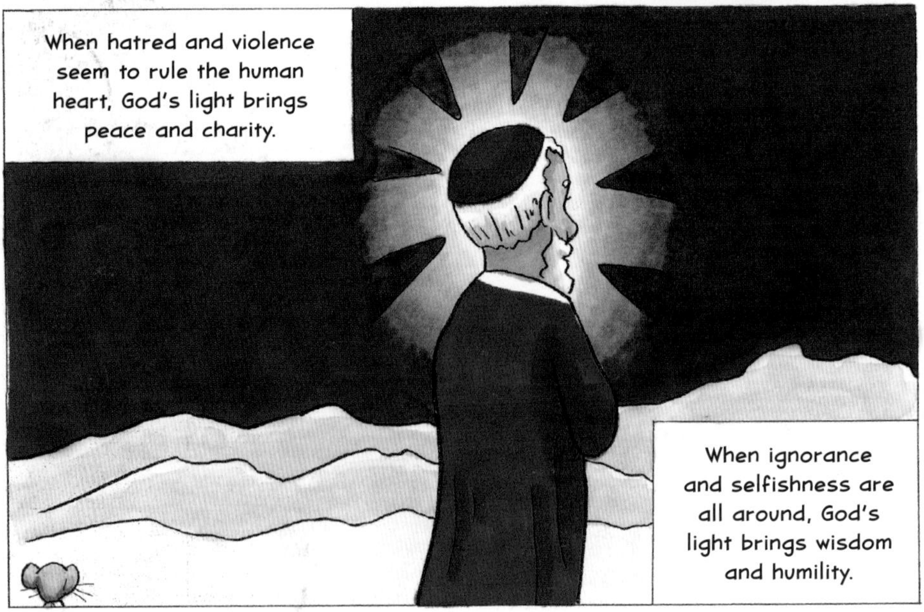
When hatred and violence seem to rule the human heart, God's light brings peace and charity.
When ignorance and selfishness are all around, God's light brings wisdom and humility.

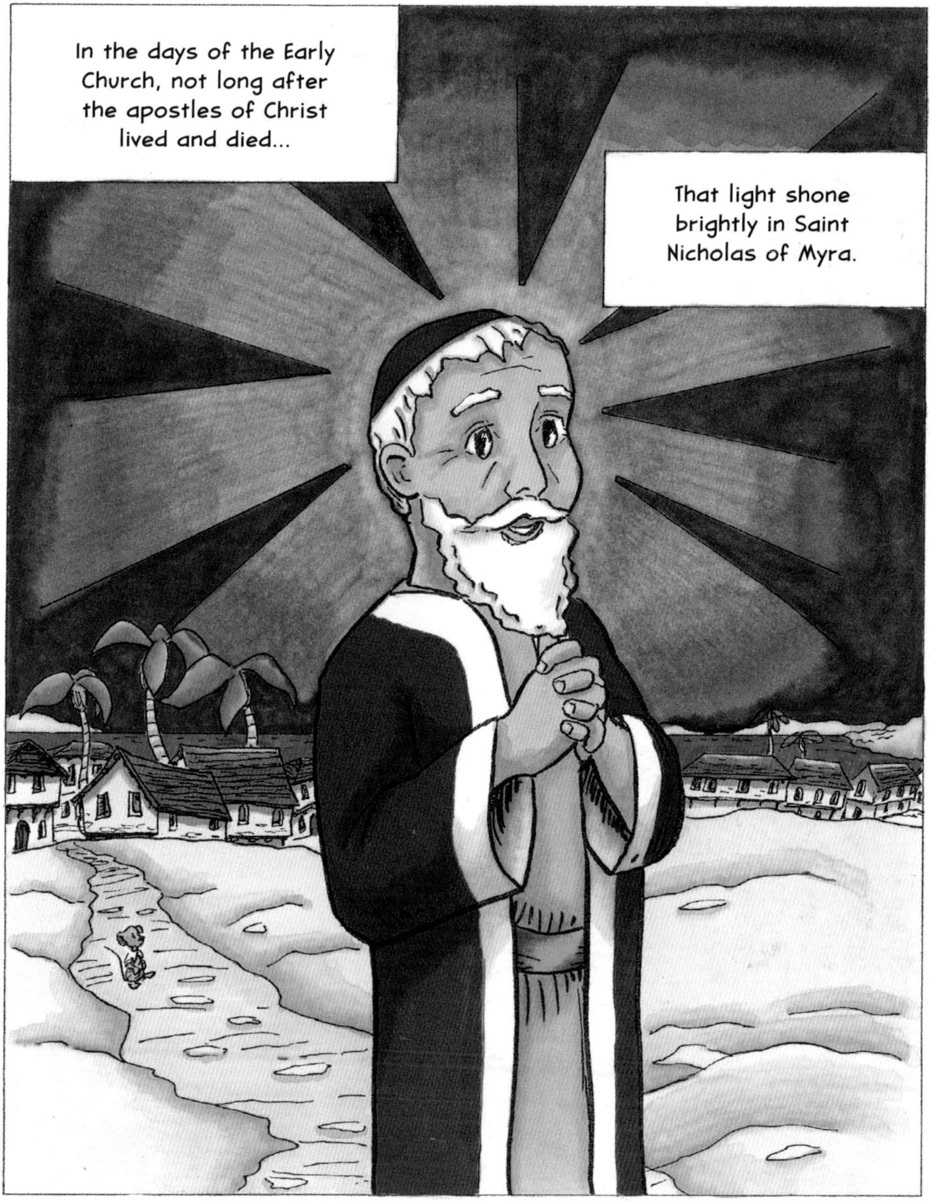
In the days of the Early Church, not long after the apostles of Christ lived and died...
That light shone brightly in Saint Nicholas of Myra.

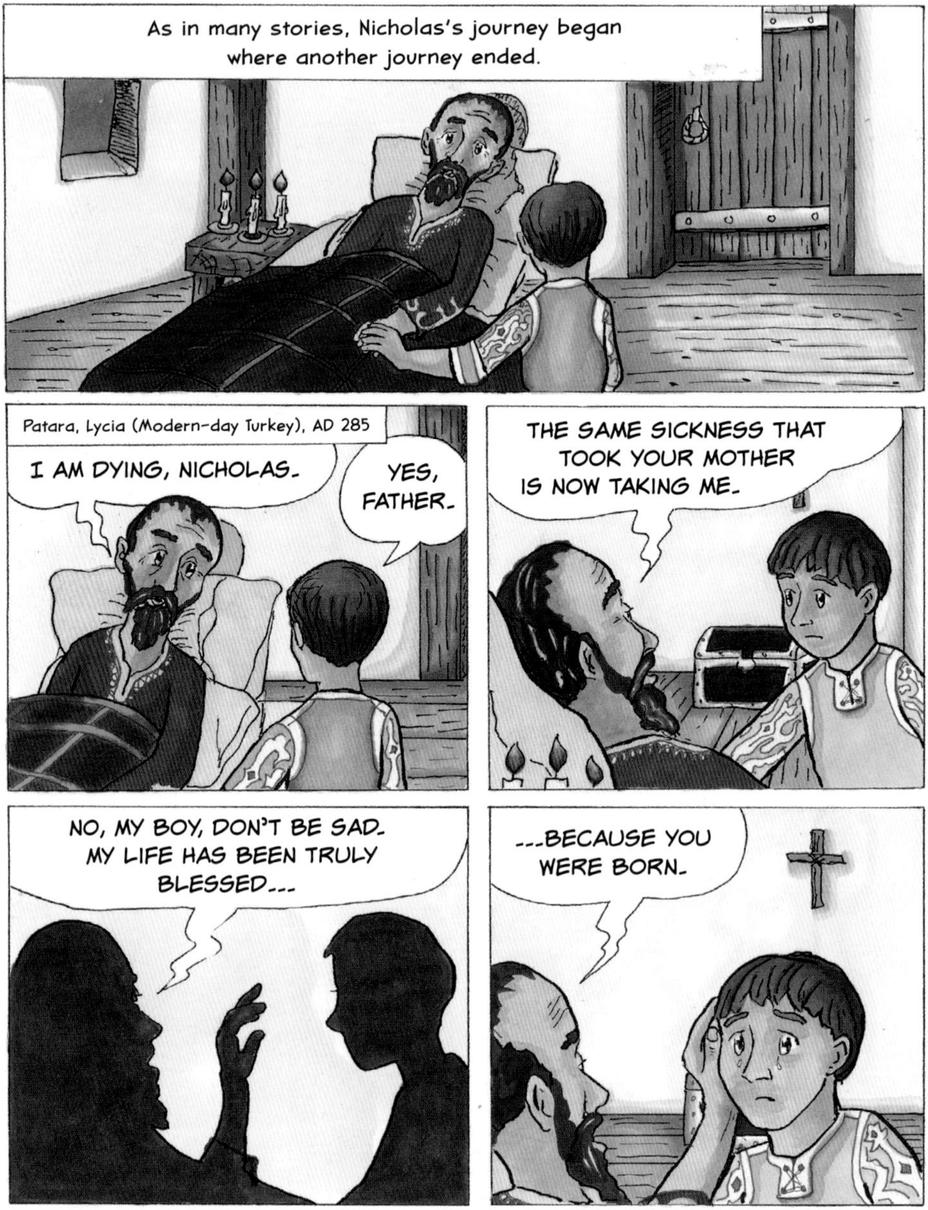
As in many stories, Nicholas's journey began where another journey ended.
Patara, Lycia (Modern-day Turkey), AD 285
I AM DYING, NICHOLAS.
YES, FATHER.
THE SAME SICKNESS THAT TOOK YOUR MOTHER IS NOW TAKING ME.
NO, MY BOY, DON'T BE SAD. MY LIFE HAS BEEN TRULY BLESSED...
...BECAUSE YOU WERE BORN.

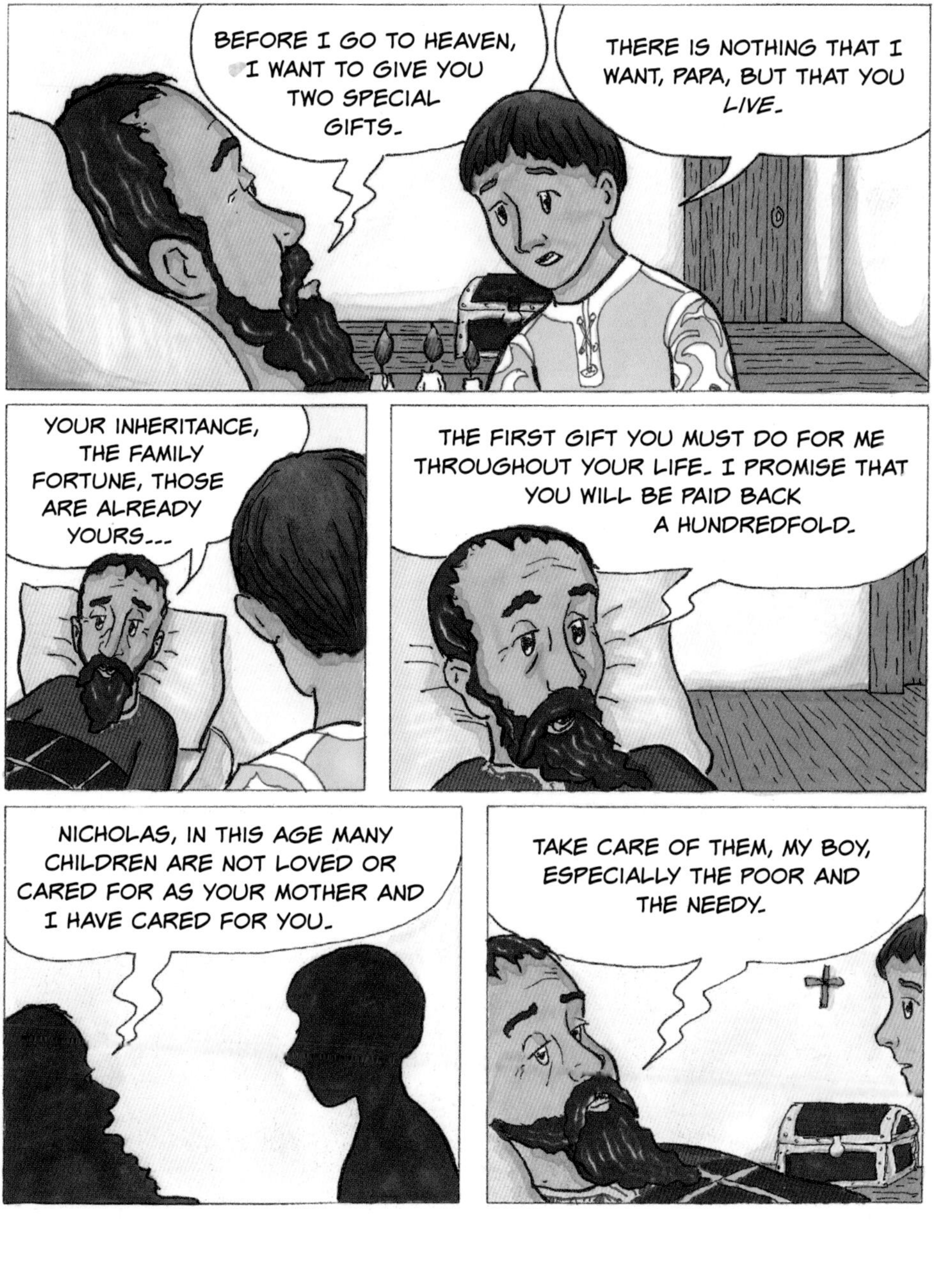
BEFORE I GO TO HEAVEN, I WANT TO GIVE YOU TWO SPECIAL GIFTS.
THERE IS NOTHING THAT I WANT, PAPA, BUT THAT YOU *LIVE*.
YOUR INHERITANCE, THE FAMILY FORTUNE, THOSE ARE ALREADY YOURS...
THE FIRST GIFT YOU MUST DO FOR ME THROUGHOUT YOUR LIFE. I PROMISE THAT YOU WILL BE PAID BACK A HUNDREDFOLD.
NICHOLAS, IN THIS AGE MANY CHILDREN ARE NOT LOVED OR CARED FOR AS YOUR MOTHER AND I HAVE CARED FOR YOU.
TAKE CARE OF THEM, MY BOY, ESPECIALLY THE POOR AND THE NEEDY.

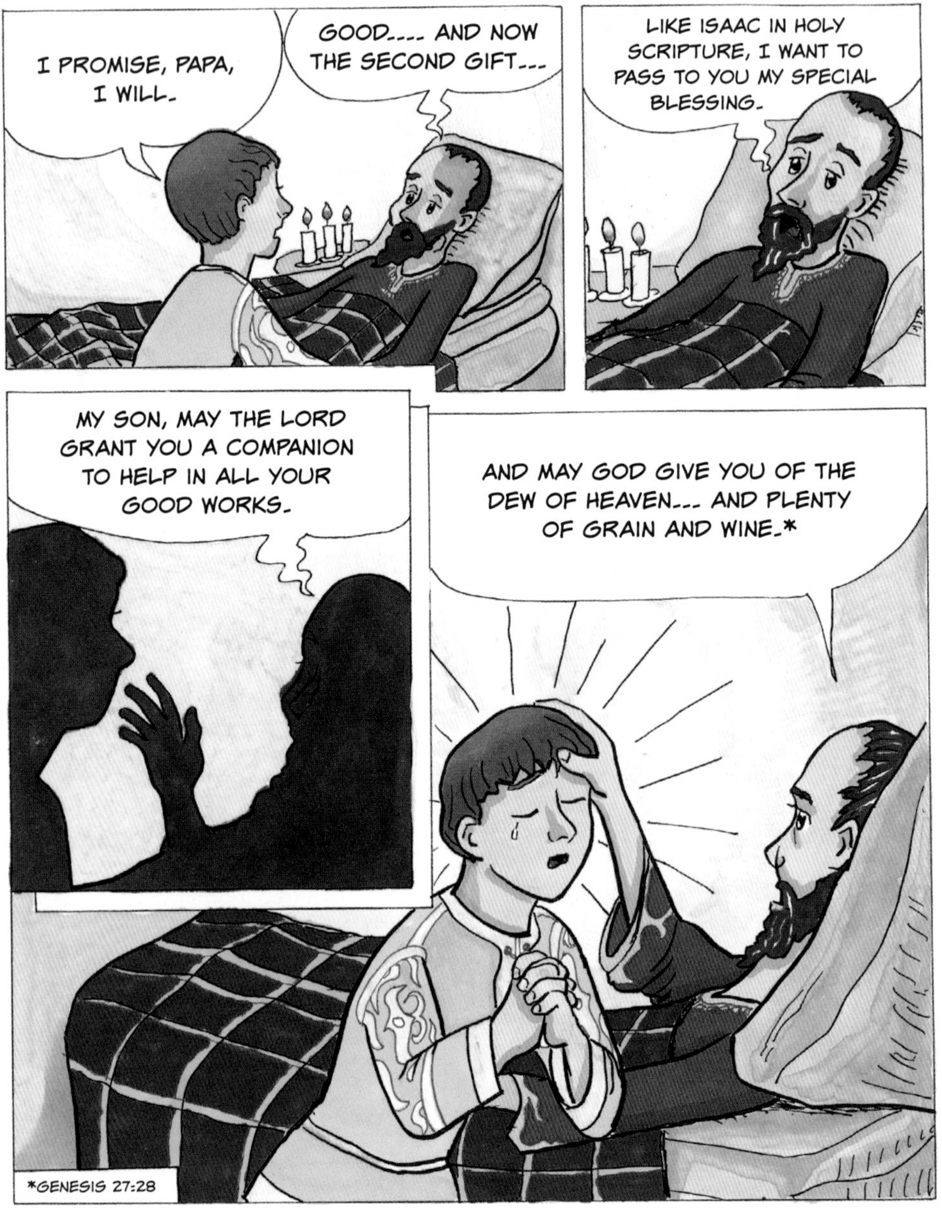
I PROMISE, PAPA, I WILL.
GOOD.... AND NOW THE SECOND GIFT...
LIKE ISAAC IN HOLY SCRIPTURE, I WANT TO PASS TO YOU MY SPECIAL BLESSING.
MY SON, MAY THE LORD GRANT YOU A COMPANION TO HELP IN ALL YOUR GOOD WORKS.
AND MAY GOD GIVE YOU OF THE DEW OF HEAVEN... AND PLENTY OF GRAIN AND WINE.*
*GENESIS 27:28

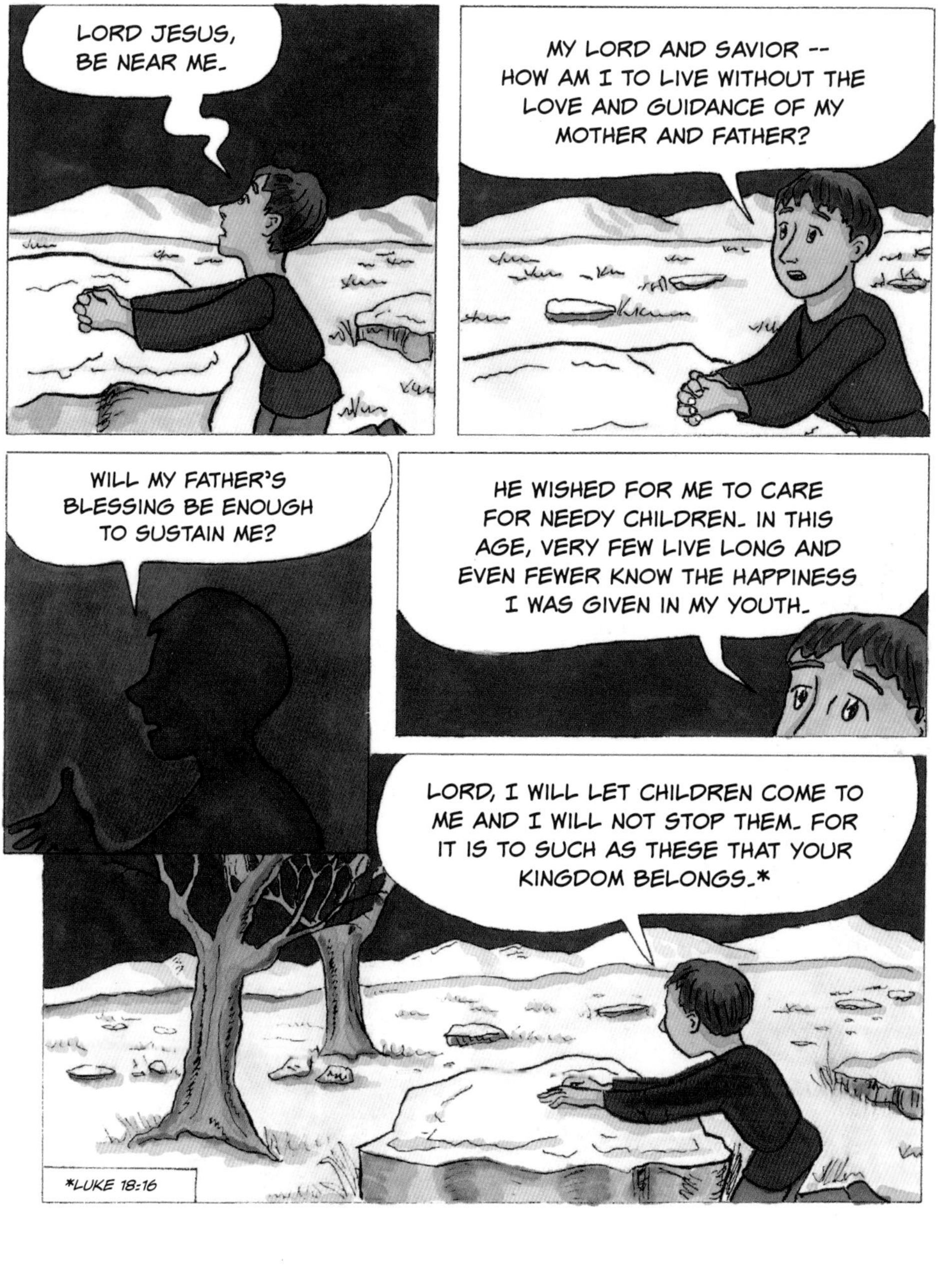
LORD JESUS, BE NEAR ME.
MY LORD AND SAVIOR -- HOW AM I TO LIVE WITHOUT THE LOVE AND GUIDANCE OF MY MOTHER AND FATHER?
WILL MY FATHER'S BLESSING BE ENOUGH TO SUSTAIN ME?
HE WISHED FOR ME TO CARE FOR NEEDY CHILDREN. IN THIS AGE, VERY FEW LIVE LONG AND EVEN FEWER KNOW THE HAPPINESS I WAS GIVEN IN MY YOUTH.
LORD, I WILL LET CHILDREN COME TO ME AND I WILL NOT STOP THEM. FOR IT IS TO SUCH AS THESE THAT YOUR KINGDOM BELONGS.*
*LUKE 18:16

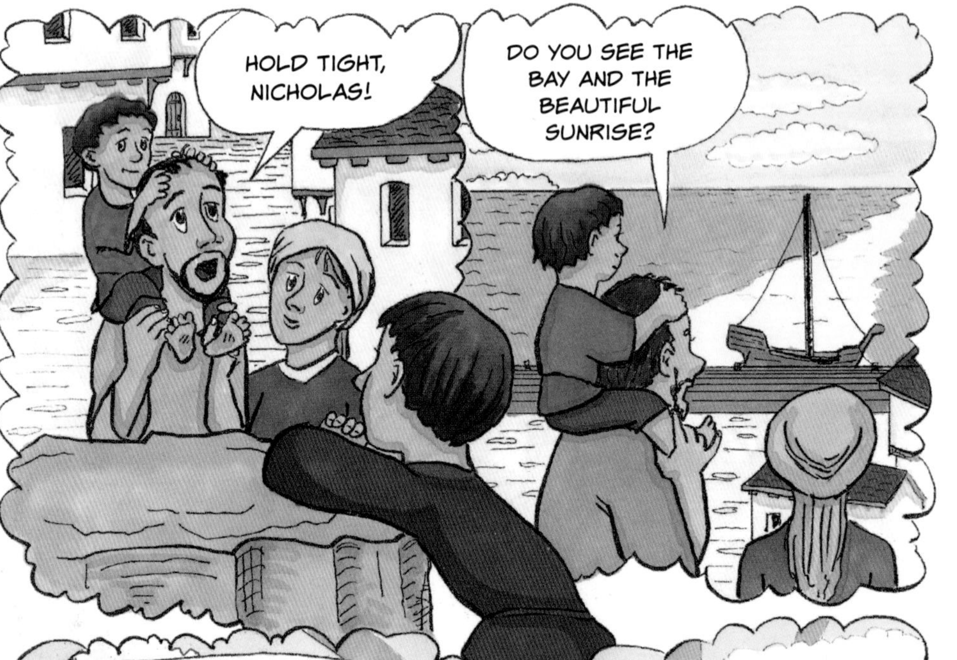
HOLD TIGHT, NICHOLAS!
DO YOU SEE THE BAY AND THE BEAUTIFUL SUNRISE?

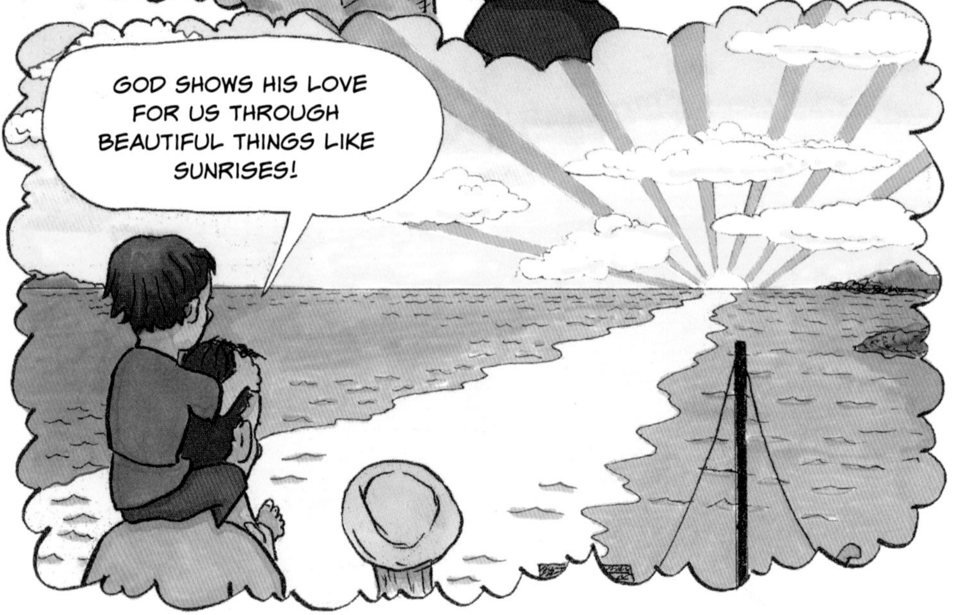
GOD SHOWS HIS LOVE FOR US THROUGH BEAUTIFUL THINGS LIKE SUNRISES!

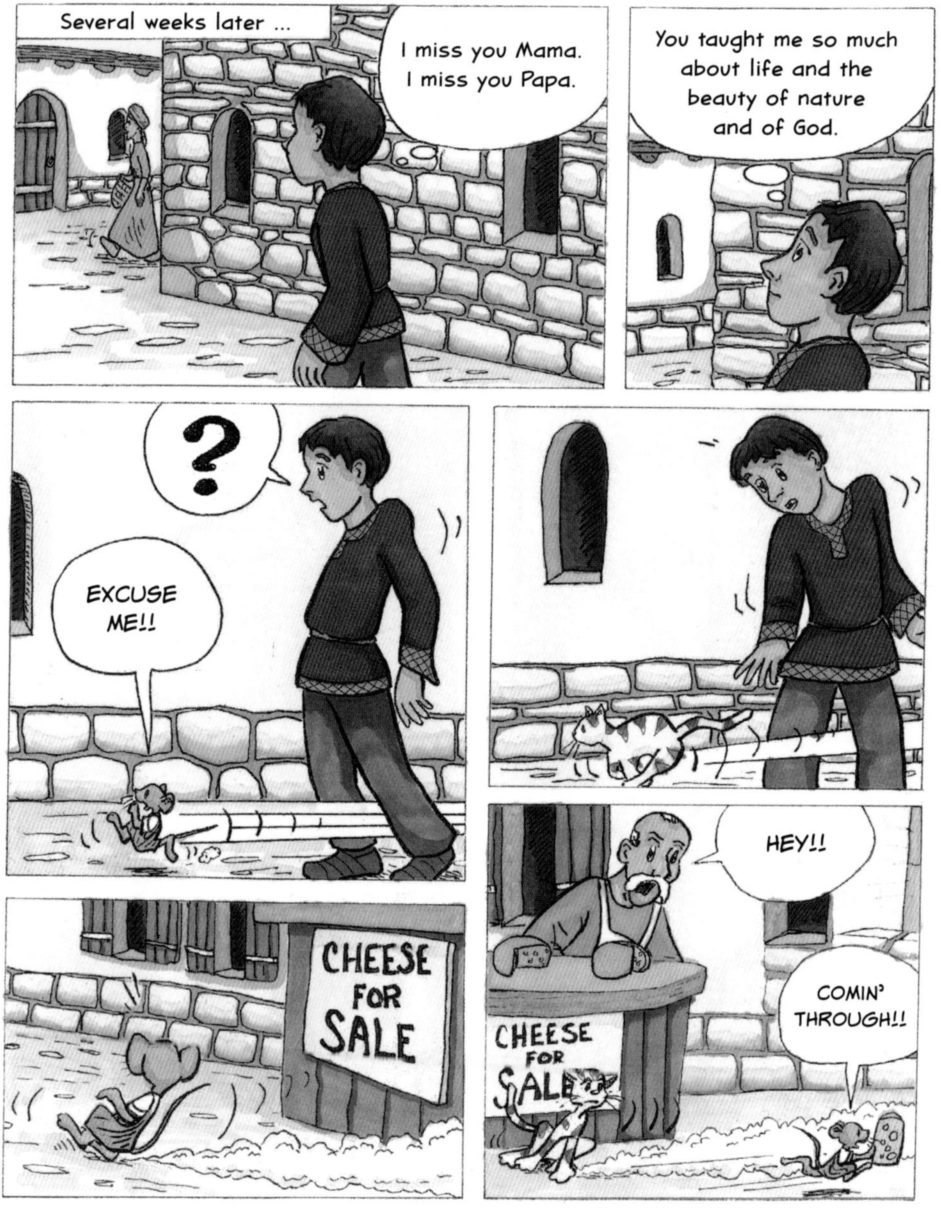
Several weeks later ...
I miss you Mama. I miss you Papa.
You taught me so much about life and the beauty of nature and of God.
?
EXCUSE ME!!
HEY!!
CHEESE FOR SALE
CHEESE FOR SALE
COMIN' THROUGH!!

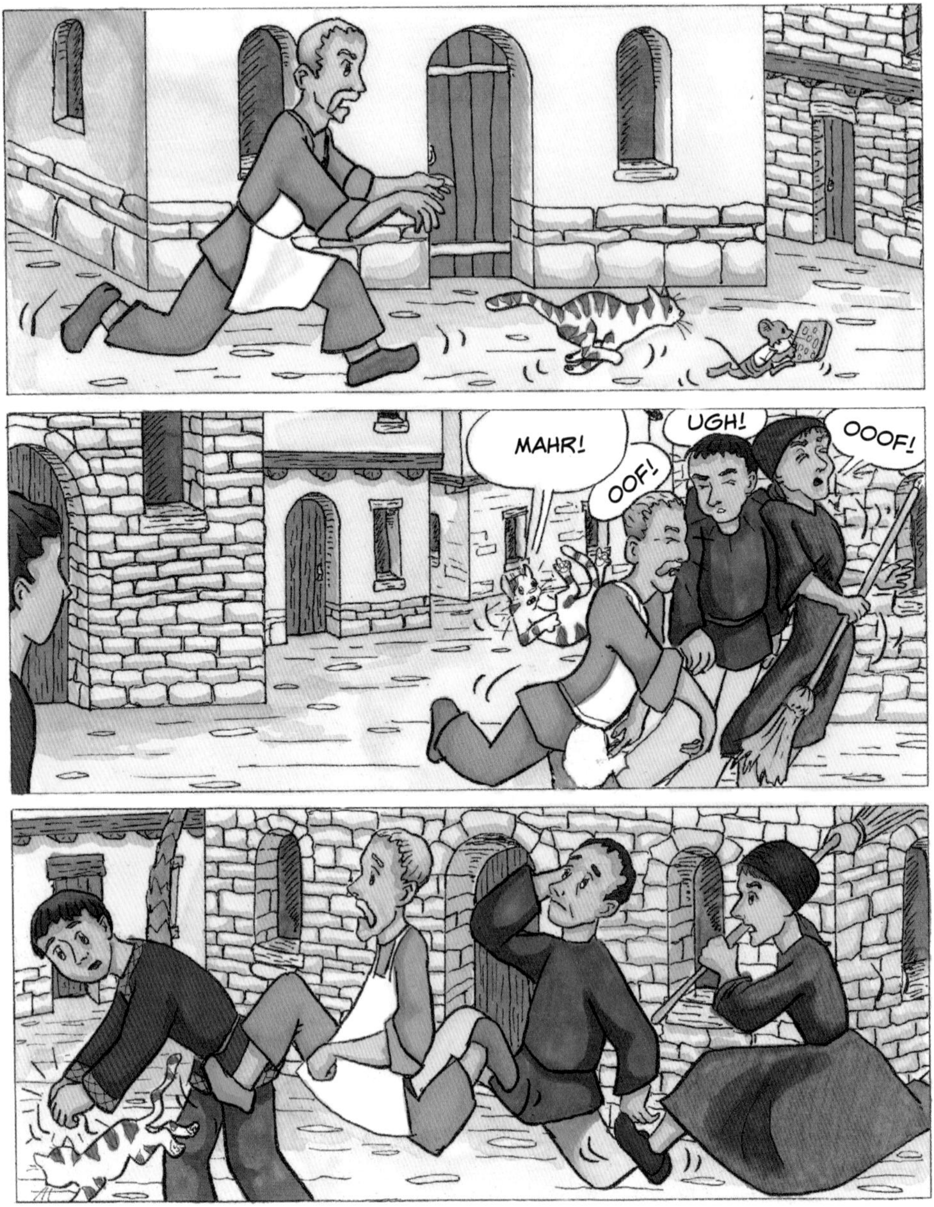
MAHR!
OOF!
UGH!
OOOF!

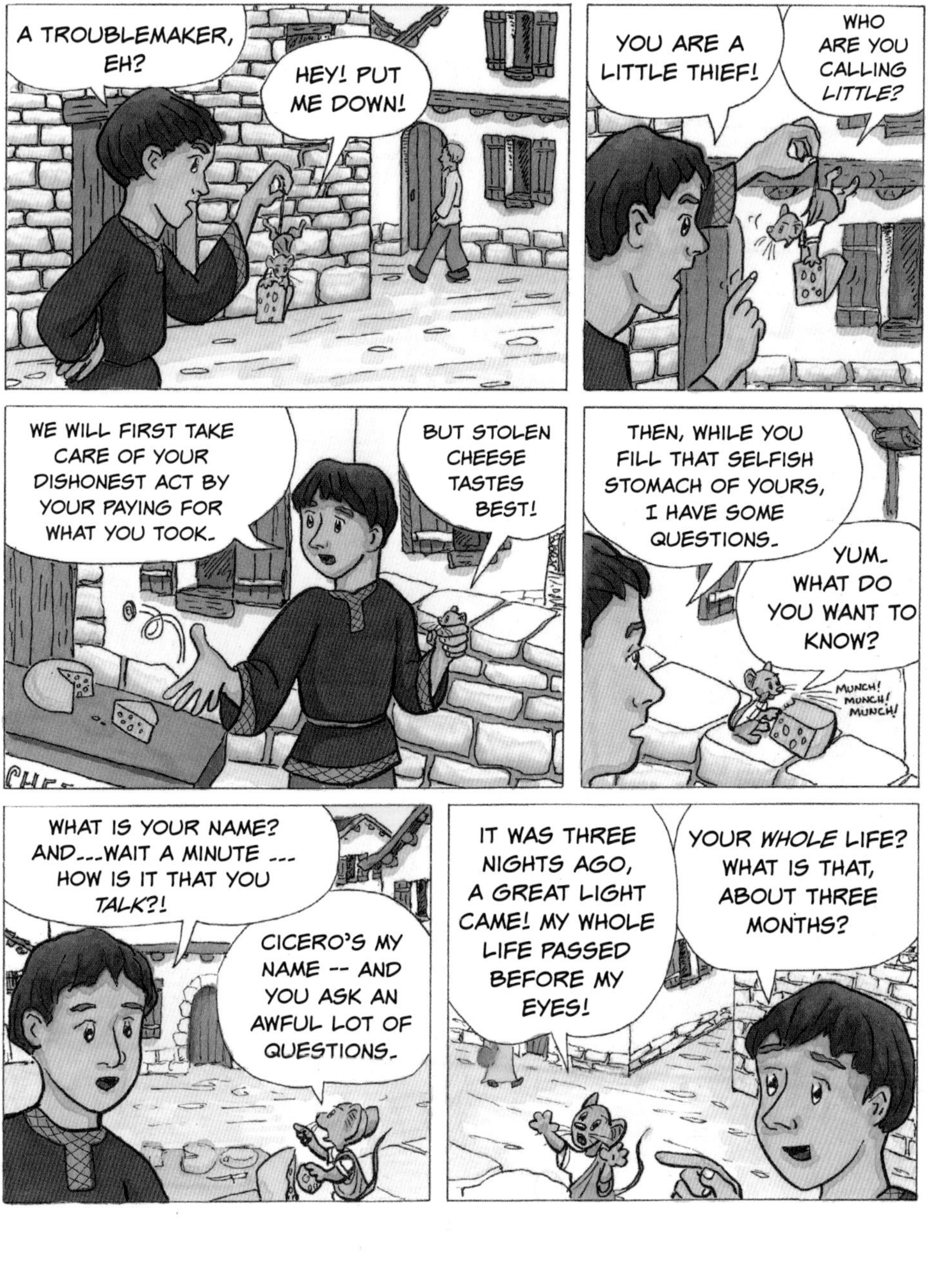

A TROUBLEMAKER, EH?
HEY! PUT ME DOWN!
YOU ARE A LITTLE THIEF!
WHO ARE YOU CALLING *LITTLE*?
WE WILL FIRST TAKE CARE OF YOUR DISHONEST ACT BY YOUR PAYING FOR WHAT YOU TOOK.
BUT STOLEN CHEESE TASTES BEST!
THEN, WHILE YOU FILL THAT SELFISH STOMACH OF YOURS, I HAVE SOME QUESTIONS.
YUM. WHAT DO YOU WANT TO KNOW?
MUNCH! MUNCH! MUNCH!
WHAT IS YOUR NAME? AND...WAIT A MINUTE ... HOW IS IT THAT YOU *TALK*?!
CICERO'S MY NAME -- AND YOU ASK AN AWFUL LOT OF QUESTIONS.
IT WAS THREE NIGHTS AGO, A GREAT LIGHT CAME! MY WHOLE LIFE PASSED BEFORE MY EYES!
YOUR *WHOLE* LIFE? WHAT IS THAT, ABOUT THREE MONTHS?

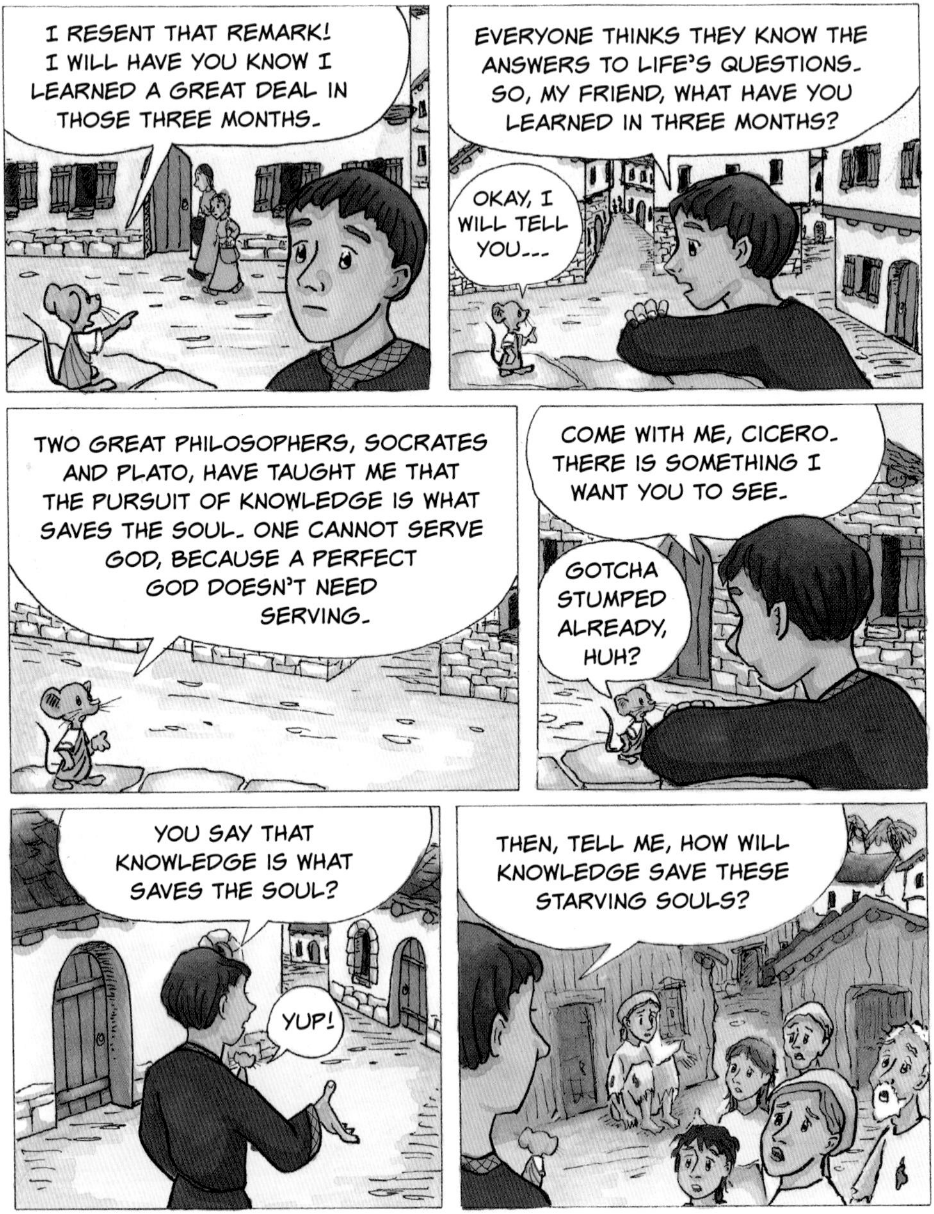
I RESENT THAT REMARK! I WILL HAVE YOU KNOW I LEARNED A GREAT DEAL IN THOSE THREE MONTHS.
EVERYONE THINKS THEY KNOW THE ANSWERS TO LIFE'S QUESTIONS. SO, MY FRIEND, WHAT HAVE YOU LEARNED IN THREE MONTHS?
OKAY, I WILL TELL YOU...
TWO GREAT PHILOSOPHERS, SOCRATES AND PLATO, HAVE TAUGHT ME THAT THE PURSUIT OF KNOWLEDGE IS WHAT SAVES THE SOUL. ONE CANNOT SERVE GOD, BECAUSE A PERFECT GOD DOESN'T NEED SERVING.
COME WITH ME, CICERO. THERE IS SOMETHING I WANT YOU TO SEE.
GOTCHA STUMPED ALREADY, HUH?
YOU SAY THAT KNOWLEDGE IS WHAT SAVES THE SOUL?
YUP!
THEN, TELL ME, HOW WILL KNOWLEDGE SAVE THESE STARVING SOULS?

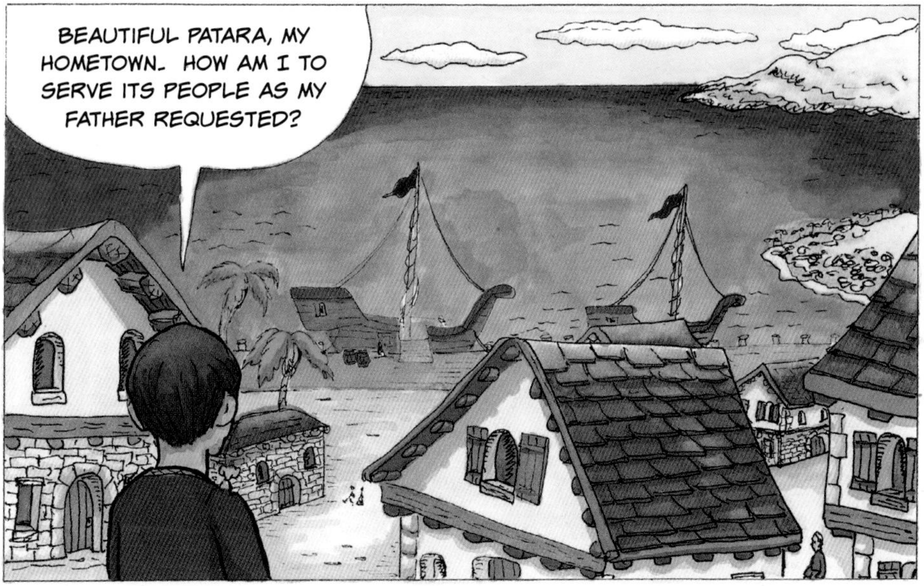
BEAUTIFUL PATARA, MY HOMETOWN. HOW AM I TO SERVE ITS PEOPLE AS MY FATHER REQUESTED?

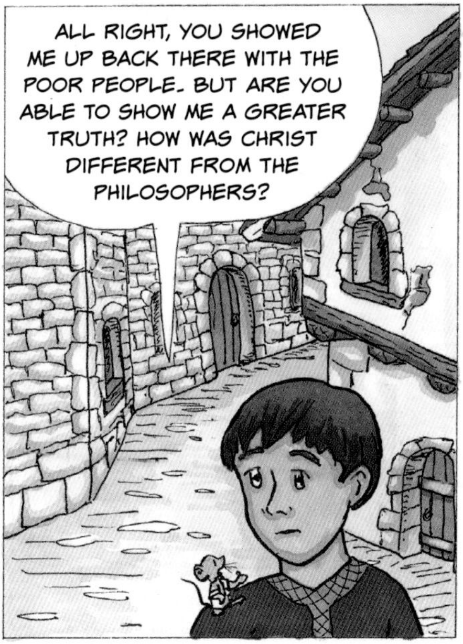
ALL RIGHT, YOU SHOWED ME UP BACK THERE WITH THE POOR PEOPLE. BUT ARE YOU ABLE TO SHOW ME A GREATER TRUTH? HOW WAS CHRIST DIFFERENT FROM THE PHILOSOPHERS?

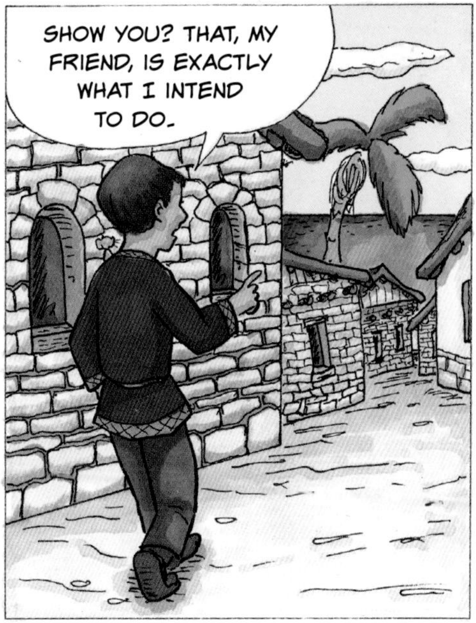
SHOW YOU? THAT, MY FRIEND, IS EXACTLY WHAT I INTEND TO DO.

CHAPTER TWO
THE THREE DOWRIES

Then I heard the voice of the Lord saying,
"Whom shall I send, and who will go for us?"
And I said, "Here am I; send me!"
—ISAIAH 6:8

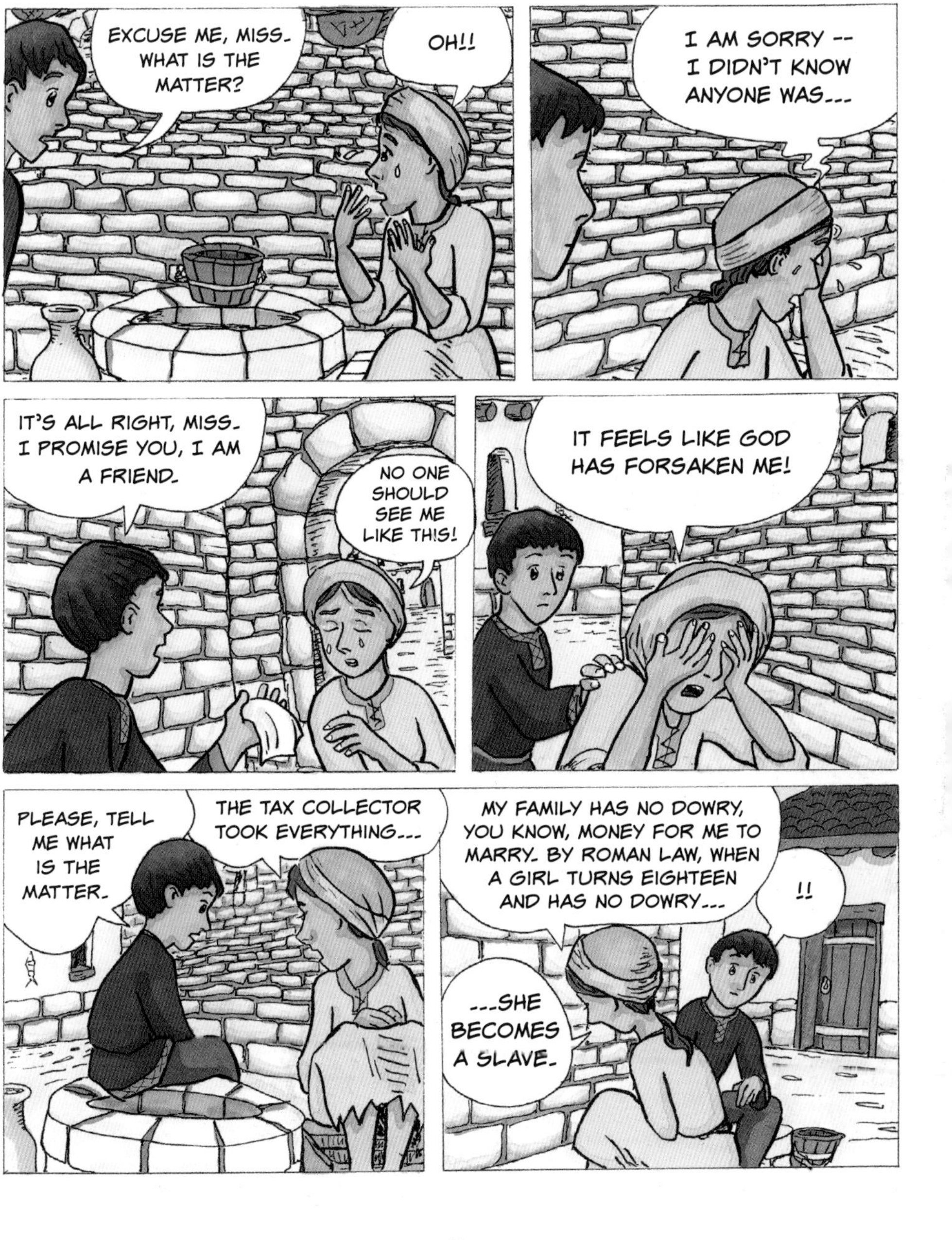

EXCUSE ME, MISS. WHAT IS THE MATTER?
OH!!
I AM SORRY -- I DIDN'T KNOW ANYONE WAS...
IT'S ALL RIGHT, MISS. I PROMISE YOU, I AM A FRIEND.
NO ONE SHOULD SEE ME LIKE THIS!
IT FEELS LIKE GOD HAS FORSAKEN ME!
PLEASE, TELL ME WHAT IS THE MATTER.
THE TAX COLLECTOR TOOK EVERYTHING...
MY FAMILY HAS NO DOWRY, YOU KNOW, MONEY FOR ME TO MARRY. BY ROMAN LAW, WHEN A GIRL TURNS EIGHTEEN AND HAS NO DOWRY...
!!
...SHE BECOMES A SLAVE.

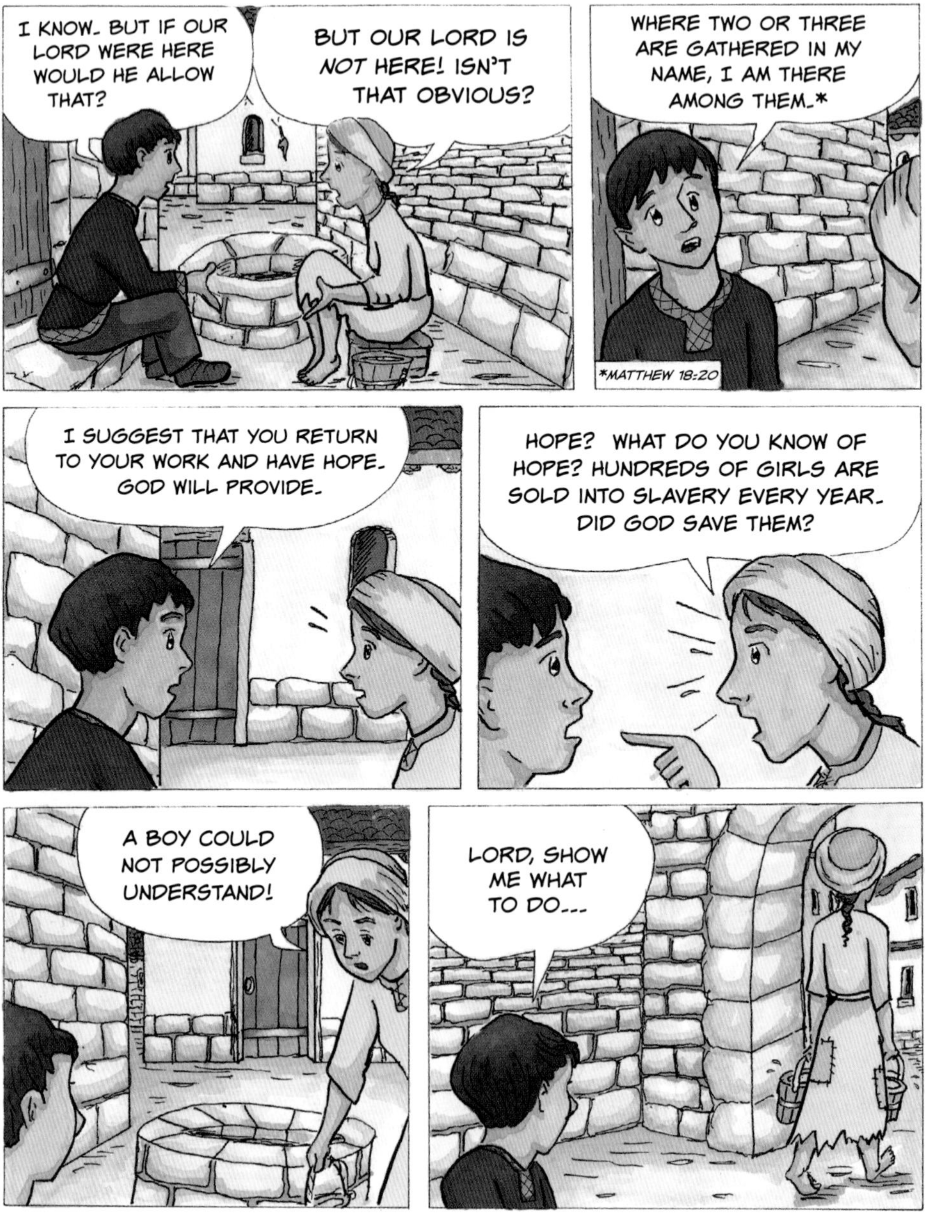
I KNOW. BUT IF OUR LORD WERE HERE WOULD HE ALLOW THAT?
BUT OUR LORD IS *NOT HERE!* ISN'T THAT OBVIOUS?
WHERE TWO OR THREE ARE GATHERED IN MY NAME, I AM THERE AMONG THEM.*
*MATTHEW 18:20
I SUGGEST THAT YOU RETURN TO YOUR WORK AND HAVE HOPE. GOD WILL PROVIDE.
HOPE? WHAT DO YOU KNOW OF HOPE? HUNDREDS OF GIRLS ARE SOLD INTO SLAVERY EVERY YEAR. DID GOD SAVE THEM?
A BOY COULD NOT POSSIBLY UNDERSTAND!
LORD, SHOW ME WHAT TO DO...

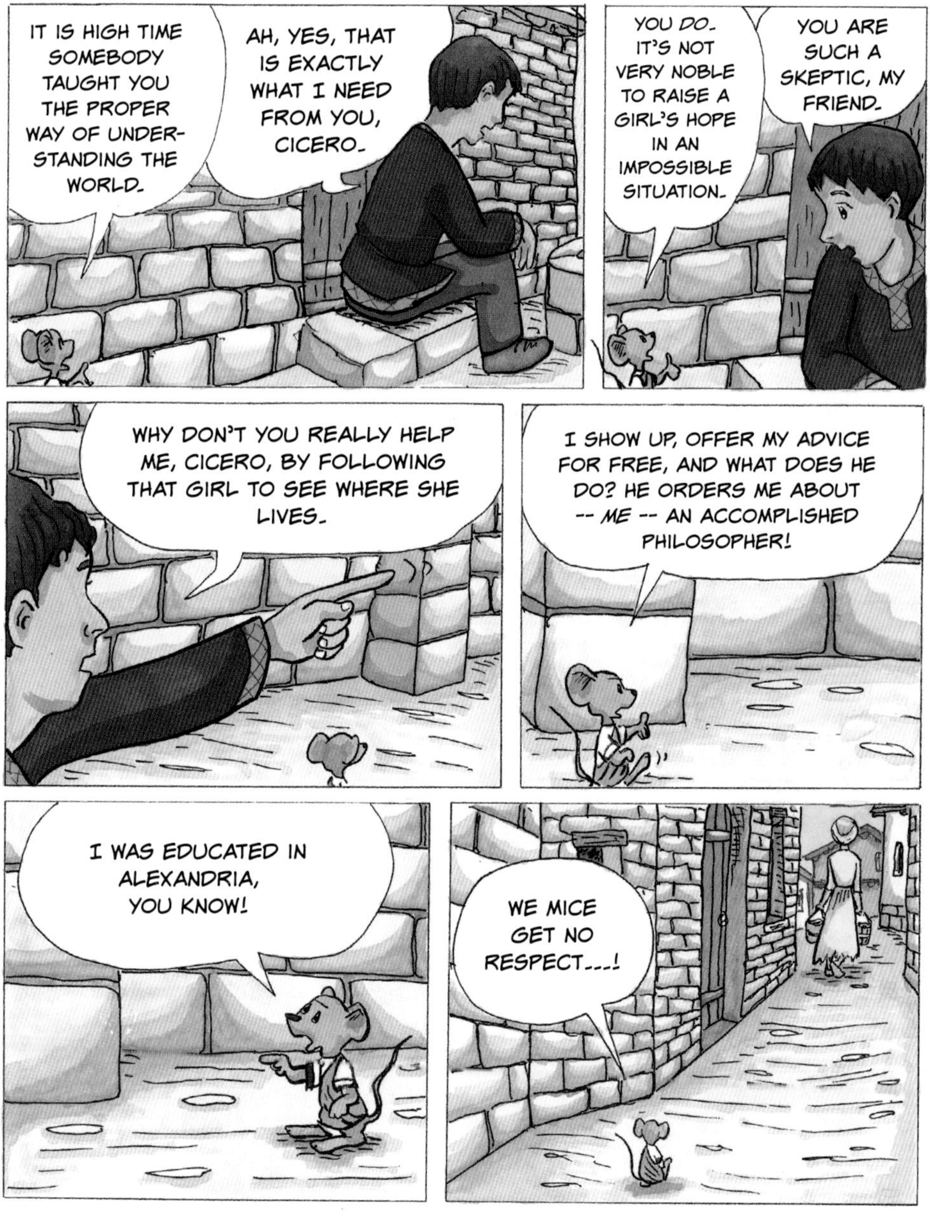
IT IS HIGH TIME SOMEBODY TAUGHT YOU THE PROPER WAY OF UNDER-STANDING THE WORLD.
AH, YES, THAT IS EXACTLY WHAT I NEED FROM YOU, CICERO.
YOU *DO*. IT'S NOT VERY NOBLE TO RAISE A GIRL'S HOPE IN AN IMPOSSIBLE SITUATION.
YOU ARE SUCH A SKEPTIC, MY FRIEND.
WHY DON'T YOU REALLY HELP ME, CICERO, BY FOLLOWING THAT GIRL TO SEE WHERE SHE LIVES.
I SHOW UP, OFFER MY ADVICE FOR FREE, AND WHAT DOES HE DO? HE ORDERS ME ABOUT -- *ME* -- AN ACCOMPLISHED PHILOSOPHER!
I WAS EDUCATED IN ALEXANDRIA, YOU KNOW!
WE MICE GET NO RESPECT...!

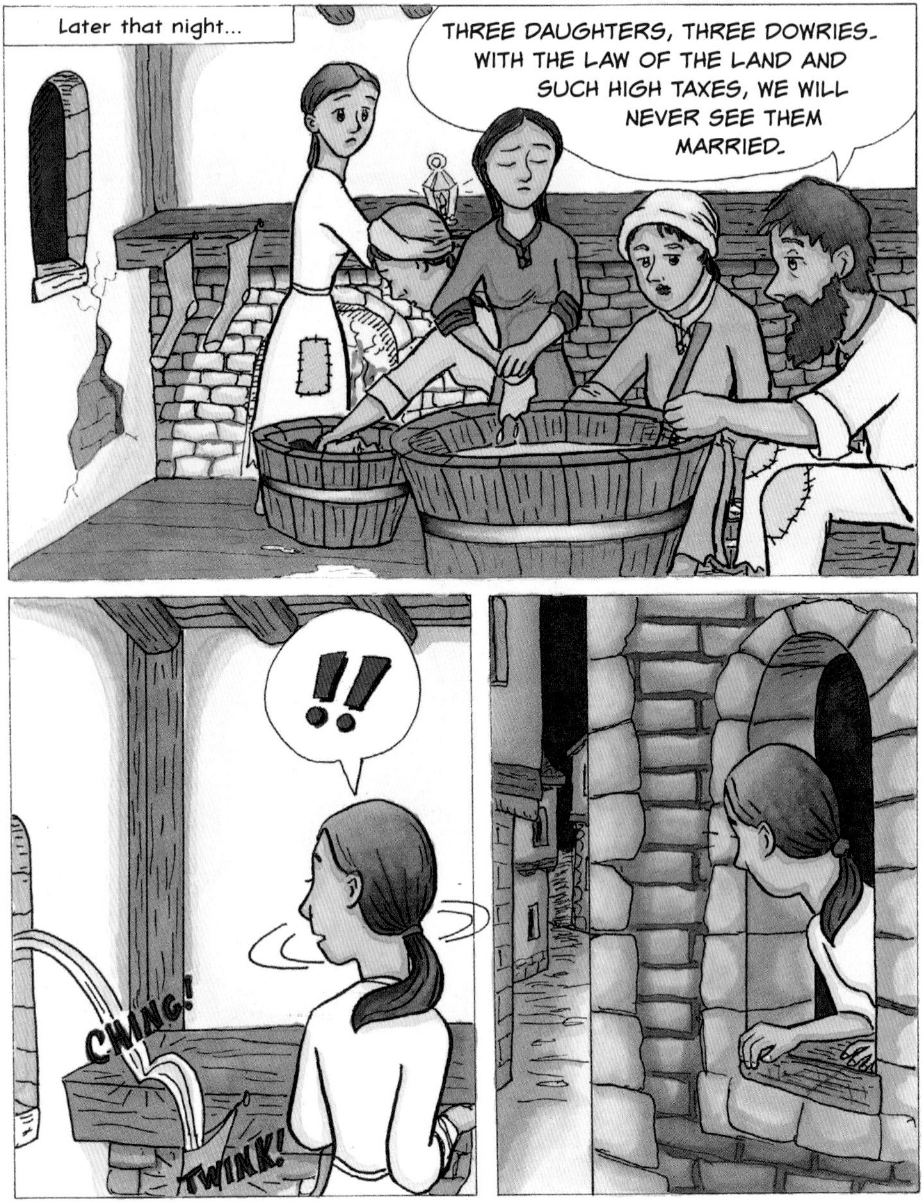
Later that night...
THREE DAUGHTERS, THREE DOWRIES. WITH THE LAW OF THE LAND AND SUCH HIGH TAXES, WE WILL NEVER SEE THEM MARRIED.
!!
CHING!
TWINK!

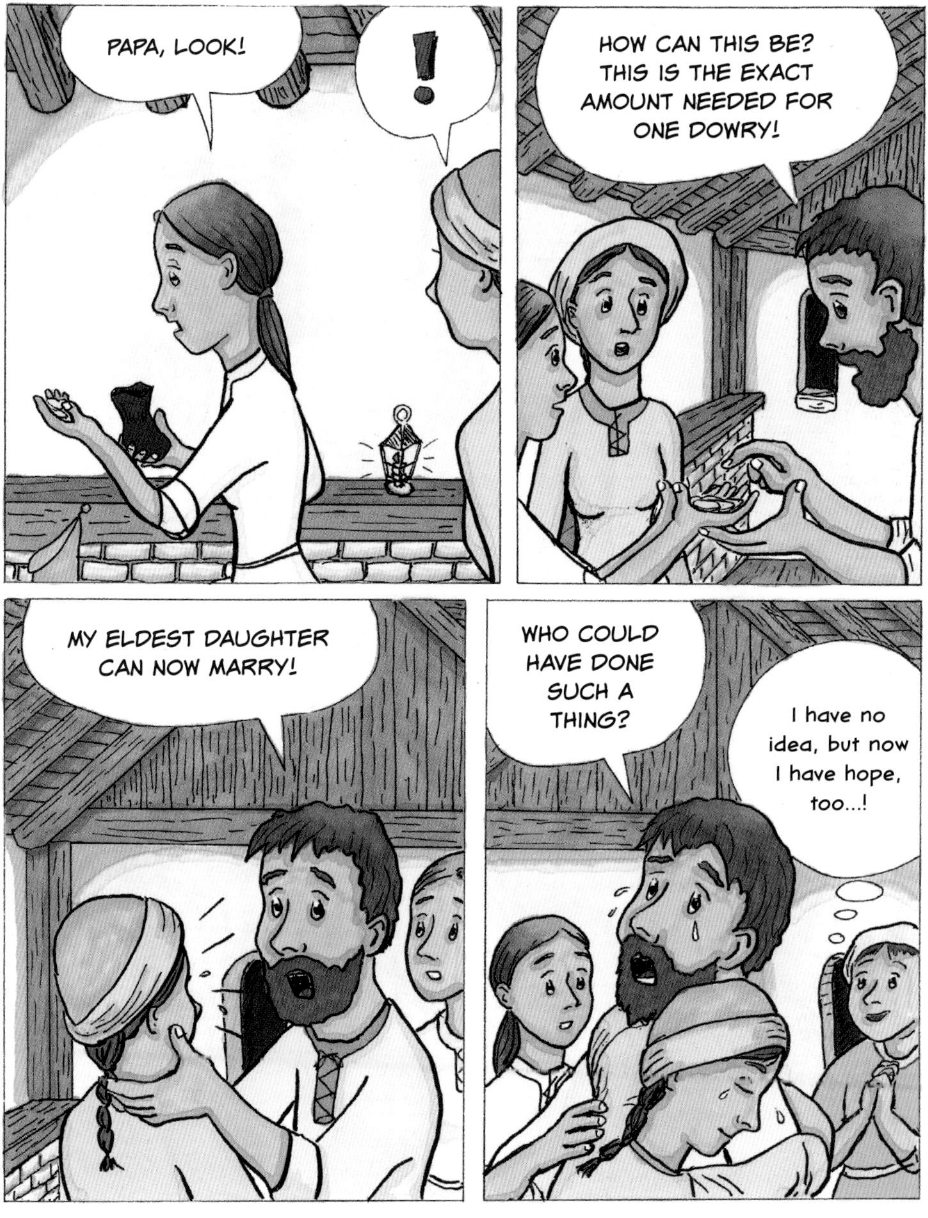
PAPA, LOOK!
!
HOW CAN THIS BE? THIS IS THE EXACT AMOUNT NEEDED FOR ONE DOWRY!
MY ELDEST DAUGHTER CAN NOW MARRY!
WHO COULD HAVE DONE SUCH A THING?
I have no idea, but now I have hope, too...!

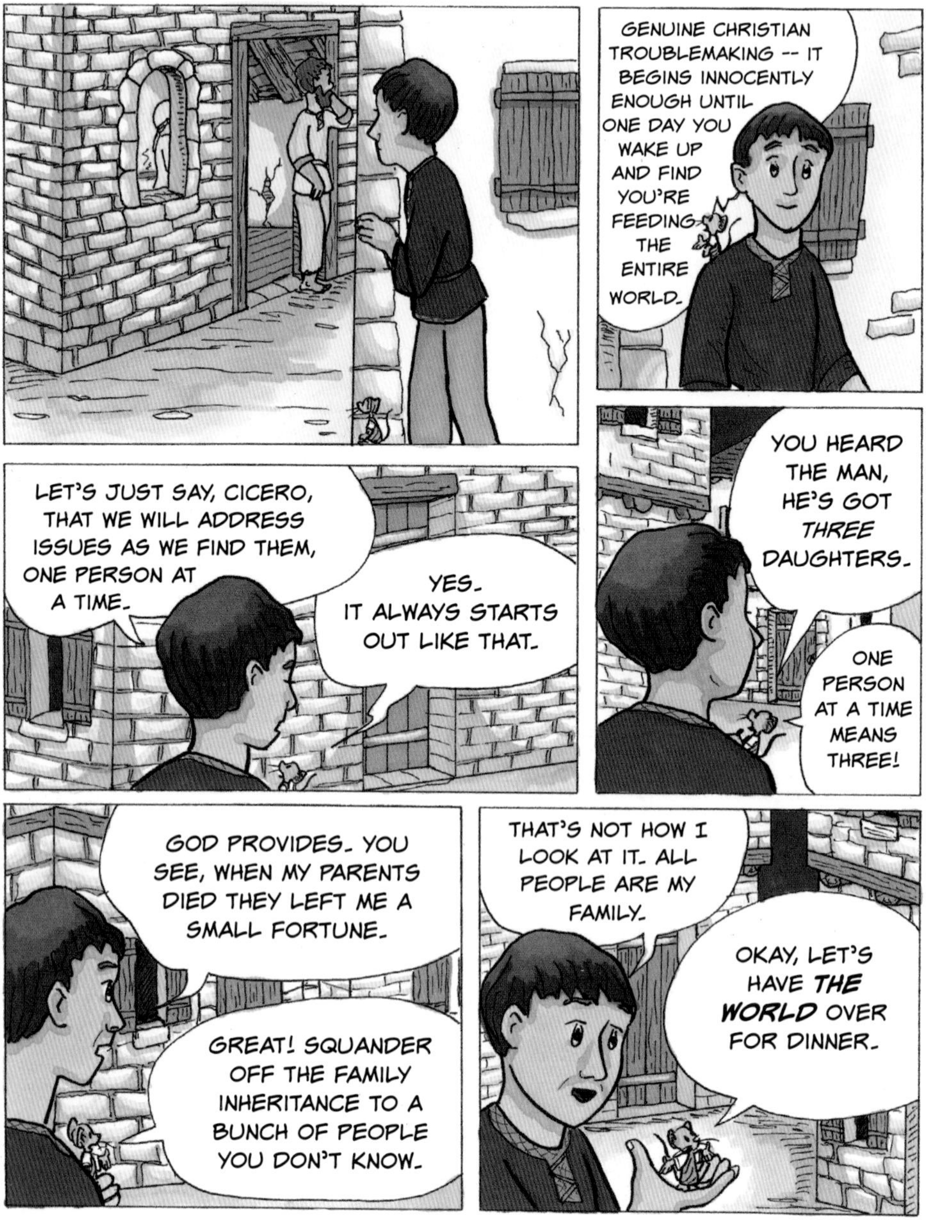
GENUINE CHRISTIAN TROUBLEMAKING -- IT BEGINS INNOCENTLY ENOUGH UNTIL ONE DAY YOU WAKE UP AND FIND YOU'RE FEEDING THE ENTIRE WORLD.
LET'S JUST SAY, CICERO, THAT WE WILL ADDRESS ISSUES AS WE FIND THEM, ONE PERSON AT A TIME.
YES. IT ALWAYS STARTS OUT LIKE THAT.
YOU HEARD THE MAN, HE'S GOT *THREE* DAUGHTERS.
ONE PERSON AT A TIME MEANS THREE!
GOD PROVIDES. YOU SEE, WHEN MY PARENTS DIED THEY LEFT ME A SMALL FORTUNE.
GREAT! SQUANDER OFF THE FAMILY INHERITANCE TO A BUNCH OF PEOPLE YOU DON'T KNOW.
THAT'S NOT HOW I LOOK AT IT. ALL PEOPLE ARE MY FAMILY.
OKAY, LET'S HAVE ***THE WORLD*** OVER FOR DINNER.

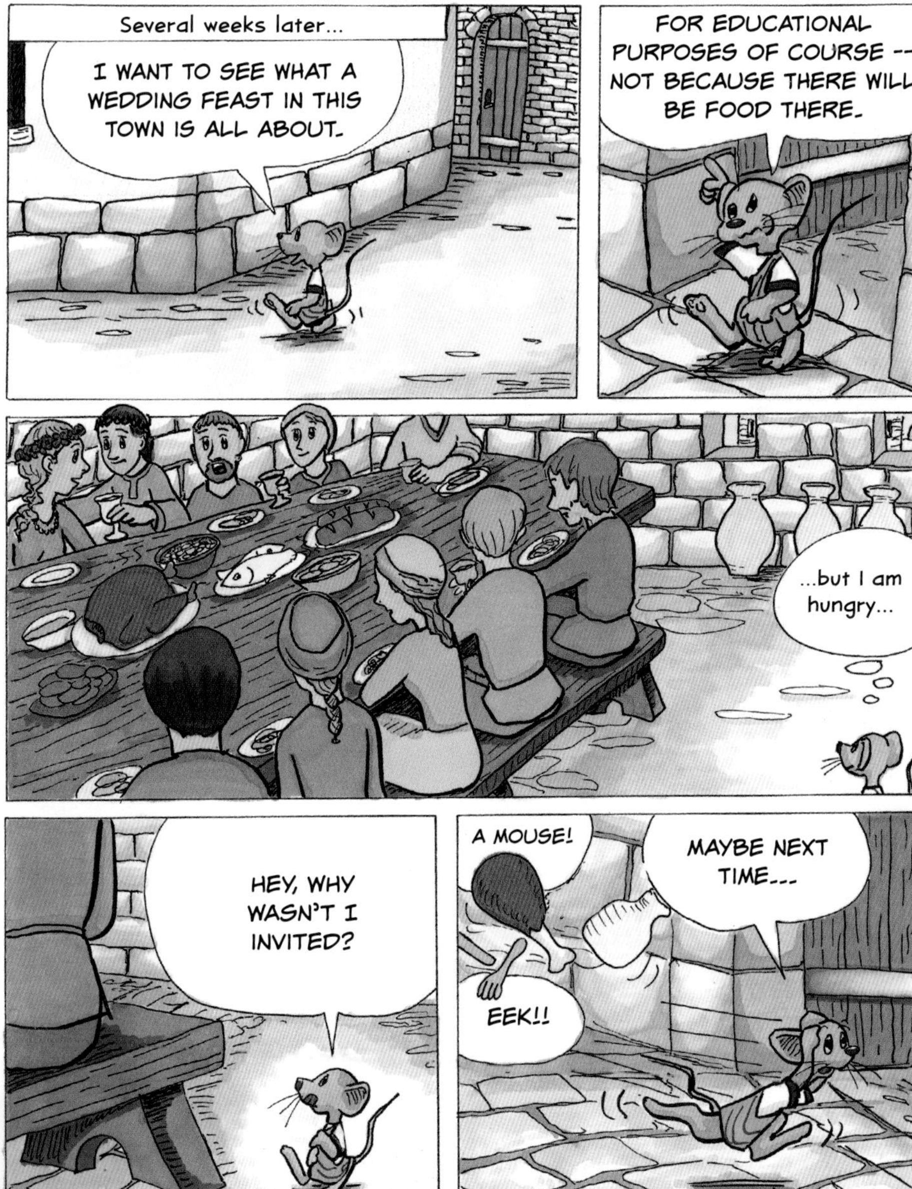
Several weeks later...
I WANT TO SEE WHAT A WEDDING FEAST IN THIS TOWN IS ALL ABOUT.
FOR EDUCATIONAL PURPOSES OF COURSE -- NOT BECAUSE THERE WILL BE FOOD THERE.
...but I am hungry...
HEY, WHY WASN'T I INVITED?
A MOUSE!
MAYBE NEXT TIME...
EEK!!

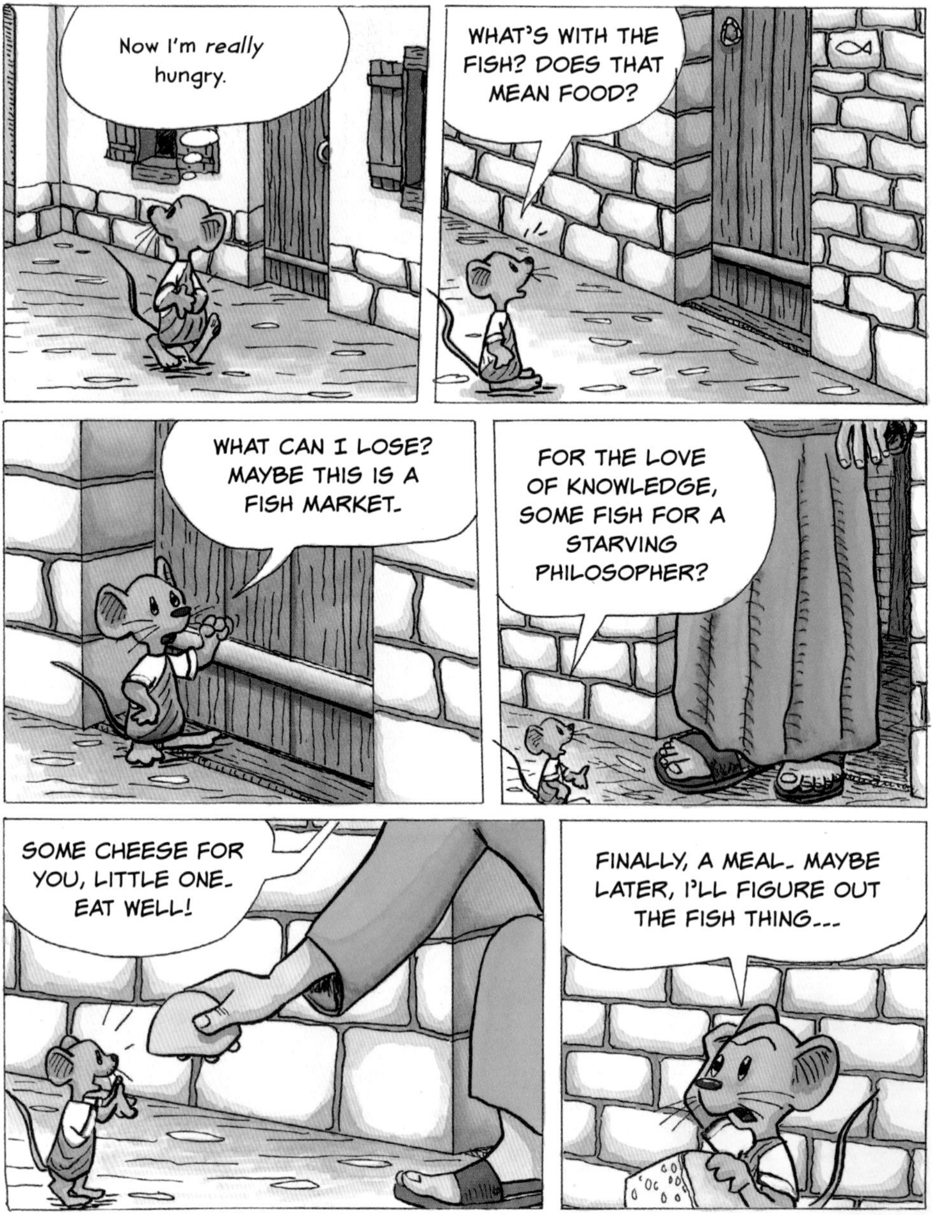
Now I'm *really* hungry.
WHAT'S WITH THE FISH? DOES THAT MEAN FOOD?
WHAT CAN I LOSE? MAYBE THIS IS A FISH MARKET.
FOR THE LOVE OF KNOWLEDGE, SOME FISH FOR A STARVING PHILOSOPHER?
SOME CHEESE FOR YOU, LITTLE ONE. EAT WELL!
FINALLY, A MEAL. MAYBE LATER, I'LL FIGURE OUT THE FISH THING...

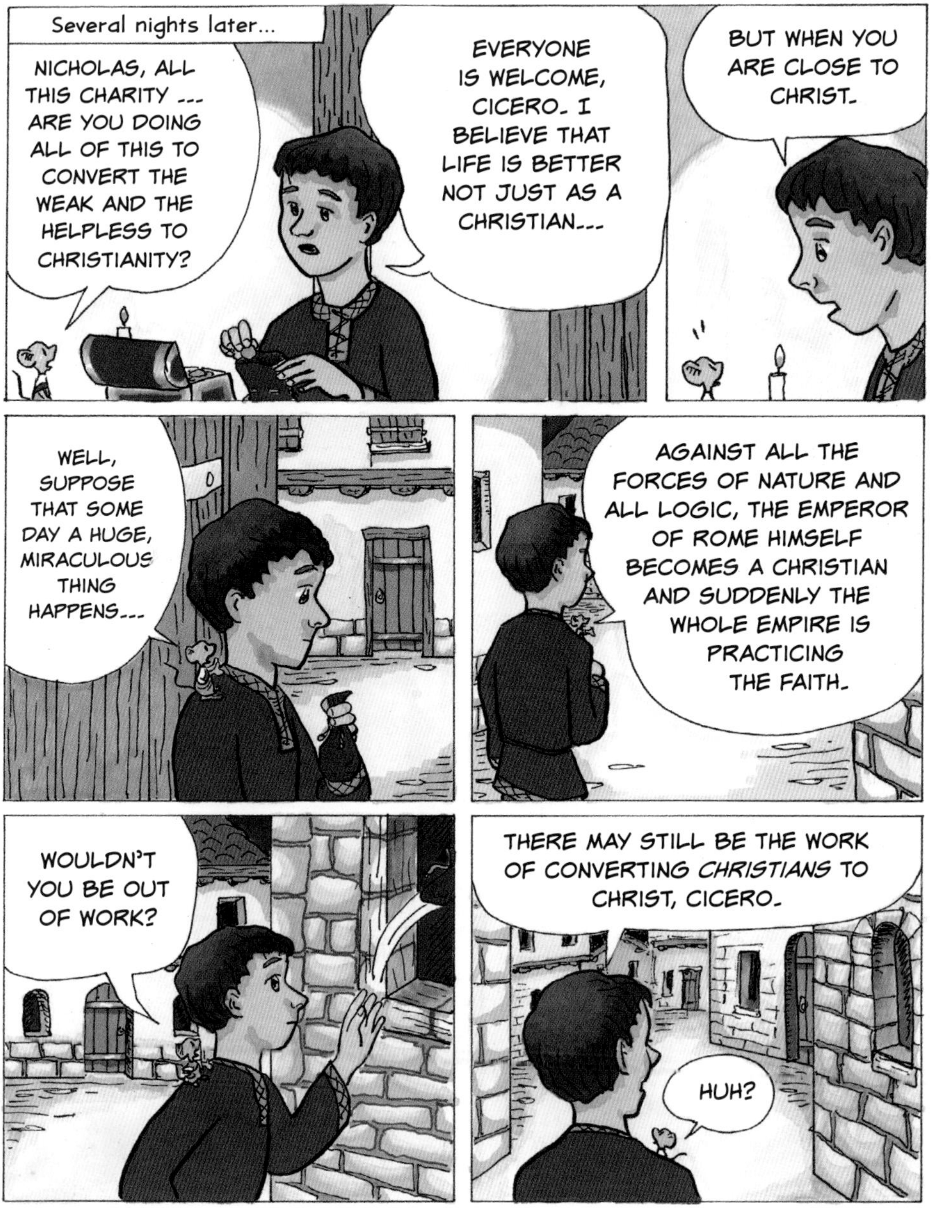
Several nights later...
NICHOLAS, ALL THIS CHARITY ... ARE YOU DOING ALL OF THIS TO CONVERT THE WEAK AND THE HELPLESS TO CHRISTIANITY?
EVERYONE IS WELCOME, CICERO. I BELIEVE THAT LIFE IS BETTER NOT JUST AS A CHRISTIAN...
BUT WHEN YOU ARE CLOSE TO CHRIST.
WELL, SUPPOSE THAT SOME DAY A HUGE, MIRACULOUS THING HAPPENS...
AGAINST ALL THE FORCES OF NATURE AND ALL LOGIC, THE EMPEROR OF ROME HIMSELF BECOMES A CHRISTIAN AND SUDDENLY THE WHOLE EMPIRE IS PRACTICING THE FAITH.
WOULDN'T YOU BE OUT OF WORK?
THERE MAY STILL BE THE WORK OF CONVERTING *CHRISTIANS* TO CHRIST, CICERO.
HUH?

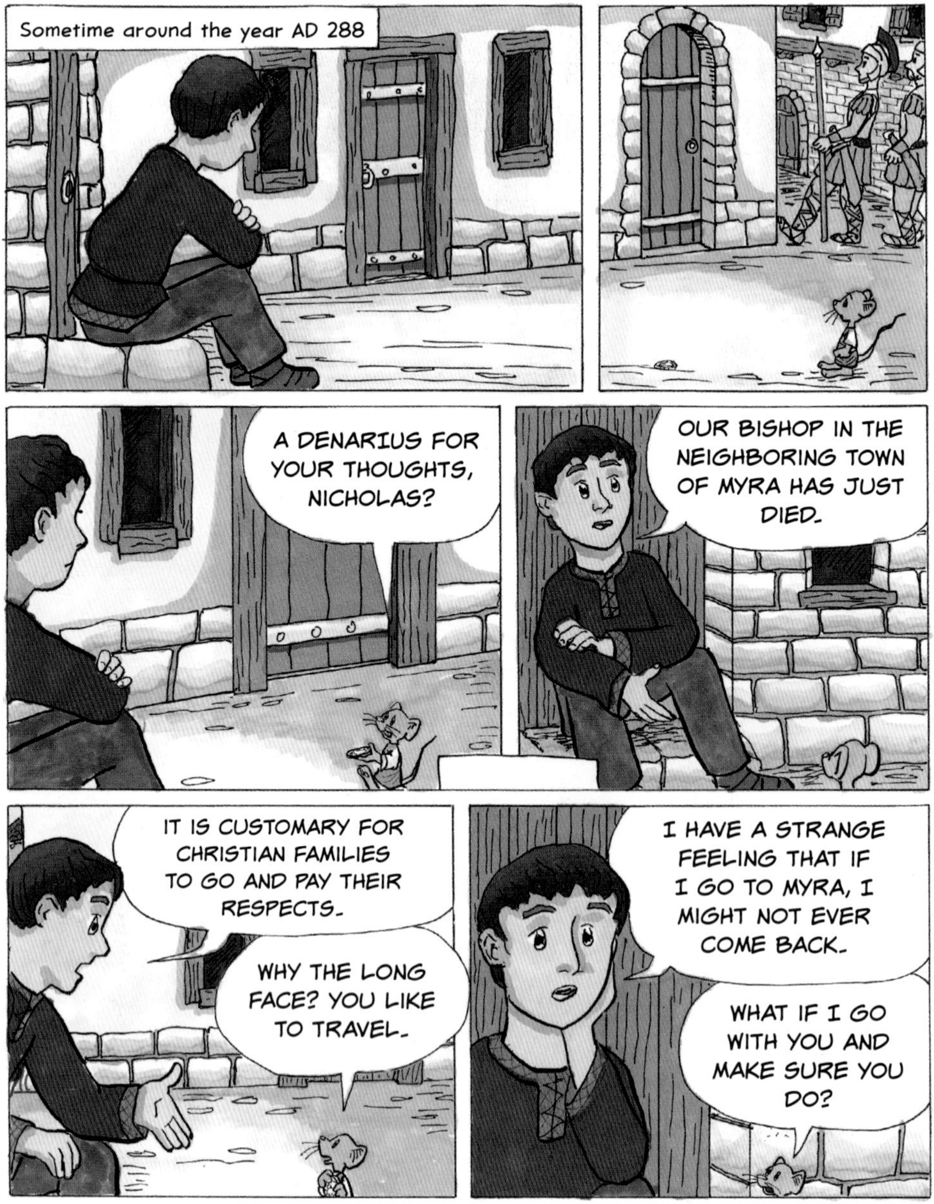
Sometime around the year AD 288
A DENARIUS FOR YOUR THOUGHTS, NICHOLAS?
OUR BISHOP IN THE NEIGHBORING TOWN OF MYRA HAS JUST DIED.
IT IS CUSTOMARY FOR CHRISTIAN FAMILIES TO GO AND PAY THEIR RESPECTS.
WHY THE LONG FACE? YOU LIKE TO TRAVEL.
I HAVE A STRANGE FEELING THAT IF I GO TO MYRA, I MIGHT NOT EVER COME BACK.
WHAT IF I GO WITH YOU AND MAKE SURE YOU DO?

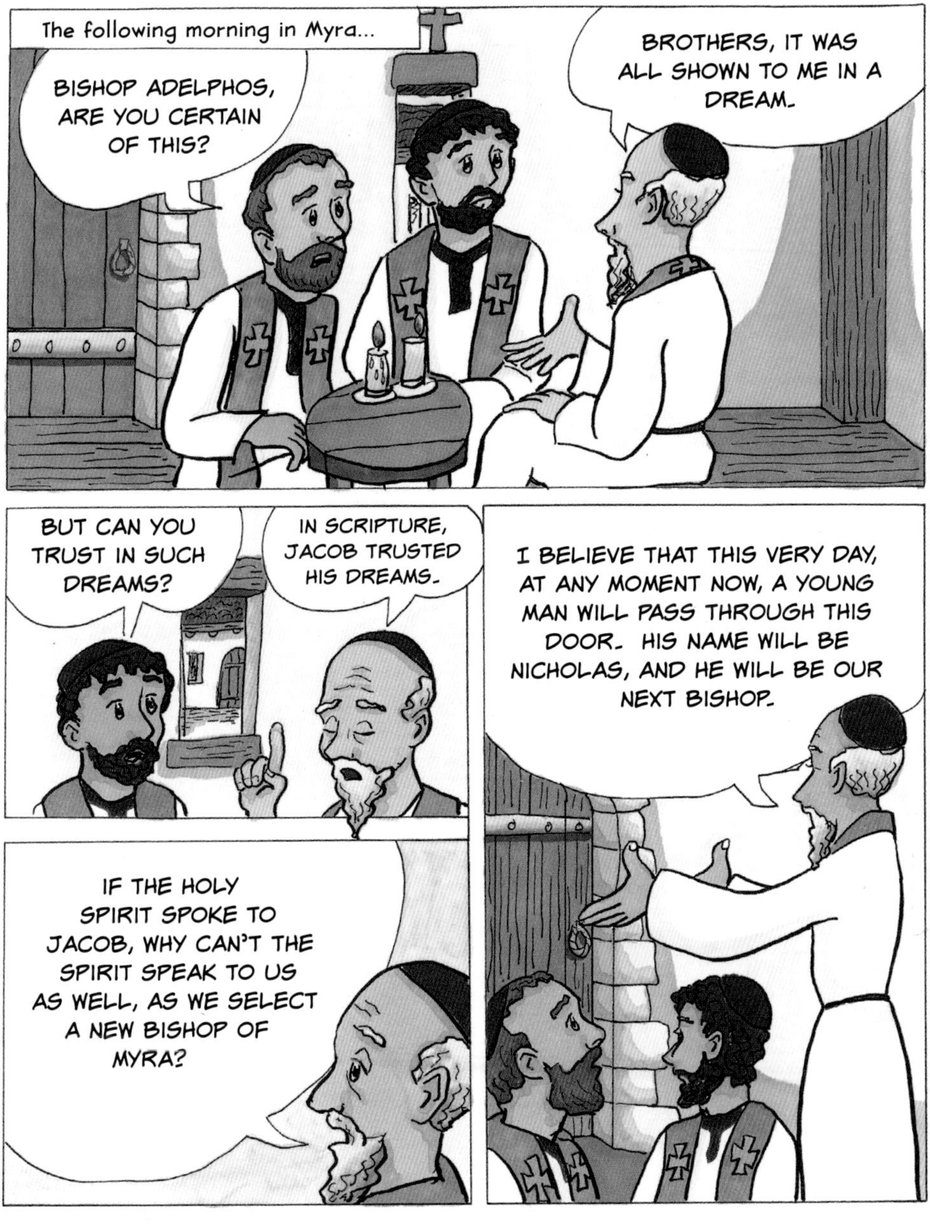
The following morning in Myra...
BISHOP ADELPHOS, ARE YOU CERTAIN OF THIS?
BROTHERS, IT WAS ALL SHOWN TO ME IN A DREAM.
BUT CAN YOU TRUST IN SUCH DREAMS?
IN SCRIPTURE, JACOB TRUSTED HIS DREAMS.
IF THE HOLY SPIRIT SPOKE TO JACOB, WHY CAN'T THE SPIRIT SPEAK TO US AS WELL, AS WE SELECT A NEW BISHOP OF MYRA?
I BELIEVE THAT THIS VERY DAY, AT ANY MOMENT NOW, A YOUNG MAN WILL PASS THROUGH THIS DOOR. HIS NAME WILL BE NICHOLAS, AND HE WILL BE OUR NEXT BISHOP.

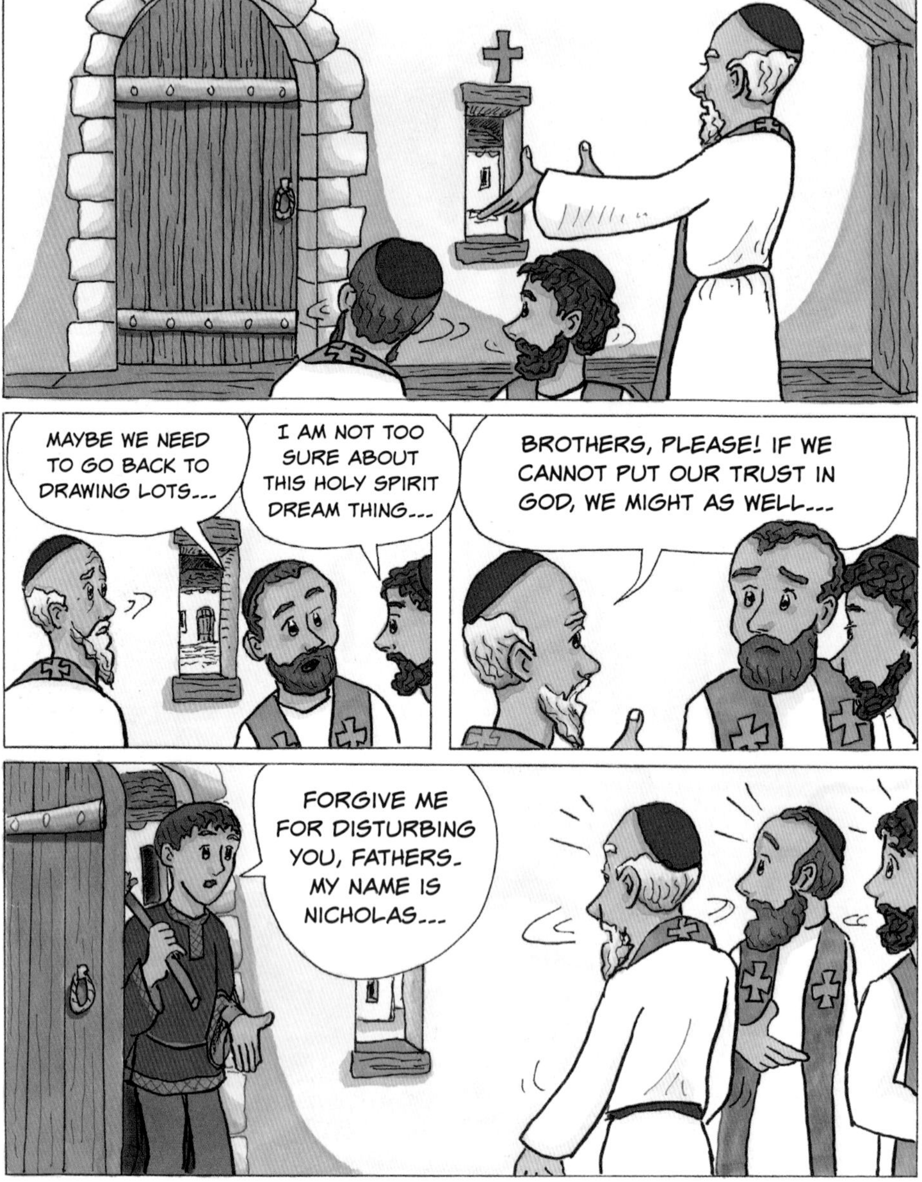
MAYBE WE NEED TO GO BACK TO DRAWING LOTS...
I AM NOT TOO SURE ABOUT THIS HOLY SPIRIT DREAM THING...
BROTHERS, PLEASE! IF WE CANNOT PUT OUR TRUST IN GOD, WE MIGHT AS WELL...
FORGIVE ME FOR DISTURBING YOU, FATHERS. MY NAME IS NICHOLAS...

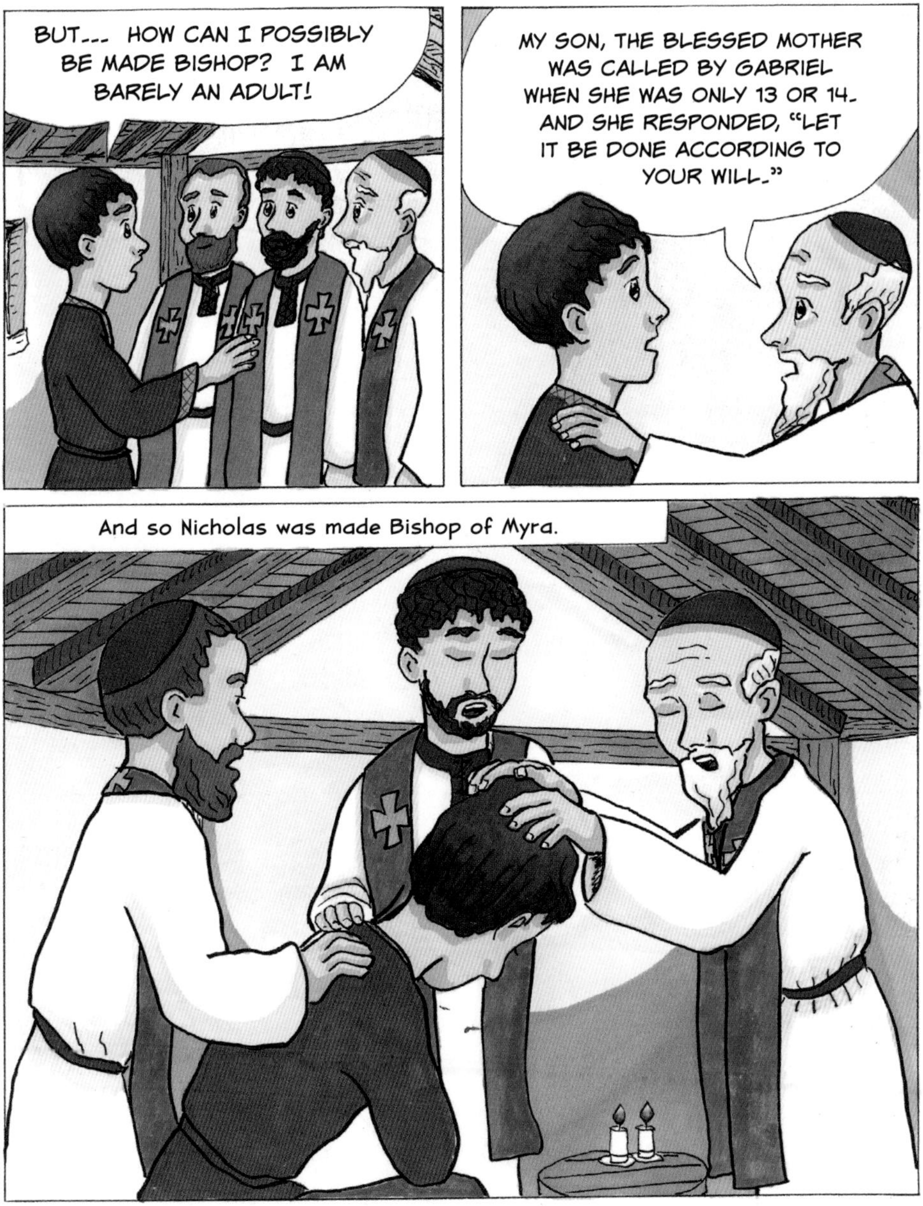
BUT... HOW CAN I POSSIBLY BE MADE BISHOP? I AM BARELY AN ADULT!
MY SON, THE BLESSED MOTHER WAS CALLED BY GABRIEL WHEN SHE WAS ONLY 13 OR 14. AND SHE RESPONDED, "LET IT BE DONE ACCORDING TO YOUR WILL."
And so Nicholas was made Bishop of Myra.

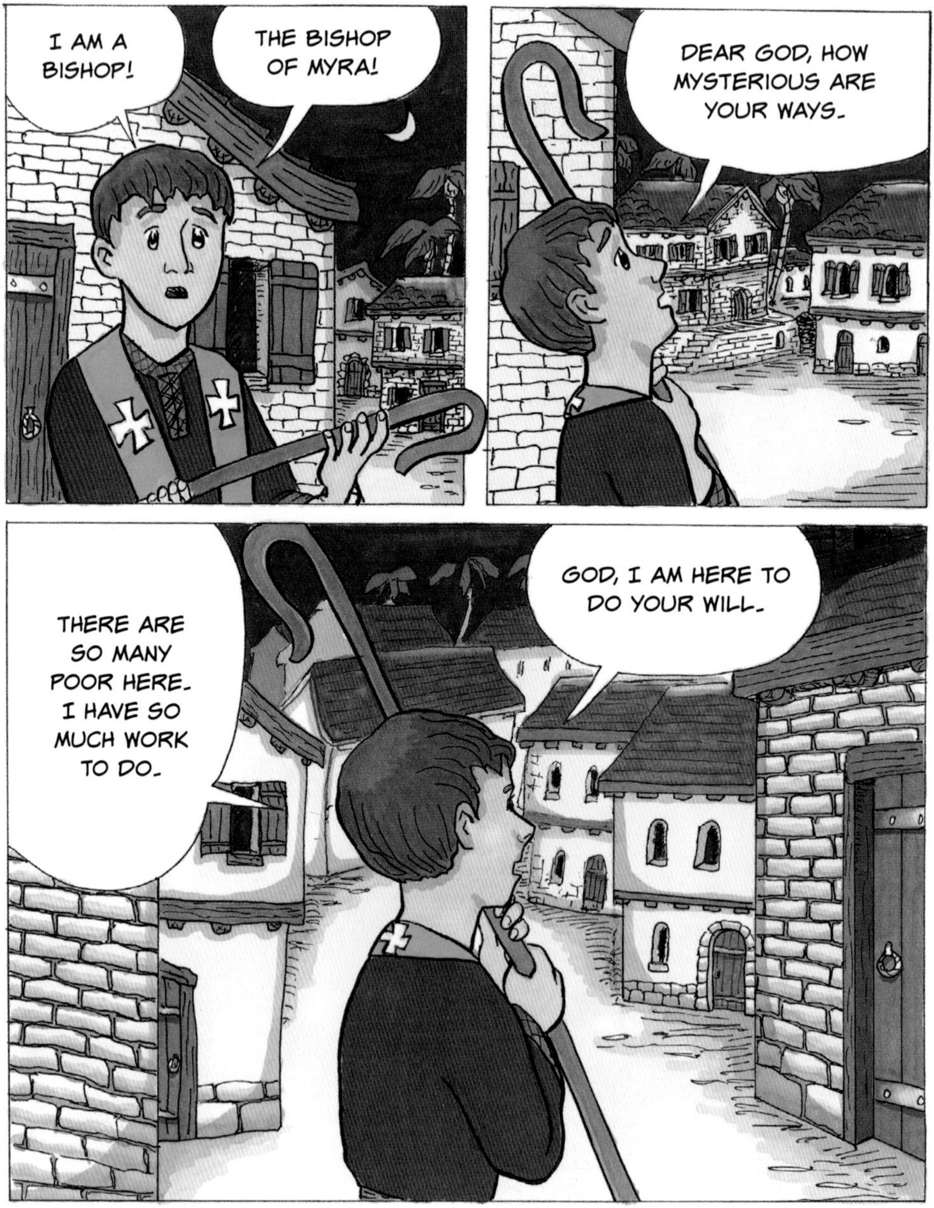
I AM A BISHOP!
THE BISHOP OF MYRA!
DEAR GOD, HOW MYSTERIOUS ARE YOUR WAYS.
THERE ARE SO MANY POOR HERE. I HAVE SO MUCH WORK TO DO.
GOD, I AM HERE TO DO YOUR WILL.

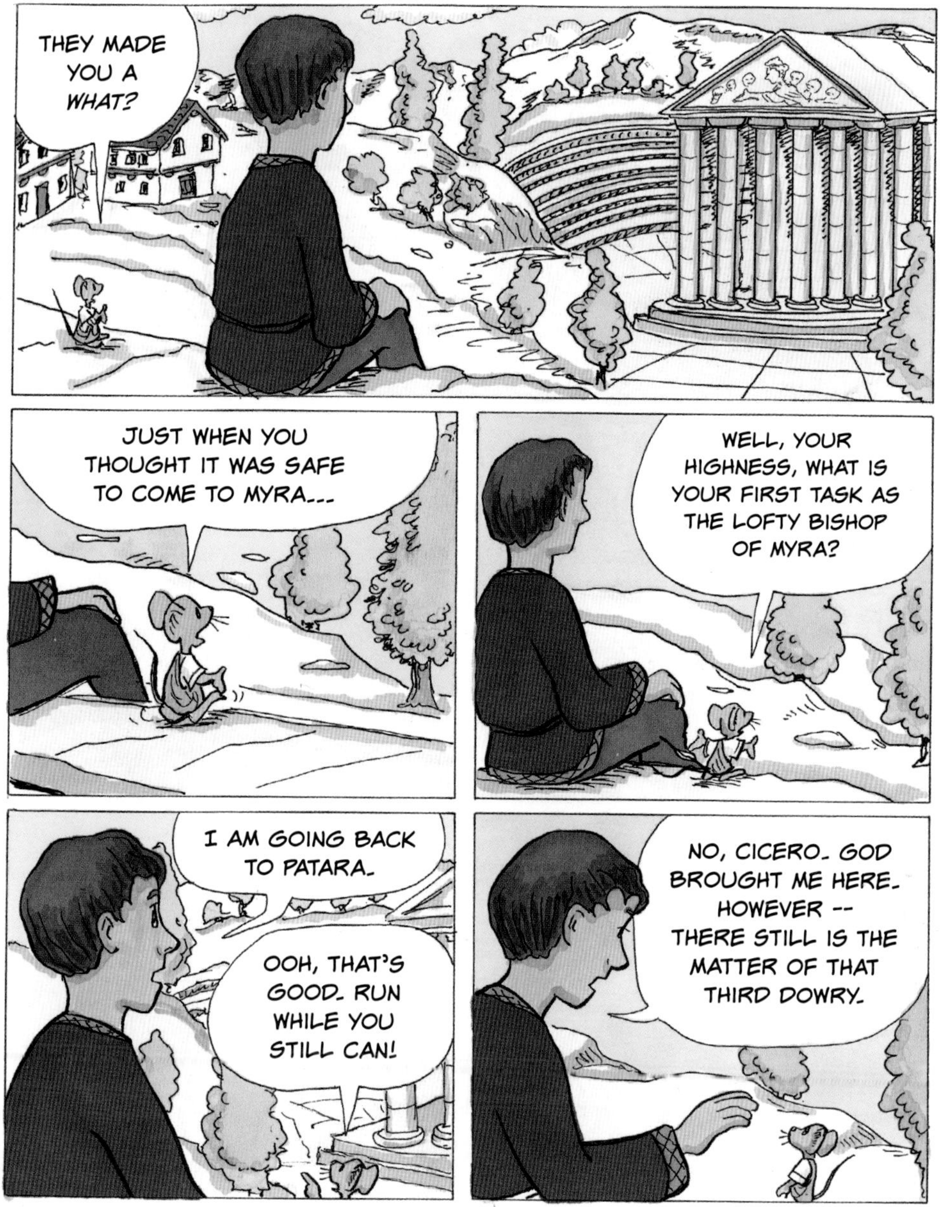
THEY MADE YOU A WHAT?
JUST WHEN YOU THOUGHT IT WAS SAFE TO COME TO MYRA...
WELL, YOUR HIGHNESS, WHAT IS YOUR FIRST TASK AS THE LOFTY BISHOP OF MYRA?
I AM GOING BACK TO PATARA.
OOH, THAT'S GOOD. RUN WHILE YOU STILL CAN!
NO, CICERO. GOD BROUGHT ME HERE. HOWEVER -- THERE STILL IS THE MATTER OF THAT THIRD DOWRY.

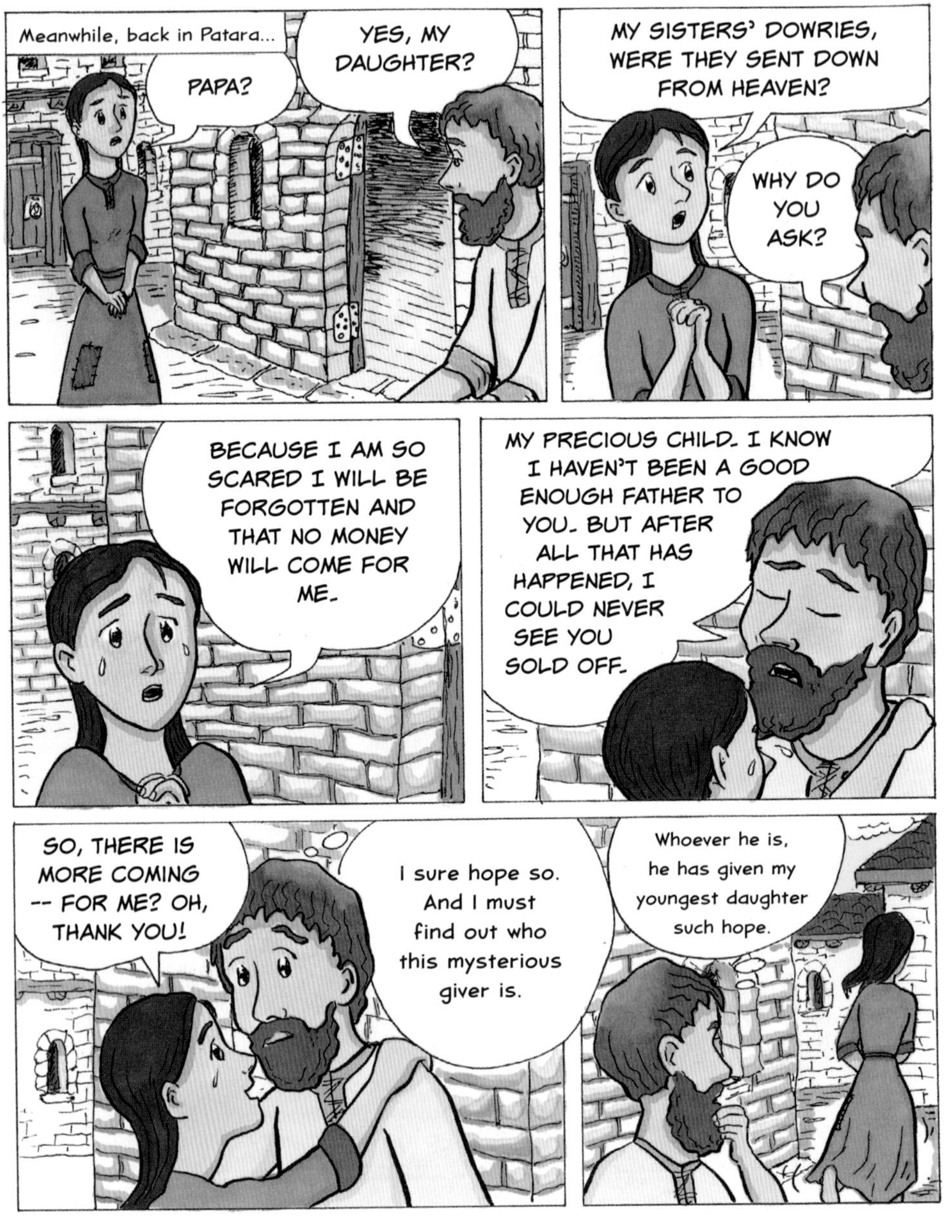
Meanwhile, back in Patara...
PAPA?
YES, MY DAUGHTER?
MY SISTERS' DOWRIES, WERE THEY SENT DOWN FROM HEAVEN?
WHY DO YOU ASK?
BECAUSE I AM SO SCARED I WILL BE FORGOTTEN AND THAT NO MONEY WILL COME FOR ME.
MY PRECIOUS CHILD. I KNOW I HAVEN'T BEEN A GOOD ENOUGH FATHER TO YOU. BUT AFTER ALL THAT HAS HAPPENED, I COULD NEVER SEE YOU SOLD OFF.
SO, THERE IS MORE COMING -- FOR ME? OH, THANK YOU!
I sure hope so. And I must find out who this mysterious giver is.
Whoever he is, he has given my youngest daughter such hope.

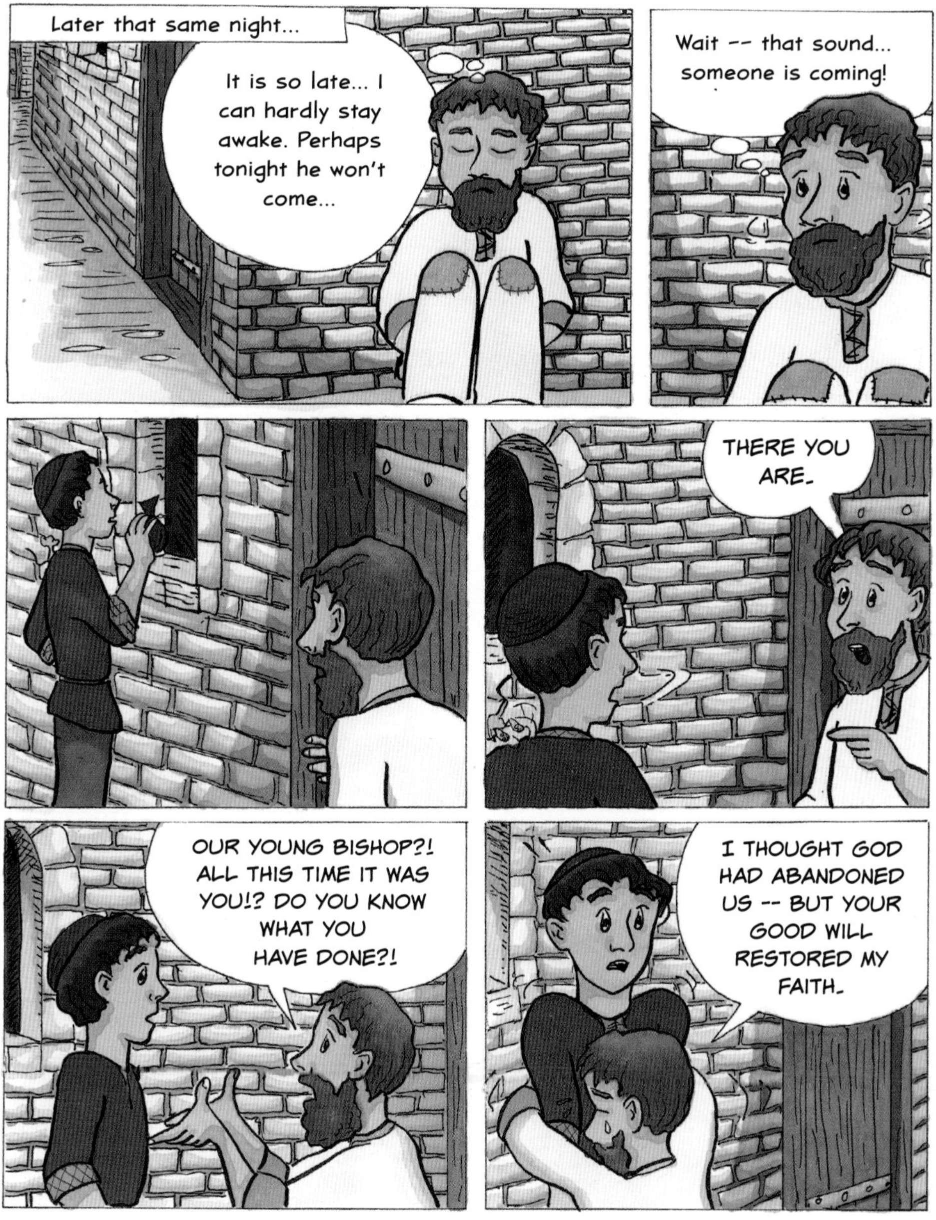
Later that same night...
It is so late... I can hardly stay awake. Perhaps tonight he won't come...
Wait -- that sound... someone is coming!
THERE YOU ARE.
OUR YOUNG BISHOP?! ALL THIS TIME IT WAS YOU!? DO YOU KNOW WHAT YOU HAVE DONE?!
I THOUGHT GOD HAD ABANDONED US -- BUT YOUR GOOD WILL RESTORED MY FAITH.

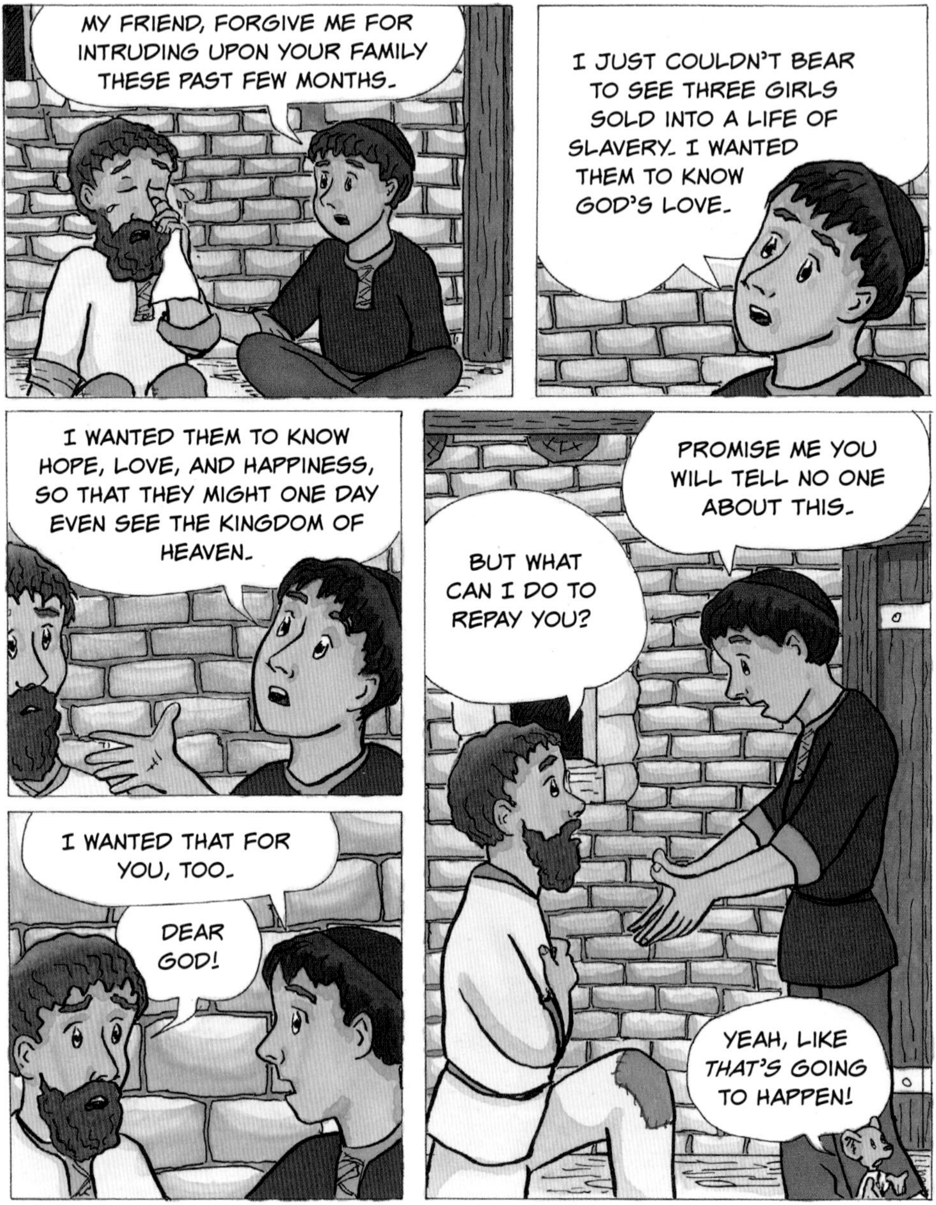
MY FRIEND, FORGIVE ME FOR INTRUDING UPON YOUR FAMILY THESE PAST FEW MONTHS.
I JUST COULDN'T BEAR TO SEE THREE GIRLS SOLD INTO A LIFE OF SLAVERY. I WANTED THEM TO KNOW GOD'S LOVE.
I WANTED THEM TO KNOW HOPE, LOVE, AND HAPPINESS, SO THAT THEY MIGHT ONE DAY EVEN SEE THE KINGDOM OF HEAVEN.
I WANTED THAT FOR YOU, TOO.
DEAR GOD!
BUT WHAT CAN I DO TO REPAY YOU?
PROMISE ME YOU WILL TELL NO ONE ABOUT THIS.
YEAH, LIKE THAT'S GOING TO HAPPEN!

CHAPTER THREE

HOW NICHOLAS BECAME A PRISONER

Do not fear, or be afraid;
have I not told you from of old and declared it?
You are my witnesses!
is there any god besides me?
There is no other rock; I know not one.
—ISAIAH 44:8

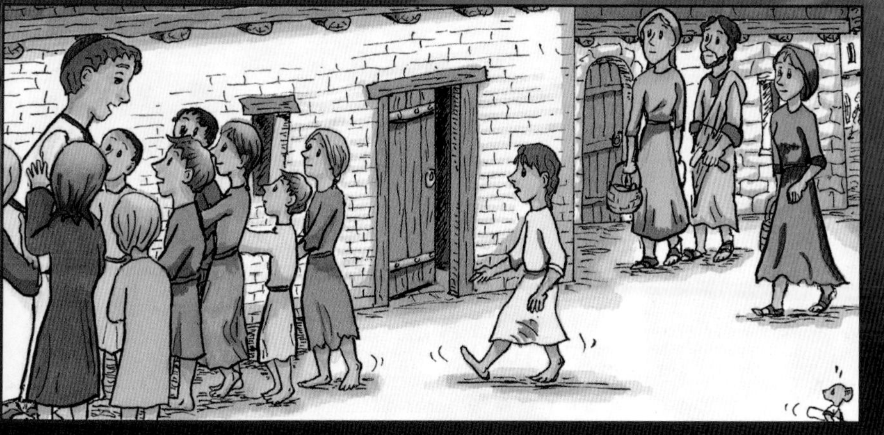

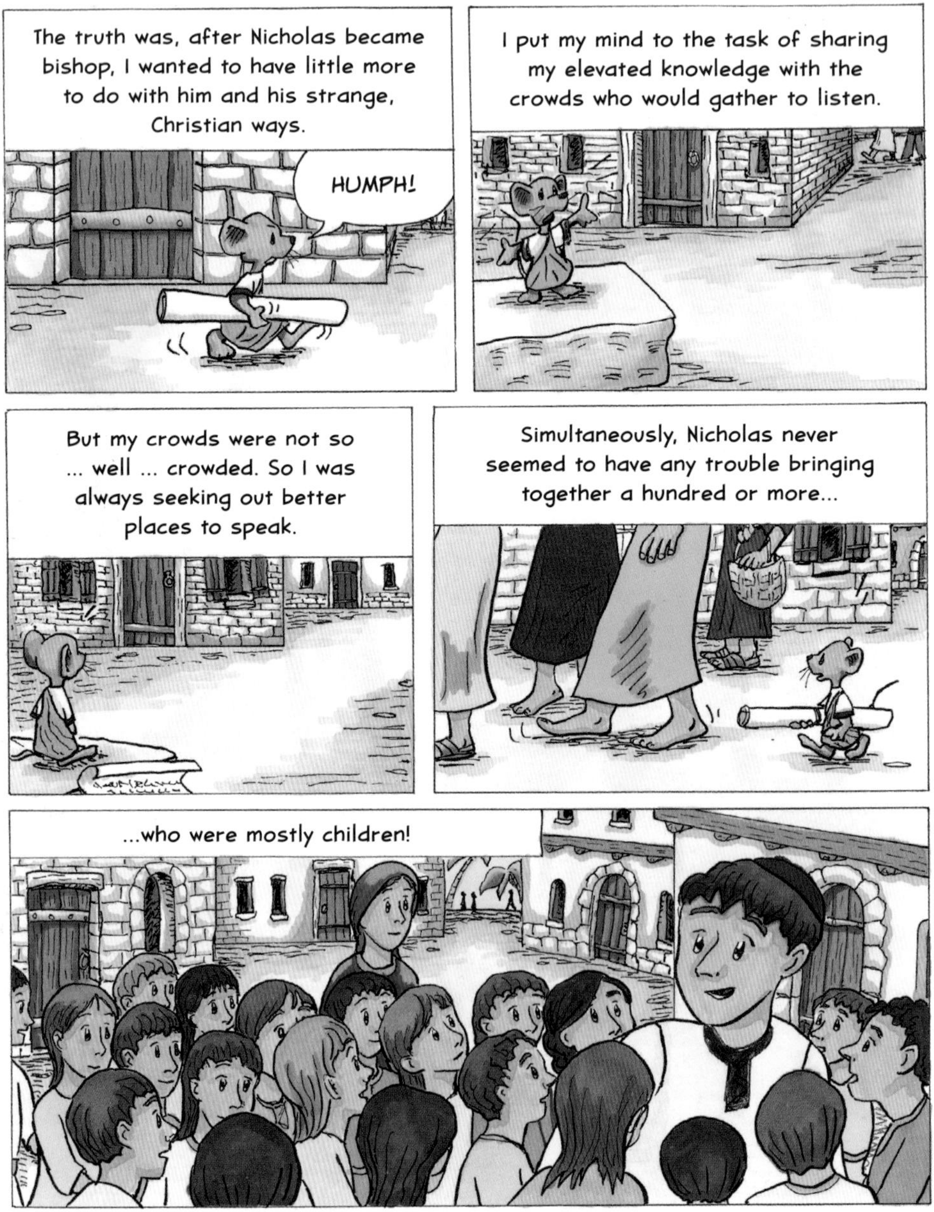
The truth was, after Nicholas became bishop, I wanted to have little more to do with him and his strange, Christian ways.
HUMPH!
I put my mind to the task of sharing my elevated knowledge with the crowds who would gather to listen.
But my crowds were not so ... well ... crowded. So I was always seeking out better places to speak.
Simultaneously, Nicholas never seemed to have any trouble bringing together a hundred or more...
...who were mostly children!

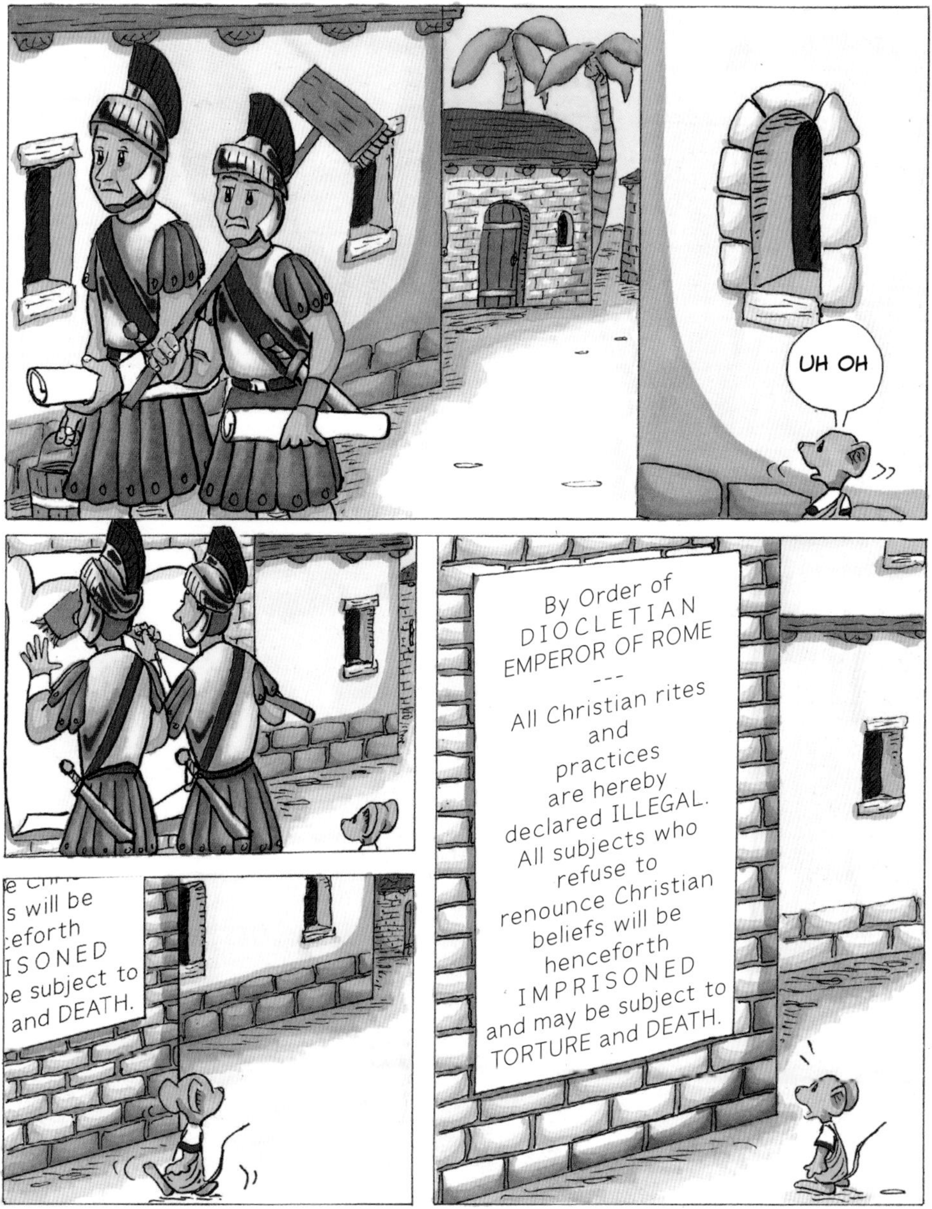
UH OH
By Order of
DIOCLETIAN
EMPEROR OF ROME

All Christian rites
and
practices
are hereby
declared ILLEGAL.
All subjects who
refuse to
renounce Christian
beliefs will be
henceforth
IMPRISONED
and may be subject to
TORTURE and DEATH.
s will be
ceforth
ISONED
e subject to
and DEATH.

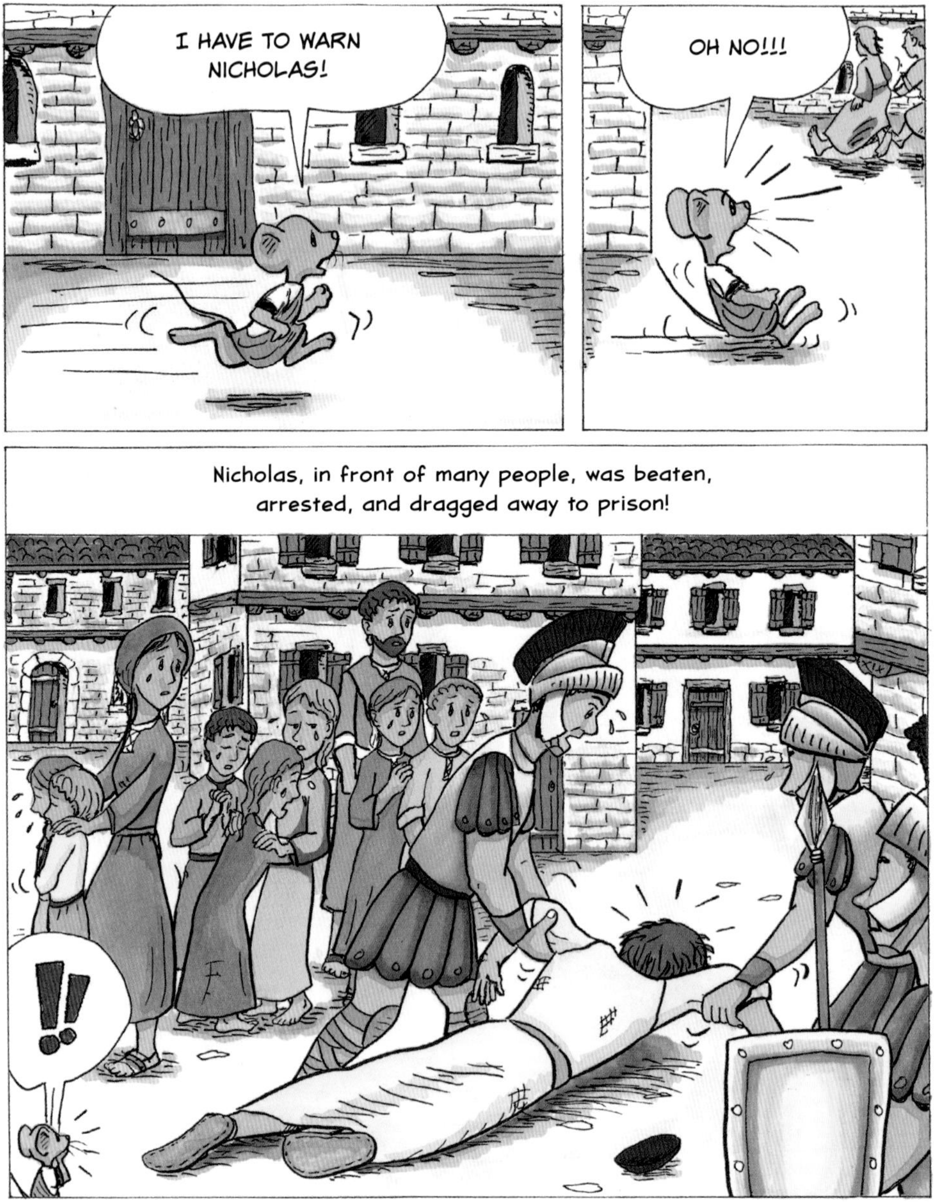
I HAVE TO WARN NICHOLAS!
OH NO!!!
Nicholas, in front of many people, was beaten, arrested, and dragged away to prison!
!!

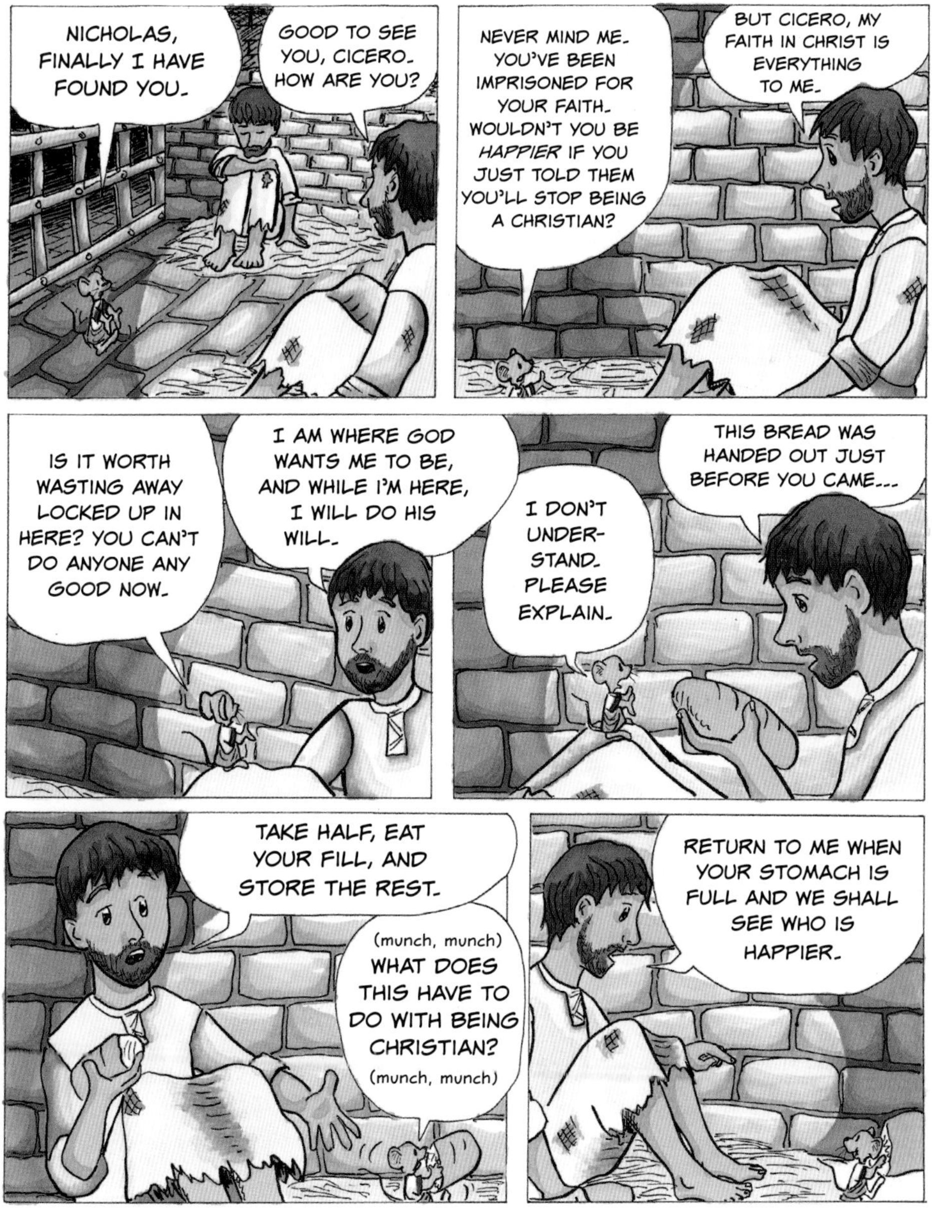
NICHOLAS, FINALLY I HAVE FOUND YOU.
GOOD TO SEE YOU, CICERO. HOW ARE YOU?
NEVER MIND ME. YOU'VE BEEN IMPRISONED FOR YOUR FAITH. WOULDN'T YOU BE *HAPPIER* IF YOU JUST TOLD THEM YOU'LL STOP BEING A CHRISTIAN?
BUT CICERO, MY FAITH IN CHRIST IS EVERYTHING TO ME.
IS IT WORTH WASTING AWAY LOCKED UP IN HERE? YOU CAN'T DO ANYONE ANY GOOD NOW.
I AM WHERE GOD WANTS ME TO BE, AND WHILE I'M HERE, I WILL DO HIS WILL.
I DON'T UNDER-STAND. PLEASE EXPLAIN.
THIS BREAD WAS HANDED OUT JUST BEFORE YOU CAME...
TAKE HALF, EAT YOUR FILL, AND STORE THE REST.
(munch, munch) WHAT DOES THIS HAVE TO DO WITH BEING CHRISTIAN? (munch, munch)
RETURN TO ME WHEN YOUR STOMACH IS FULL AND WE SHALL SEE WHO IS HAPPIER.

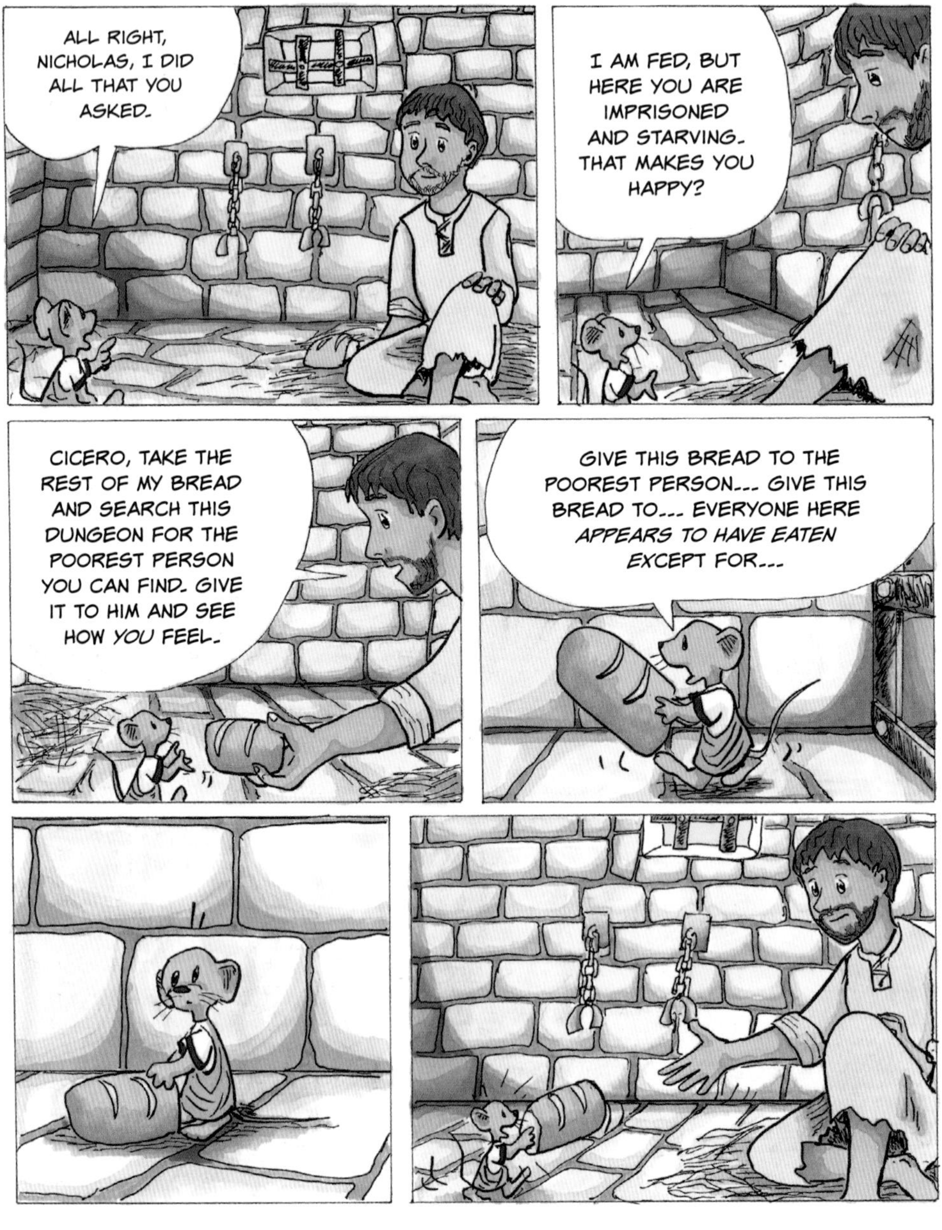
ALL RIGHT, NICHOLAS, I DID ALL THAT YOU ASKED.
I AM FED, BUT HERE YOU ARE IMPRISONED AND STARVING. THAT MAKES YOU HAPPY?
CICERO, TAKE THE REST OF MY BREAD AND SEARCH THIS DUNGEON FOR THE POOREST PERSON YOU CAN FIND. GIVE IT TO HIM AND SEE HOW *YOU* FEEL.
GIVE THIS BREAD TO THE POOREST PERSON... GIVE THIS BREAD TO... EVERYONE HERE *APPEARS TO HAVE EATEN* EXCEPT FOR...

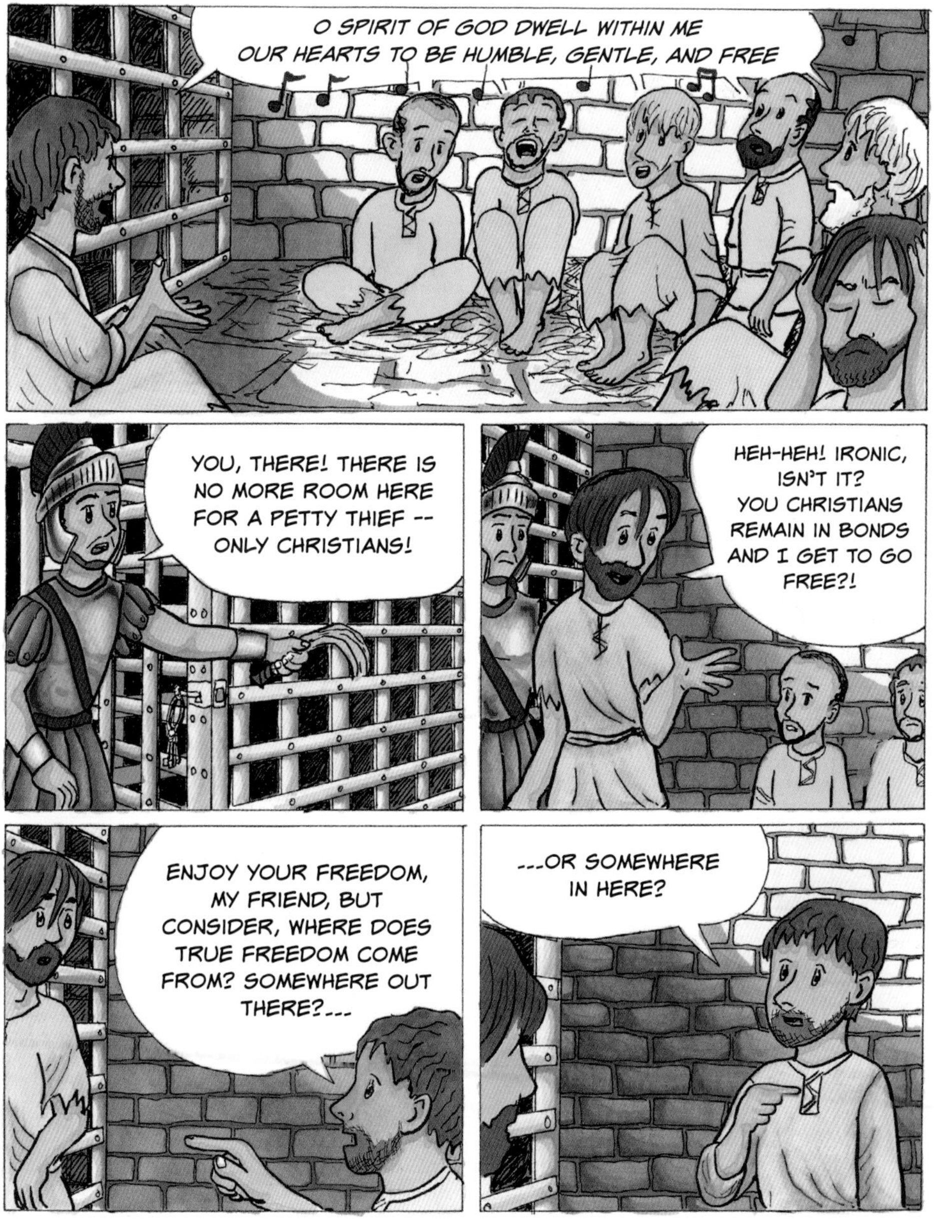
O SPIRIT OF GOD DWELL WITHIN ME
OUR HEARTS TO BE HUMBLE, GENTLE, AND FREE
YOU, THERE! THERE IS NO MORE ROOM HERE FOR A PETTY THIEF -- ONLY CHRISTIANS!
HEH-HEH! IRONIC, ISN'T IT? YOU CHRISTIANS REMAIN IN BONDS AND I GET TO GO FREE?!
ENJOY YOUR FREEDOM, MY FRIEND, BUT CONSIDER, WHERE DOES TRUE FREEDOM COME FROM? SOMEWHERE OUT THERE?...
...OR SOMEWHERE IN HERE?

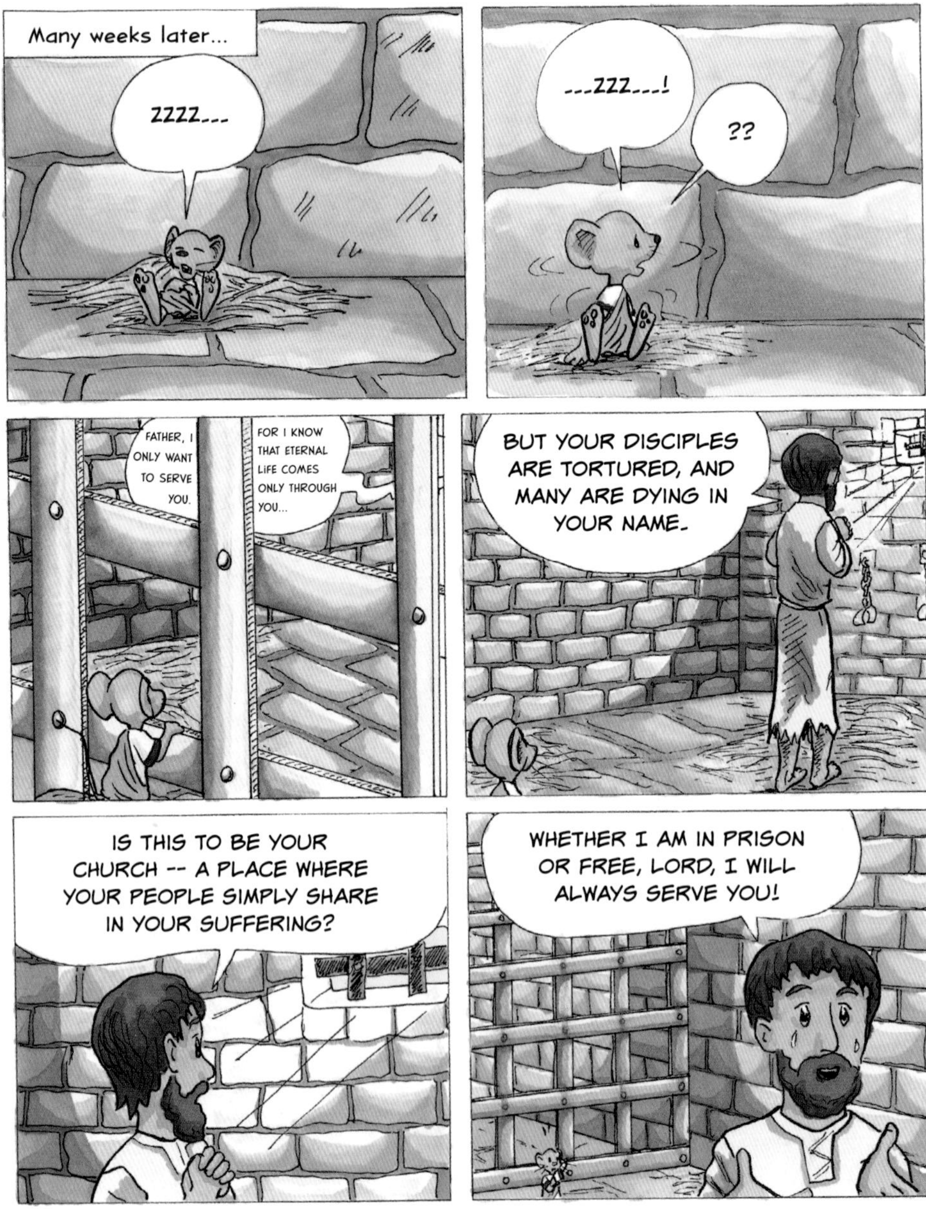
Many weeks later...
ZZZZ...
...ZZZ...!
??
FATHER, I ONLY WANT TO SERVE YOU.
FOR I KNOW THAT ETERNAL LIFE COMES ONLY THROUGH YOU...
BUT YOUR DISCIPLES ARE TORTURED, AND MANY ARE DYING IN YOUR NAME.
IS THIS TO BE YOUR CHURCH -- A PLACE WHERE YOUR PEOPLE SIMPLY SHARE IN YOUR SUFFERING?
WHETHER I AM IN PRISON OR FREE, LORD, I WILL ALWAYS SERVE YOU!

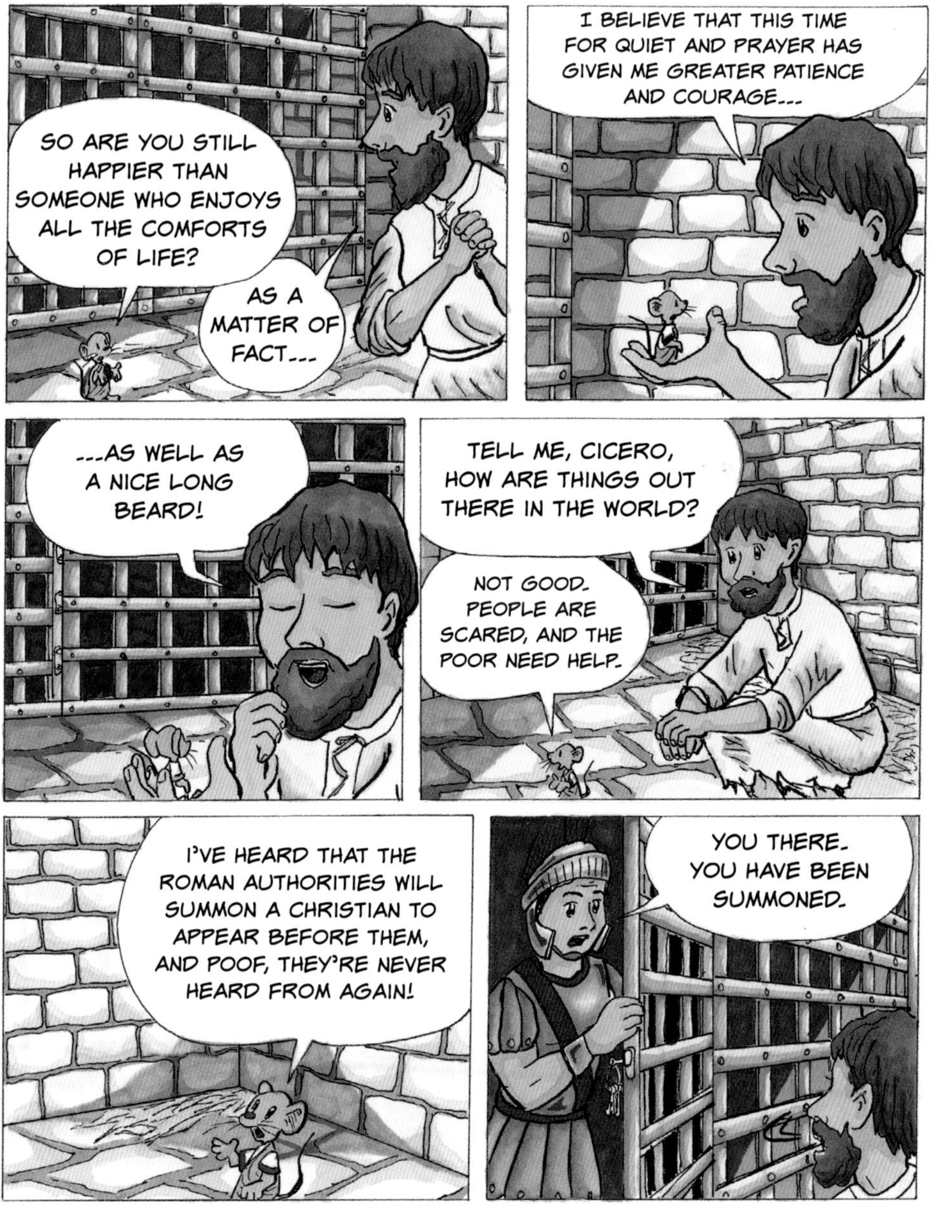
SO ARE YOU STILL HAPPIER THAN SOMEONE WHO ENJOYS ALL THE COMFORTS OF LIFE?
AS A MATTER OF FACT...
I BELIEVE THAT THIS TIME FOR QUIET AND PRAYER HAS GIVEN ME GREATER PATIENCE AND COURAGE...
...AS WELL AS A NICE LONG BEARD!
TELL ME, CICERO, HOW ARE THINGS OUT THERE IN THE WORLD?
NOT GOOD. PEOPLE ARE SCARED, AND THE POOR NEED HELP.
I'VE HEARD THAT THE ROMAN AUTHORITIES WILL SUMMON A CHRISTIAN TO APPEAR BEFORE THEM, AND POOF, THEY'RE NEVER HEARD FROM AGAIN!
YOU THERE. YOU HAVE BEEN SUMMONED.

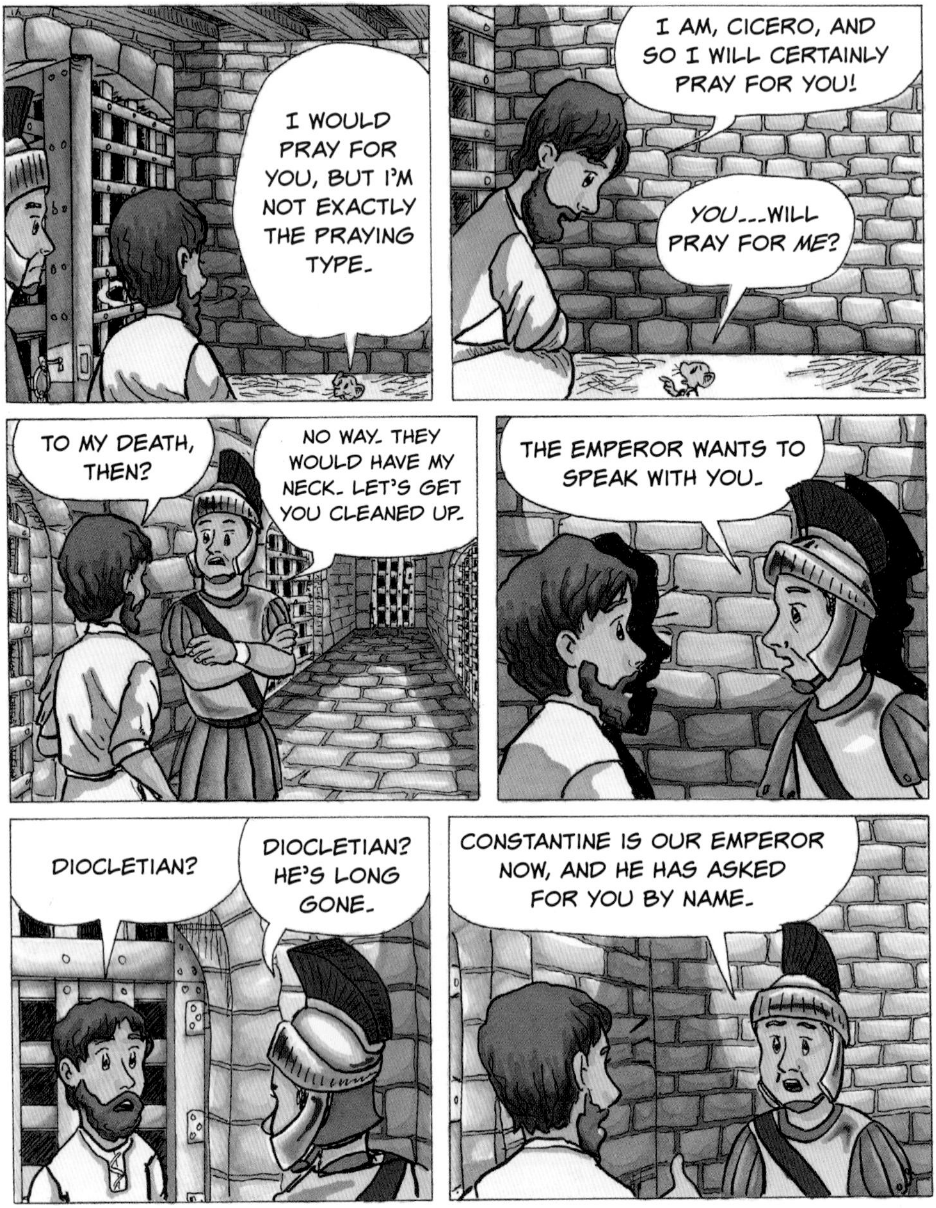
I WOULD PRAY FOR YOU, BUT I'M NOT EXACTLY THE PRAYING TYPE.
I AM, CICERO, AND SO I WILL CERTAINLY PRAY FOR YOU!
YOU...WILL PRAY FOR ME?
TO MY DEATH, THEN?
NO WAY. THEY WOULD HAVE MY NECK. LET'S GET YOU CLEANED UP.
THE EMPEROR WANTS TO SPEAK WITH YOU.
DIOCLETIAN?
DIOCLETIAN? HE'S LONG GONE.
CONSTANTINE IS OUR EMPEROR NOW, AND HE HAS ASKED FOR YOU BY NAME.

Emperor Constantine's Palace, AD 300

CONSTANTINE THE FIRST, EMPEROR OF ROME, I PRESENT NICHOLAS, BISHOP OF MYRA IN LYCIA.

YOU! BOW BEFORE YOUR EMPEROR!

THAT WON'T BE NECESSARY, TRIBUNE. DISMISSED.

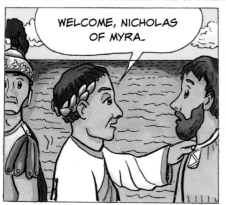

WELCOME, NICHOLAS OF MYRA.

PLEASE DINE WITH ME. I HAVE MUCH TO DISCUSS WITH YOU. TELL ME, HOW ARE YOU WITH MIRACLES?

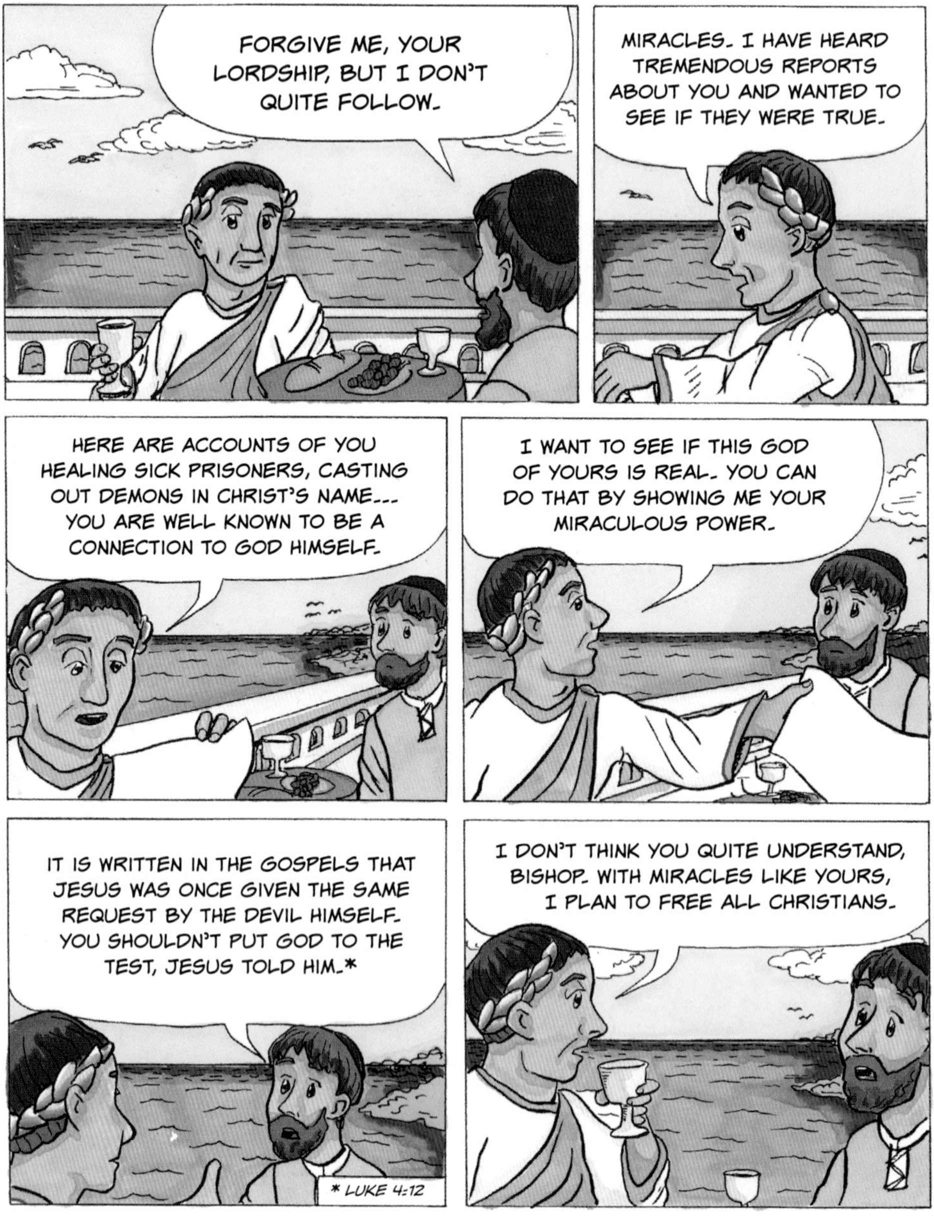
FORGIVE ME, YOUR LORDSHIP, BUT I DON'T QUITE FOLLOW.
MIRACLES. I HAVE HEARD TREMENDOUS REPORTS ABOUT YOU AND WANTED TO SEE IF THEY WERE TRUE.
HERE ARE ACCOUNTS OF YOU HEALING SICK PRISONERS, CASTING OUT DEMONS IN CHRIST'S NAME... YOU ARE WELL KNOWN TO BE A CONNECTION TO GOD HIMSELF.
I WANT TO SEE IF THIS GOD OF YOURS IS REAL. YOU CAN DO THAT BY SHOWING ME YOUR MIRACULOUS POWER.
IT IS WRITTEN IN THE GOSPELS THAT JESUS WAS ONCE GIVEN THE SAME REQUEST BY THE DEVIL HIMSELF. YOU SHOULDN'T PUT GOD TO THE TEST, JESUS TOLD HIM.*
* LUKE 4:12
I DON'T THINK YOU QUITE UNDERSTAND, BISHOP. WITH MIRACLES LIKE YOURS, I PLAN TO FREE ALL CHRISTIANS.

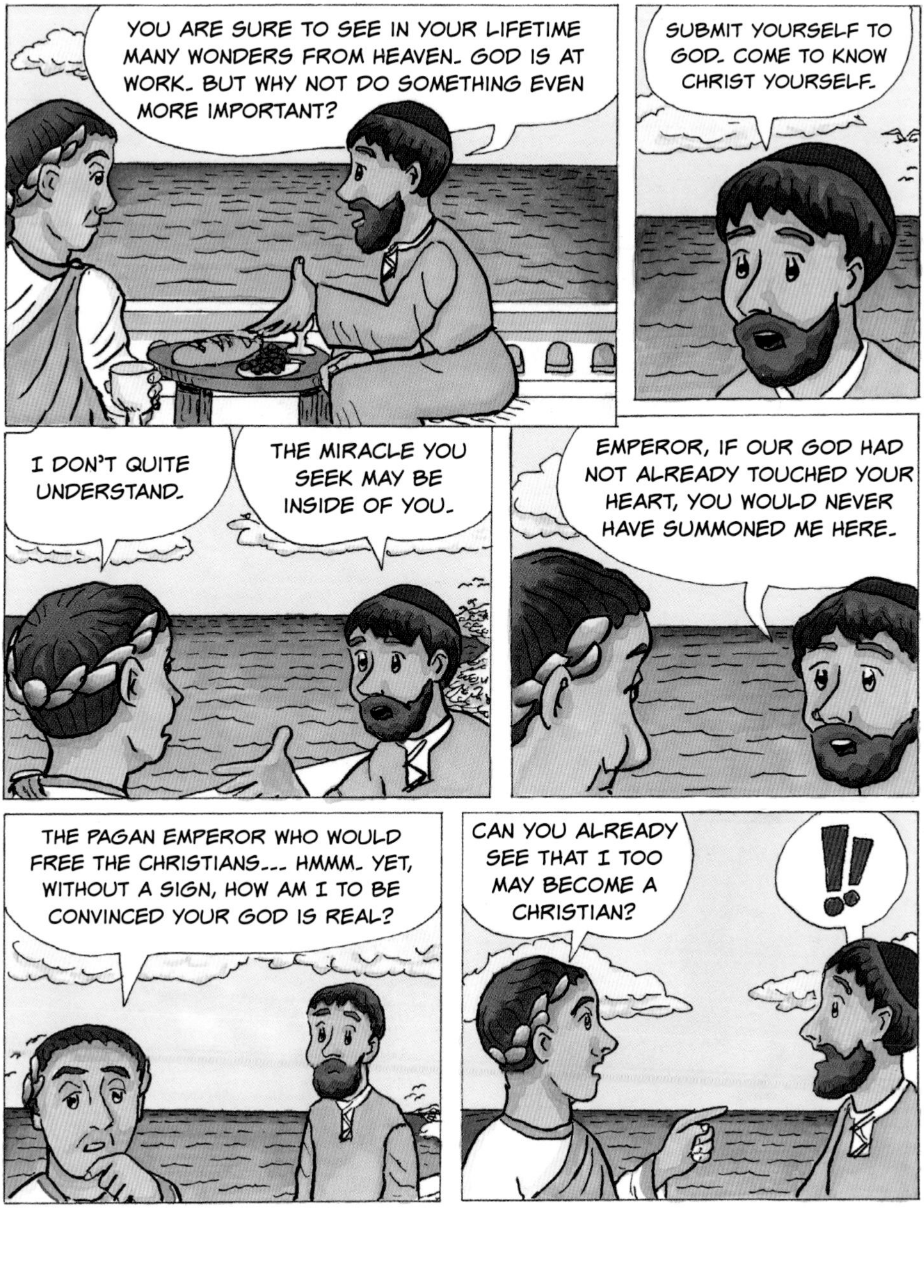
YOU ARE SURE TO SEE IN YOUR LIFETIME MANY WONDERS FROM HEAVEN. GOD IS AT WORK. BUT WHY NOT DO SOMETHING EVEN MORE IMPORTANT?
SUBMIT YOURSELF TO GOD. COME TO KNOW CHRIST YOURSELF.
I DON'T QUITE UNDERSTAND.
THE MIRACLE YOU SEEK MAY BE INSIDE OF YOU.
EMPEROR, IF OUR GOD HAD NOT ALREADY TOUCHED YOUR HEART, YOU WOULD NEVER HAVE SUMMONED ME HERE.
THE PAGAN EMPEROR WHO WOULD FREE THE CHRISTIANS... HMMM. YET, WITHOUT A SIGN, HOW AM I TO BE CONVINCED YOUR GOD IS REAL?
CAN YOU ALREADY SEE THAT I TOO MAY BECOME A CHRISTIAN?
!!

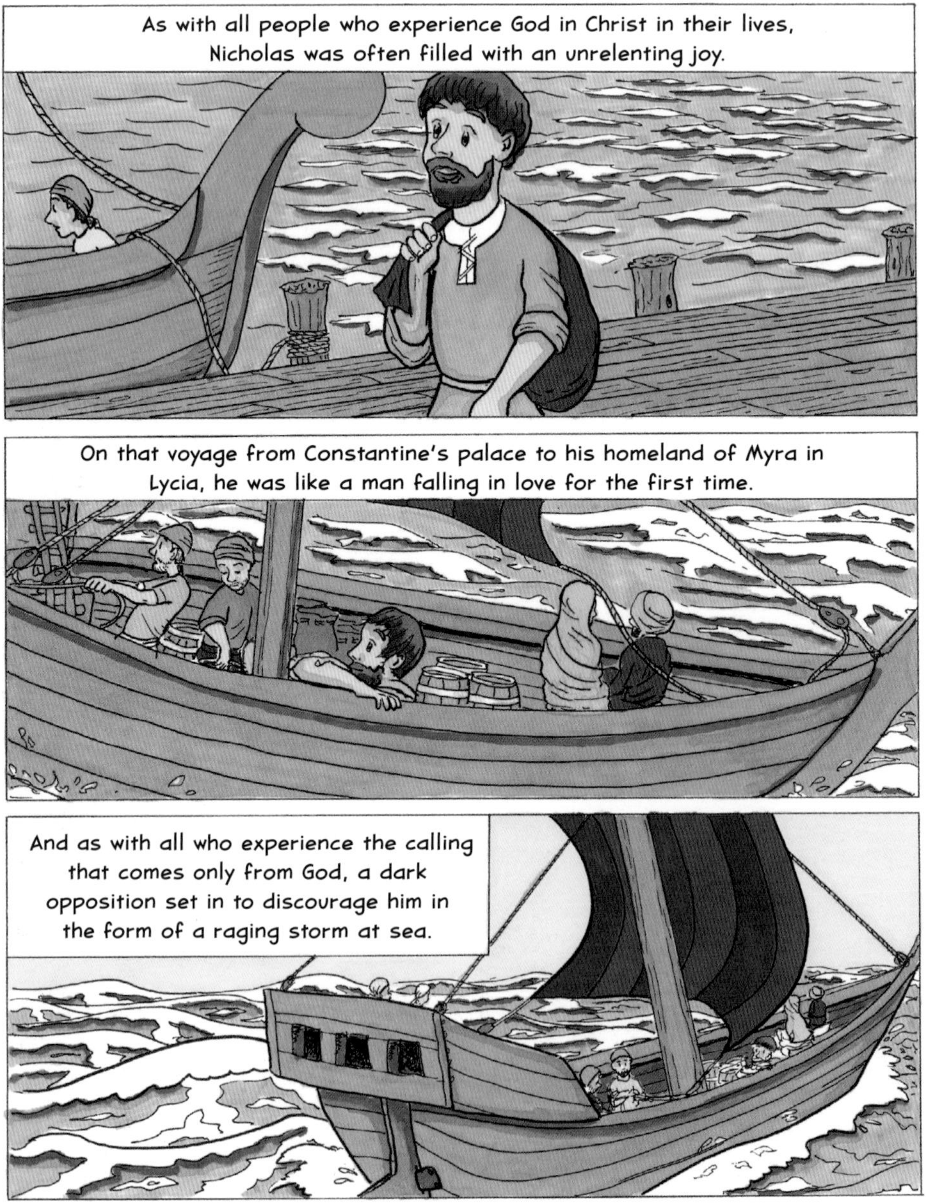
As with all people who experience God in Christ in their lives, Nicholas was often filled with an unrelenting joy.
On that voyage from Constantine's palace to his homeland of Myra in Lycia, he was like a man falling in love for the first time.
And as with all who experience the calling that comes only from God, a dark opposition set in to discourage him in the form of a raging storm at sea.

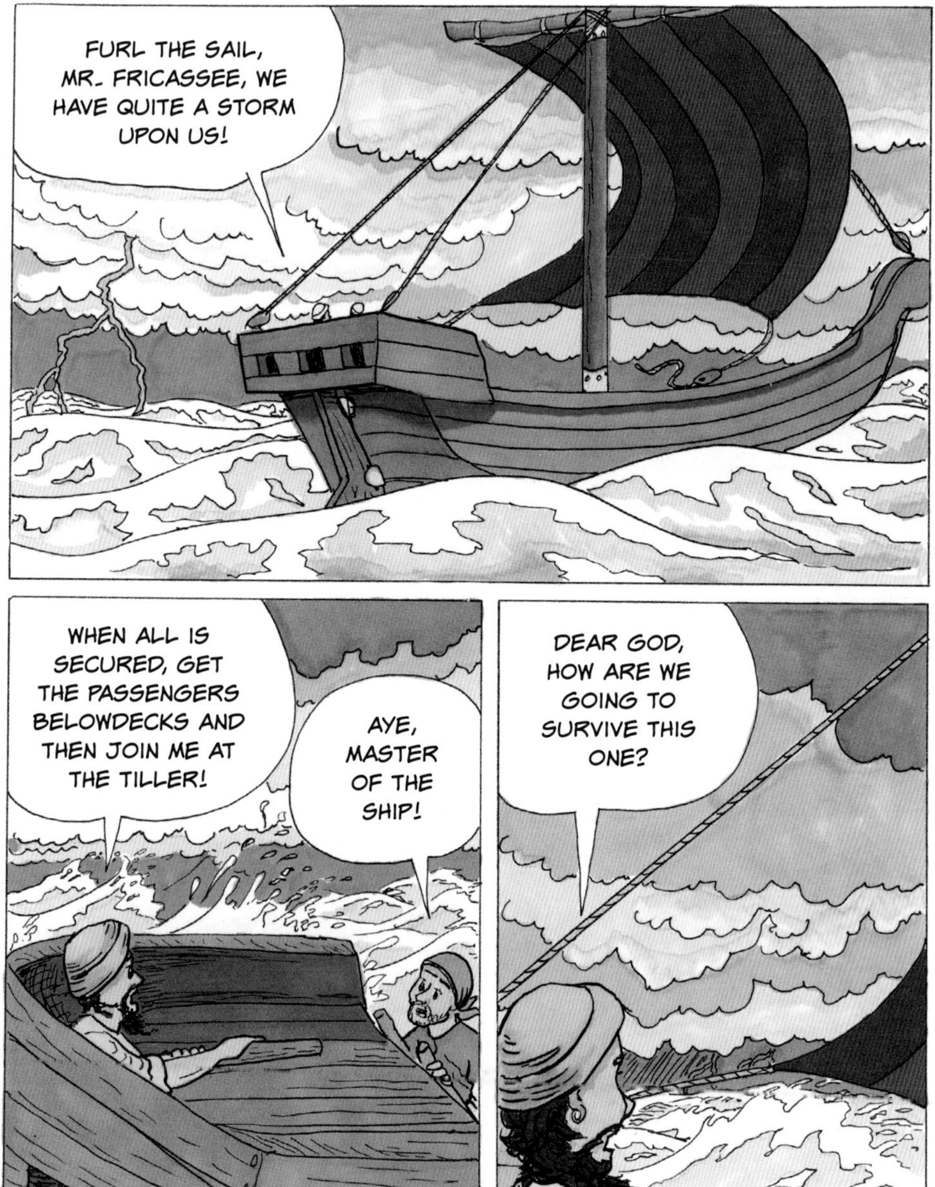
FURL THE SAIL, MR. FRICASSEE, WE HAVE QUITE A STORM UPON US!
WHEN ALL IS SECURED, GET THE PASSENGERS BELOWDECKS AND THEN JOIN ME AT THE TILLER!
AYE, MASTER OF THE SHIP!
DEAR GOD, HOW ARE WE GOING TO SURVIVE THIS ONE?

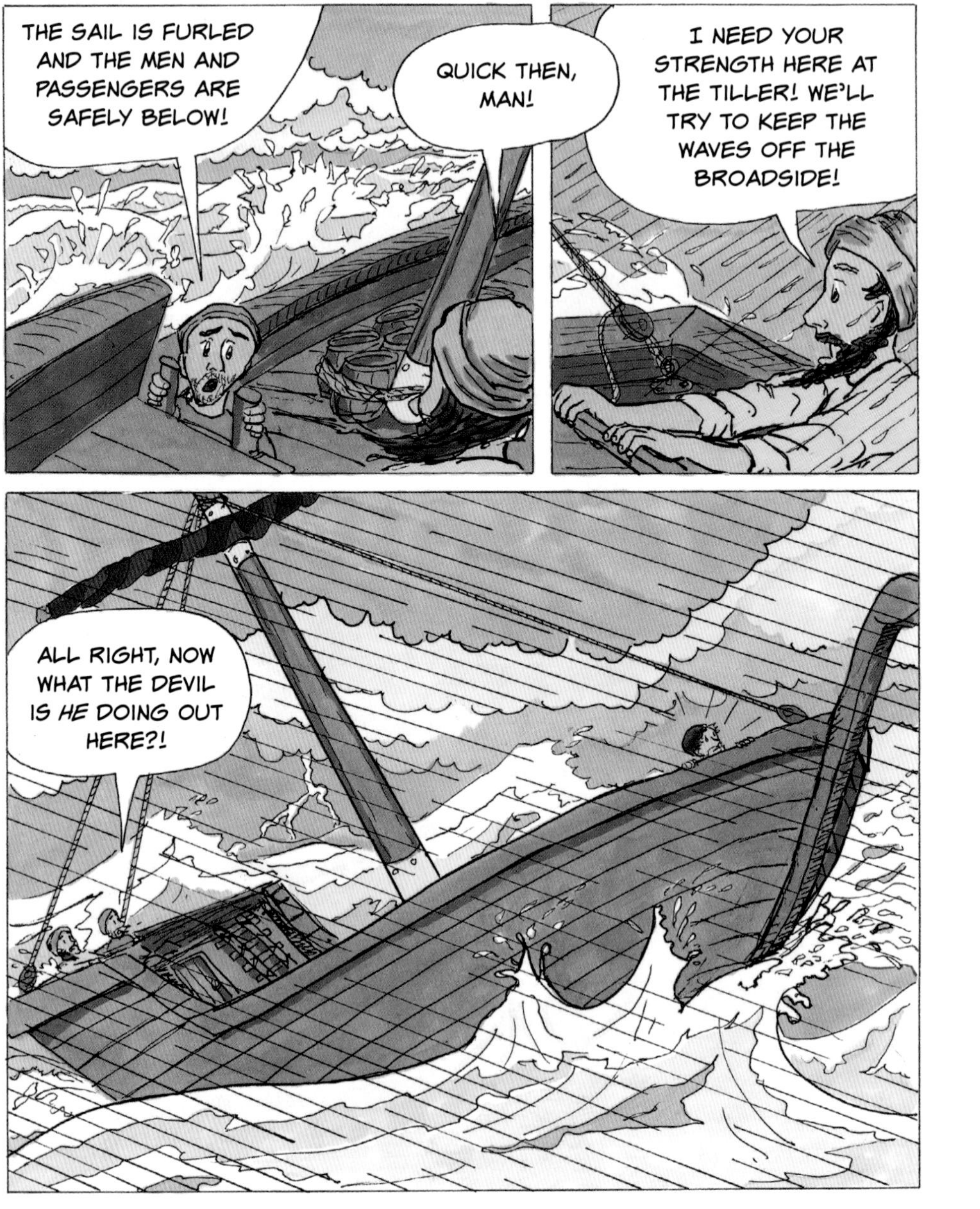
THE SAIL IS FURLED AND THE MEN AND PASSENGERS ARE SAFELY BELOW!
QUICK THEN, MAN!
I NEED YOUR STRENGTH HERE AT THE TILLER! WE'LL TRY TO KEEP THE WAVES OFF THE BROADSIDE!
ALL RIGHT, NOW WHAT THE DEVIL IS *HE* DOING OUT HERE?!

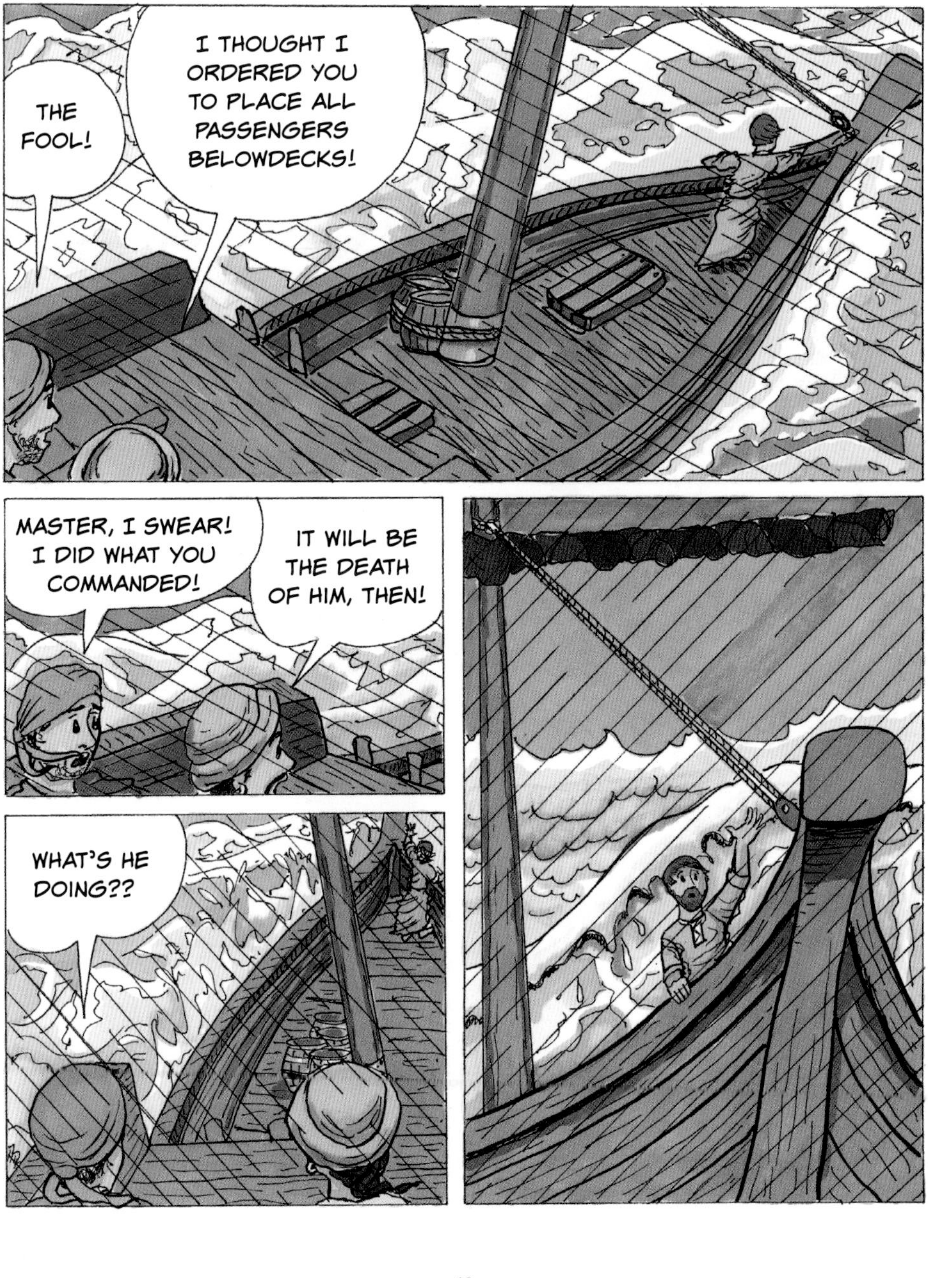
THE FOOL!
I THOUGHT I ORDERED YOU TO PLACE ALL PASSENGERS BELOWDECKS!
MASTER, I SWEAR! I DID WHAT YOU COMMANDED!
IT WILL BE THE DEATH OF HIM, THEN!
WHAT'S HE DOING??

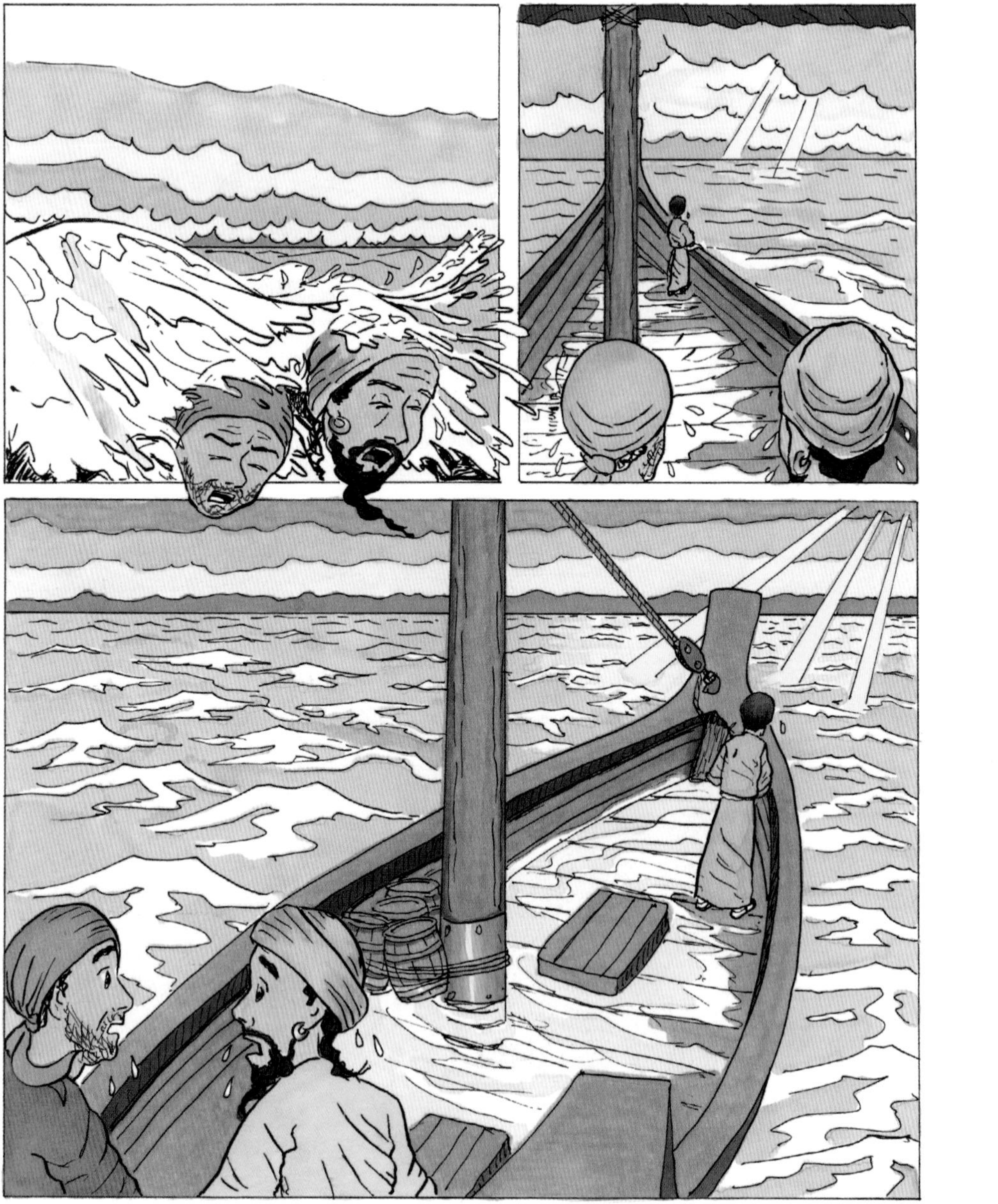

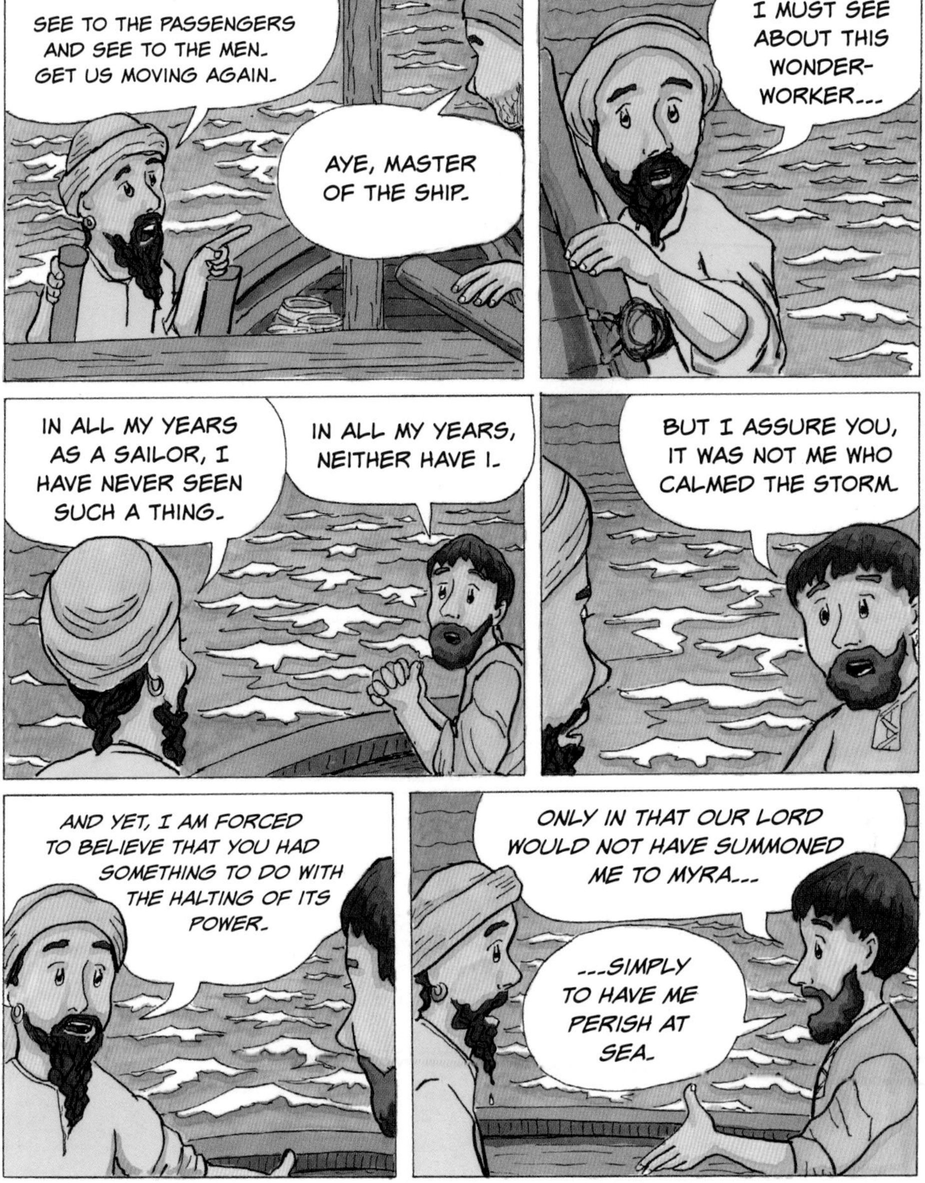
SEE TO THE PASSENGERS AND SEE TO THE MEN. GET US MOVING AGAIN.
AYE, MASTER OF THE SHIP.
I MUST SEE ABOUT THIS WONDER-WORKER...
IN ALL MY YEARS AS A SAILOR, I HAVE NEVER SEEN SUCH A THING.
IN ALL MY YEARS, NEITHER HAVE I.
BUT I ASSURE YOU, IT WAS NOT ME WHO CALMED THE STORM.
AND YET, I AM FORCED TO BELIEVE THAT YOU HAD SOMETHING TO DO WITH THE HALTING OF ITS POWER.
ONLY IN THAT OUR LORD WOULD NOT HAVE SUMMONED ME TO MYRA...
...SIMPLY TO HAVE ME PERISH AT SEA.

CHAPTER FOUR
THE GIVER OF GIFTS

Trust in the LORD with all your heart,
and do not rely on your own insight.
in all your ways acknowledge him,
and he will make straight your paths.
--PROVERBS 3:5-6

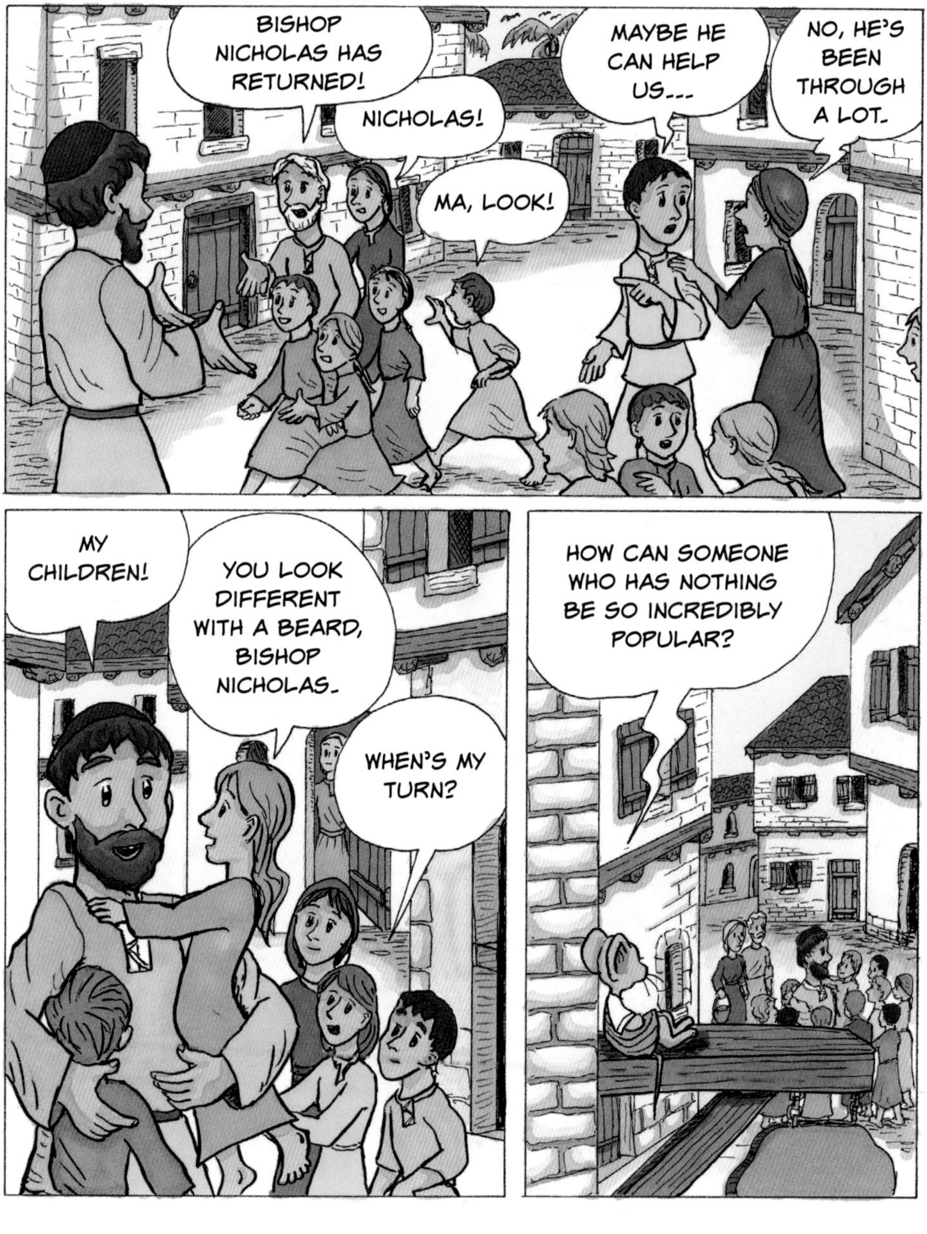
BISHOP NICHOLAS HAS RETURNED!
NICHOLAS!
MA, LOOK!
MAYBE HE CAN HELP US...
NO, HE'S BEEN THROUGH A LOT.
MY CHILDREN!
YOU LOOK DIFFERENT WITH A BEARD, BISHOP NICHOLAS.
WHEN'S MY TURN?
HOW CAN SOMEONE WHO HAS NOTHING BE SO INCREDIBLY POPULAR?

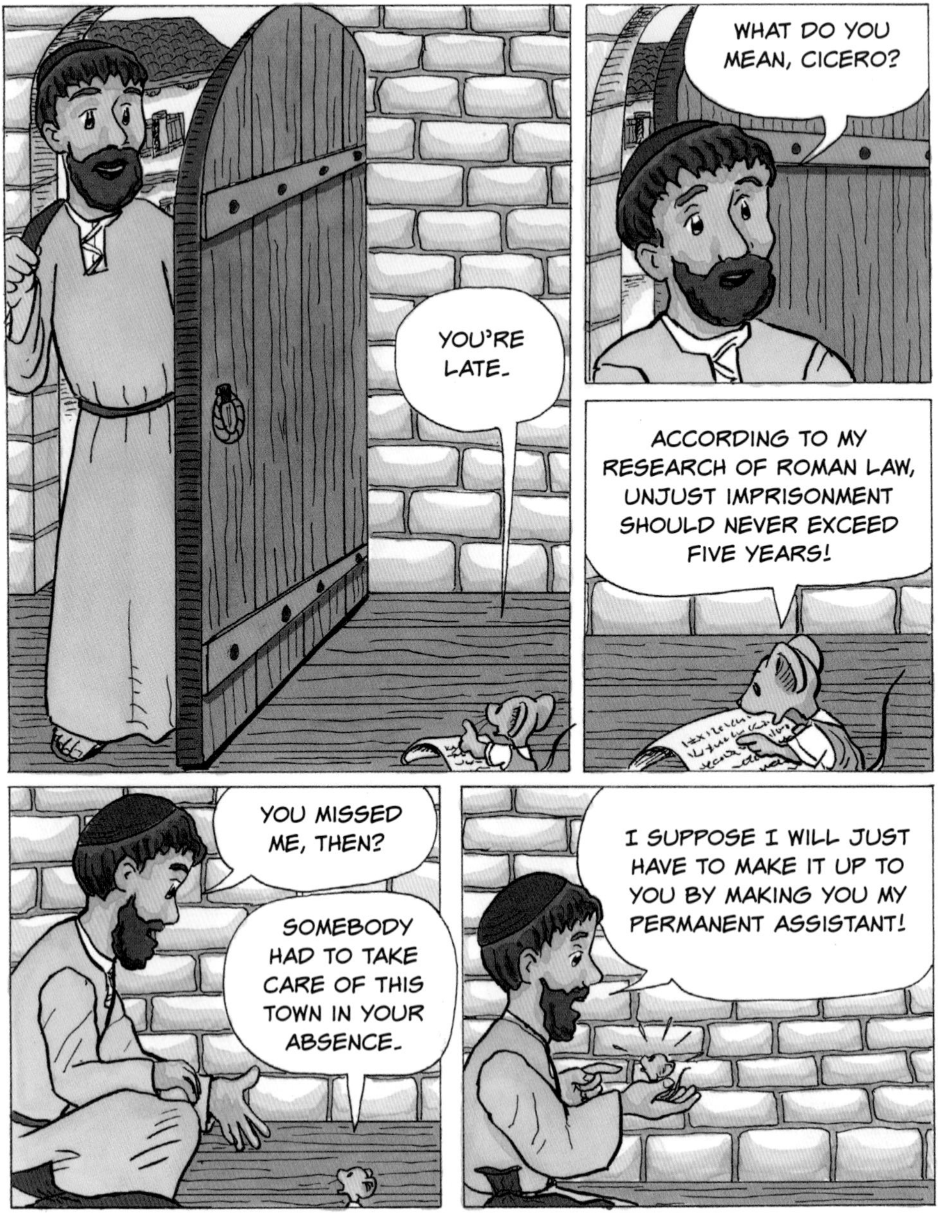
YOU'RE LATE.
WHAT DO YOU MEAN, CICERO?
ACCORDING TO MY RESEARCH OF ROMAN LAW, UNJUST IMPRISONMENT SHOULD NEVER EXCEED FIVE YEARS!
YOU MISSED ME, THEN?
SOMEBODY HAD TO TAKE CARE OF THIS TOWN IN YOUR ABSENCE.
I SUPPOSE I WILL JUST HAVE TO MAKE IT UP TO YOU BY MAKING YOU MY PERMANENT ASSISTANT!

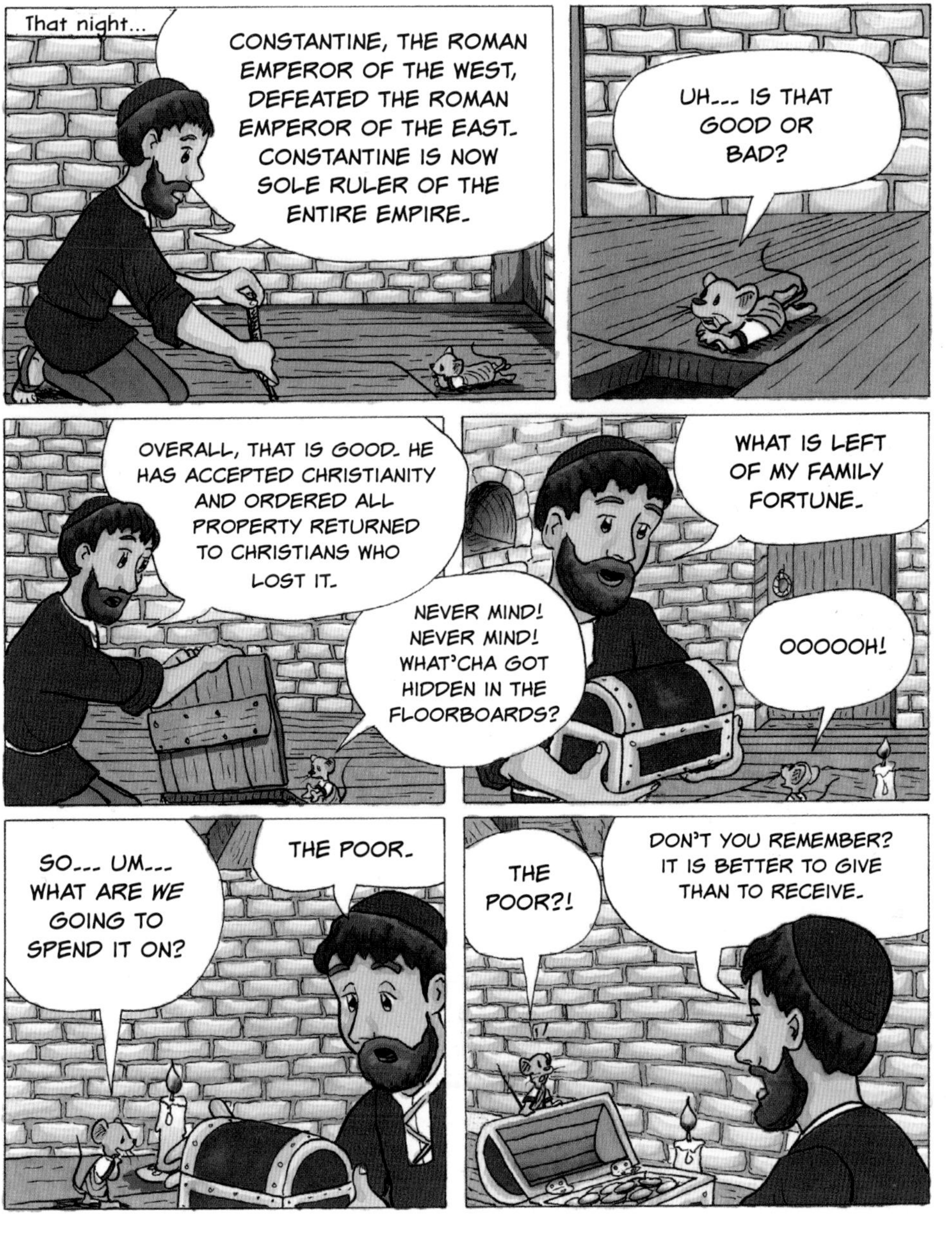
That night...
CONSTANTINE, THE ROMAN EMPEROR OF THE WEST, DEFEATED THE ROMAN EMPEROR OF THE EAST. CONSTANTINE IS NOW SOLE RULER OF THE ENTIRE EMPIRE.
UH... IS THAT GOOD OR BAD?
OVERALL, THAT IS GOOD. HE HAS ACCEPTED CHRISTIANITY AND ORDERED ALL PROPERTY RETURNED TO CHRISTIANS WHO LOST IT.
NEVER MIND! NEVER MIND! WHAT'CHA GOT HIDDEN IN THE FLOORBOARDS?
WHAT IS LEFT OF MY FAMILY FORTUNE.
OOOOOH!
SO... UM... WHAT ARE WE GOING TO SPEND IT ON?
THE POOR.
THE POOR?!
DON'T YOU REMEMBER? IT IS BETTER TO GIVE THAN TO RECEIVE.

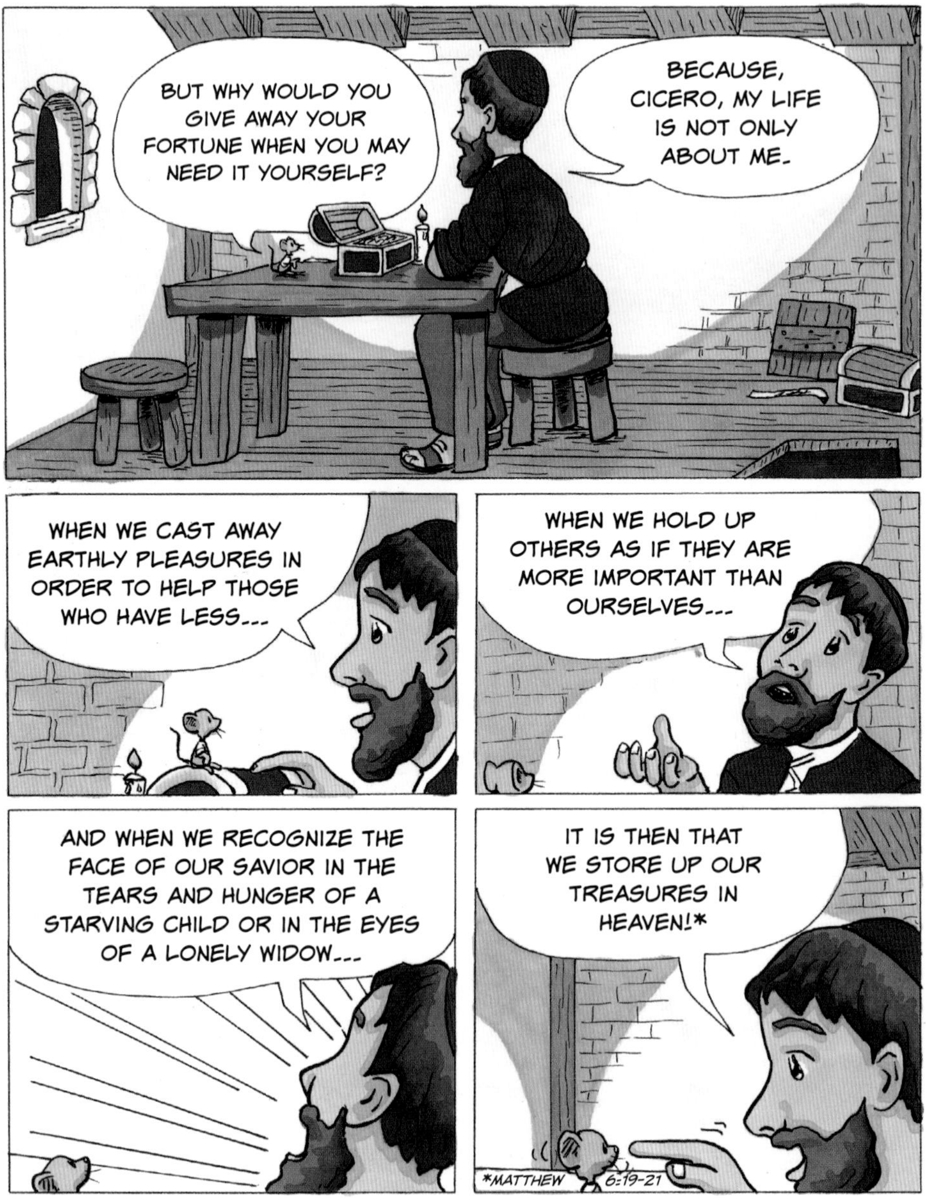

BUT WHY WOULD YOU GIVE AWAY YOUR FORTUNE WHEN YOU MAY NEED IT YOURSELF?
BECAUSE, CICERO, MY LIFE IS NOT ONLY ABOUT ME.
WHEN WE CAST AWAY EARTHLY PLEASURES IN ORDER TO HELP THOSE WHO HAVE LESS...
WHEN WE HOLD UP OTHERS AS IF THEY ARE MORE IMPORTANT THAN OURSELVES...
AND WHEN WE RECOGNIZE THE FACE OF OUR SAVIOR IN THE TEARS AND HUNGER OF A STARVING CHILD OR IN THE EYES OF A LONELY WIDOW...
IT IS THEN THAT WE STORE UP OUR TREASURES IN HEAVEN!*
*MATTHEW 6:19-21

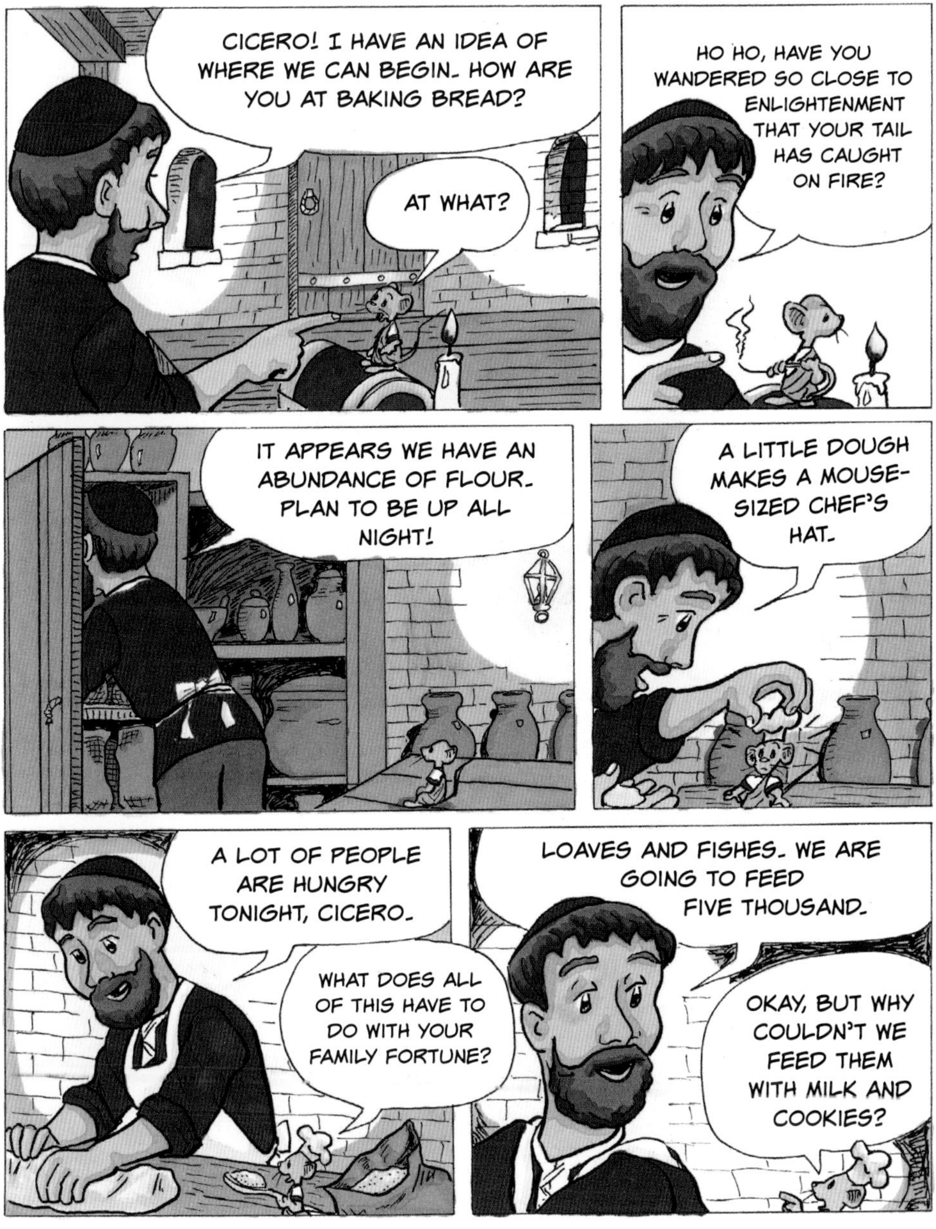
CICERO! I HAVE AN IDEA OF WHERE WE CAN BEGIN. HOW ARE YOU AT BAKING BREAD?
AT WHAT?
HO HO, HAVE YOU WANDERED SO CLOSE TO ENLIGHTENMENT THAT YOUR TAIL HAS CAUGHT ON FIRE?
IT APPEARS WE HAVE AN ABUNDANCE OF FLOUR. PLAN TO BE UP ALL NIGHT!
A LITTLE DOUGH MAKES A MOUSE-SIZED CHEF'S HAT.
A LOT OF PEOPLE ARE HUNGRY TONIGHT, CICERO.
WHAT DOES ALL OF THIS HAVE TO DO WITH YOUR FAMILY FORTUNE?
LOAVES AND FISHES. WE ARE GOING TO FEED FIVE THOUSAND.
OKAY, BUT WHY COULDN'T WE FEED THEM WITH MILK AND COOKIES?

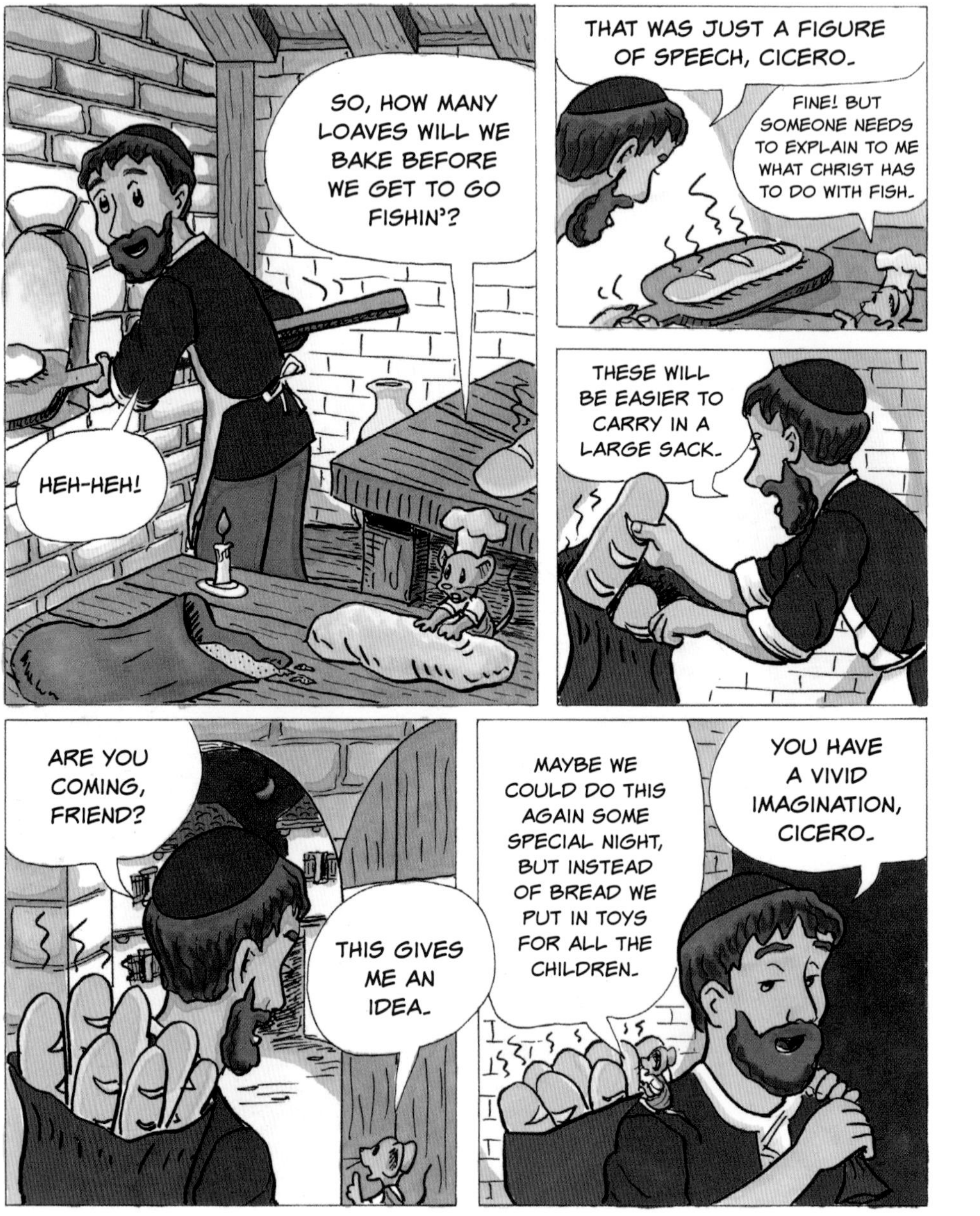
SO, HOW MANY LOAVES WILL WE BAKE BEFORE WE GET TO GO FISHIN'?
HEH-HEH!
THAT WAS JUST A FIGURE OF SPEECH, CICERO.
FINE! BUT SOMEONE NEEDS TO EXPLAIN TO ME WHAT CHRIST HAS TO DO WITH FISH.
THESE WILL BE EASIER TO CARRY IN A LARGE SACK.
ARE YOU COMING, FRIEND?
THIS GIVES ME AN IDEA.
MAYBE WE COULD DO THIS AGAIN SOME SPECIAL NIGHT, BUT INSTEAD OF BREAD WE PUT IN TOYS FOR ALL THE CHILDREN.
YOU HAVE A VIVID IMAGINATION, CICERO.

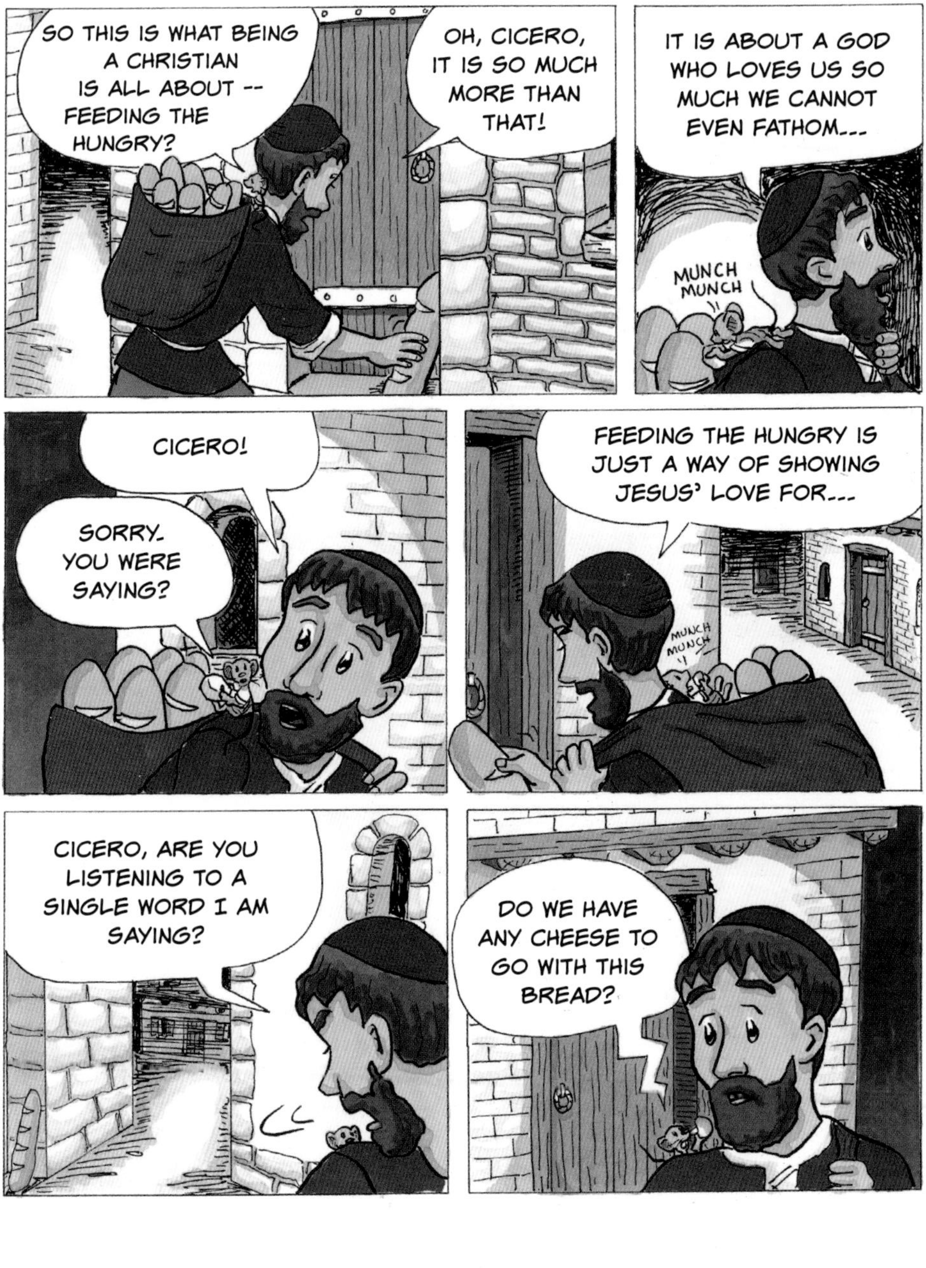
SO THIS IS WHAT BEING A CHRISTIAN IS ALL ABOUT -- FEEDING THE HUNGRY?
OH, CICERO, IT IS SO MUCH MORE THAN THAT!
IT IS ABOUT A GOD WHO LOVES US SO MUCH WE CANNOT EVEN FATHOM...
MUNCH MUNCH
CICERO!
SORRY. YOU WERE SAYING?
FEEDING THE HUNGRY IS JUST A WAY OF SHOWING JESUS' LOVE FOR...
MUNCH MUNCH
CICERO, ARE YOU LISTENING TO A SINGLE WORD I AM SAYING?
DO WE HAVE ANY CHEESE TO GO WITH THIS BREAD?

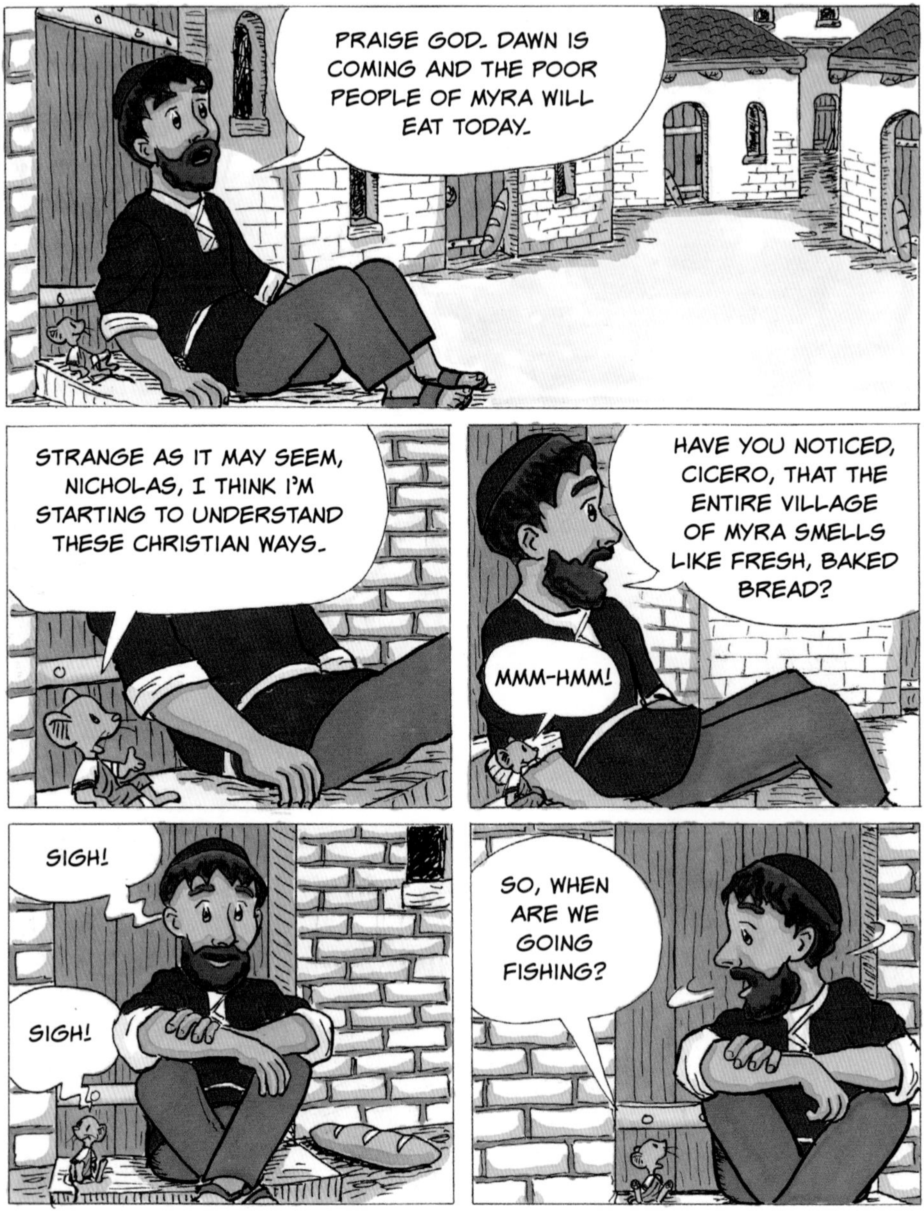
PRAISE GOD. DAWN IS COMING AND THE POOR PEOPLE OF MYRA WILL EAT TODAY.
STRANGE AS IT MAY SEEM, NICHOLAS, I THINK I'M STARTING TO UNDERSTAND THESE CHRISTIAN WAYS.
HAVE YOU NOTICED, CICERO, THAT THE ENTIRE VILLAGE OF MYRA SMELLS LIKE FRESH, BAKED BREAD?
MMM-HMM!
SIGH!
SIGH!
SO, WHEN ARE WE GOING FISHING?

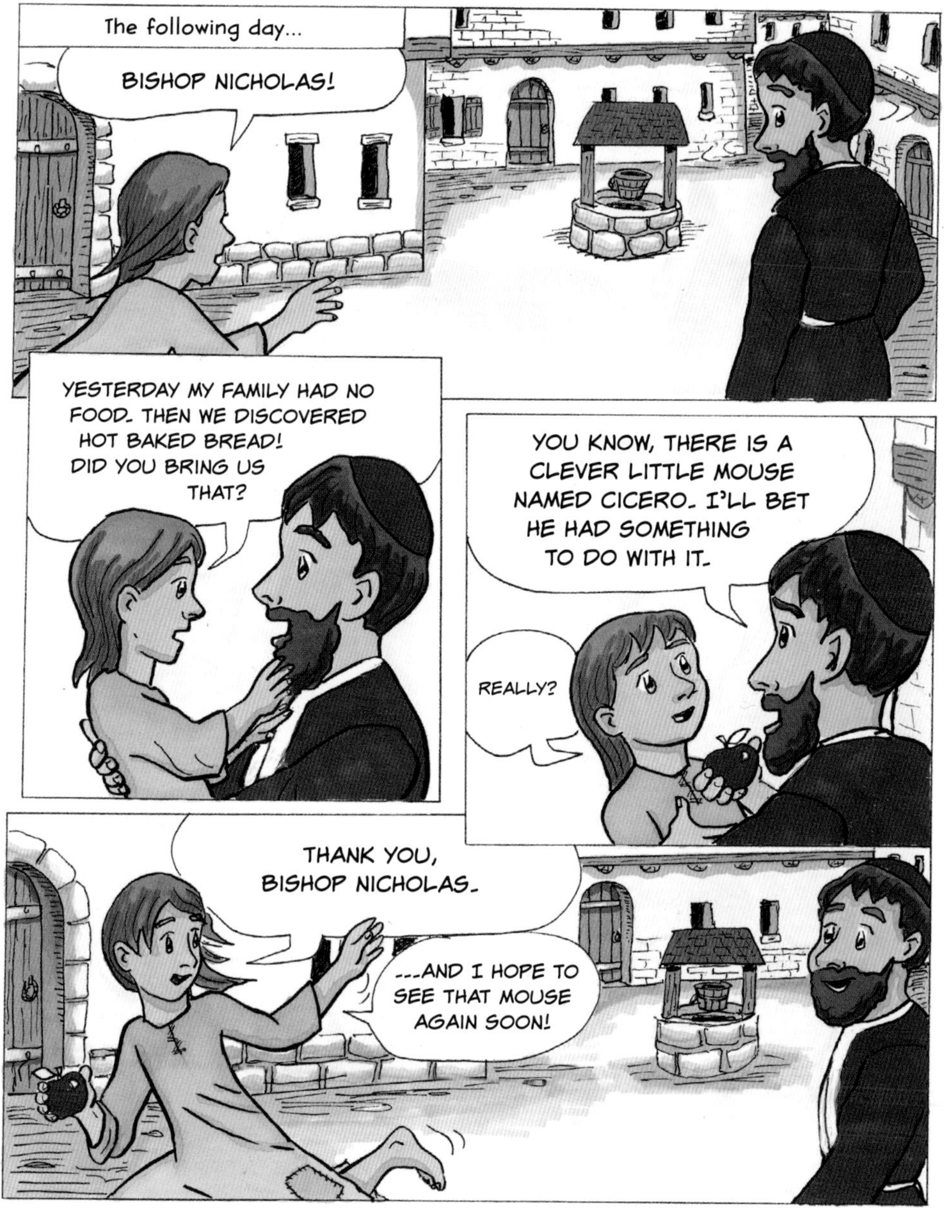
The following day...
BISHOP NICHOLAS!
YESTERDAY MY FAMILY HAD NO FOOD. THEN WE DISCOVERED HOT BAKED BREAD! DID YOU BRING US THAT?
YOU KNOW, THERE IS A CLEVER LITTLE MOUSE NAMED CICERO. I'LL BET HE HAD SOMETHING TO DO WITH IT.
REALLY?
THANK YOU, BISHOP NICHOLAS.
...AND I HOPE TO SEE THAT MOUSE AGAIN SOON!

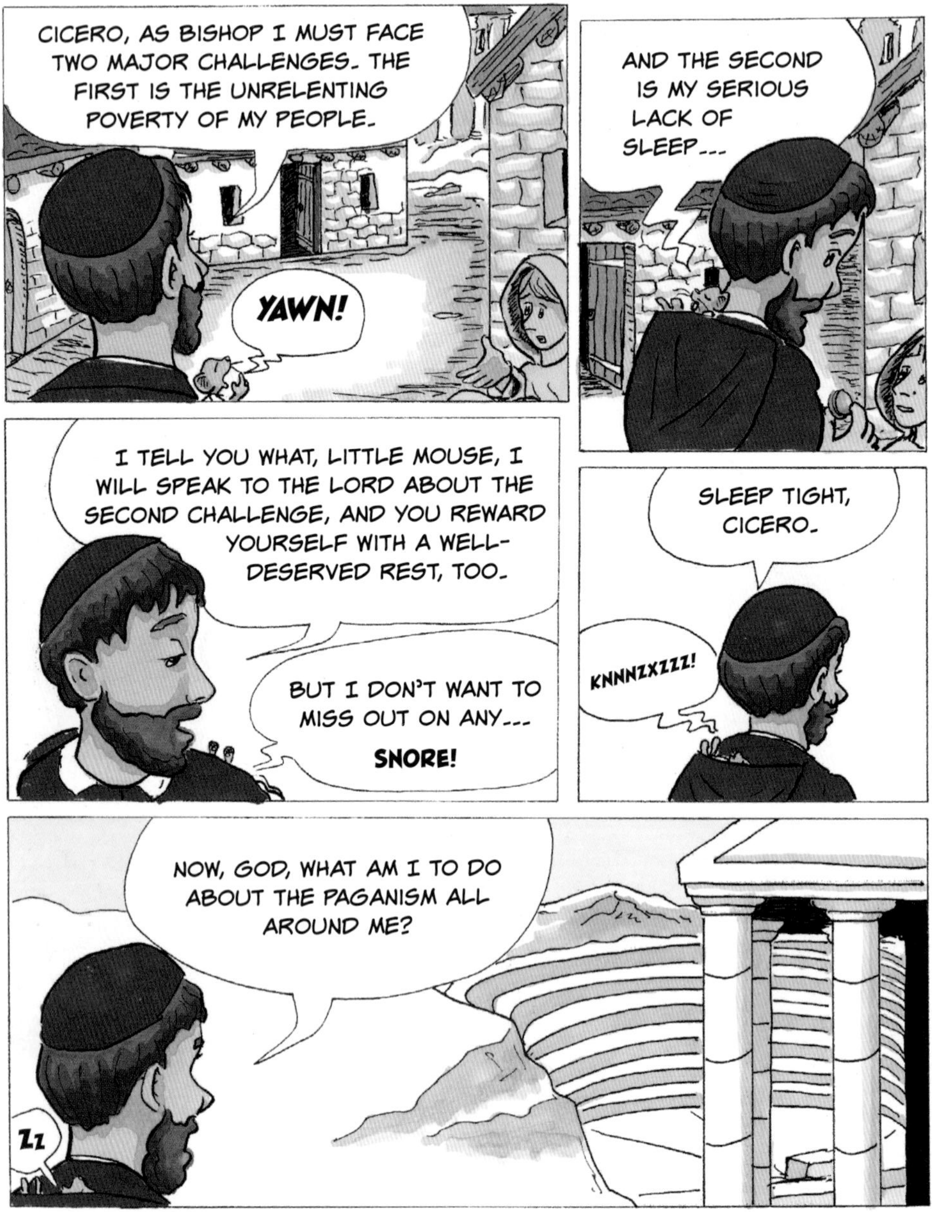
CICERO, AS BISHOP I MUST FACE TWO MAJOR CHALLENGES. THE FIRST IS THE UNRELENTING POVERTY OF MY PEOPLE.
YAWN!
AND THE SECOND IS MY SERIOUS LACK OF SLEEP...
I TELL YOU WHAT, LITTLE MOUSE, I WILL SPEAK TO THE LORD ABOUT THE SECOND CHALLENGE, AND YOU REWARD YOURSELF WITH A WELL-DESERVED REST, TOO.
BUT I DON'T WANT TO MISS OUT ON ANY...
SNORE!
SLEEP TIGHT, CICERO.
KNNNZXZZZ!
NOW, GOD, WHAT AM I TO DO ABOUT THE PAGANISM ALL AROUND ME?
Zz

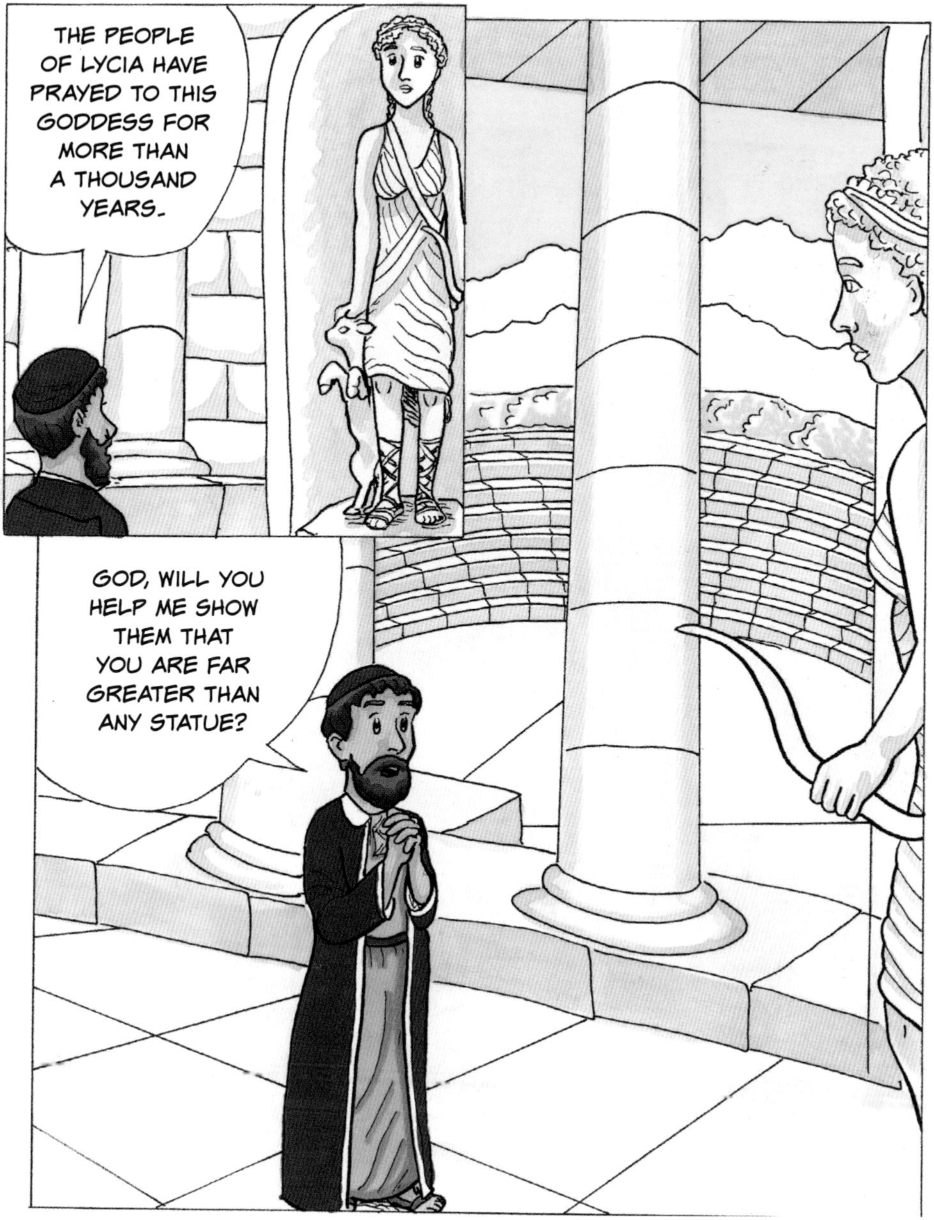
THE PEOPLE OF LYCIA HAVE PRAYED TO THIS GODDESS FOR MORE THAN A THOUSAND YEARS.
GOD, WILL YOU HELP ME SHOW THEM THAT YOU ARE FAR GREATER THAN ANY STATUE?

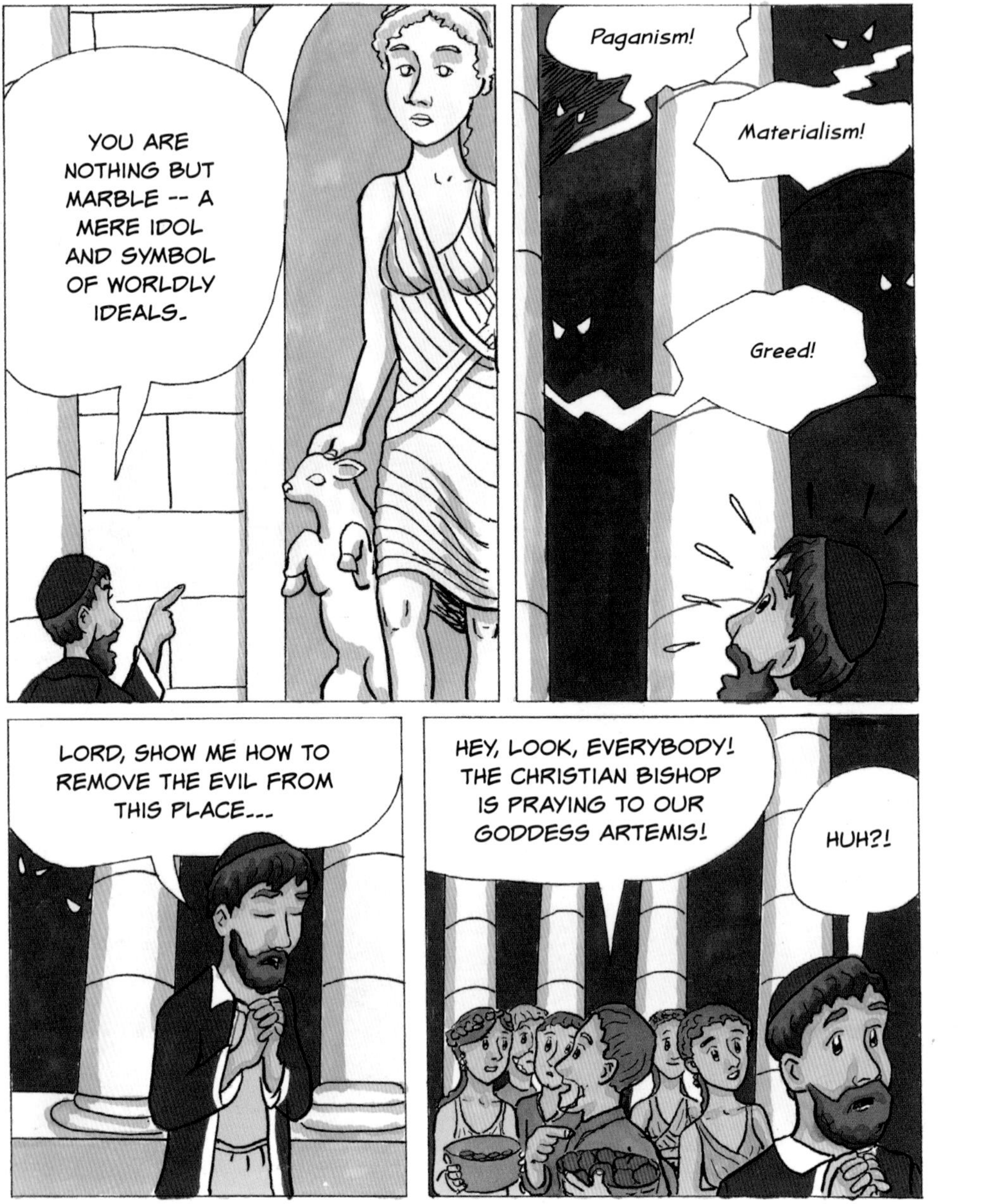
YOU ARE NOTHING BUT MARBLE -- A MERE IDOL AND SYMBOL OF WORLDLY IDEALS.
Paganism!
Materialism!
Greed!
LORD, SHOW ME HOW TO REMOVE THE EVIL FROM THIS PLACE...
HEY, LOOK, EVERYBODY! THE CHRISTIAN BISHOP IS PRAYING TO OUR GODDESS ARTEMIS!
HUH?!

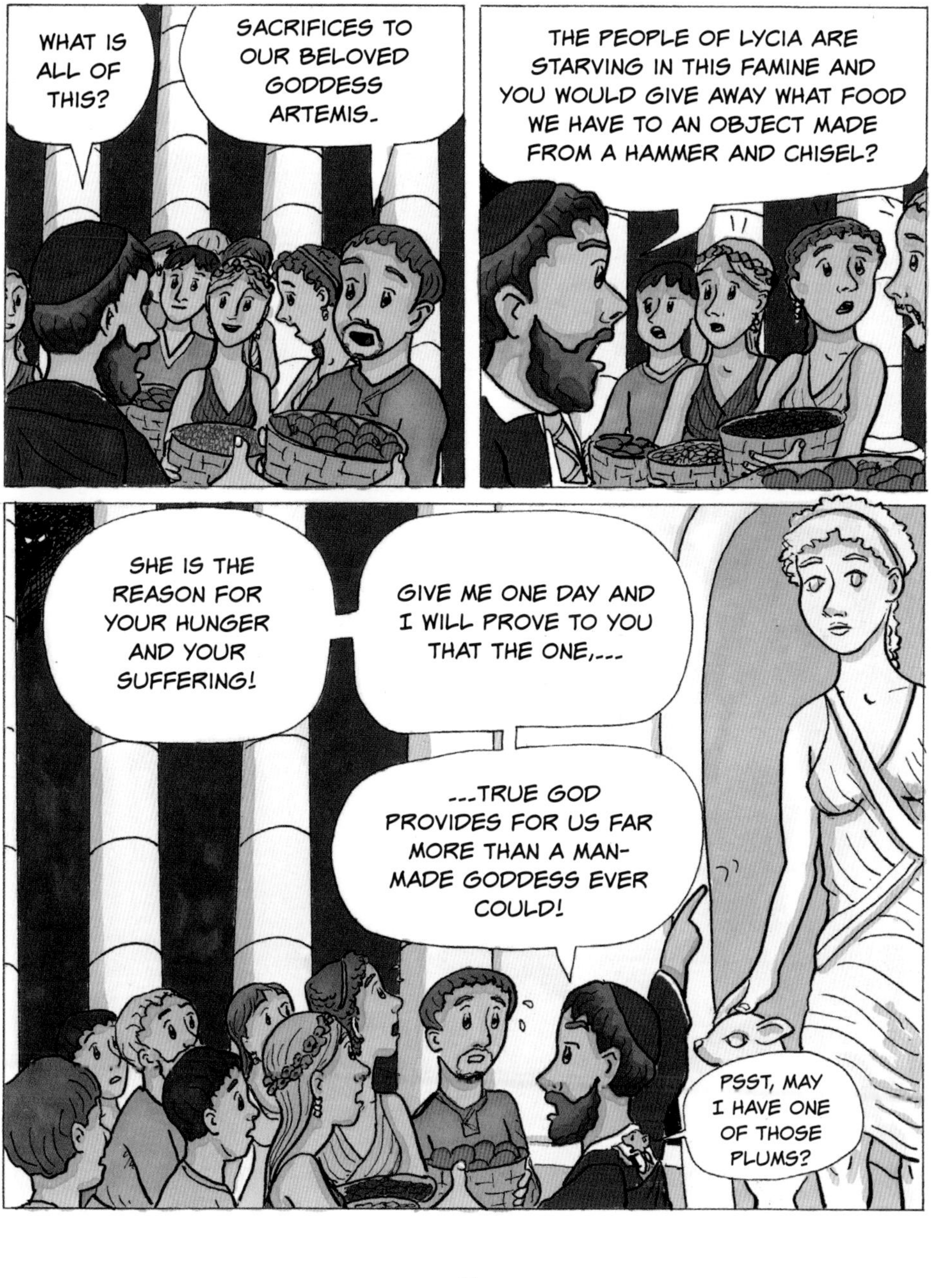
WHAT IS ALL OF THIS?
SACRIFICES TO OUR BELOVED GODDESS ARTEMIS.
THE PEOPLE OF LYCIA ARE STARVING IN THIS FAMINE AND YOU WOULD GIVE AWAY WHAT FOOD WE HAVE TO AN OBJECT MADE FROM A HAMMER AND CHISEL?
SHE IS THE REASON FOR YOUR HUNGER AND YOUR SUFFERING!
GIVE ME ONE DAY AND I WILL PROVE TO YOU THAT THE ONE,...
...TRUE GOD PROVIDES FOR US FAR MORE THAN A MAN-MADE GODDESS EVER COULD!
PSST, MAY I HAVE ONE OF THOSE PLUMS?

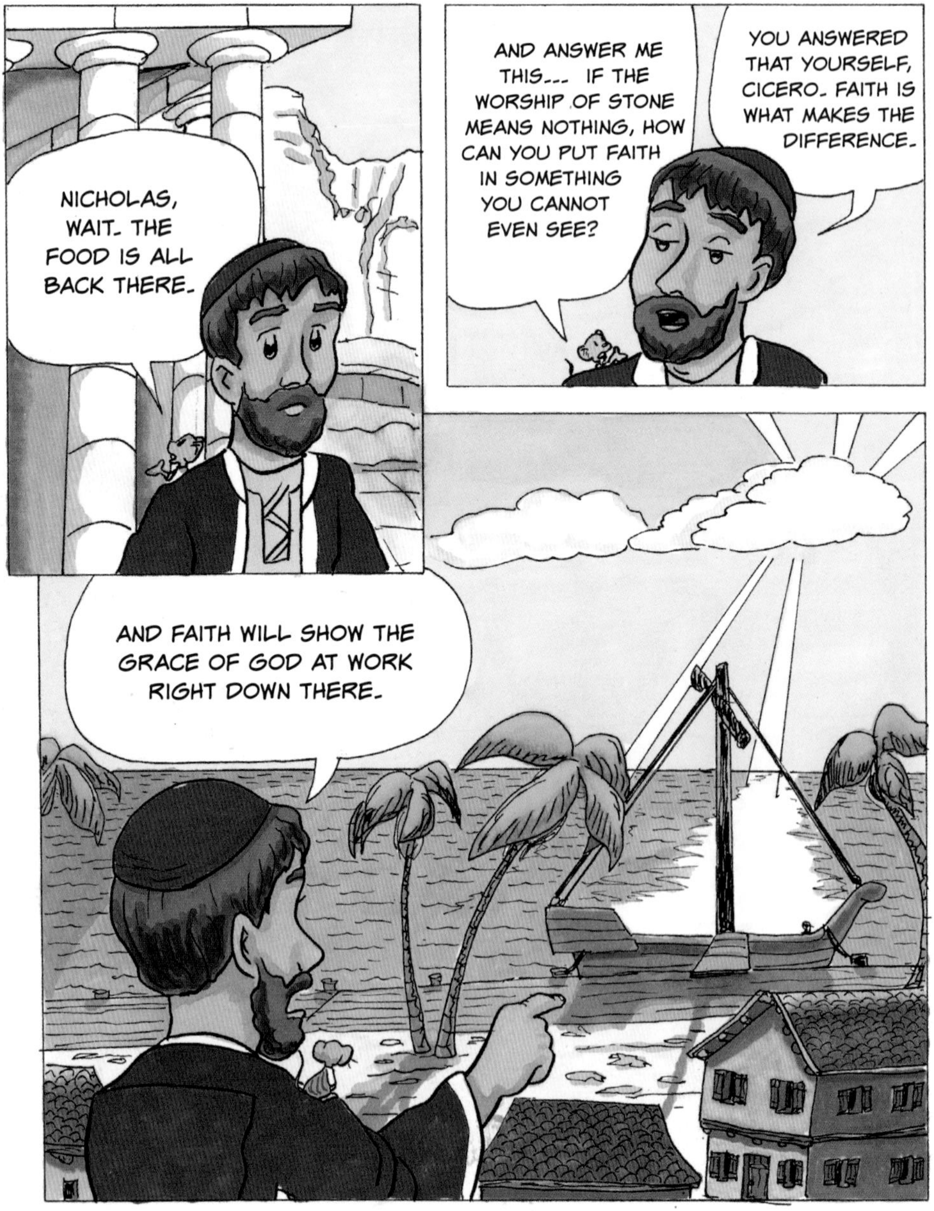
NICHOLAS, WAIT. THE FOOD IS ALL BACK THERE.
AND ANSWER ME THIS... IF THE WORSHIP OF STONE MEANS NOTHING, HOW CAN YOU PUT FAITH IN SOMETHING YOU CANNOT EVEN SEE?
YOU ANSWERED THAT YOURSELF, CICERO. FAITH IS WHAT MAKES THE DIFFERENCE.
AND FAITH WILL SHOW THE GRACE OF GOD AT WORK RIGHT DOWN THERE.

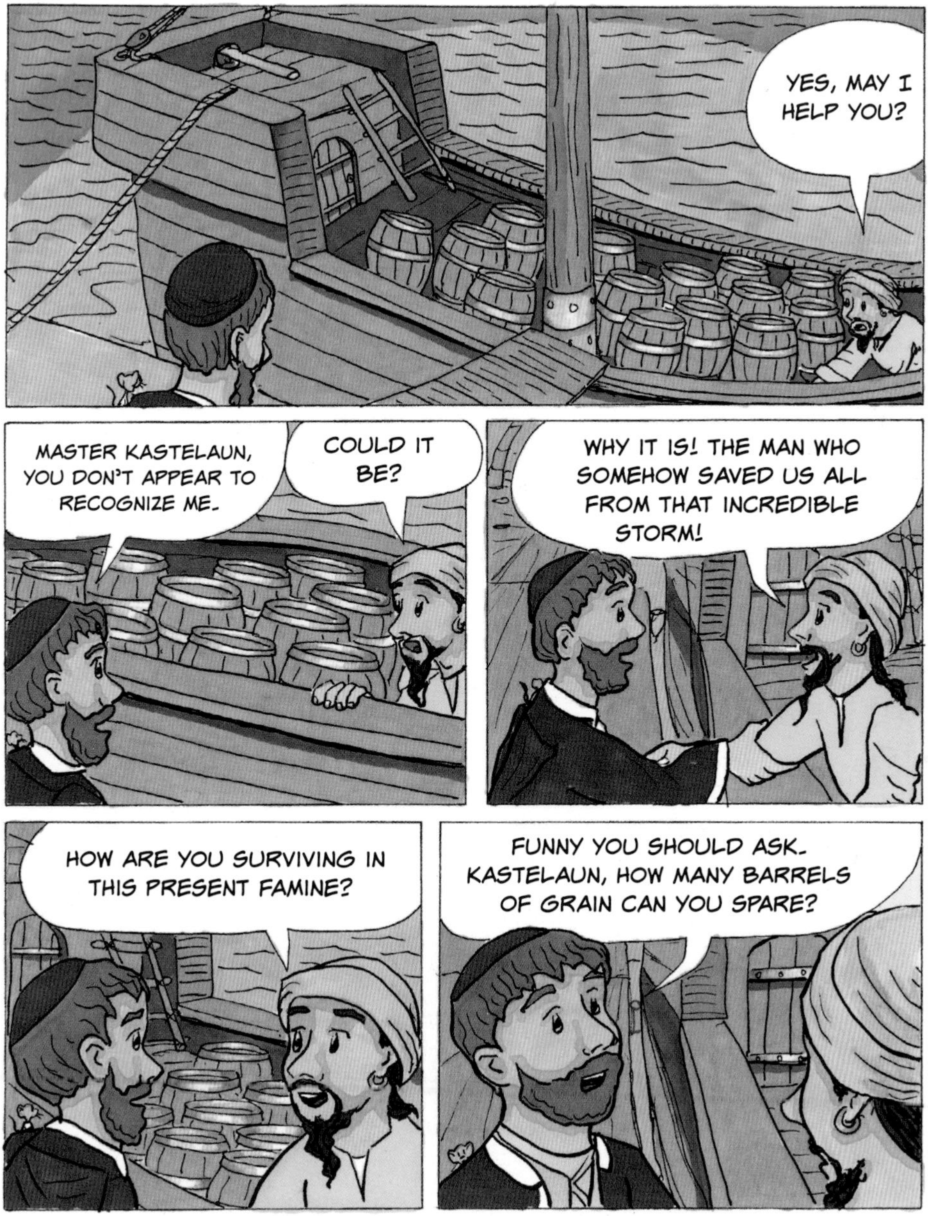
YES, MAY I HELP YOU?
MASTER KASTELAUN, YOU DON'T APPEAR TO RECOGNIZE ME.
COULD IT BE?
WHY IT IS! THE MAN WHO SOMEHOW SAVED US ALL FROM THAT INCREDIBLE STORM!
HOW ARE YOU SURVIVING IN THIS PRESENT FAMINE?
FUNNY YOU SHOULD ASK. KASTELAUN, HOW MANY BARRELS OF GRAIN CAN YOU SPARE?

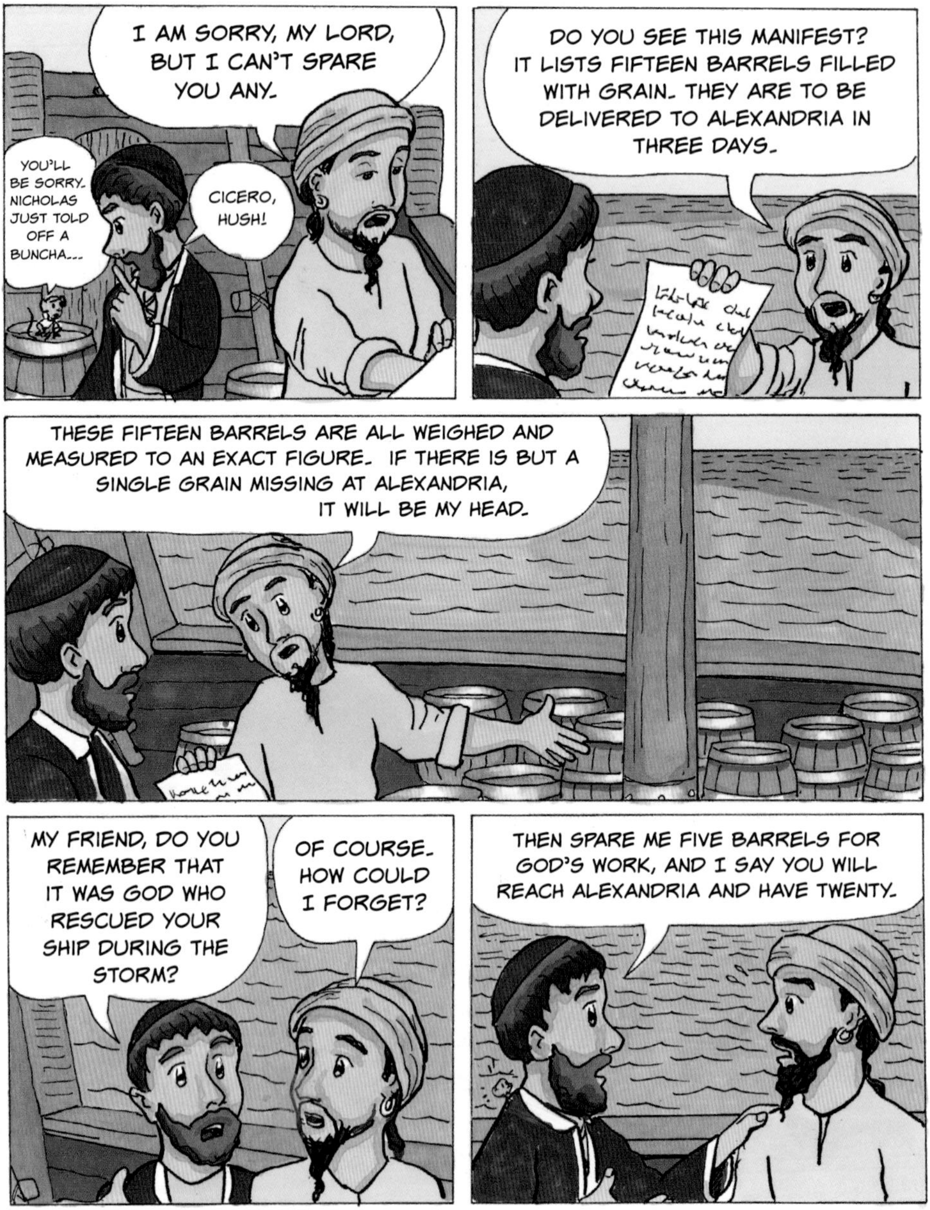
I AM SORRY, MY LORD, BUT I CAN'T SPARE YOU ANY.
YOU'LL BE SORRY. NICHOLAS JUST TOLD OFF A BUNCHA...
CICERO, HUSH!
DO YOU SEE THIS MANIFEST? IT LISTS FIFTEEN BARRELS FILLED WITH GRAIN. THEY ARE TO BE DELIVERED TO ALEXANDRIA IN THREE DAYS.
THESE FIFTEEN BARRELS ARE ALL WEIGHED AND MEASURED TO AN EXACT FIGURE. IF THERE IS BUT A SINGLE GRAIN MISSING AT ALEXANDRIA, IT WILL BE MY HEAD.
MY FRIEND, DO YOU REMEMBER THAT IT WAS GOD WHO RESCUED YOUR SHIP DURING THE STORM?
OF COURSE. HOW COULD I FORGET?
THEN SPARE ME FIVE BARRELS FOR GOD'S WORK, AND I SAY YOU WILL REACH ALEXANDRIA AND HAVE TWENTY.

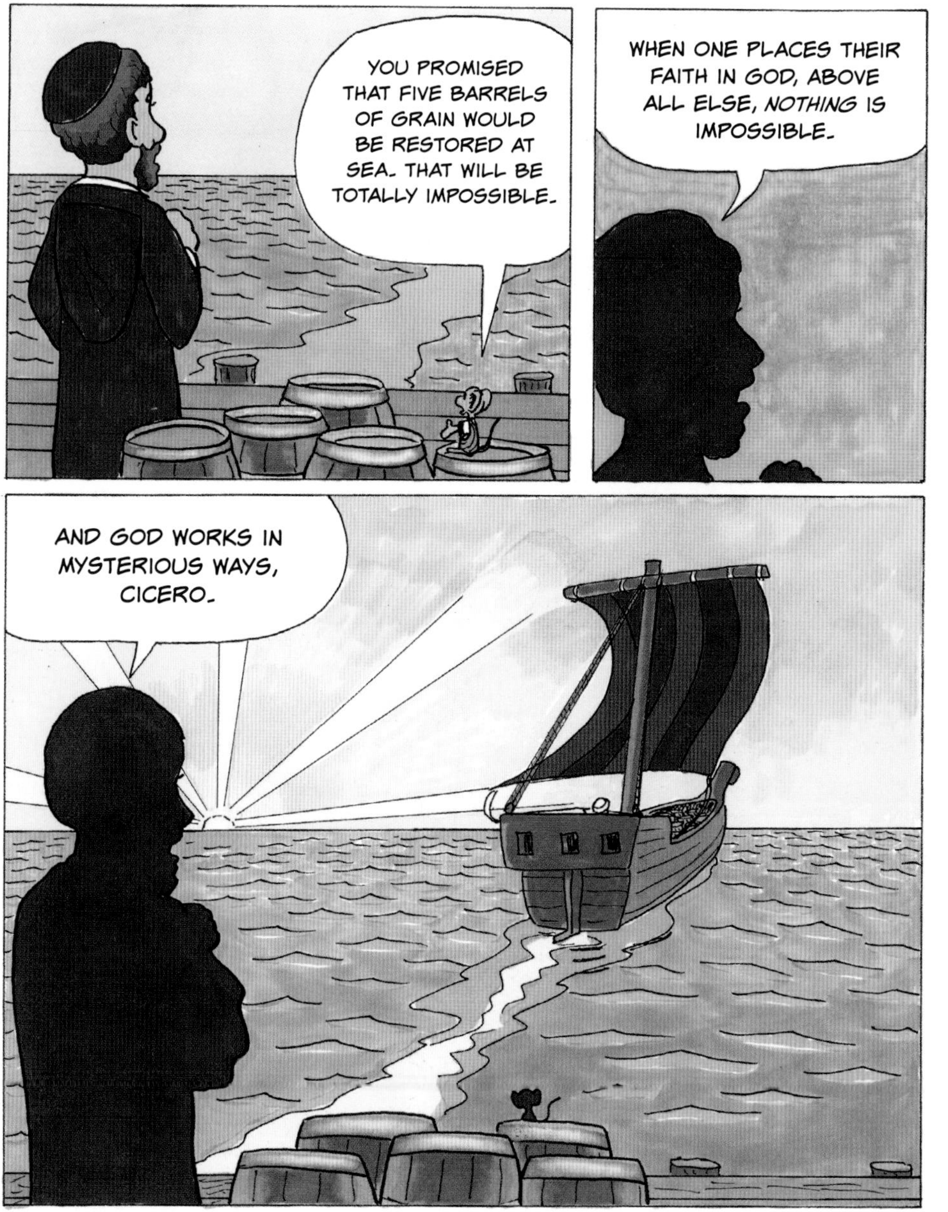
YOU PROMISED THAT FIVE BARRELS OF GRAIN WOULD BE RESTORED AT SEA. THAT WILL BE TOTALLY IMPOSSIBLE.
WHEN ONE PLACES THEIR FAITH IN GOD, ABOVE ALL ELSE, *NOTHING* IS IMPOSSIBLE.
AND GOD WORKS IN MYSTERIOUS WAYS, CICERO.

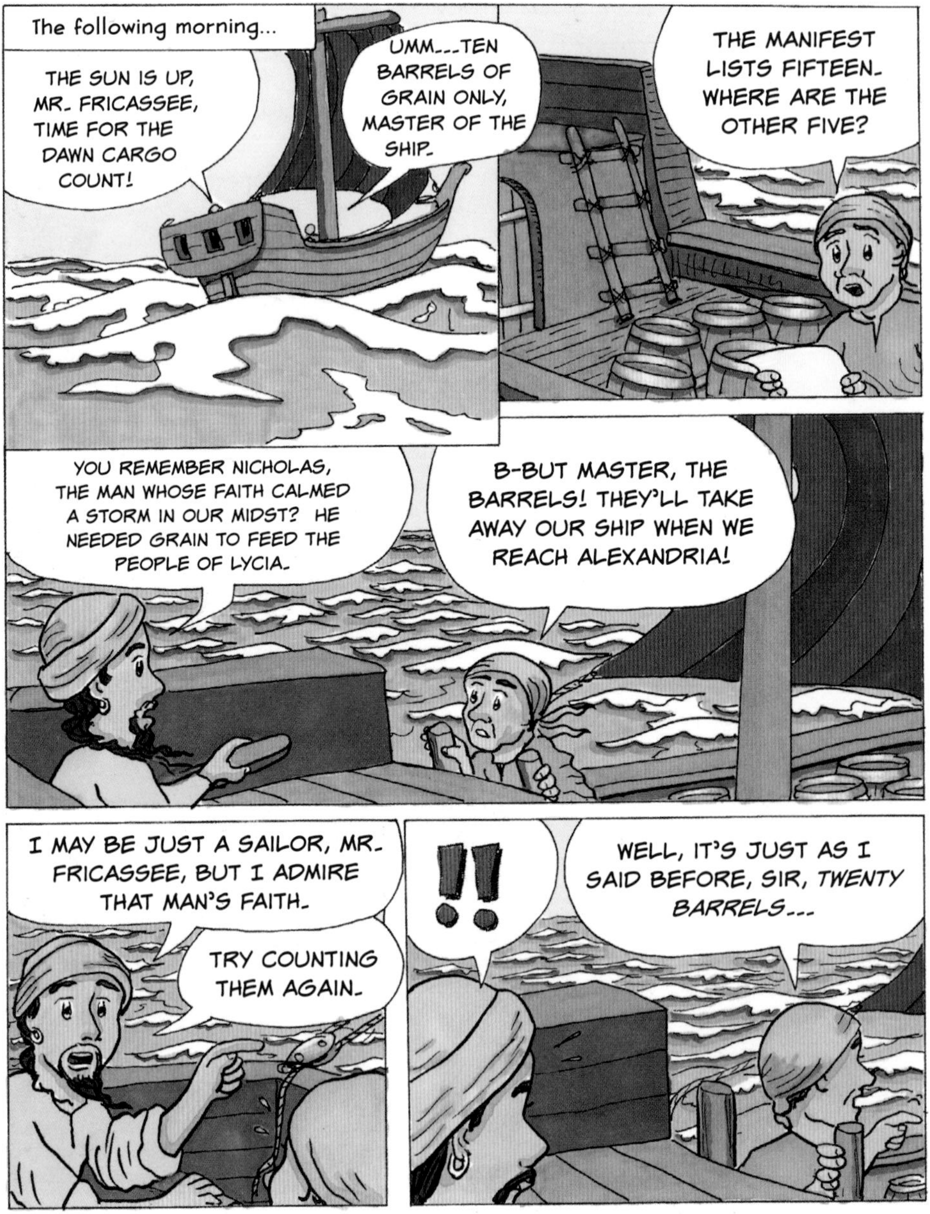
The following morning...
THE SUN IS UP, MR. FRICASSEE, TIME FOR THE DAWN CARGO COUNT!
UMM...TEN BARRELS OF GRAIN ONLY, MASTER OF THE SHIP.
THE MANIFEST LISTS FIFTEEN. WHERE ARE THE OTHER FIVE?
YOU REMEMBER NICHOLAS, THE MAN WHOSE FAITH CALMED A STORM IN OUR MIDST? HE NEEDED GRAIN TO FEED THE PEOPLE OF LYCIA.
B-BUT MASTER, THE BARRELS! THEY'LL TAKE AWAY OUR SHIP WHEN WE REACH ALEXANDRIA!
I MAY BE JUST A SAILOR, MR. FRICASSEE, BUT I ADMIRE THAT MAN'S FAITH.
TRY COUNTING THEM AGAIN.
!!
WELL, IT'S JUST AS I SAID BEFORE, SIR, *TWENTY BARRELS...*

CHAPTER FIVE

THE REAL MEANING
OF CHRISTMAS

And suddenly there was with the angel
a multitude of the heavenly host,
praising God and saying,
"Glory to God in the highest heaven,
and on earth peace among those whom he favors!"
—LUKE 2:13-14

HEY, WHAT GIVES? YOU HAVE BEEN NOTHING BUT SMILES ALL DAY.

OH, CICERO, IT IS CHRISTMAS EVE!

KASTELAUN TOLD THE PAGANS ABOUT GOD'S MIRACLE WITH THE GRAIN AND MANY OF THEM HAVE BECOME CHRISTIANS!

OH, I GET IT. YOU'RE PUTTING MONEY TOGETHER SO WE CAN GO OUT AND CELEBRATE.

NO, CICERO, ALTHOUGH THAT'S NOT A BAD IDEA.

WHAT IS CHRISTMAS EVE, ANYWAY?

IT IS THE NIGHT BEFORE OUR SAVIOR WAS BORN. A SOLEMN, BEAUTIFUL NIGHT.

IN THE SPIRIT OF SHEPHERDS AND KINGS WHO BORE GIFTS TO THE CHRIST CHILD, I WANT TO GIVE TO THOSE WHO HAVE NOTHING.

AFTER THAT, WE CELEBRATE!

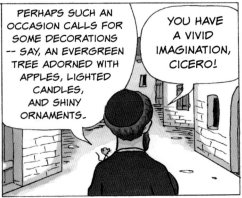

PERHAPS SUCH AN OCCASION CALLS FOR SOME DECORATIONS -- SAY, AN EVERGREEN TREE ADORNED WITH APPLES, LIGHTED CANDLES, AND SHINY ORNAMENTS.

YOU HAVE A VIVID IMAGINATION, CICERO!

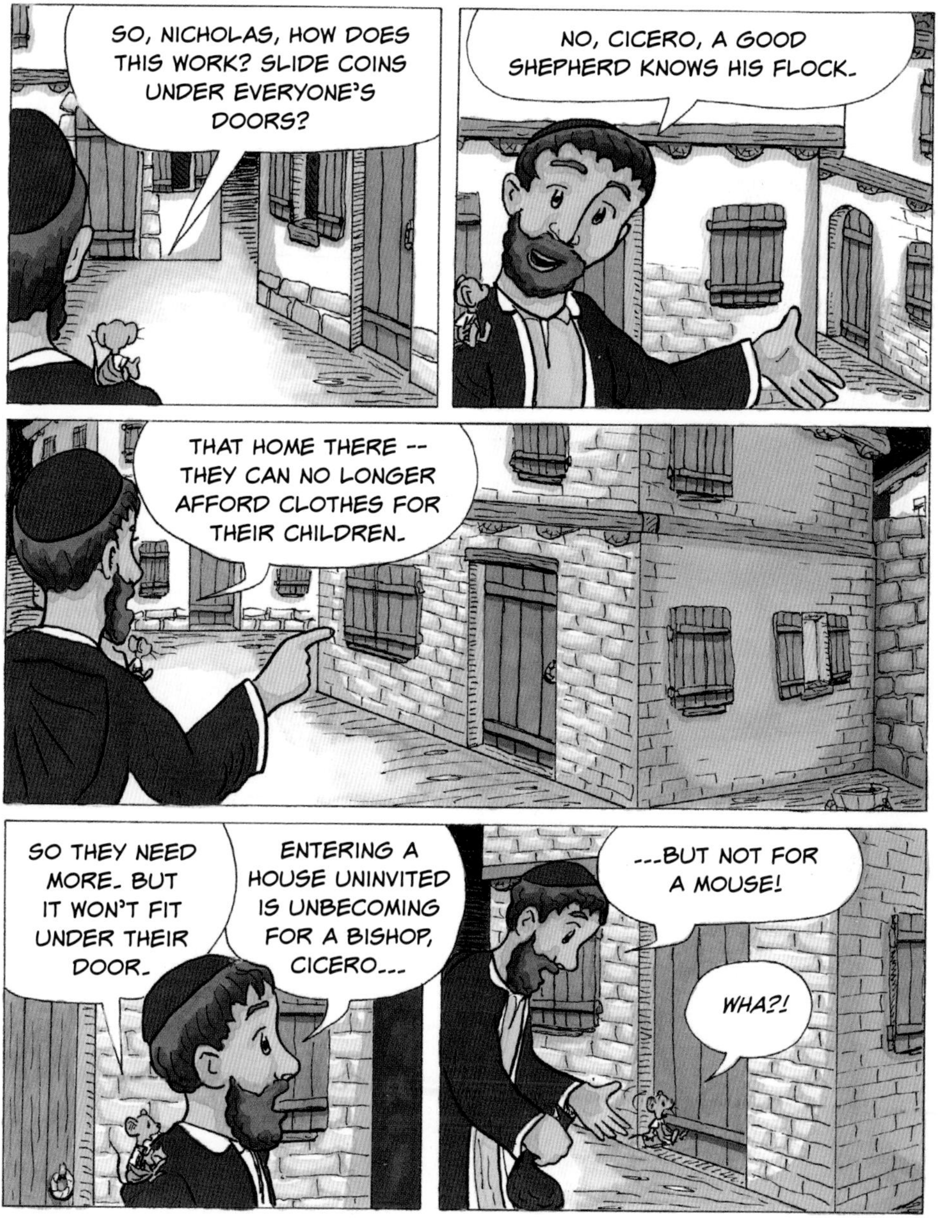
SO, NICHOLAS, HOW DOES THIS WORK? SLIDE COINS UNDER EVERYONE'S DOORS?
NO, CICERO, A GOOD SHEPHERD KNOWS HIS FLOCK.
THAT HOME THERE -- THEY CAN NO LONGER AFFORD CLOTHES FOR THEIR CHILDREN.
SO THEY NEED MORE. BUT IT WON'T FIT UNDER THEIR DOOR.
ENTERING A HOUSE UNINVITED IS UNBECOMING FOR A BISHOP, CICERO...
...BUT NOT FOR A MOUSE!
WHA?!

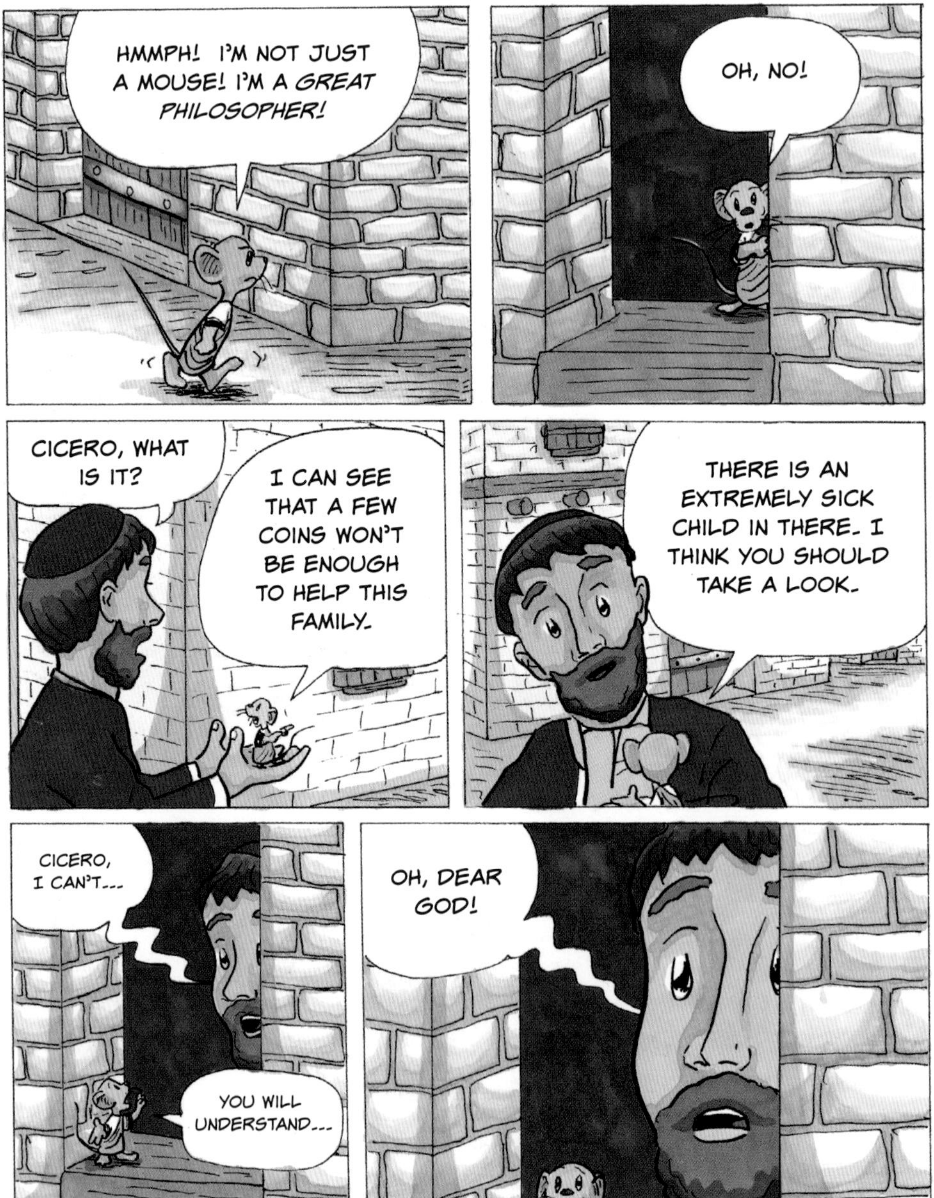
HMMPH! I'M NOT JUST A MOUSE! I'M A *GREAT PHILOSOPHER!*
OH, NO!
CICERO, WHAT IS IT?
I CAN SEE THAT A FEW COINS WON'T BE ENOUGH TO HELP THIS FAMILY.
THERE IS AN EXTREMELY SICK CHILD IN THERE. I THINK YOU SHOULD TAKE A LOOK.
CICERO, I CAN'T...
YOU WILL UNDERSTAND...
OH, DEAR GOD!

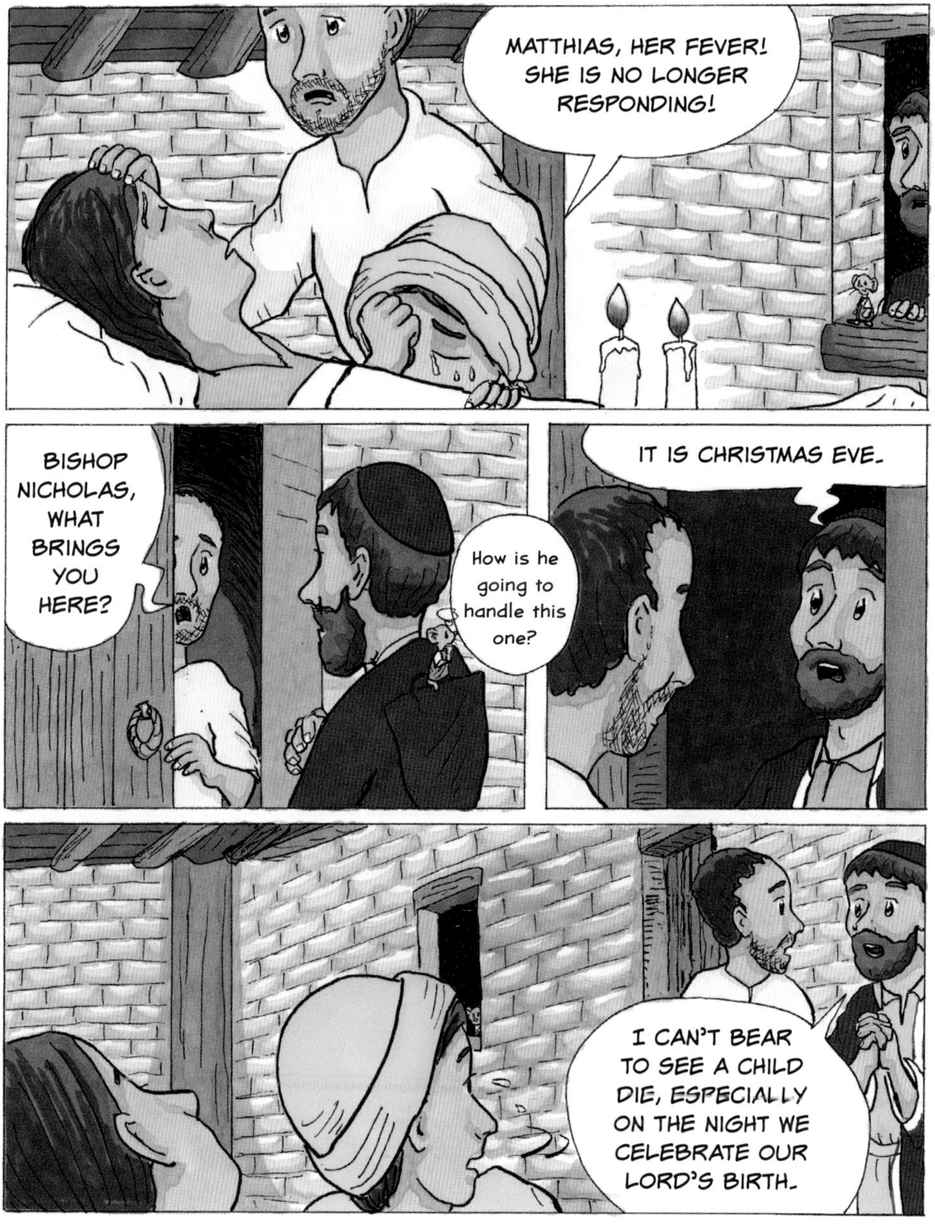
MATTHIAS, HER FEVER! SHE IS NO LONGER RESPONDING!
BISHOP NICHOLAS, WHAT BRINGS YOU HERE?
How is he going to handle this one?
IT IS CHRISTMAS EVE.
I CAN'T BEAR TO SEE A CHILD DIE, ESPECIALLY ON THE NIGHT WE CELEBRATE OUR LORD'S BIRTH.

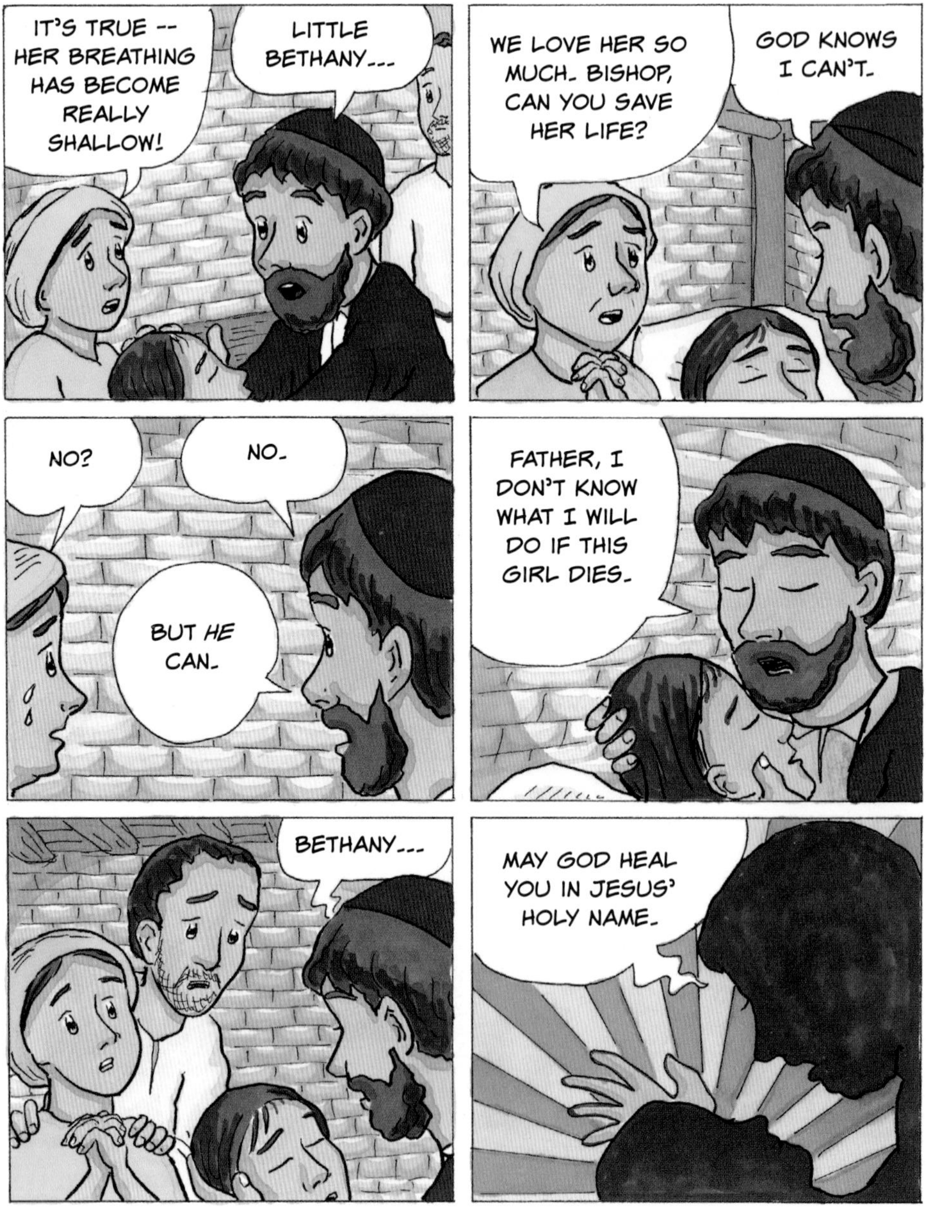
IT'S TRUE -- HER BREATHING HAS BECOME REALLY SHALLOW!
LITTLE BETHANY...
WE LOVE HER SO MUCH. BISHOP, CAN YOU SAVE HER LIFE?
GOD KNOWS I CAN'T.
NO?
NO.
BUT HE CAN.
FATHER, I DON'T KNOW WHAT I WILL DO IF THIS GIRL DIES.
BETHANY...
MAY GOD HEAL YOU IN JESUS' HOLY NAME.

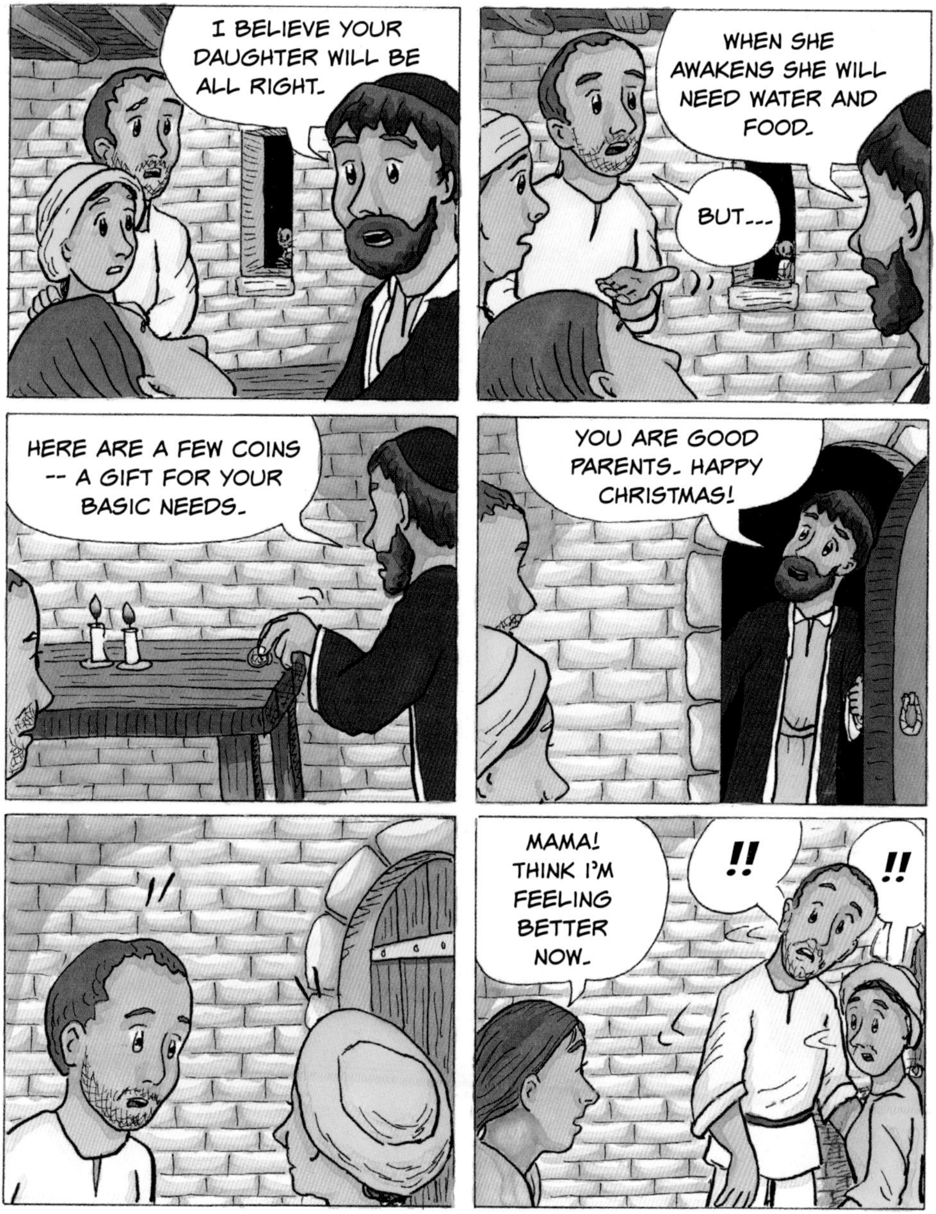
I BELIEVE YOUR DAUGHTER WILL BE ALL RIGHT.
WHEN SHE AWAKENS SHE WILL NEED WATER AND FOOD.
BUT...
HERE ARE A FEW COINS -- A GIFT FOR YOUR BASIC NEEDS.
YOU ARE GOOD PARENTS. HAPPY CHRISTMAS!
MAMA! THINK I'M FEELING BETTER NOW.
!!
!!

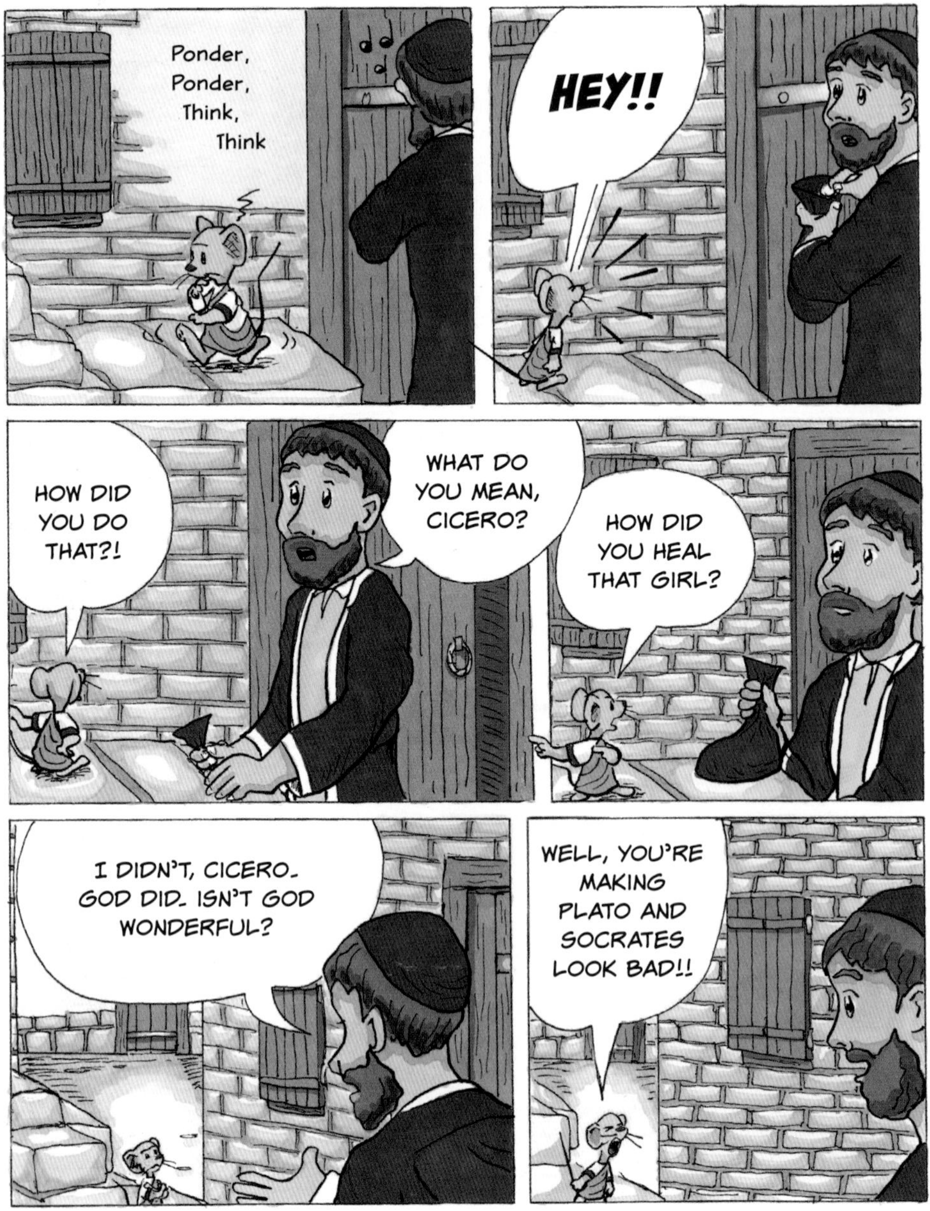
Ponder, Ponder, Think, Think
HEY!!
HOW DID YOU DO THAT?!
WHAT DO YOU MEAN, CICERO?
HOW DID YOU HEAL THAT GIRL?
I DIDN'T, CICERO. GOD DID. ISN'T GOD WONDERFUL?
WELL, YOU'RE MAKING PLATO AND SOCRATES LOOK BAD!!

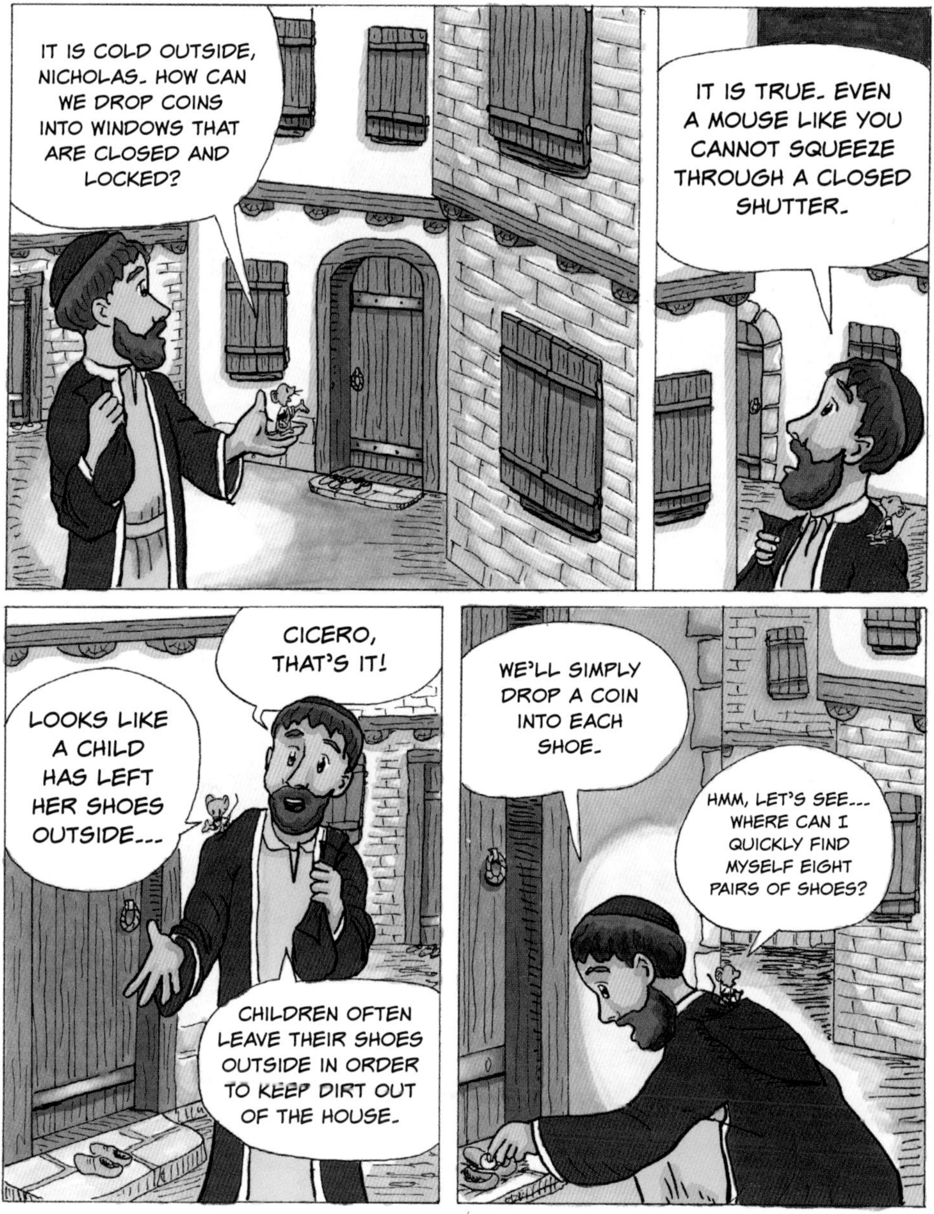
IT IS COLD OUTSIDE, NICHOLAS. HOW CAN WE DROP COINS INTO WINDOWS THAT ARE CLOSED AND LOCKED?
IT IS TRUE. EVEN A MOUSE LIKE YOU CANNOT SQUEEZE THROUGH A CLOSED SHUTTER.
LOOKS LIKE A CHILD HAS LEFT HER SHOES OUTSIDE...
CICERO, THAT'S IT!
CHILDREN OFTEN LEAVE THEIR SHOES OUTSIDE IN ORDER TO KEEP DIRT OUT OF THE HOUSE.
WE'LL SIMPLY DROP A COIN INTO EACH SHOE.
HMM, LET'S SEE... WHERE CAN I QUICKLY FIND MYSELF EIGHT PAIRS OF SHOES?

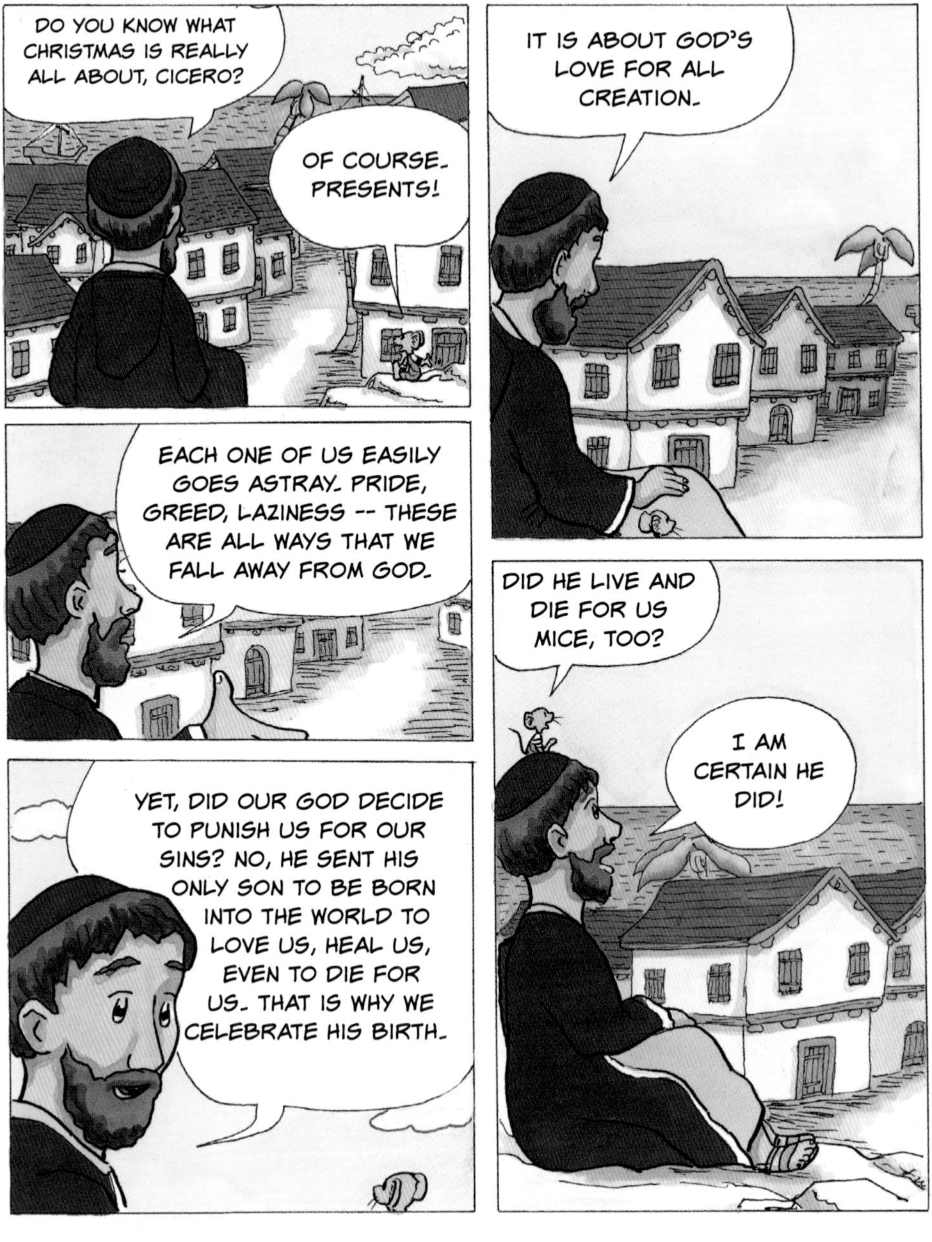
DO YOU KNOW WHAT CHRISTMAS IS REALLY ALL ABOUT, CICERO?
OF COURSE. PRESENTS!
IT IS ABOUT GOD'S LOVE FOR ALL CREATION.
EACH ONE OF US EASILY GOES ASTRAY. PRIDE, GREED, LAZINESS -- THESE ARE ALL WAYS THAT WE FALL AWAY FROM GOD.
DID HE LIVE AND DIE FOR US MICE, TOO?
I AM CERTAIN HE DID!
YET, DID OUR GOD DECIDE TO PUNISH US FOR OUR SINS? NO, HE SENT HIS ONLY SON TO BE BORN INTO THE WORLD TO LOVE US, HEAL US, EVEN TO DIE FOR US. THAT IS WHY WE CELEBRATE HIS BIRTH.

CHAPTER SIX
DEFENDER OF THE PEOPLE

He has told you, O mortal, what is good;
and what does the LORD require of you
but to do justice, and to love kindness,
and to walk humbly with your God?
--MICAH 6:8

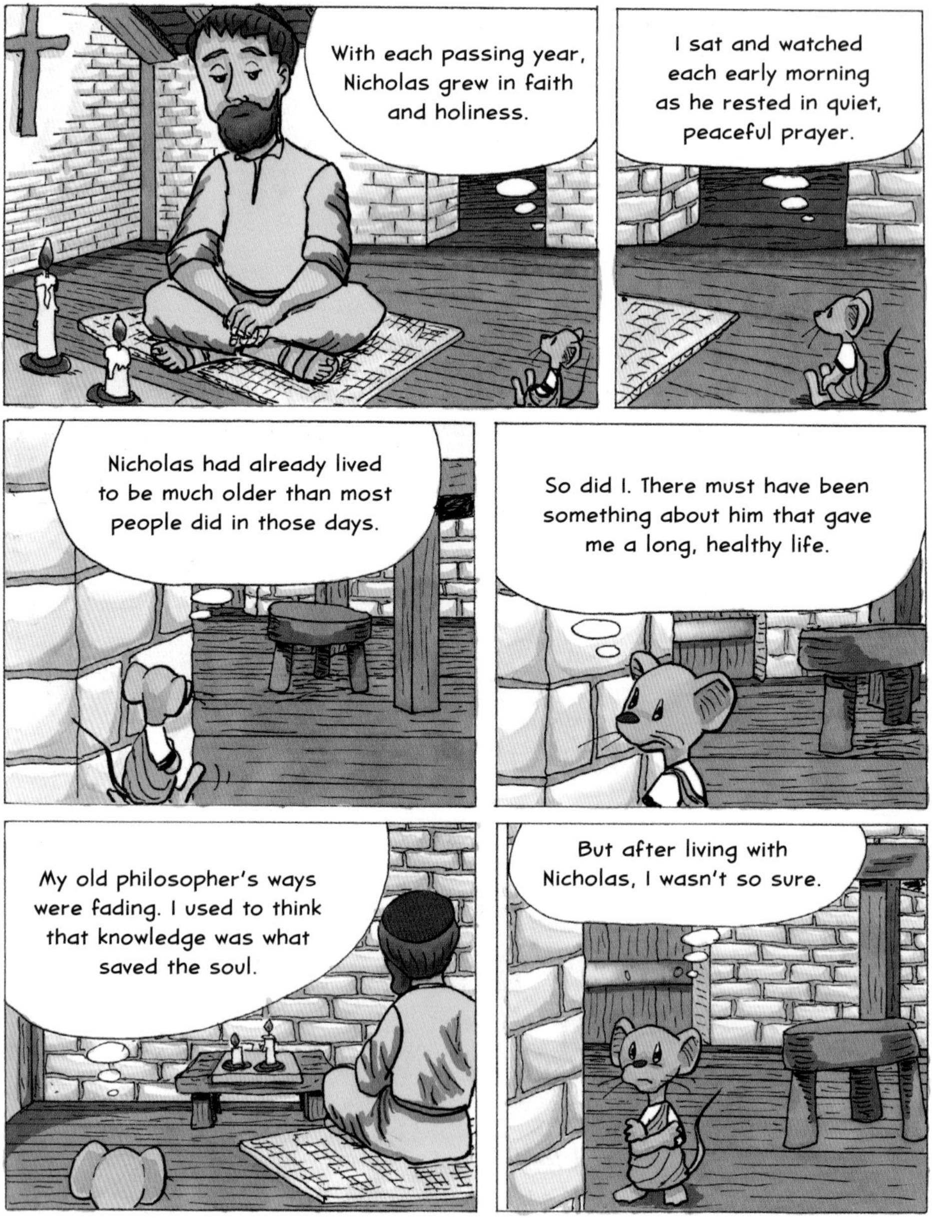
With each passing year, Nicholas grew in faith and holiness.
I sat and watched each early morning as he rested in quiet, peaceful prayer.
Nicholas had already lived to be much older than most people did in those days.
So did I. There must have been something about him that gave me a long, healthy life.
My old philosopher's ways were fading. I used to think that knowledge was what saved the soul.
But after living with Nicholas, I wasn't so sure.

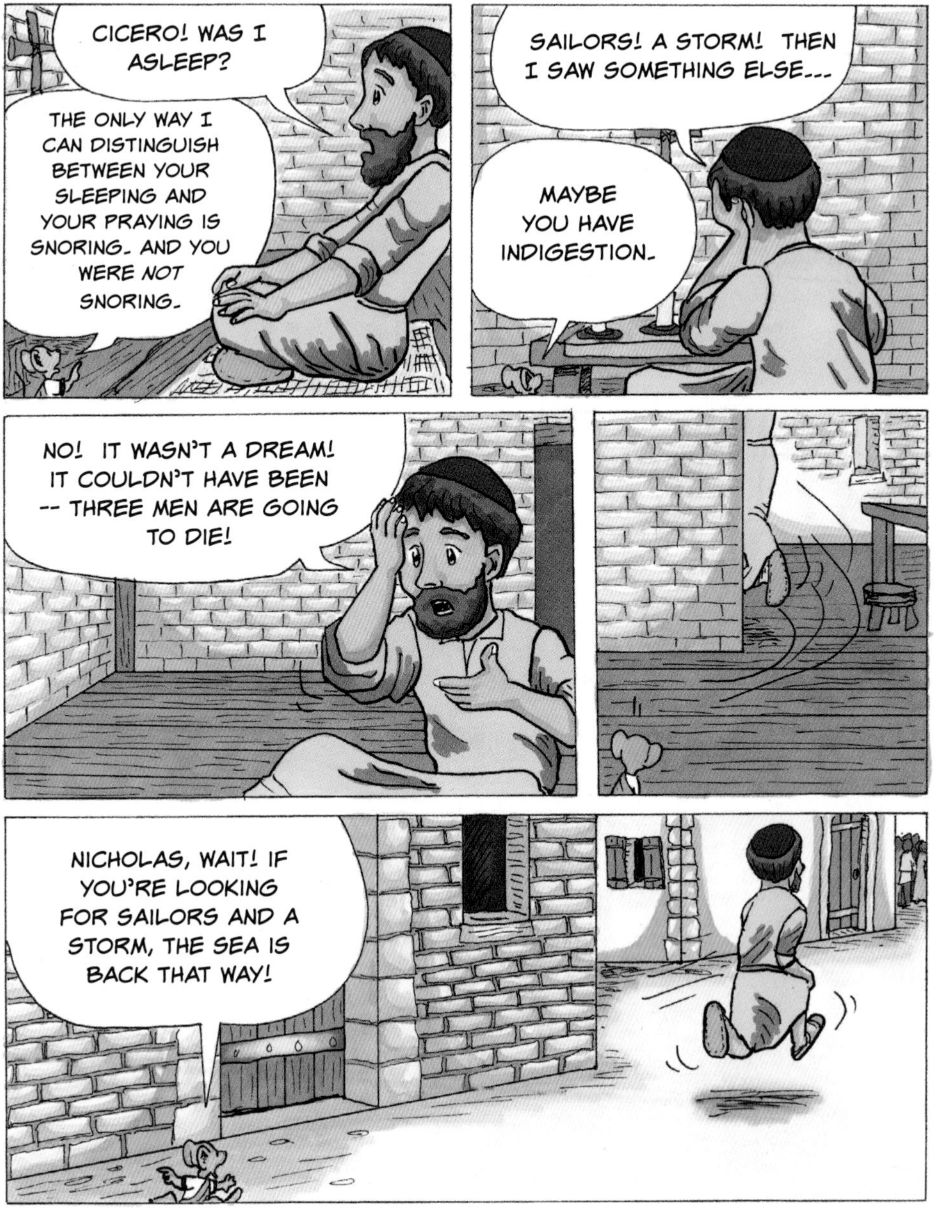

CICERO! WAS I ASLEEP?
THE ONLY WAY I CAN DISTINGUISH BETWEEN YOUR SLEEPING AND YOUR PRAYING IS SNORING. AND YOU WERE *NOT* SNORING.
SAILORS! A STORM! THEN I SAW SOMETHING ELSE...
MAYBE YOU HAVE INDIGESTION.
NO! IT WASN'T A DREAM! IT COULDN'T HAVE BEEN -- THREE MEN ARE GOING TO DIE!
NICHOLAS, WAIT! IF YOU'RE LOOKING FOR SAILORS AND A STORM, THE SEA IS BACK THAT WAY!

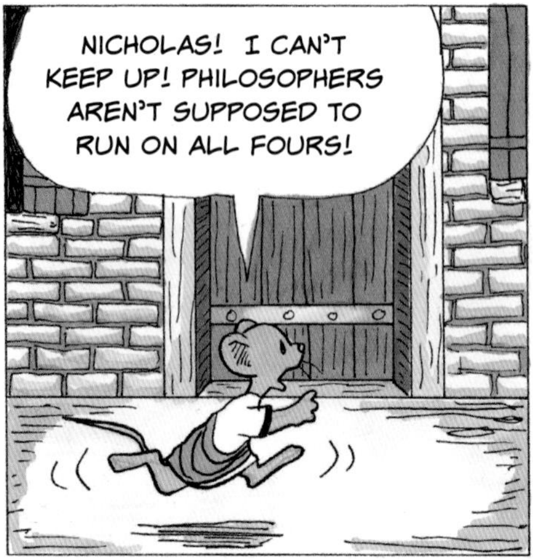
NICHOLAS! I CAN'T KEEP UP! PHILOSOPHERS AREN'T SUPPOSED TO RUN ON ALL FOURS!

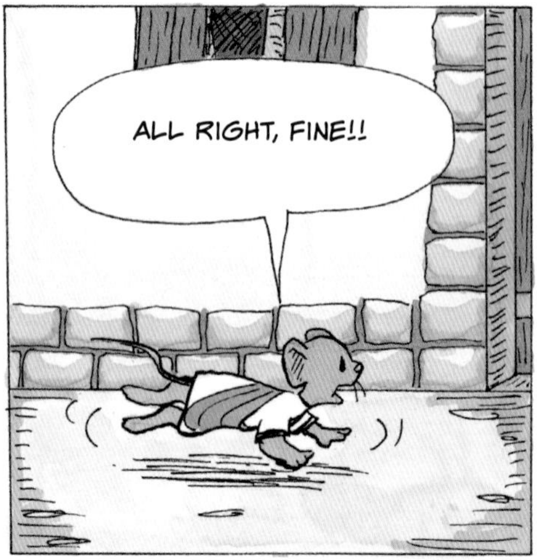
ALL RIGHT, FINE!!

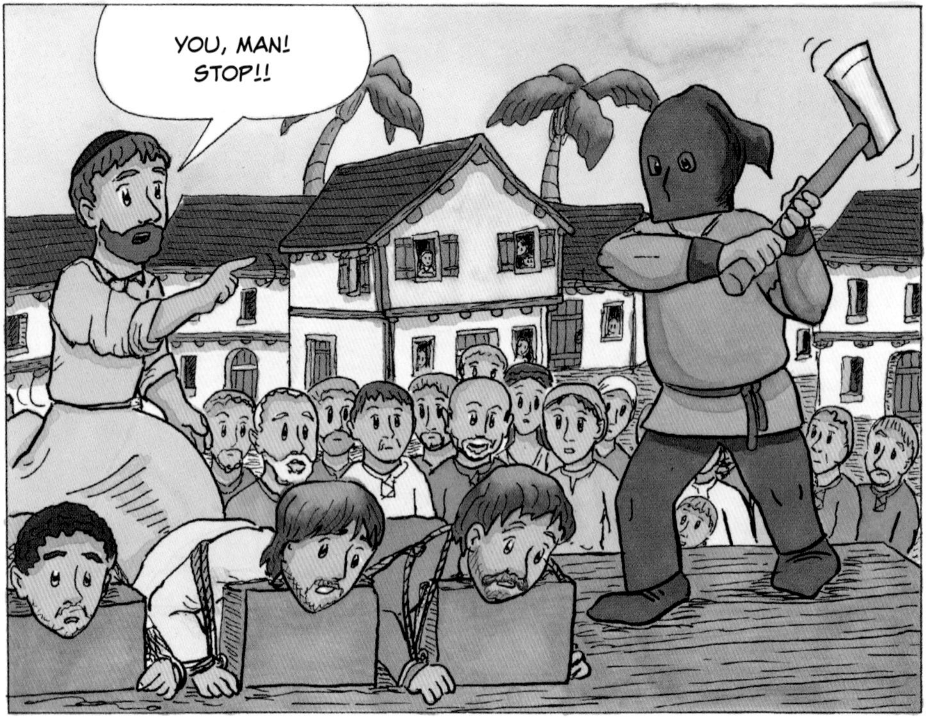
YOU, MAN! STOP!!

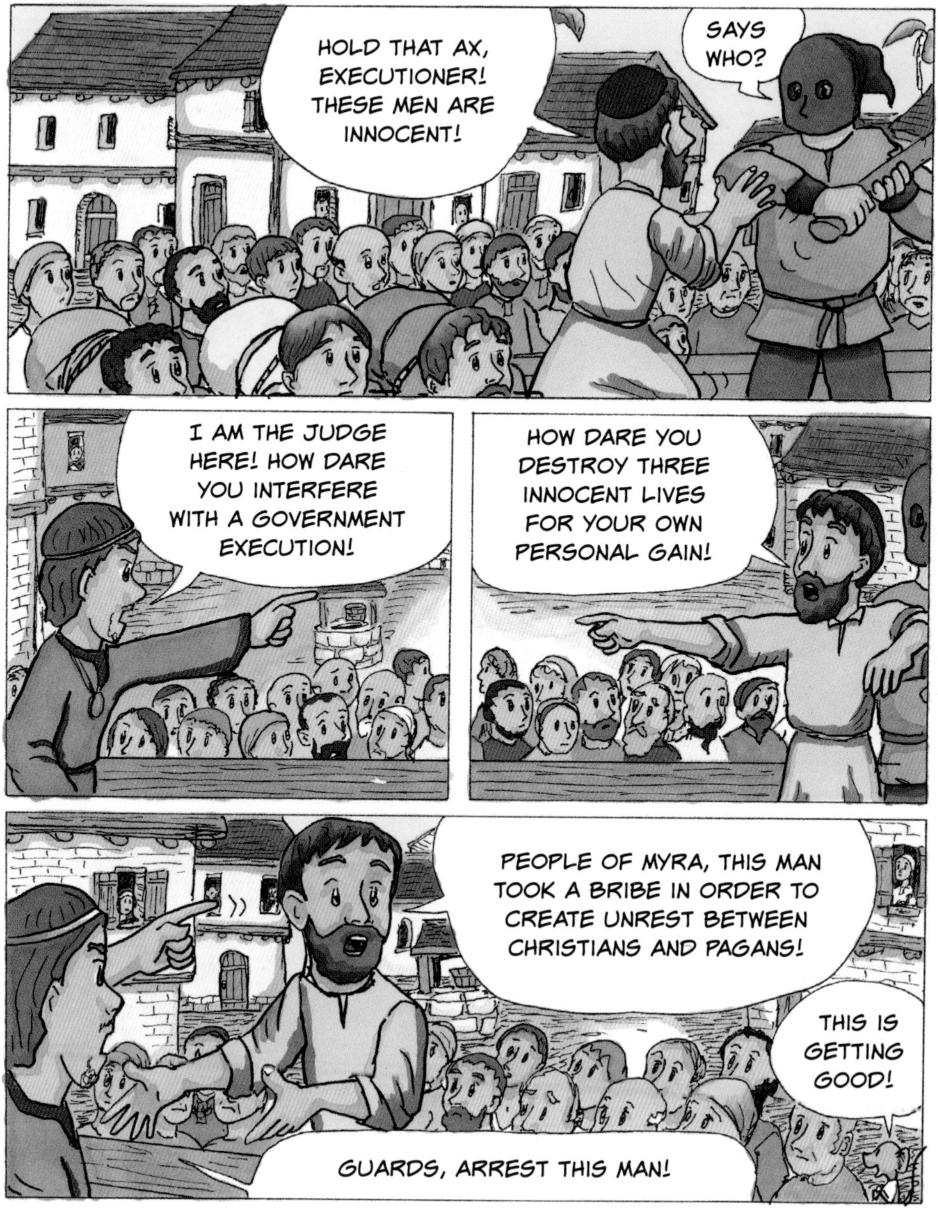
HOLD THAT AX, EXECUTIONER! THESE MEN ARE INNOCENT!
SAYS WHO?
I AM THE JUDGE HERE! HOW DARE YOU INTERFERE WITH A GOVERNMENT EXECUTION!
HOW DARE YOU DESTROY THREE INNOCENT LIVES FOR YOUR OWN PERSONAL GAIN!
PEOPLE OF MYRA, THIS MAN TOOK A BRIBE IN ORDER TO CREATE UNREST BETWEEN CHRISTIANS AND PAGANS!
THIS IS GETTING GOOD!
GUARDS, ARREST THIS MAN!

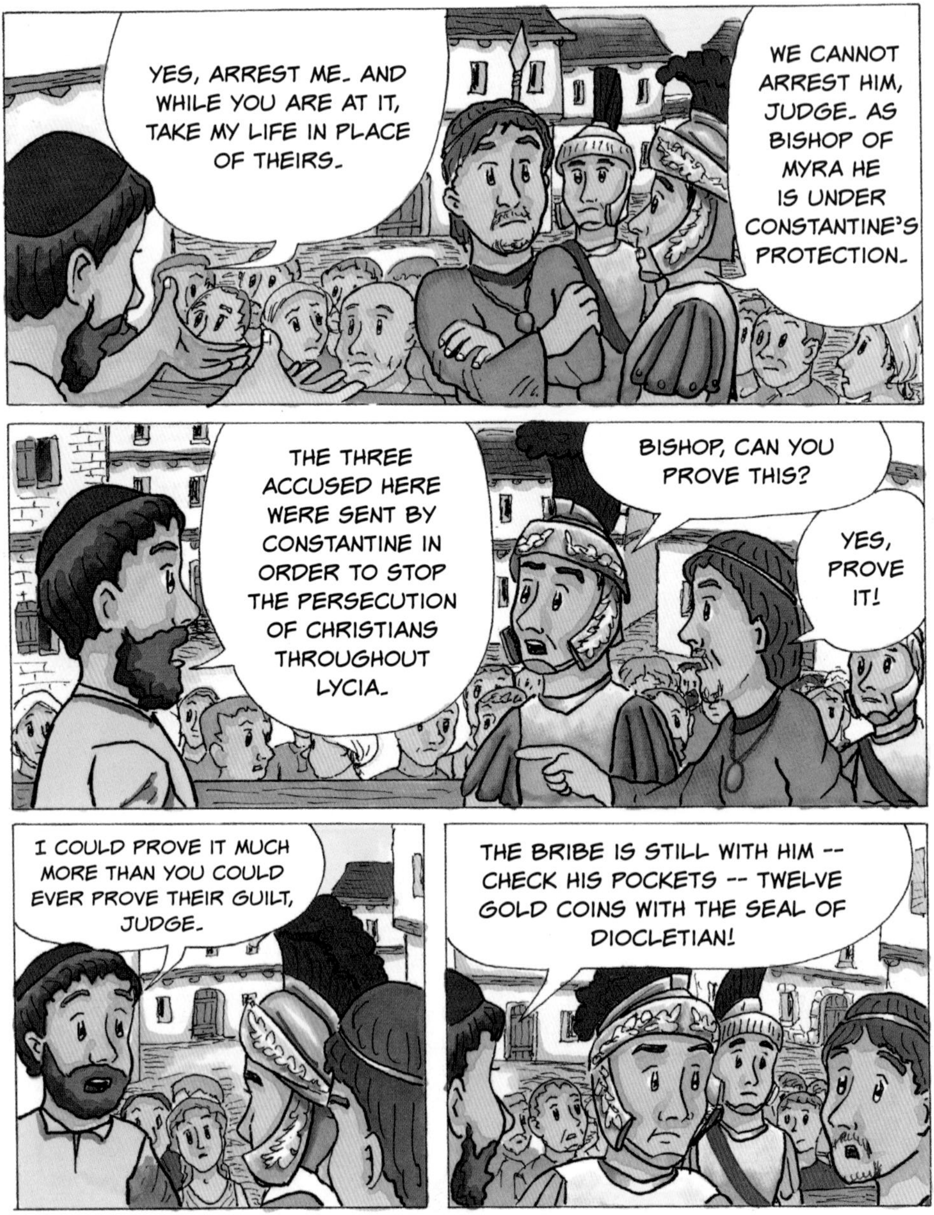
YES, ARREST ME. AND WHILE YOU ARE AT IT, TAKE MY LIFE IN PLACE OF THEIRS.
WE CANNOT ARREST HIM, JUDGE. AS BISHOP OF MYRA HE IS UNDER CONSTANTINE'S PROTECTION.
THE THREE ACCUSED HERE WERE SENT BY CONSTANTINE IN ORDER TO STOP THE PERSECUTION OF CHRISTIANS THROUGHOUT LYCIA.
BISHOP, CAN YOU PROVE THIS?
YES, PROVE IT!
I COULD PROVE IT MUCH MORE THAN YOU COULD EVER PROVE THEIR GUILT, JUDGE.
THE BRIBE IS STILL WITH HIM -- CHECK HIS POCKETS -- TWELVE GOLD COINS WITH THE SEAL OF DIOCLETIAN!

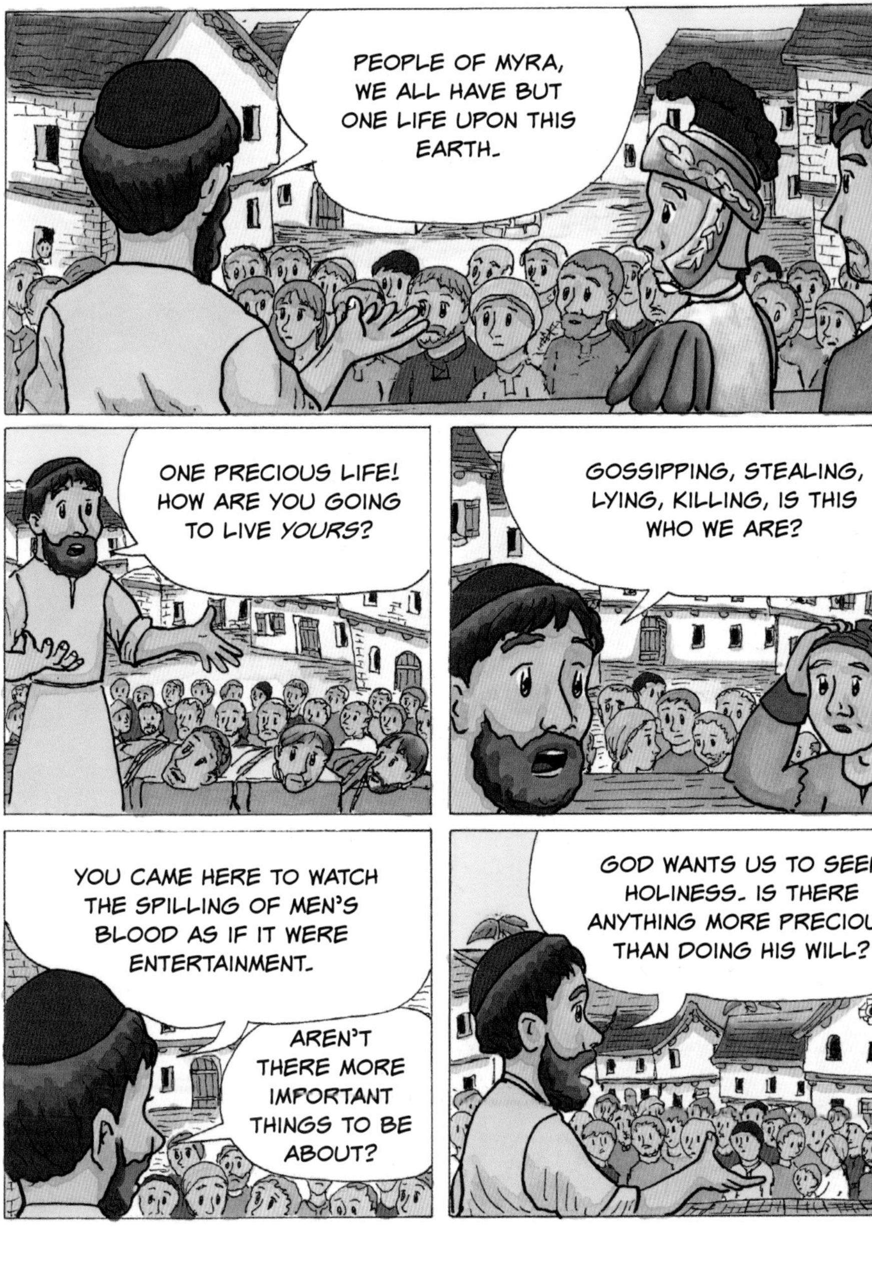
PEOPLE OF MYRA, WE ALL HAVE BUT ONE LIFE UPON THIS EARTH.
ONE PRECIOUS LIFE! HOW ARE YOU GOING TO LIVE *YOURS*?
GOSSIPPING, STEALING, LYING, KILLING, IS THIS WHO WE ARE?
YOU CAME HERE TO WATCH THE SPILLING OF MEN'S BLOOD AS IF IT WERE ENTERTAINMENT.
AREN'T THERE MORE IMPORTANT THINGS TO BE ABOUT?
GOD WANTS US TO SEEK HOLINESS. IS THERE ANYTHING MORE PRECIOUS THAN DOING HIS WILL?

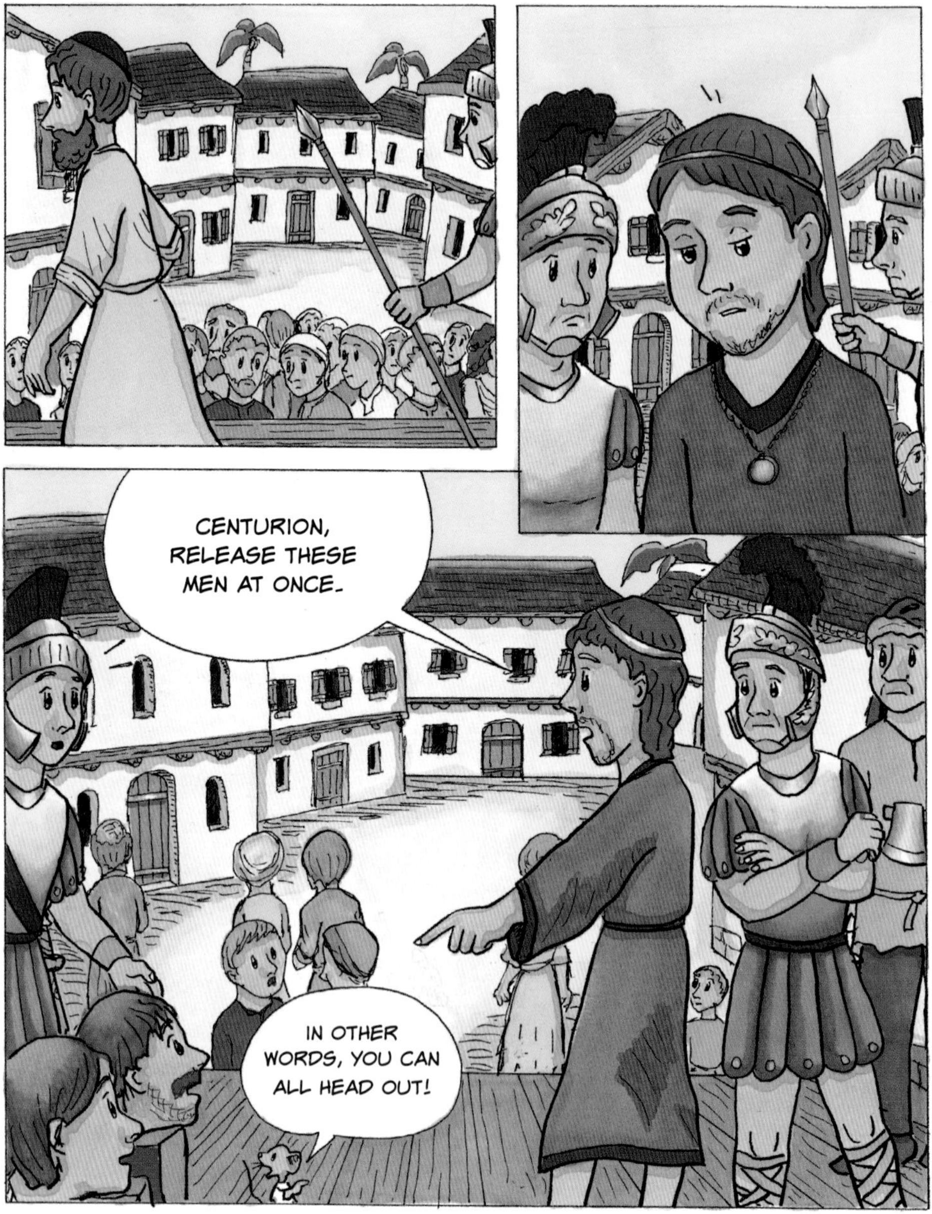
CENTURION, RELEASE THESE MEN AT ONCE.
IN OTHER WORDS, YOU CAN ALL HEAD OUT!

Many months later...

PLEASE FORGIVE THE INTRUSION, BISHOP...

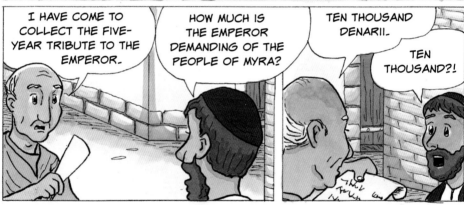

I HAVE COME TO COLLECT THE FIVE-YEAR TRIBUTE TO THE EMPEROR.

HOW MUCH IS THE EMPEROR DEMANDING OF THE PEOPLE OF MYRA?

TEN THOUSAND DENARII.

TEN THOUSAND?!

SIR, MYRA CANNOT AFFORD EVEN HALF THAT SUM! WE HAVE MANY POOR PEOPLE WHO ARE BARELY SCRAPING BY WITH THE FRUIT AND GRAIN GOD HAS PROVIDED.

ANY APPEAL MUST BE TAKEN DIRECTLY TO CONSTANTINE HIMSELF.

VERY WELL, I WILL BE BACK WITHIN THE WEEK.

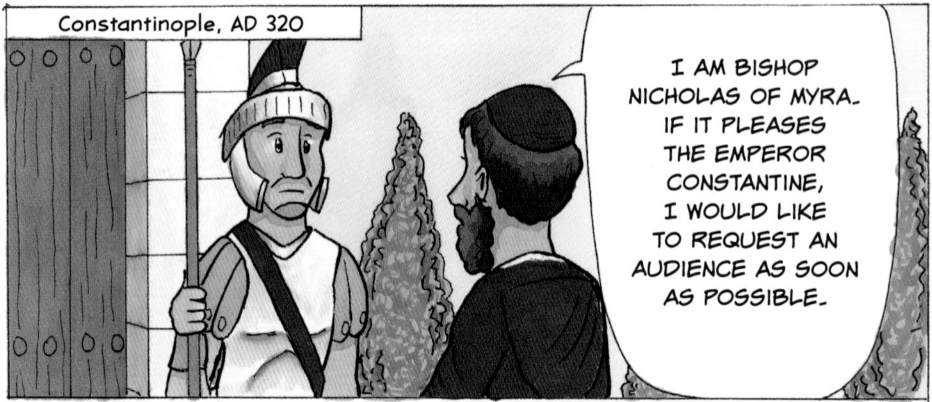
Constantinople, AD 320
I AM BISHOP NICHOLAS OF MYRA. IF IT PLEASES THE EMPEROR CONSTANTINE, I WOULD LIKE TO REQUEST AN AUDIENCE AS SOON AS POSSIBLE.

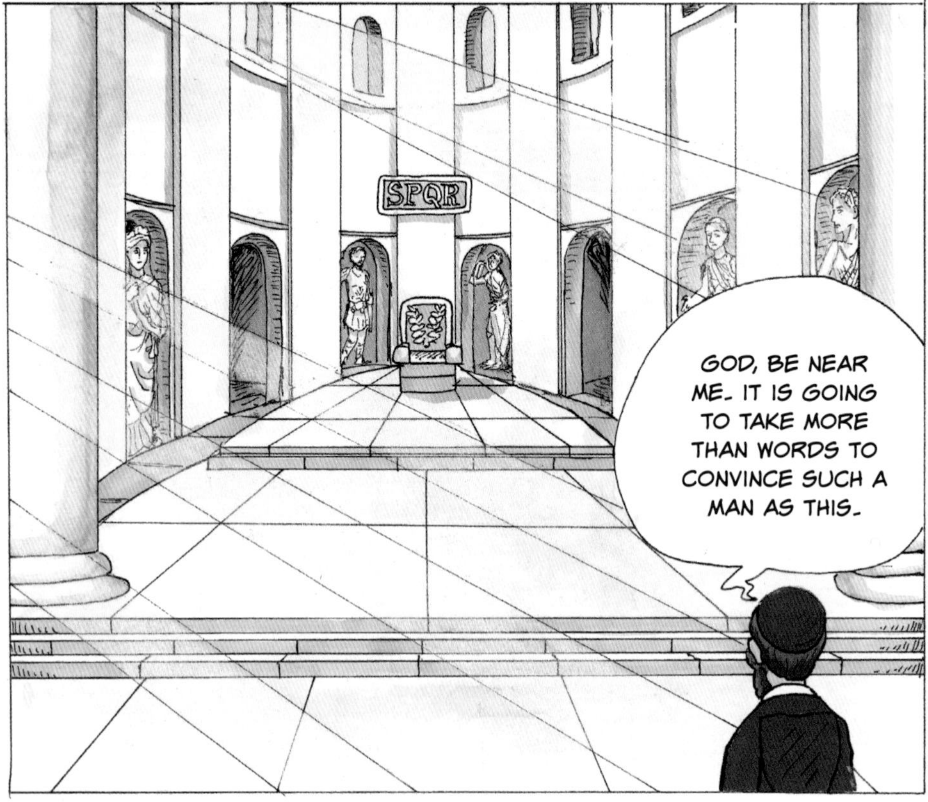
SPQR
GOD, BE NEAR ME. IT IS GOING TO TAKE MORE THAN WORDS TO CONVINCE SUCH A MAN AS THIS.

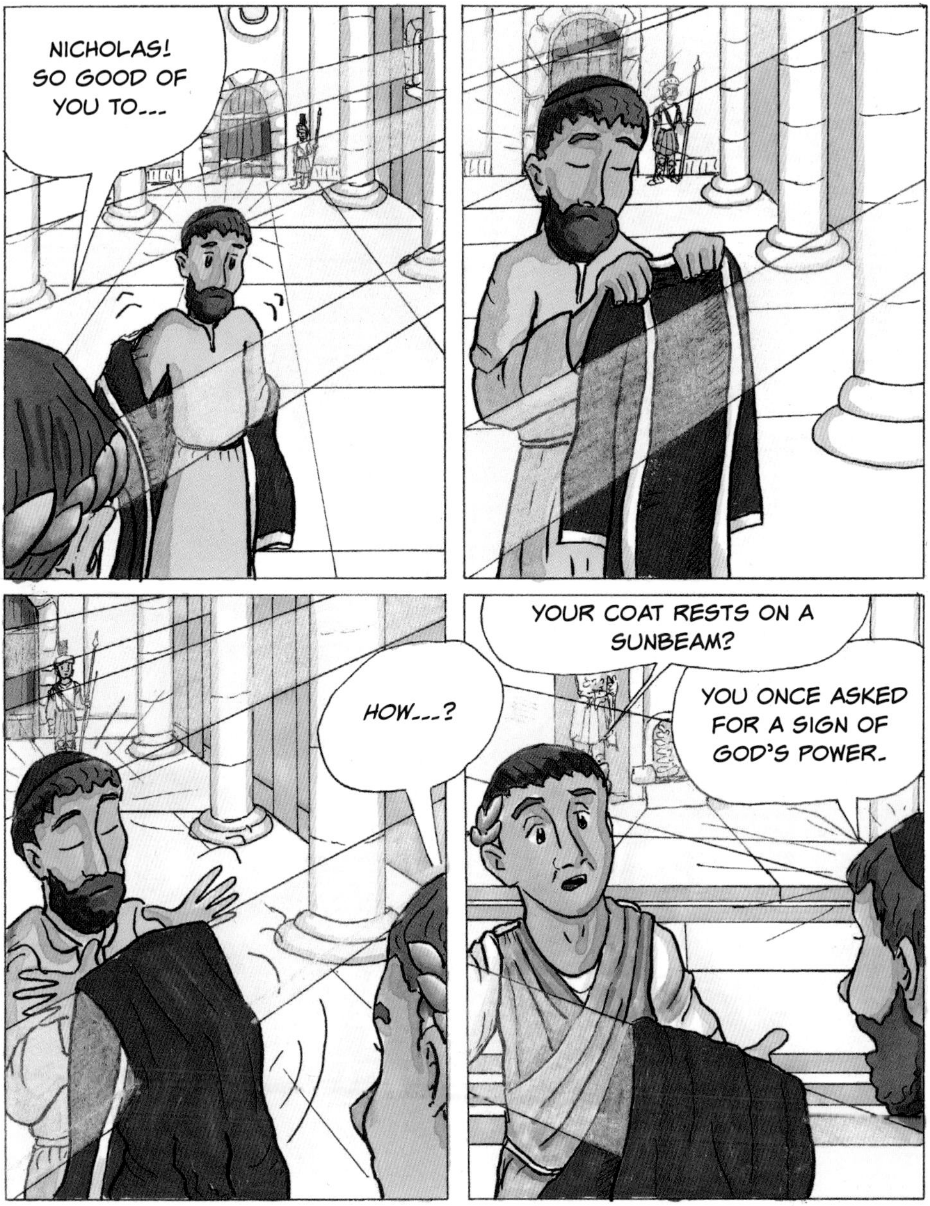
NICHOLAS! SO GOOD OF YOU TO...
HOW...?
YOUR COAT RESTS ON A SUNBEAM?
YOU ONCE ASKED FOR A SIGN OF GOD'S POWER.

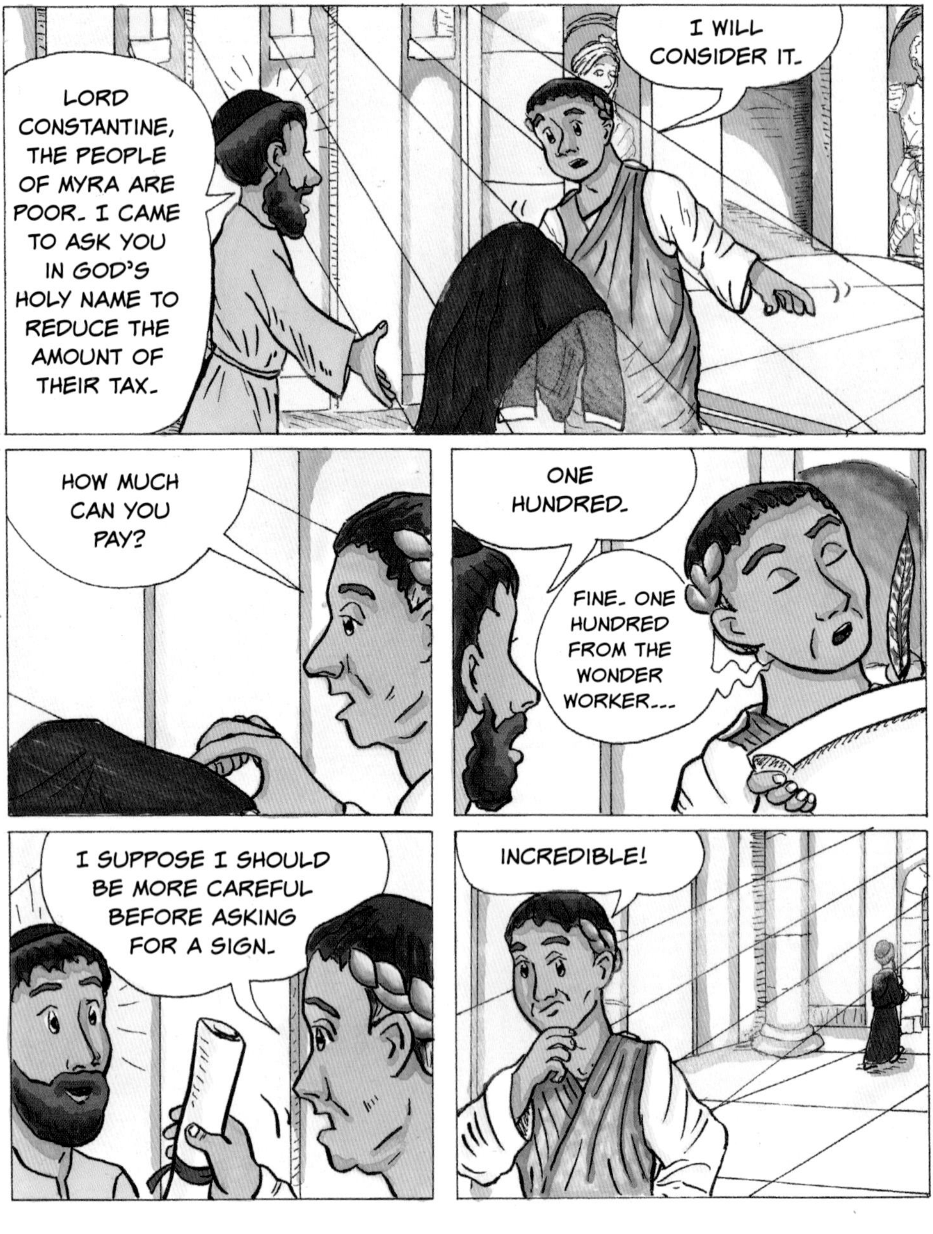
LORD CONSTANTINE, THE PEOPLE OF MYRA ARE POOR. I CAME TO ASK YOU IN GOD'S HOLY NAME TO REDUCE THE AMOUNT OF THEIR TAX.
I WILL CONSIDER IT.
HOW MUCH CAN YOU PAY?
ONE HUNDRED.
FINE. ONE HUNDRED FROM THE WONDER WORKER...
I SUPPOSE I SHOULD BE MORE CAREFUL BEFORE ASKING FOR A SIGN.
INCREDIBLE!

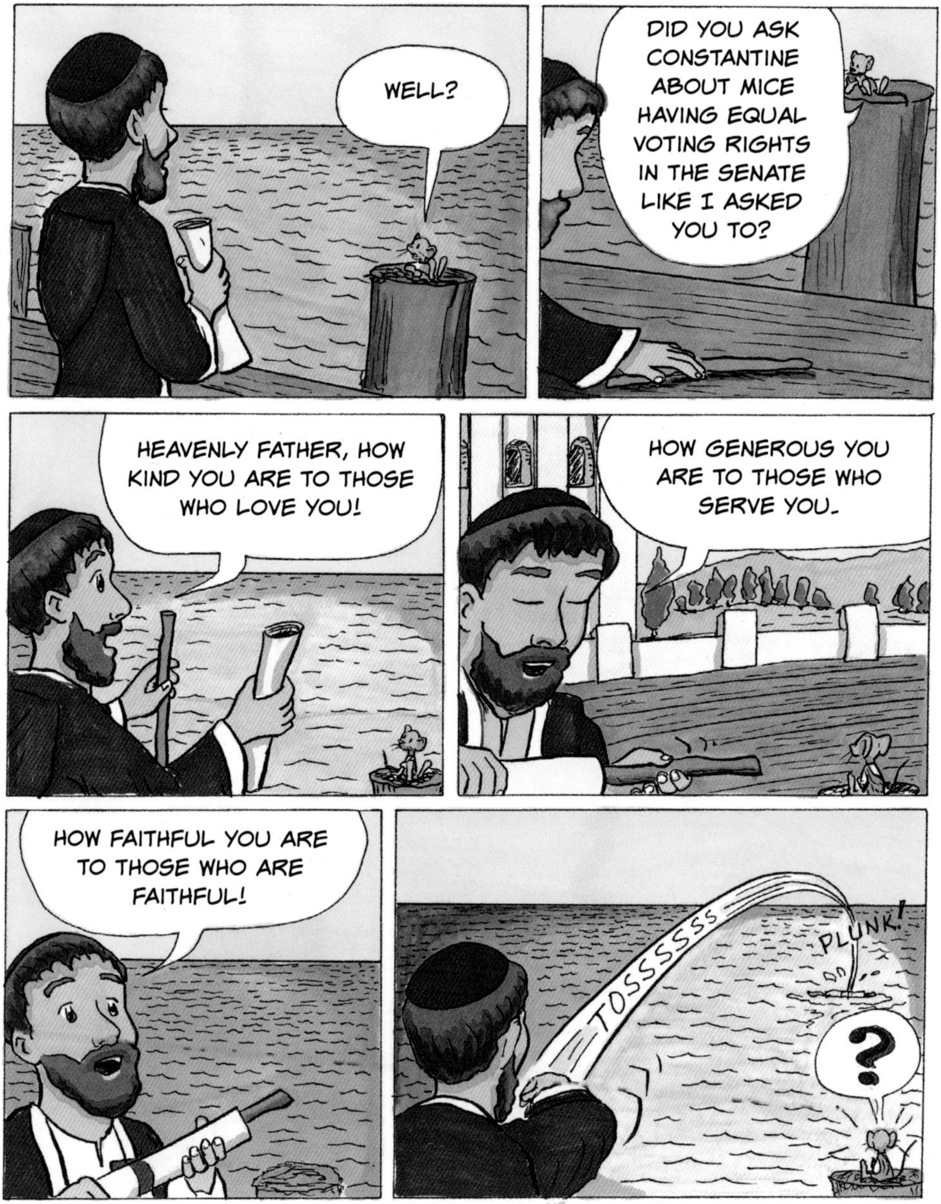
WELL?
DID YOU ASK CONSTANTINE ABOUT MICE HAVING EQUAL VOTING RIGHTS IN THE SENATE LIKE I ASKED YOU TO?
HEAVENLY FATHER, HOW KIND YOU ARE TO THOSE WHO LOVE YOU!
HOW GENEROUS YOU ARE TO THOSE WHO SERVE YOU.
HOW FAITHFUL YOU ARE TO THOSE WHO ARE FAITHFUL!
TOSSSSSS
PLUNK!
?

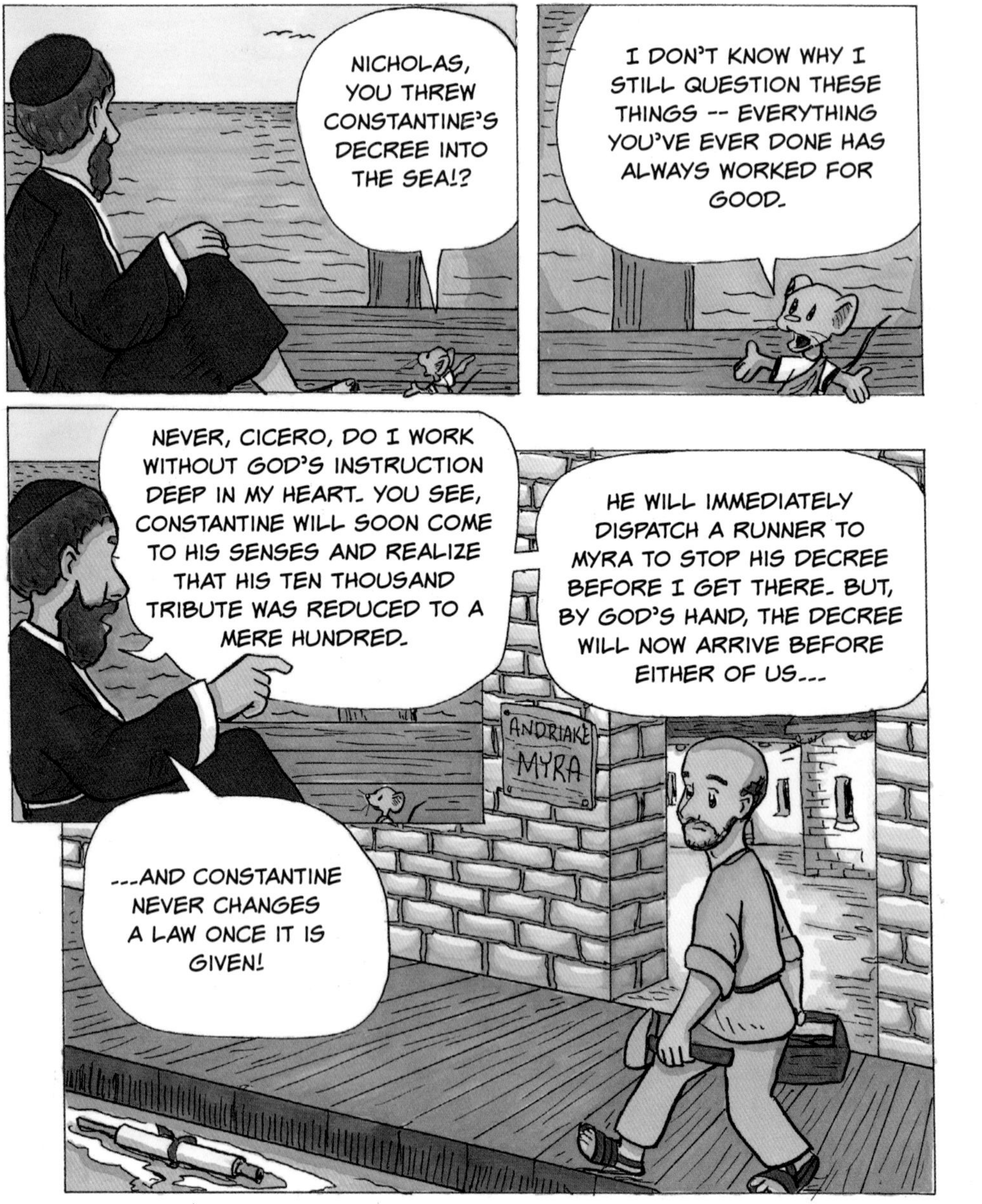
NICHOLAS, YOU THREW CONSTANTINE'S DECREE INTO THE SEA!?
I DON'T KNOW WHY I STILL QUESTION THESE THINGS -- EVERYTHING YOU'VE EVER DONE HAS ALWAYS WORKED FOR GOOD.
NEVER, CICERO, DO I WORK WITHOUT GOD'S INSTRUCTION DEEP IN MY HEART. YOU SEE, CONSTANTINE WILL SOON COME TO HIS SENSES AND REALIZE THAT HIS TEN THOUSAND TRIBUTE WAS REDUCED TO A MERE HUNDRED.
HE WILL IMMEDIATELY DISPATCH A RUNNER TO MYRA TO STOP HIS DECREE BEFORE I GET THERE. BUT, BY GOD'S HAND, THE DECREE WILL NOW ARRIVE BEFORE EITHER OF US...
ANDRIAKE
MYRA
...AND CONSTANTINE NEVER CHANGES A LAW ONCE IT IS GIVEN!

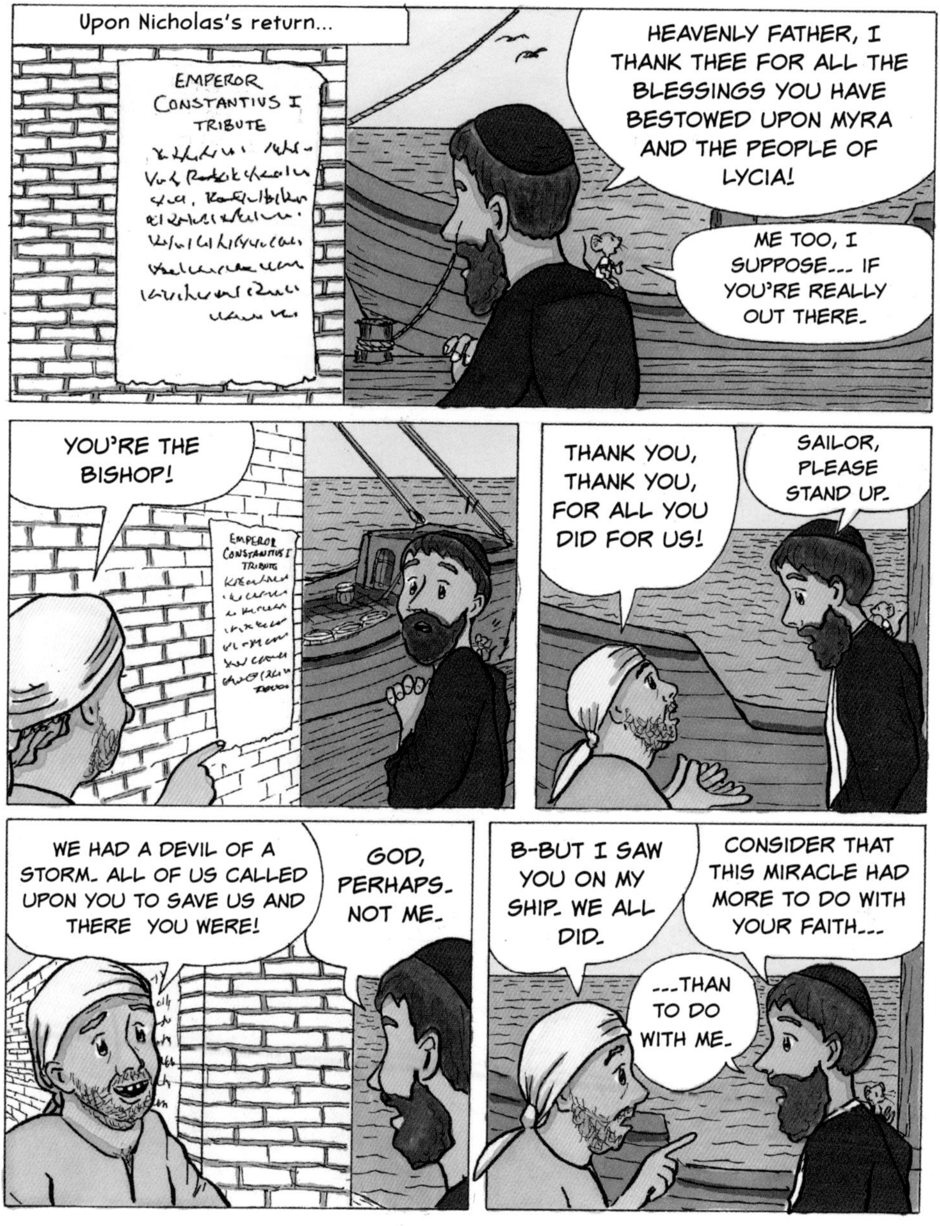
Upon Nicholas's return...
EMPEROR CONSTANTIUS I TRIBUTE
HEAVENLY FATHER, I THANK THEE FOR ALL THE BLESSINGS YOU HAVE BESTOWED UPON MYRA AND THE PEOPLE OF LYCIA!
ME TOO, I SUPPOSE... IF YOU'RE REALLY OUT THERE.
YOU'RE THE BISHOP!
EMPEROR CONSTANTIUS I TRIBUTE
THANK YOU, THANK YOU, FOR ALL YOU DID FOR US!
SAILOR, PLEASE STAND UP.
WE HAD A DEVIL OF A STORM. ALL OF US CALLED UPON YOU TO SAVE US AND THERE YOU WERE!
GOD, PERHAPS. NOT ME.
B-BUT I SAW YOU ON MY SHIP. WE ALL DID.
CONSIDER THAT THIS MIRACLE HAD MORE TO DO WITH YOUR FAITH...
...THAN TO DO WITH ME.

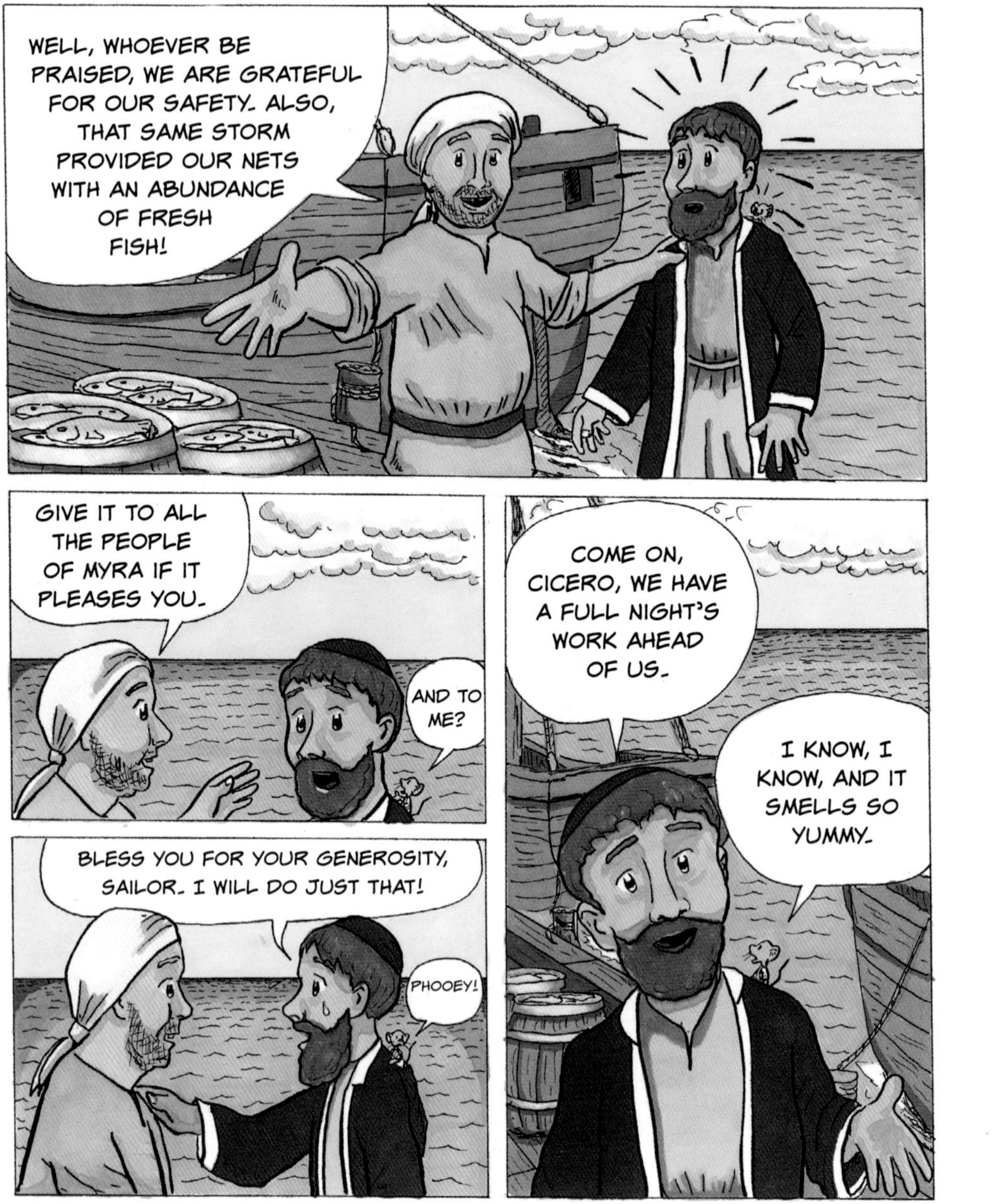
WELL, WHOEVER BE PRAISED, WE ARE GRATEFUL FOR OUR SAFETY. ALSO, THAT SAME STORM PROVIDED OUR NETS WITH AN ABUNDANCE OF FRESH FISH!
GIVE IT TO ALL THE PEOPLE OF MYRA IF IT PLEASES YOU.
AND TO ME?
BLESS YOU FOR YOUR GENEROSITY, SAILOR. I WILL DO JUST THAT!
PHOOEY!
COME ON, CICERO, WE HAVE A FULL NIGHT'S WORK AHEAD OF US.
I KNOW, I KNOW, AND IT SMELLS SO YUMMY.

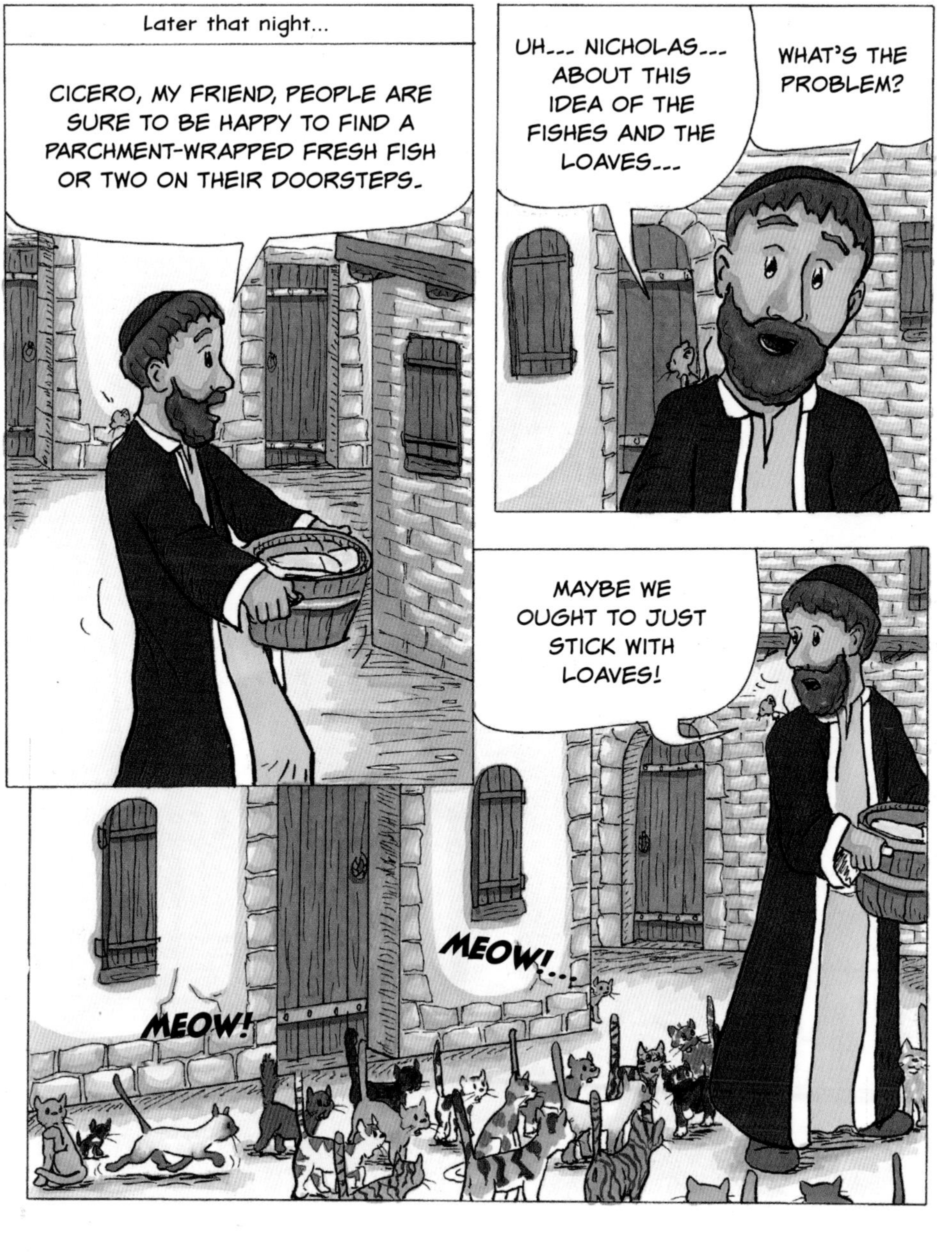
Later that night...
CICERO, MY FRIEND, PEOPLE ARE SURE TO BE HAPPY TO FIND A PARCHMENT-WRAPPED FRESH FISH OR TWO ON THEIR DOORSTEPS.
UH... NICHOLAS... ABOUT THIS IDEA OF THE FISHES AND THE LOAVES...
WHAT'S THE PROBLEM?
MAYBE WE OUGHT TO JUST STICK WITH LOAVES!
MEOW!...
MEOW!

CHAPTER SEVEN
DEFENDER OF THE FAITH

You are the light of the world.
A city built on a hill cannot be hidden.
in the same way, let your light shine before others,
so that they may see your good works
and give glory to your Father in heaven.
—MATTHEW 5:14, 16

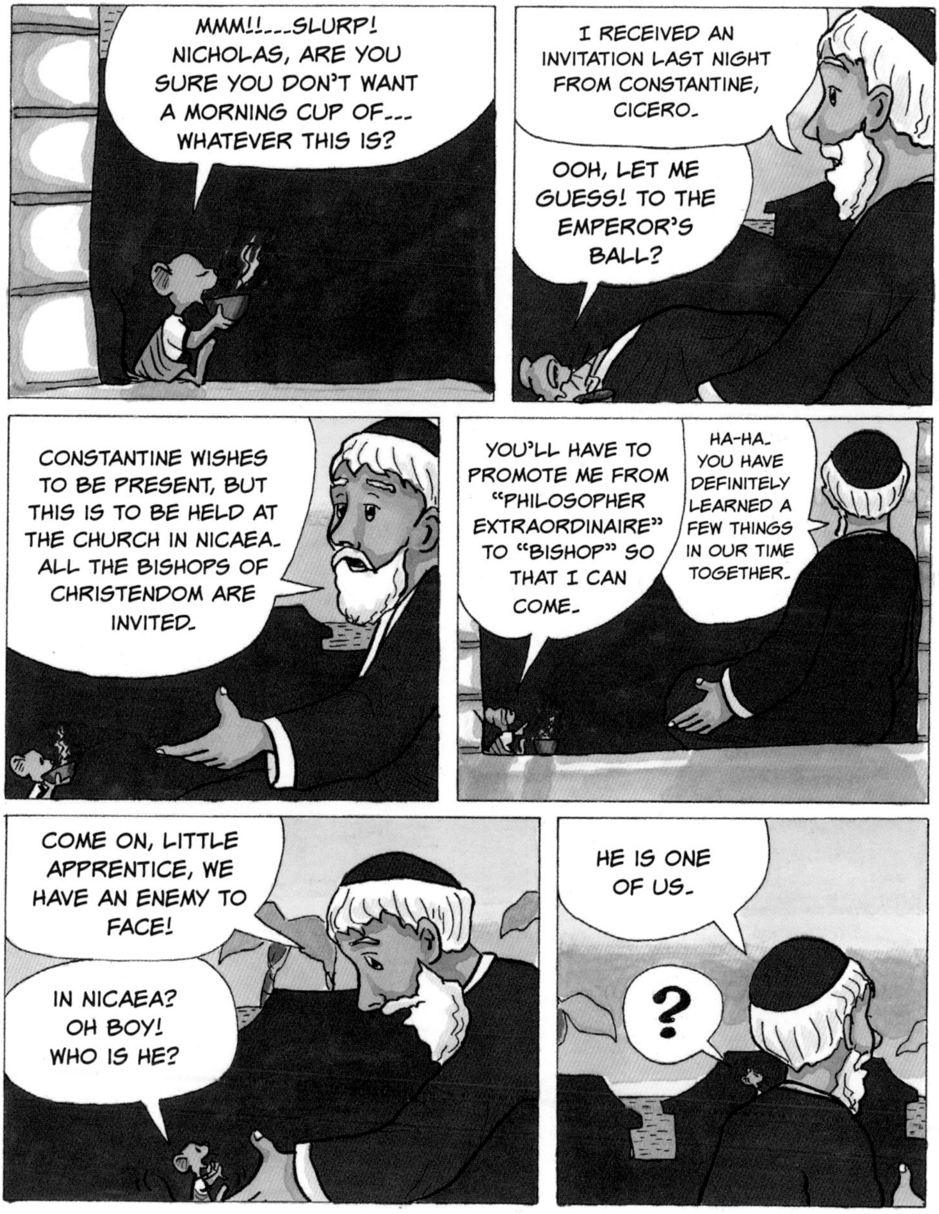
MMM!!...SLURP! NICHOLAS, ARE YOU SURE YOU DON'T WANT A MORNING CUP OF... WHATEVER THIS IS?
I RECEIVED AN INVITATION LAST NIGHT FROM CONSTANTINE, CICERO.
OOH, LET ME GUESS! TO THE EMPEROR'S BALL?
CONSTANTINE WISHES TO BE PRESENT, BUT THIS IS TO BE HELD AT THE CHURCH IN NICAEA. ALL THE BISHOPS OF CHRISTENDOM ARE INVITED.
YOU'LL HAVE TO PROMOTE ME FROM "PHILOSOPHER EXTRAORDINAIRE" TO "BISHOP" SO THAT I CAN COME.
HA-HA. YOU HAVE DEFINITELY LEARNED A FEW THINGS IN OUR TIME TOGETHER.
COME ON, LITTLE APPRENTICE, WE HAVE AN ENEMY TO FACE!
IN NICAEA? OH BOY! WHO IS HE?
HE IS ONE OF US.
?

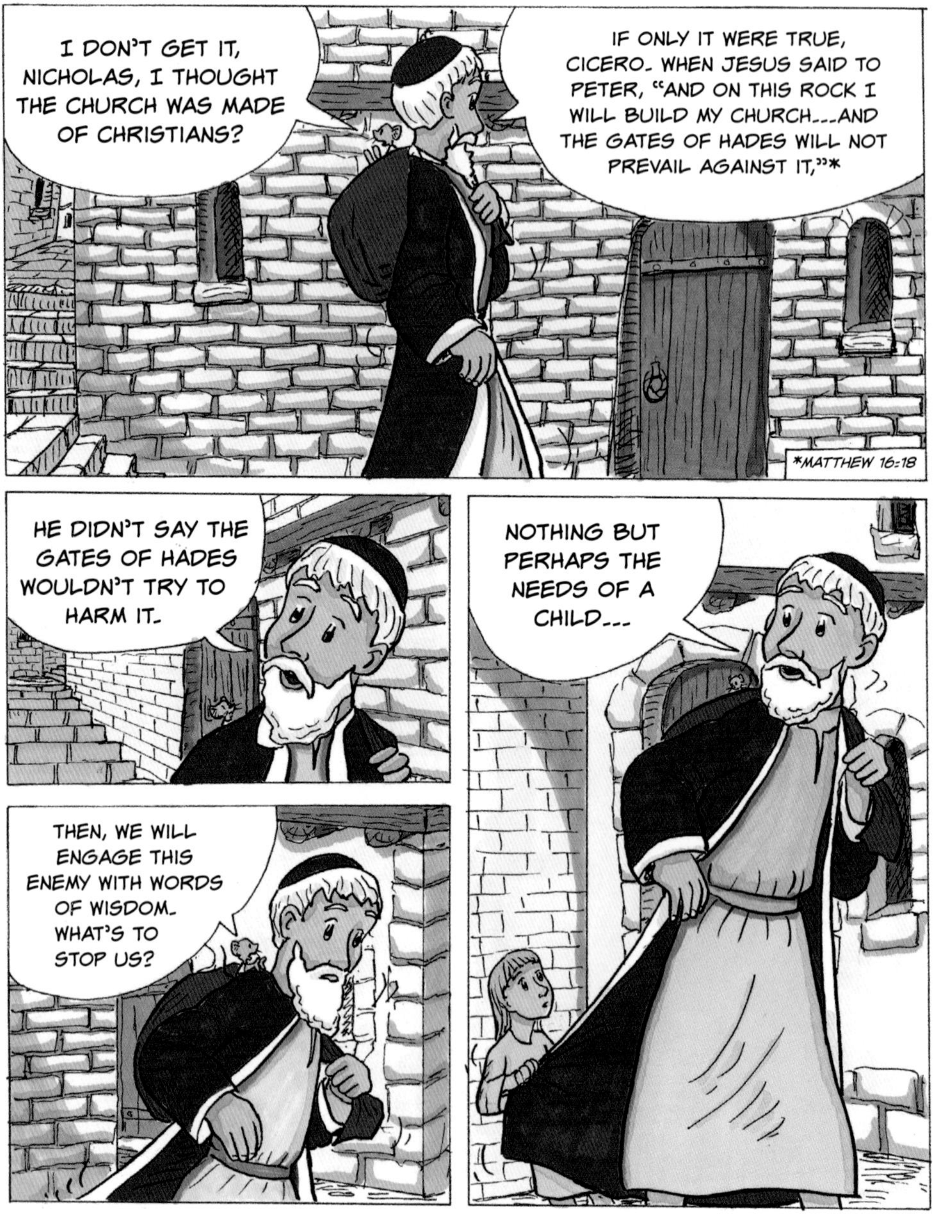
I DON'T GET IT, NICHOLAS, I THOUGHT THE CHURCH WAS MADE OF CHRISTIANS?
IF ONLY IT WERE TRUE, CICERO. WHEN JESUS SAID TO PETER, "AND ON THIS ROCK I WILL BUILD MY CHURCH...AND THE GATES OF HADES WILL NOT PREVAIL AGAINST IT,"*
*MATTHEW 16:18
HE DIDN'T SAY THE GATES OF HADES WOULDN'T TRY TO HARM IT.
NOTHING BUT PERHAPS THE NEEDS OF A CHILD...
THEN, WE WILL ENGAGE THIS ENEMY WITH WORDS OF WISDOM. WHAT'S TO STOP US?

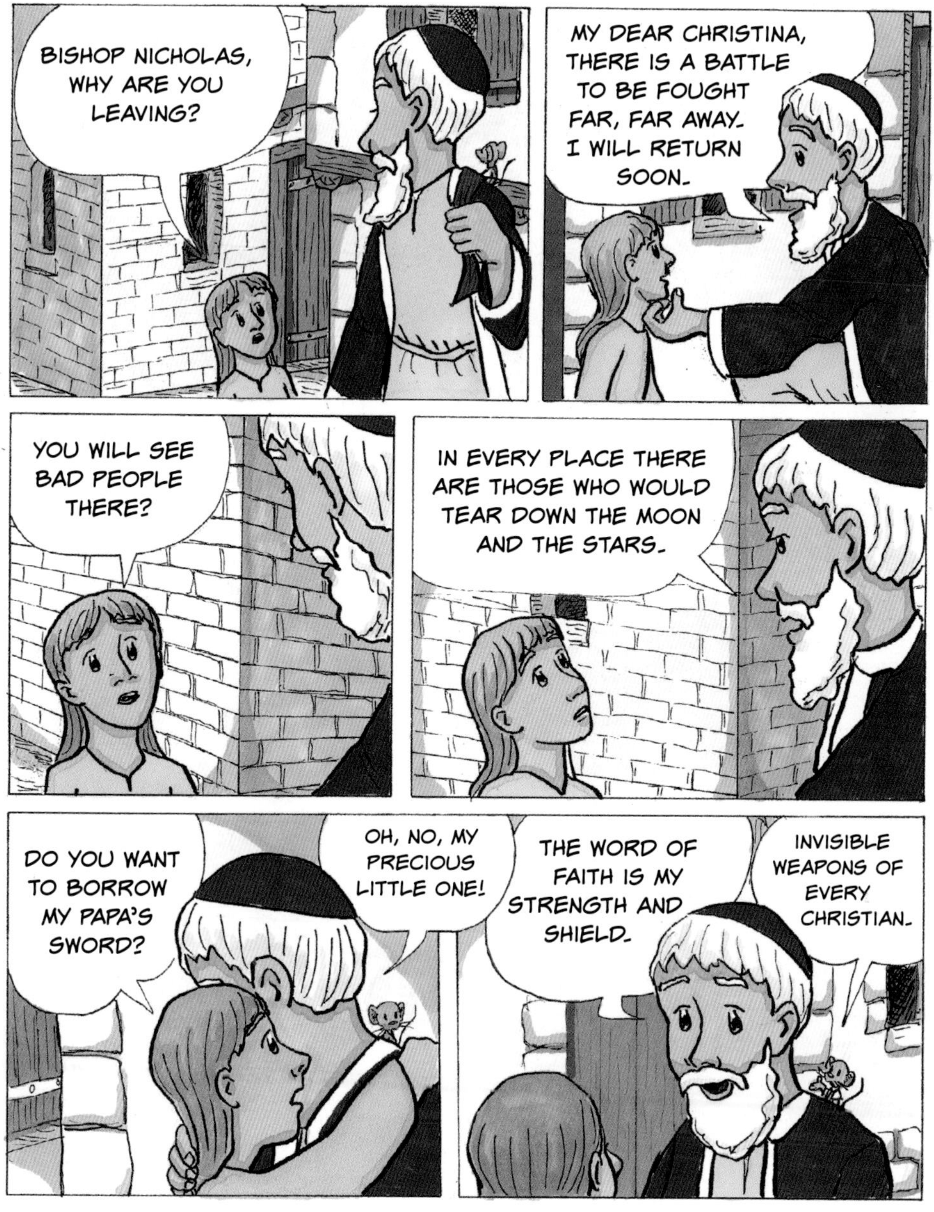
BISHOP NICHOLAS, WHY ARE YOU LEAVING?
MY DEAR CHRISTINA, THERE IS A BATTLE TO BE FOUGHT FAR, FAR AWAY. I WILL RETURN SOON.
YOU WILL SEE BAD PEOPLE THERE?
IN EVERY PLACE THERE ARE THOSE WHO WOULD TEAR DOWN THE MOON AND THE STARS.
DO YOU WANT TO BORROW MY PAPA'S SWORD?
OH, NO, MY PRECIOUS LITTLE ONE!
THE WORD OF FAITH IS MY STRENGTH AND SHIELD.
INVISIBLE WEAPONS OF EVERY CHRISTIAN.

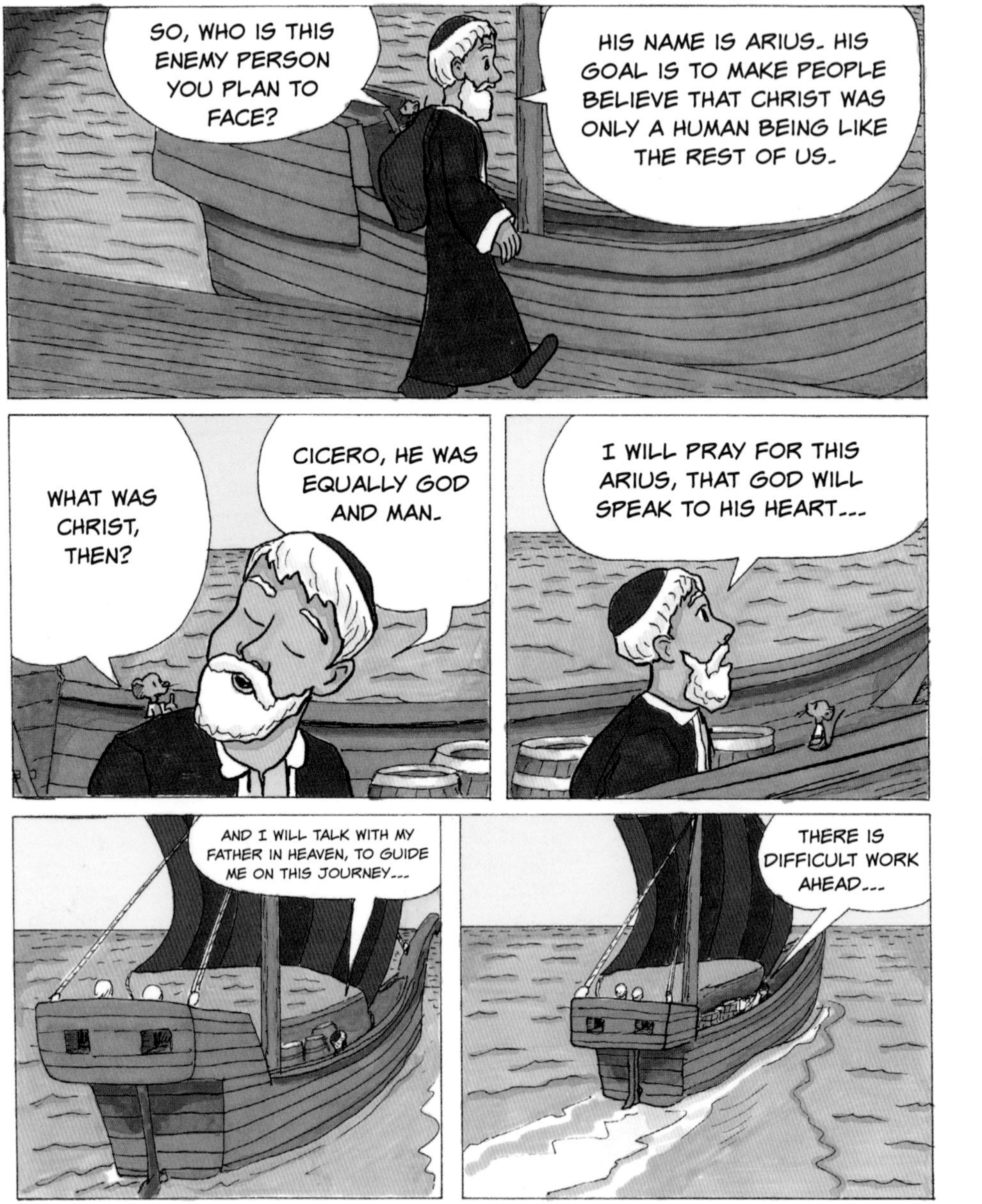
SO, WHO IS THIS ENEMY PERSON YOU PLAN TO FACE?
HIS NAME IS ARIUS. HIS GOAL IS TO MAKE PEOPLE BELIEVE THAT CHRIST WAS ONLY A HUMAN BEING LIKE THE REST OF US.
WHAT WAS CHRIST, THEN?
CICERO, HE WAS EQUALLY GOD AND MAN.
I WILL PRAY FOR THIS ARIUS, THAT GOD WILL SPEAK TO HIS HEART...
AND I WILL TALK WITH MY FATHER IN HEAVEN, TO GUIDE ME ON THIS JOURNEY...
THERE IS DIFFICULT WORK AHEAD...

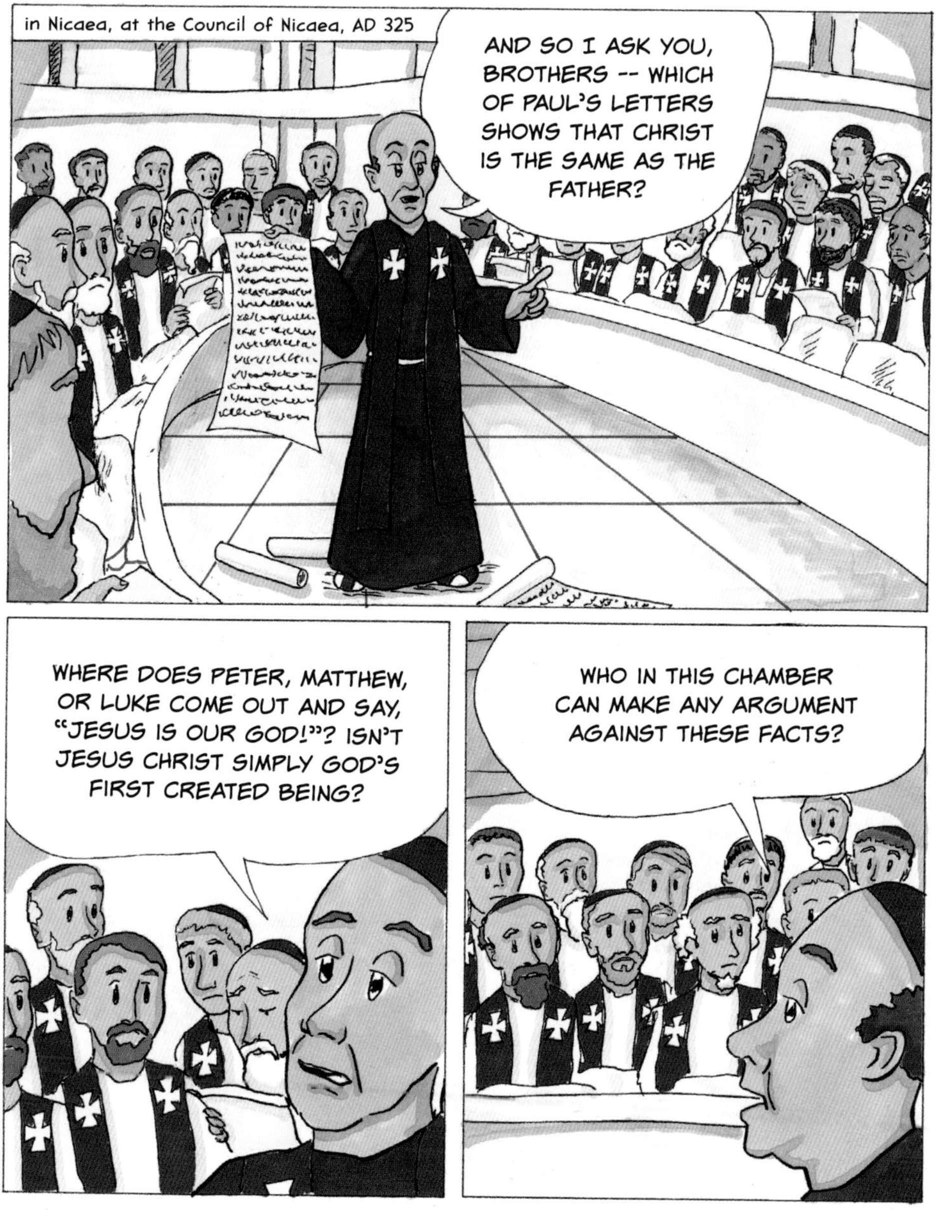
in Nicaea, at the Council of Nicaea, AD 325
AND SO I ASK YOU, BROTHERS -- WHICH OF PAUL'S LETTERS SHOWS THAT CHRIST IS THE SAME AS THE FATHER?
WHERE DOES PETER, MATTHEW, OR LUKE COME OUT AND SAY, "JESUS IS OUR GOD!"? ISN'T JESUS CHRIST SIMPLY GOD'S FIRST CREATED BEING?
WHO IN THIS CHAMBER CAN MAKE ANY ARGUMENT AGAINST THESE FACTS?

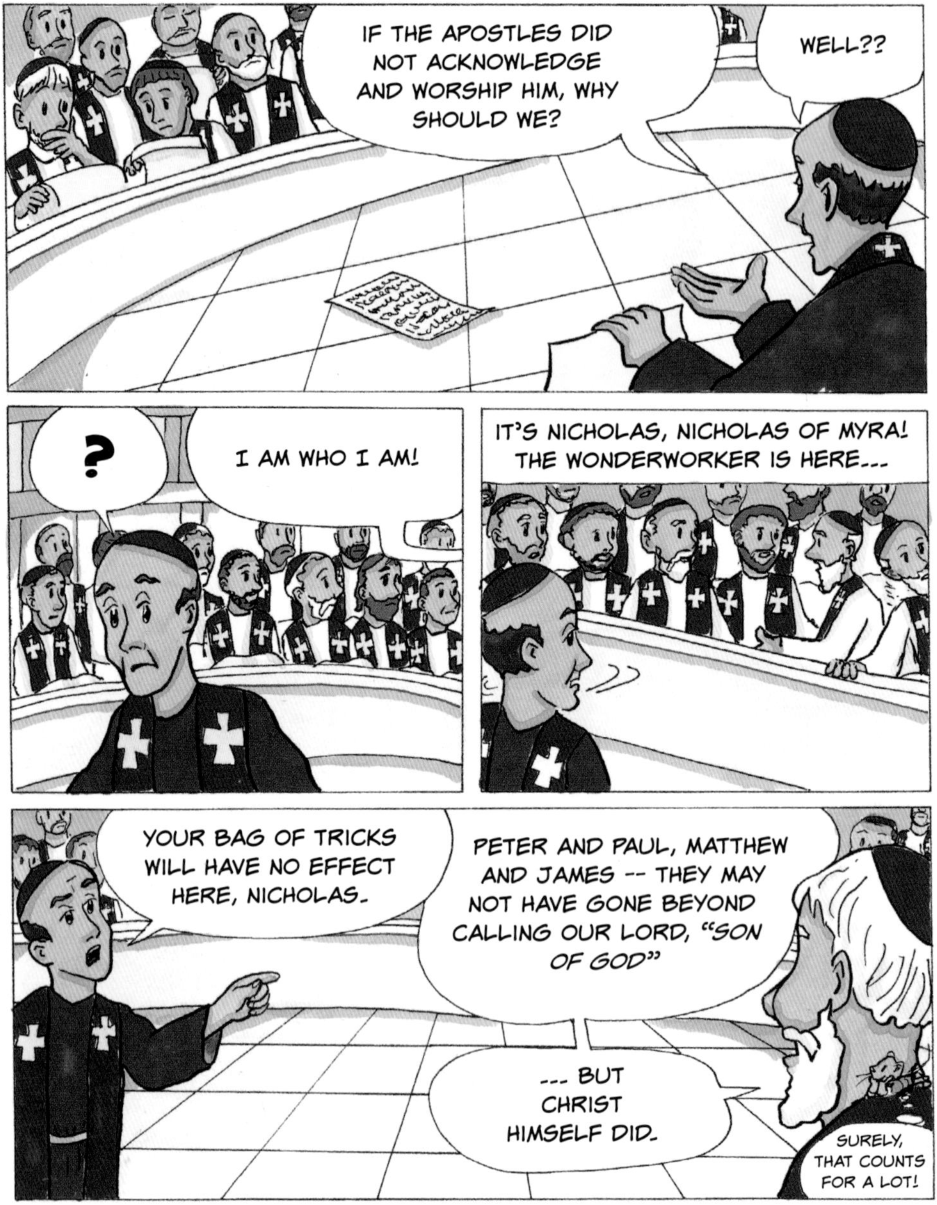
IF THE APOSTLES DID NOT ACKNOWLEDGE AND WORSHIP HIM, WHY SHOULD WE?
WELL??
?
I AM WHO I AM!
IT'S NICHOLAS, NICHOLAS OF MYRA! THE WONDERWORKER IS HERE...
YOUR BAG OF TRICKS WILL HAVE NO EFFECT HERE, NICHOLAS.
PETER AND PAUL, MATTHEW AND JAMES -- THEY MAY NOT HAVE GONE BEYOND CALLING OUR LORD, "SON OF GOD"
... BUT CHRIST HIMSELF DID.
SURELY, THAT COUNTS FOR A LOT!

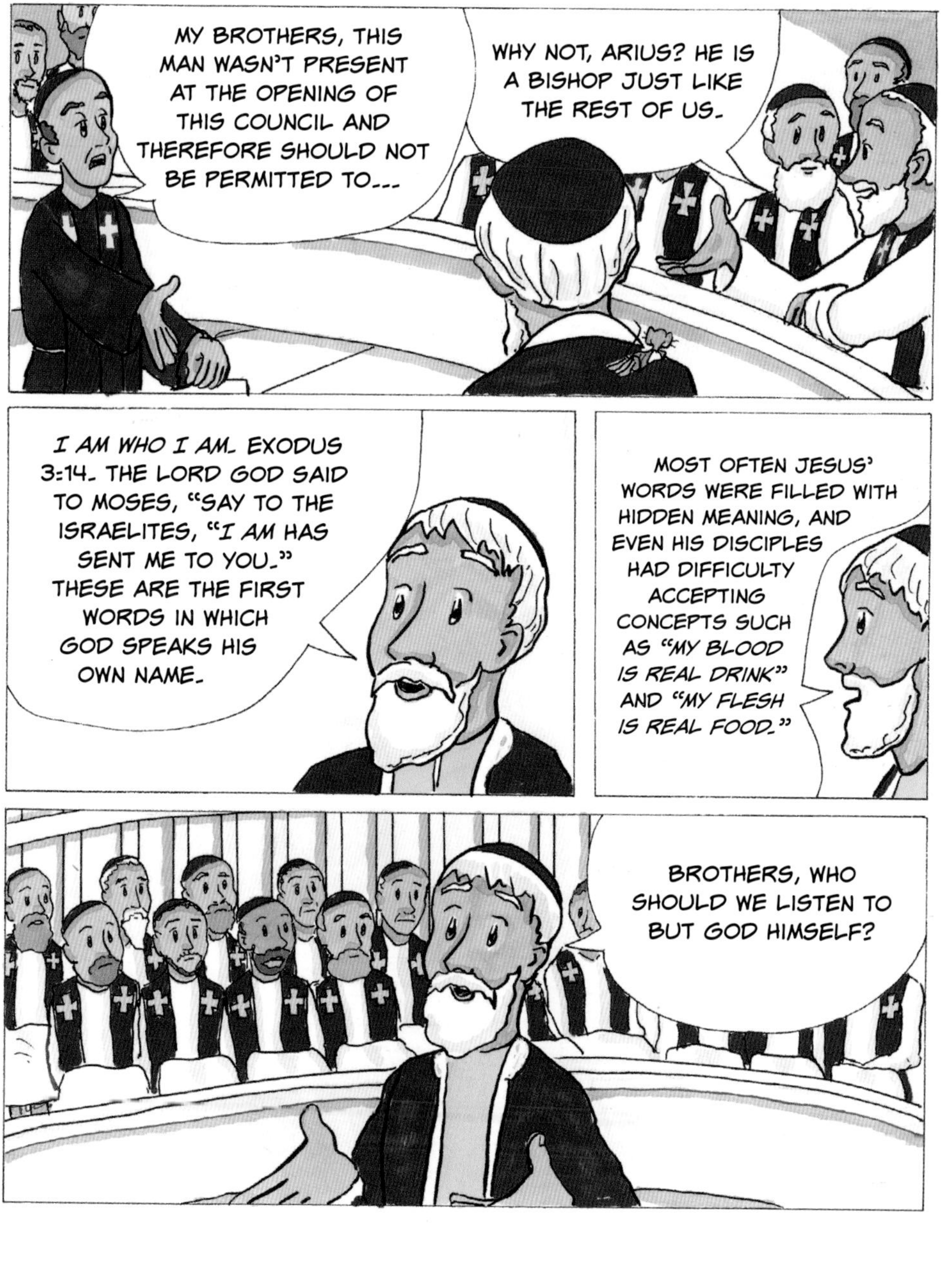
MY BROTHERS, THIS MAN WASN'T PRESENT AT THE OPENING OF THIS COUNCIL AND THEREFORE SHOULD NOT BE PERMITTED TO...
WHY NOT, ARIUS? HE IS A BISHOP JUST LIKE THE REST OF US.
I AM WHO I AM. EXODUS 3:14. THE LORD GOD SAID TO MOSES, "SAY TO THE ISRAELITES, "I AM HAS SENT ME TO YOU."" THESE ARE THE FIRST WORDS IN WHICH GOD SPEAKS HIS OWN NAME.
MOST OFTEN JESUS' WORDS WERE FILLED WITH HIDDEN MEANING, AND EVEN HIS DISCIPLES HAD DIFFICULTY ACCEPTING CONCEPTS SUCH AS "MY BLOOD IS REAL DRINK" AND "MY FLESH IS REAL FOOD."
BROTHERS, WHO SHOULD WE LISTEN TO BUT GOD HIMSELF?

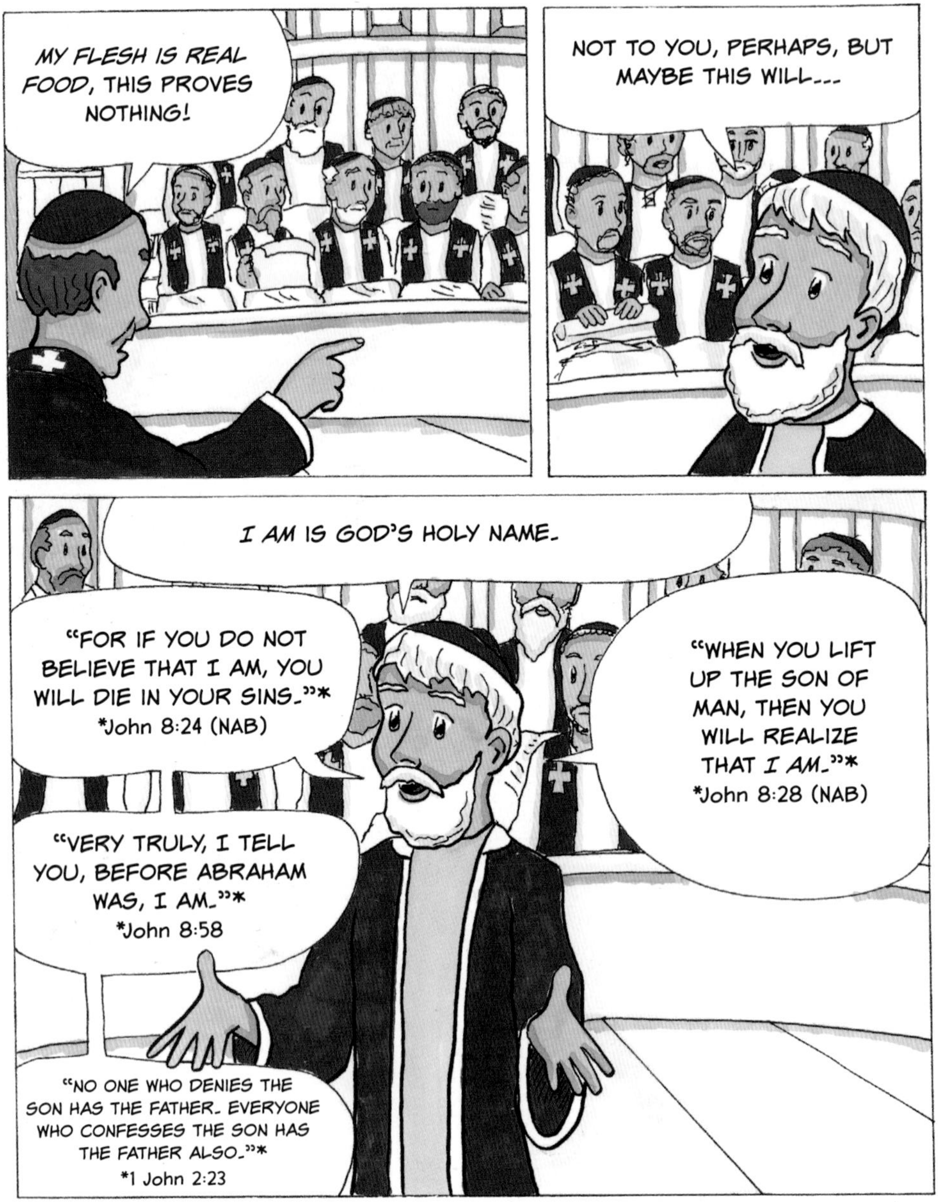
MY FLESH IS REAL FOOD, THIS PROVES NOTHING!
NOT TO YOU, PERHAPS, BUT MAYBE THIS WILL...
I AM IS GOD'S HOLY NAME.
"FOR IF YOU DO NOT BELIEVE THAT I AM, YOU WILL DIE IN YOUR SINS."* *John 8:24 (NAB)
"WHEN YOU LIFT UP THE SON OF MAN, THEN YOU WILL REALIZE THAT I AM."* *John 8:28 (NAB)
"VERY TRULY, I TELL YOU, BEFORE ABRAHAM WAS, I AM."* *John 8:58
"NO ONE WHO DENIES THE SON HAS THE FATHER. EVERYONE WHO CONFESSES THE SON HAS THE FATHER ALSO."* *1 John 2:23

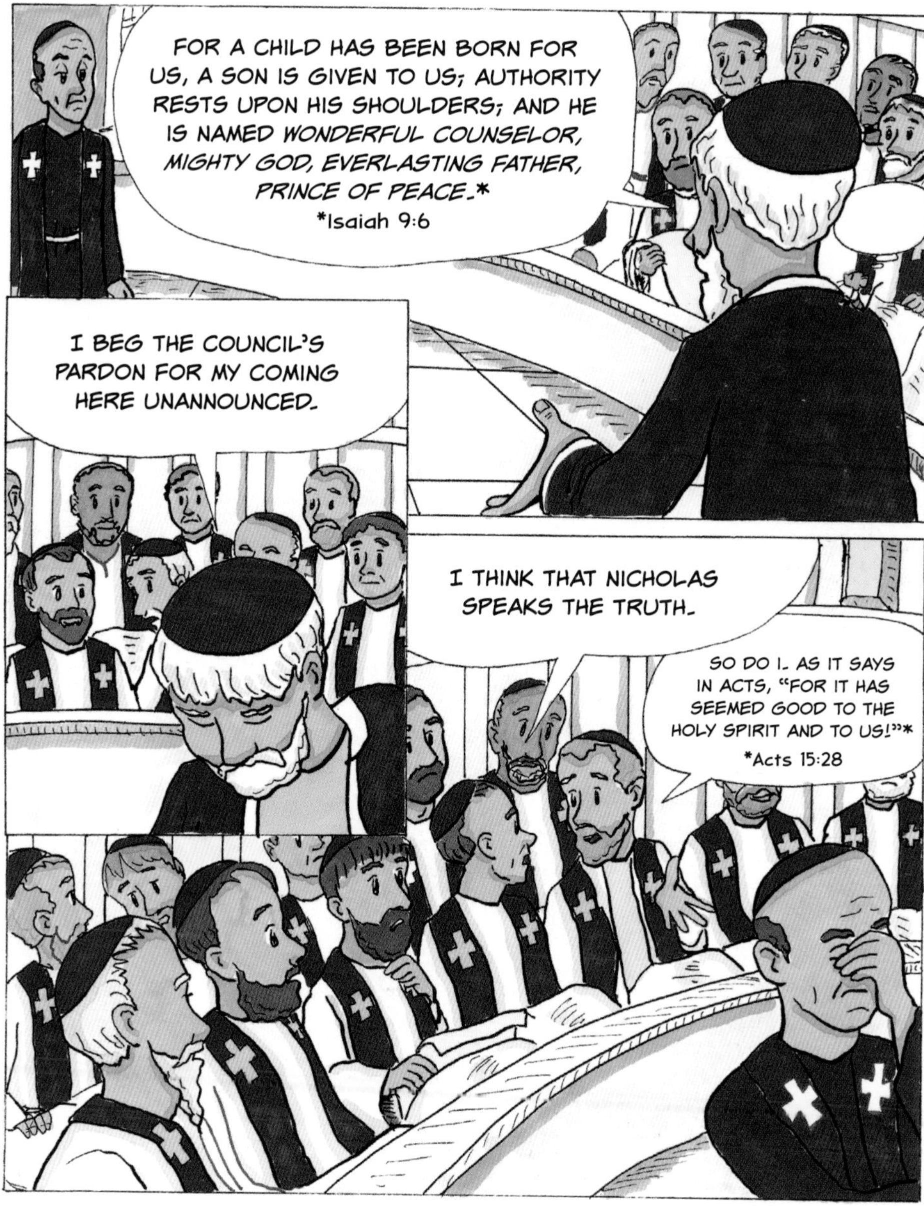
FOR A CHILD HAS BEEN BORN FOR US, A SON IS GIVEN TO US; AUTHORITY RESTS UPON HIS SHOULDERS; AND HE IS NAMED *WONDERFUL COUNSELOR, MIGHTY GOD, EVERLASTING FATHER, PRINCE OF PEACE*.*
*Isaiah 9:6
I BEG THE COUNCIL'S PARDON FOR MY COMING HERE UNANNOUNCED.
I THINK THAT NICHOLAS SPEAKS THE TRUTH.
SO DO I. AS IT SAYS IN ACTS, "FOR IT HAS SEEMED GOOD TO THE HOLY SPIRIT AND TO US!"*
*Acts 15:28

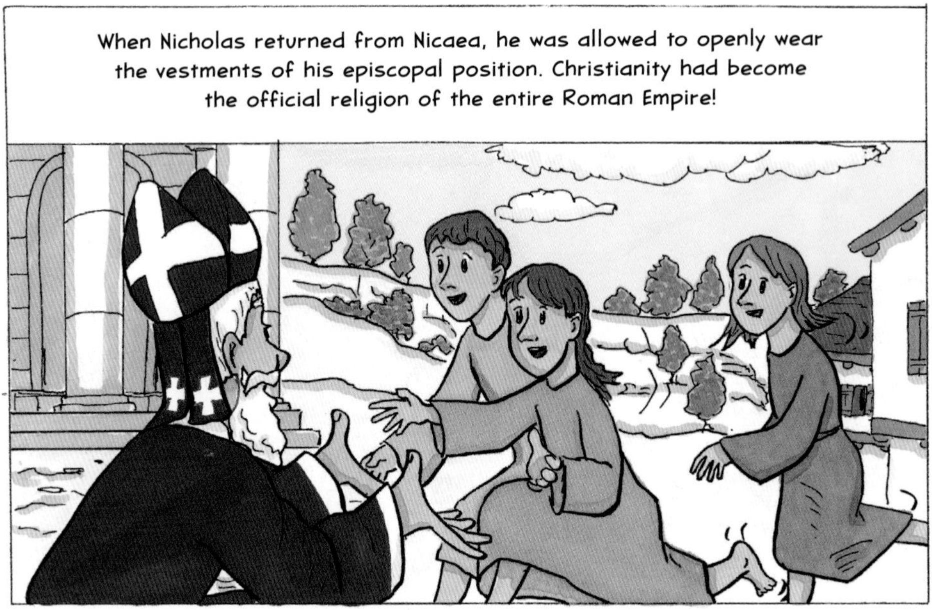
When Nicholas returned from Nicaea, he was allowed to openly wear the vestments of his episcopal position. Christianity had become the official religion of the entire Roman Empire!

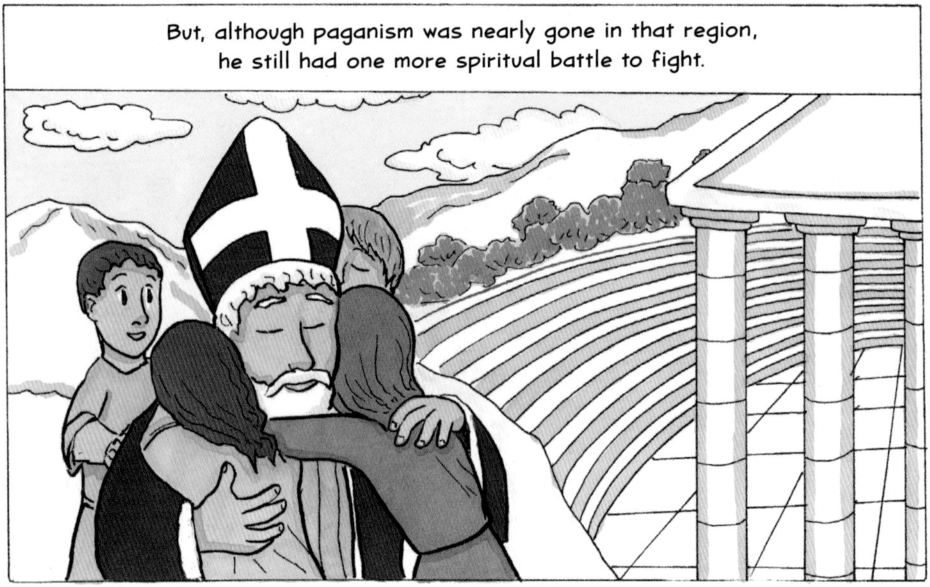
But, although paganism was nearly gone in that region, he still had one more spiritual battle to fight.

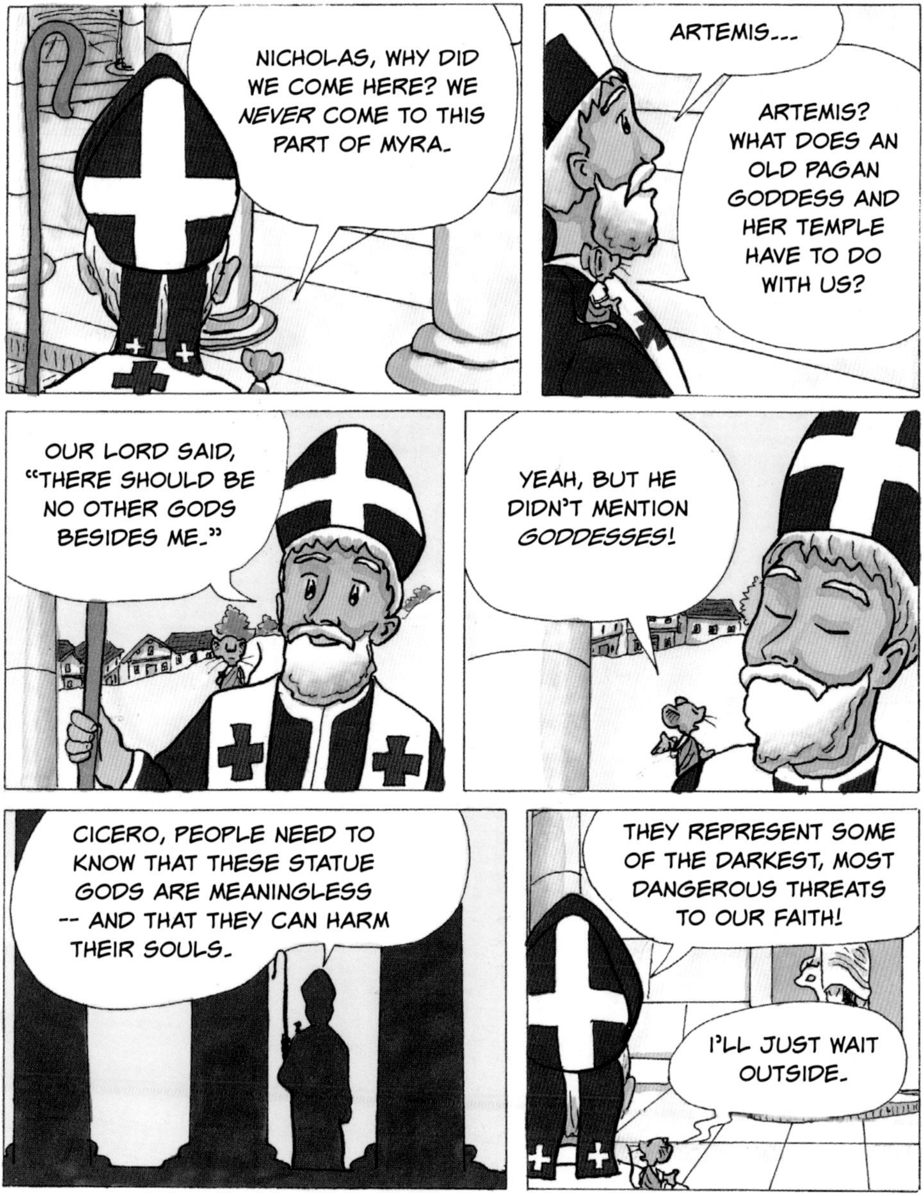
NICHOLAS, WHY DID WE COME HERE? WE *NEVER* COME TO THIS PART OF MYRA.
ARTEMIS...
ARTEMIS? WHAT DOES AN OLD PAGAN GODDESS AND HER TEMPLE HAVE TO DO WITH US?
OUR LORD SAID, "THERE SHOULD BE NO OTHER GODS BESIDES ME."
YEAH, BUT HE DIDN'T MENTION *GODDESSES*!
CICERO, PEOPLE NEED TO KNOW THAT THESE STATUE GODS ARE MEANINGLESS -- AND THAT THEY CAN HARM THEIR SOULS.
THEY REPRESENT SOME OF THE DARKEST, MOST DANGEROUS THREATS TO OUR FAITH!
I'LL JUST WAIT OUTSIDE.

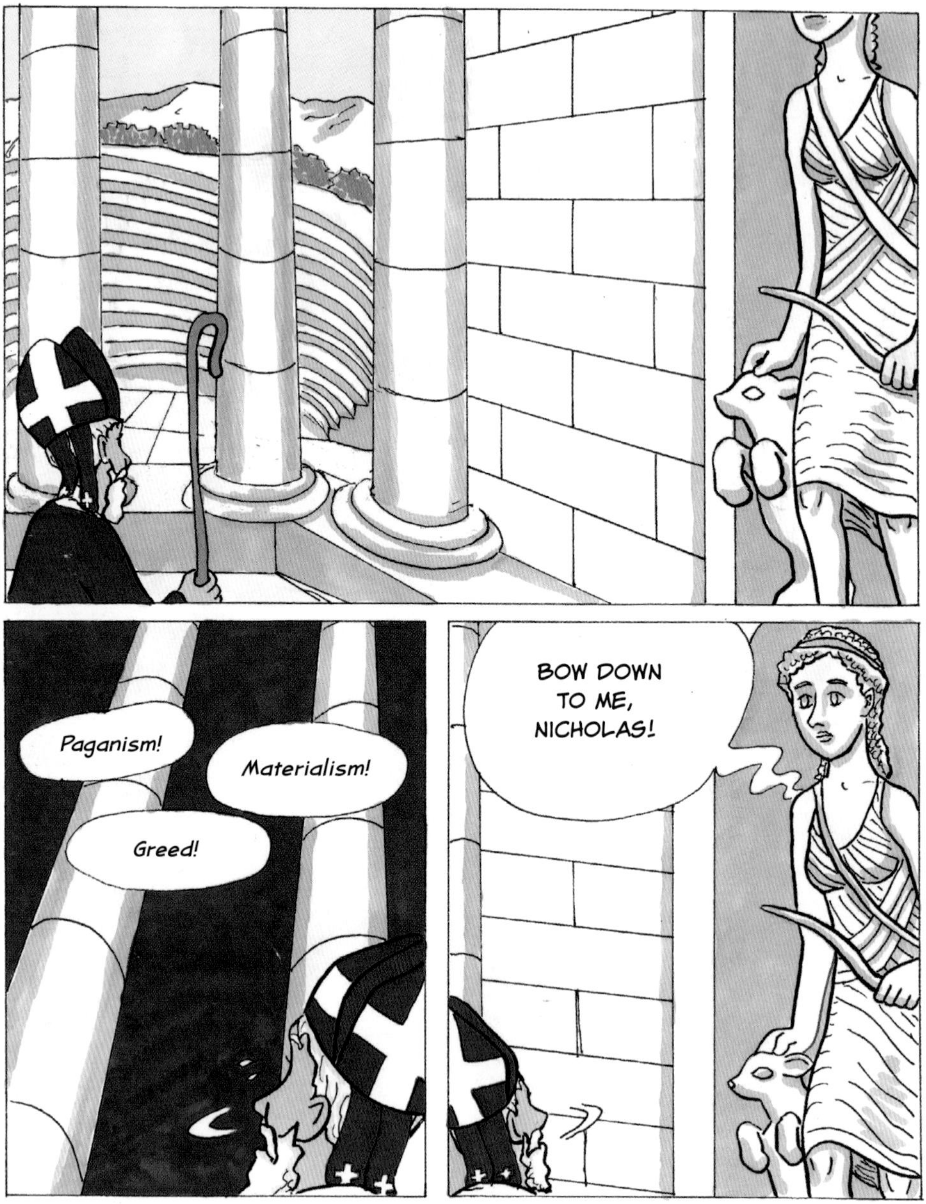
Paganism!
Materialism!
Greed!
BOW DOWN TO ME, NICHOLAS!

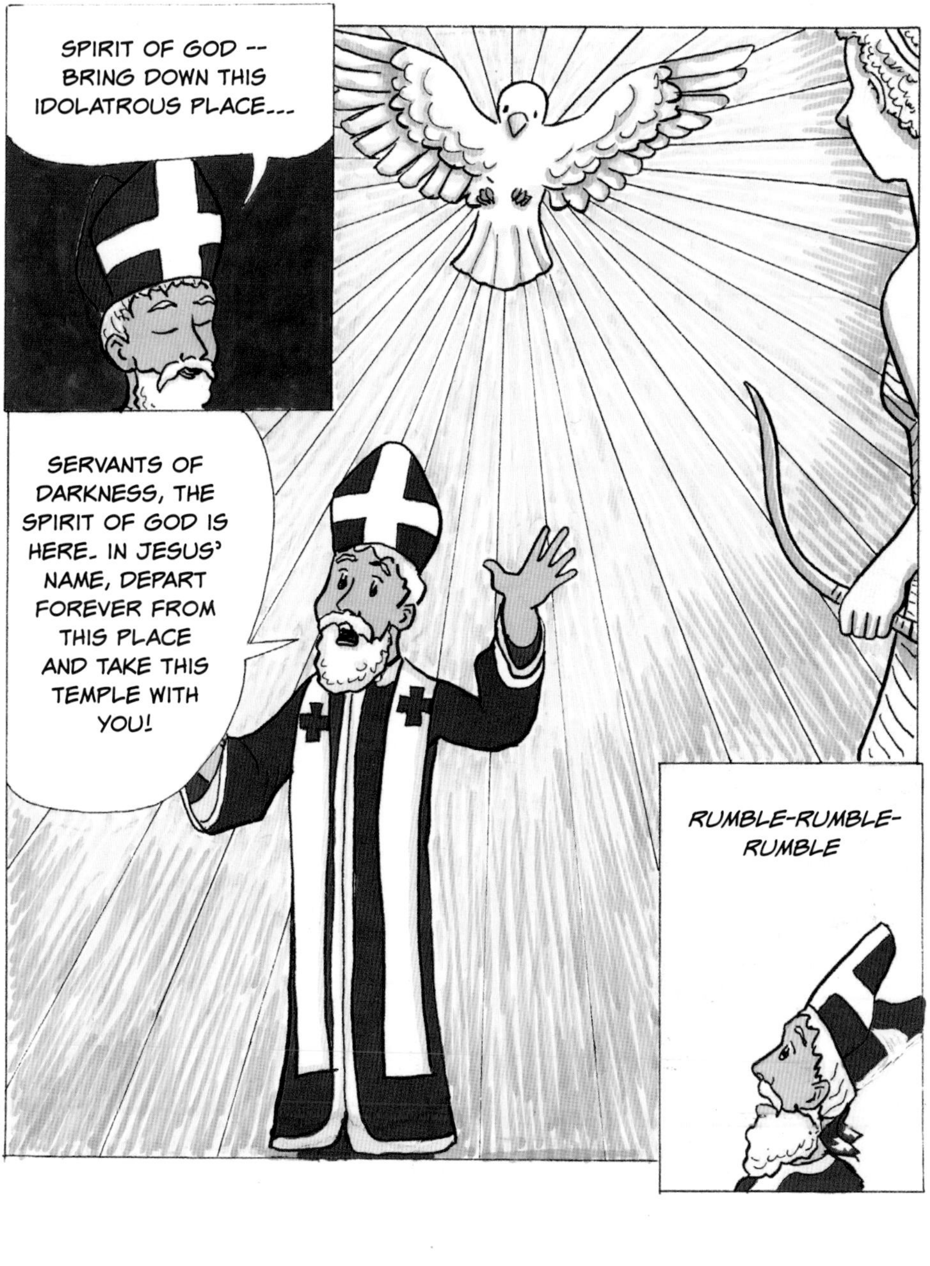
SPIRIT OF GOD -- BRING DOWN THIS IDOLATROUS PLACE...
SERVANTS OF DARKNESS, THE SPIRIT OF GOD IS HERE. IN JESUS' NAME, DEPART FOREVER FROM THIS PLACE AND TAKE THIS TEMPLE WITH YOU!
RUMBLE-RUMBLE-RUMBLE

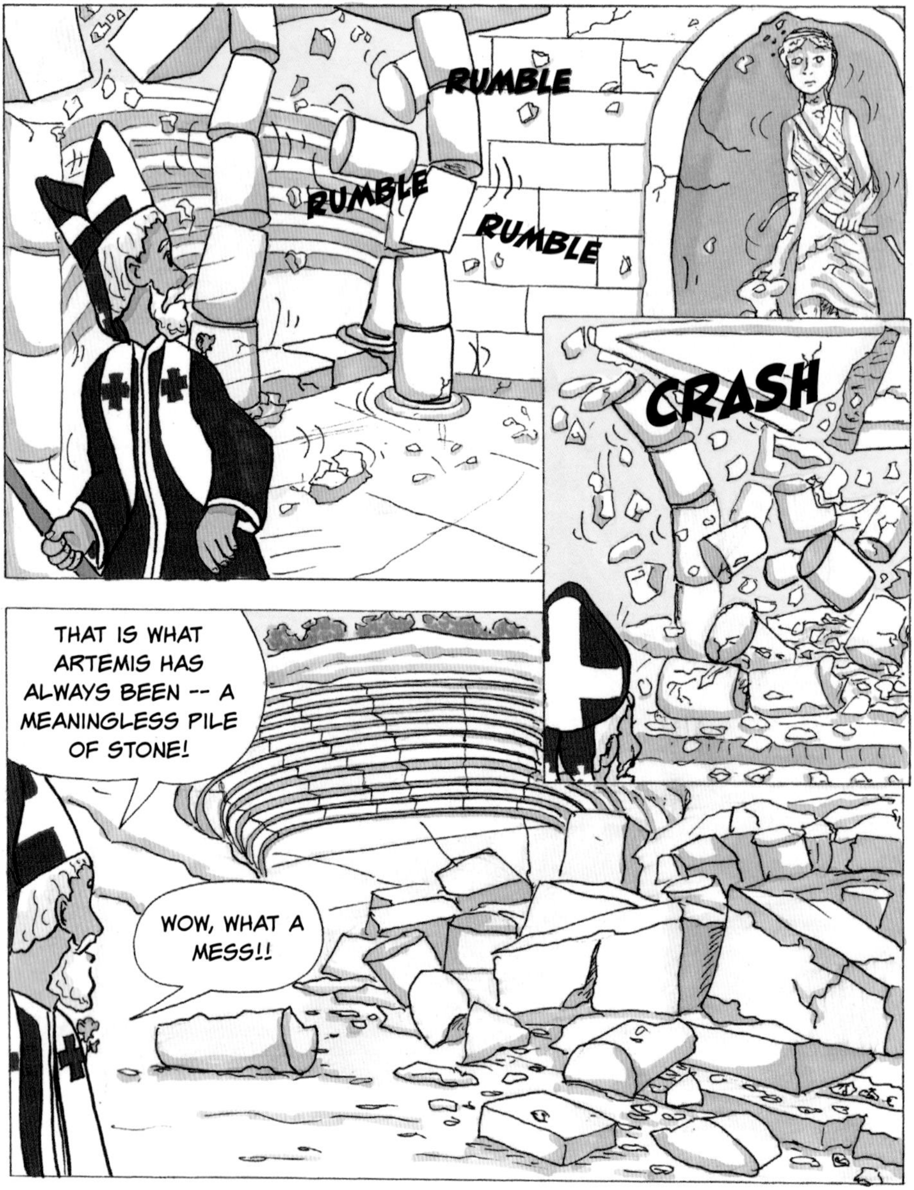
RUMBLE
RUMBLE
RUMBLE
CRASH
THAT IS WHAT ARTEMIS HAS ALWAYS BEEN -- A MEANINGLESS PILE OF STONE!
WOW, WHAT A MESS!!

CHAPTER EIGHT
THE ADVENT OF SANTA CLAUS

Before I formed you in the womb I knew you,
and before you were born I consecrated you;
I appointed you a prophet to the nations.
--JEREMIAH 1:5

MYRA, LYCIA, AD 342

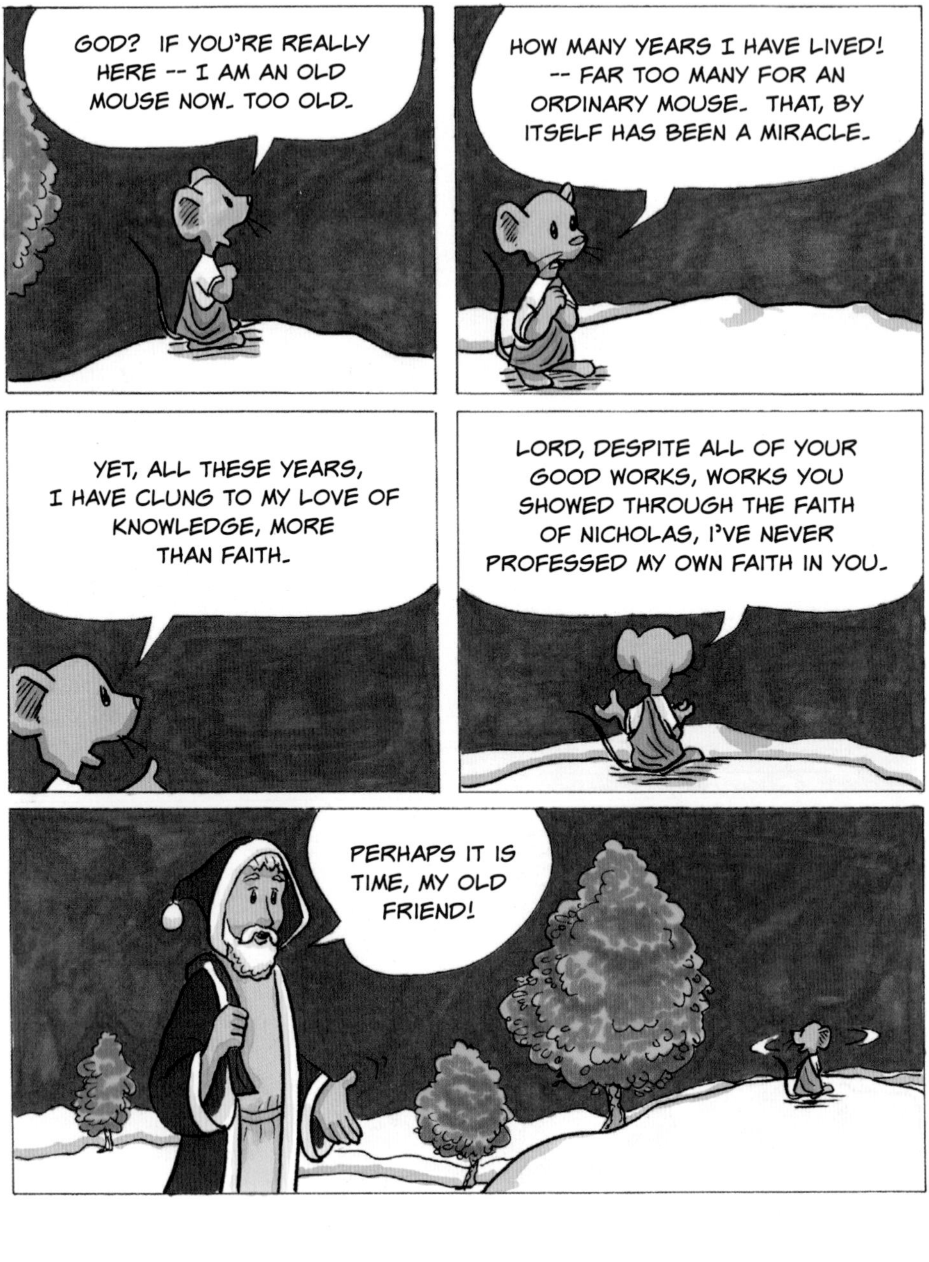
GOD? IF YOU'RE REALLY HERE -- I AM AN OLD MOUSE NOW. TOO OLD.
HOW MANY YEARS I HAVE LIVED! -- FAR TOO MANY FOR AN ORDINARY MOUSE. THAT, BY ITSELF HAS BEEN A MIRACLE.
YET, ALL THESE YEARS, I HAVE CLUNG TO MY LOVE OF KNOWLEDGE, MORE THAN FAITH.
LORD, DESPITE ALL OF YOUR GOOD WORKS, WORKS YOU SHOWED THROUGH THE FAITH OF NICHOLAS, I'VE NEVER PROFESSED MY OWN FAITH IN YOU.
PERHAPS IT IS TIME, MY OLD FRIEND!

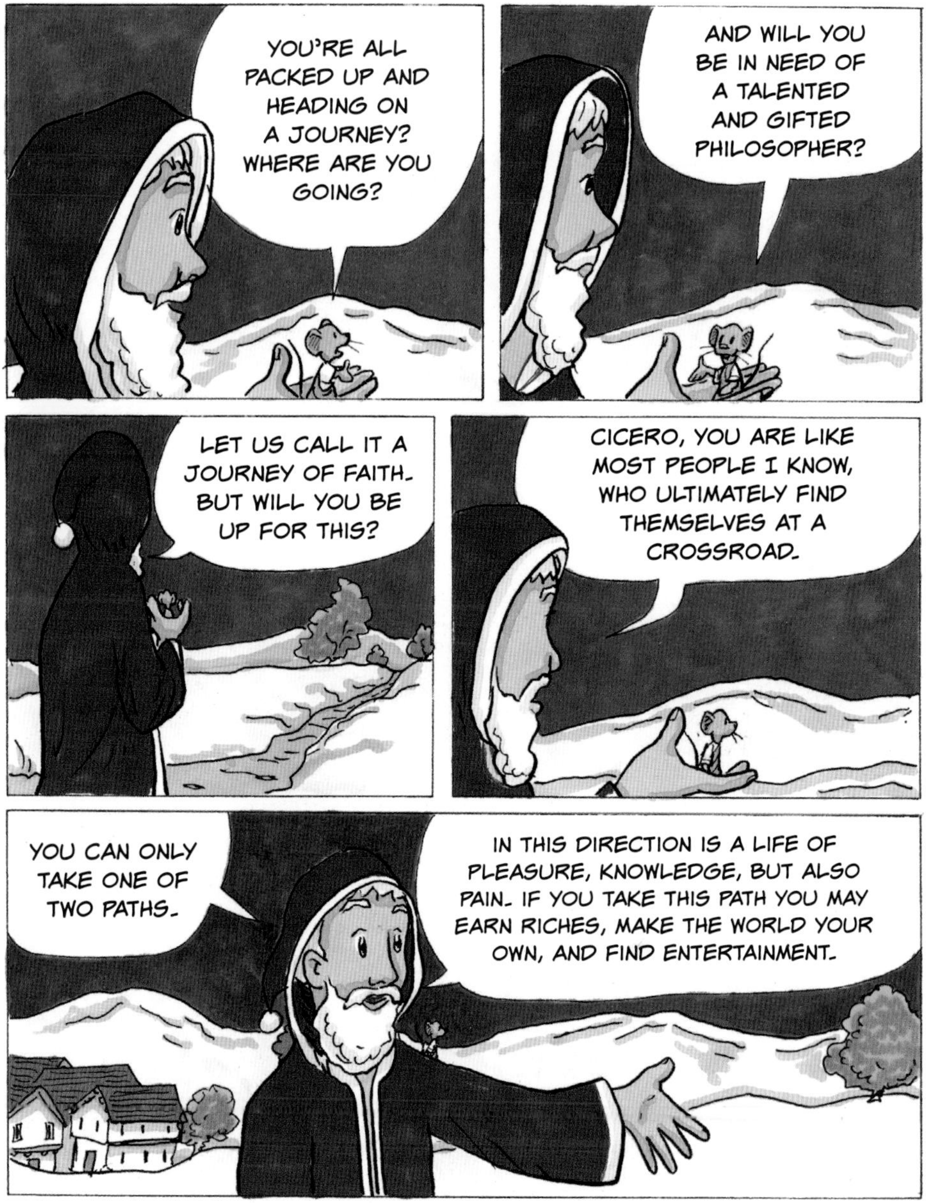
YOU'RE ALL PACKED UP AND HEADING ON A JOURNEY? WHERE ARE YOU GOING?
AND WILL YOU BE IN NEED OF A TALENTED AND GIFTED PHILOSOPHER?
LET US CALL IT A JOURNEY OF FAITH. BUT WILL YOU BE UP FOR THIS?
CICERO, YOU ARE LIKE MOST PEOPLE I KNOW, WHO ULTIMATELY FIND THEMSELVES AT A CROSSROAD.
YOU CAN ONLY TAKE ONE OF TWO PATHS.
IN THIS DIRECTION IS A LIFE OF PLEASURE, KNOWLEDGE, BUT ALSO PAIN. IF YOU TAKE THIS PATH YOU MAY EARN RICHES, MAKE THE WORLD YOUR OWN, AND FIND ENTERTAINMENT.

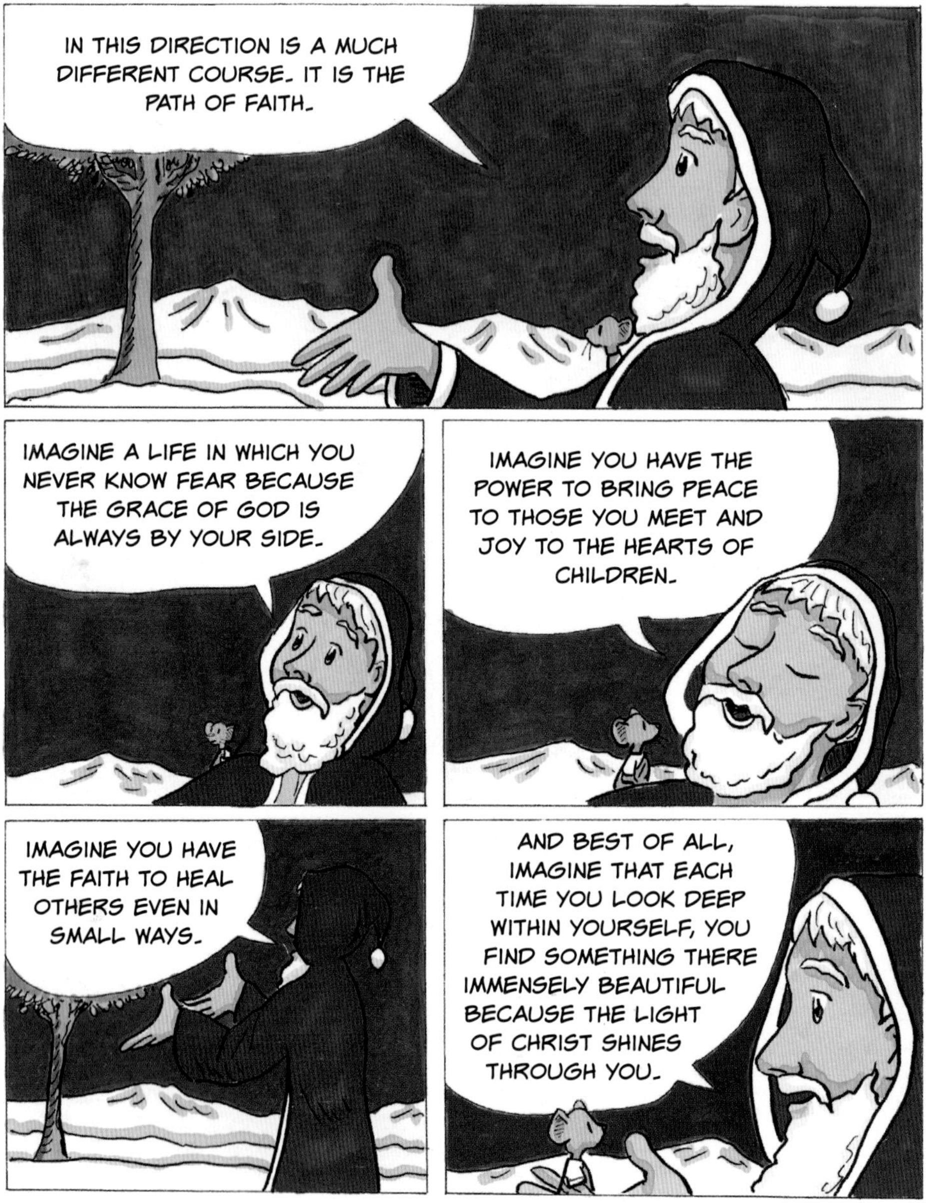
IN THIS DIRECTION IS A MUCH DIFFERENT COURSE. IT IS THE PATH OF FAITH.
IMAGINE A LIFE IN WHICH YOU NEVER KNOW FEAR BECAUSE THE GRACE OF GOD IS ALWAYS BY YOUR SIDE.
IMAGINE YOU HAVE THE POWER TO BRING PEACE TO THOSE YOU MEET AND JOY TO THE HEARTS OF CHILDREN.
IMAGINE YOU HAVE THE FAITH TO HEAL OTHERS EVEN IN SMALL WAYS.
AND BEST OF ALL, IMAGINE THAT EACH TIME YOU LOOK DEEP WITHIN YOURSELF, YOU FIND SOMETHING THERE IMMENSELY BEAUTIFUL BECAUSE THE LIGHT OF CHRIST SHINES THROUGH YOU.

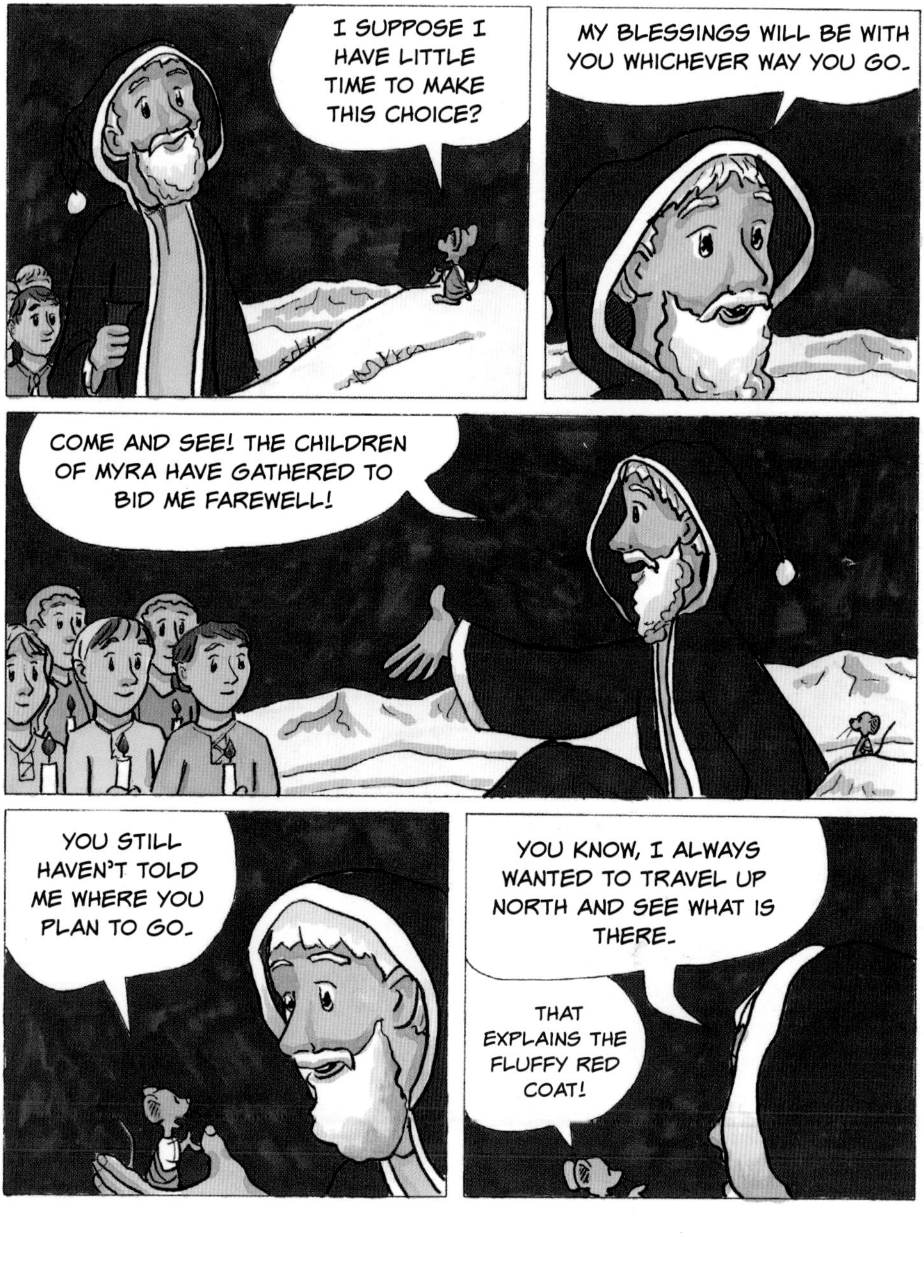

I SUPPOSE I HAVE LITTLE TIME TO MAKE THIS CHOICE?
MY BLESSINGS WILL BE WITH YOU WHICHEVER WAY YOU GO.
COME AND SEE! THE CHILDREN OF MYRA HAVE GATHERED TO BID ME FAREWELL!
YOU STILL HAVEN'T TOLD ME WHERE YOU PLAN TO GO.
YOU KNOW, I ALWAYS WANTED TO TRAVEL UP NORTH AND SEE WHAT IS THERE.
THAT EXPLAINS THE FLUFFY RED COAT!

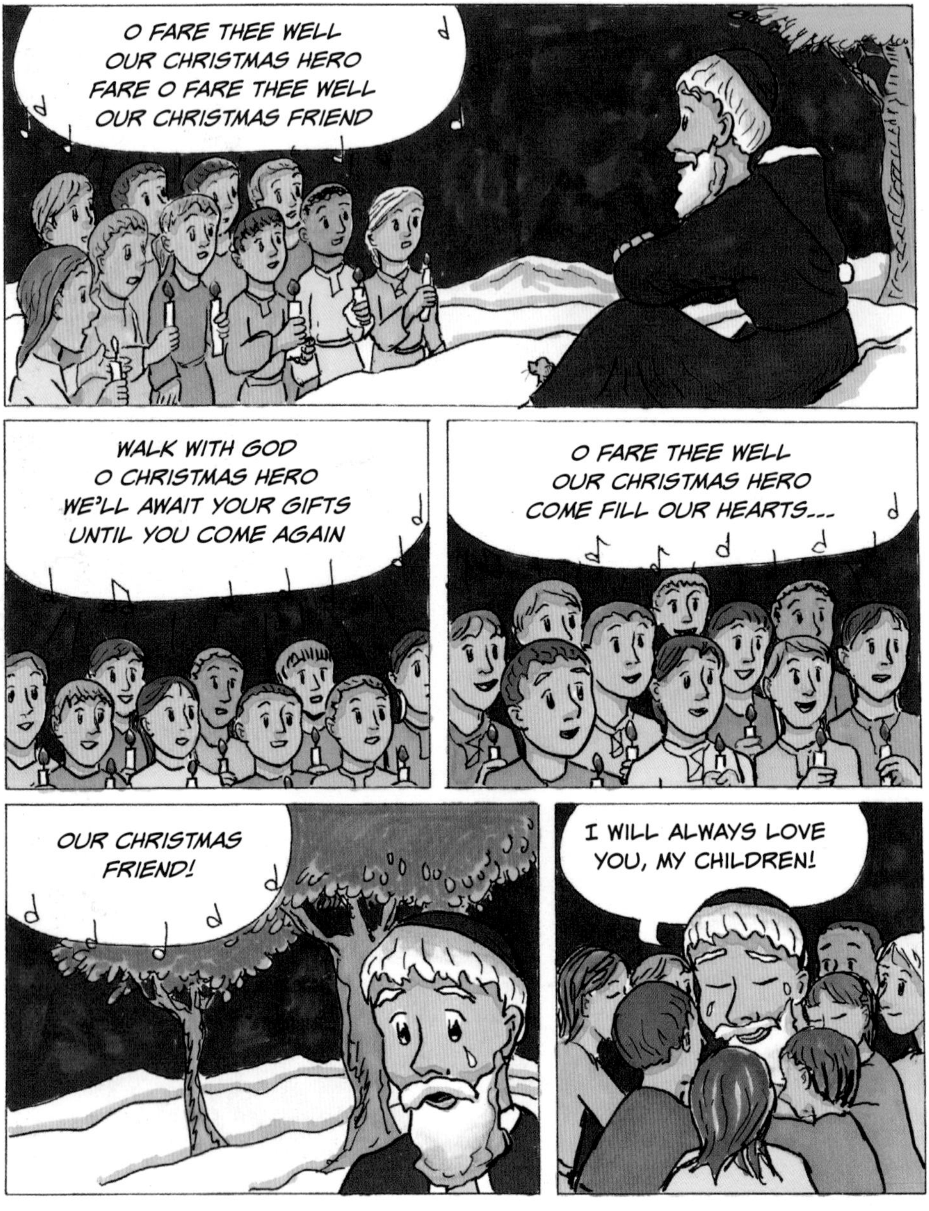
O FARE THEE WELL OUR CHRISTMAS HERO FARE O FARE THEE WELL OUR CHRISTMAS FRIEND
WALK WITH GOD O CHRISTMAS HERO WE'LL AWAIT YOUR GIFTS UNTIL YOU COME AGAIN
O FARE THEE WELL OUR CHRISTMAS HERO COME FILL OUR HEARTS...
OUR CHRISTMAS FRIEND!
I WILL ALWAYS LOVE YOU, MY CHILDREN!

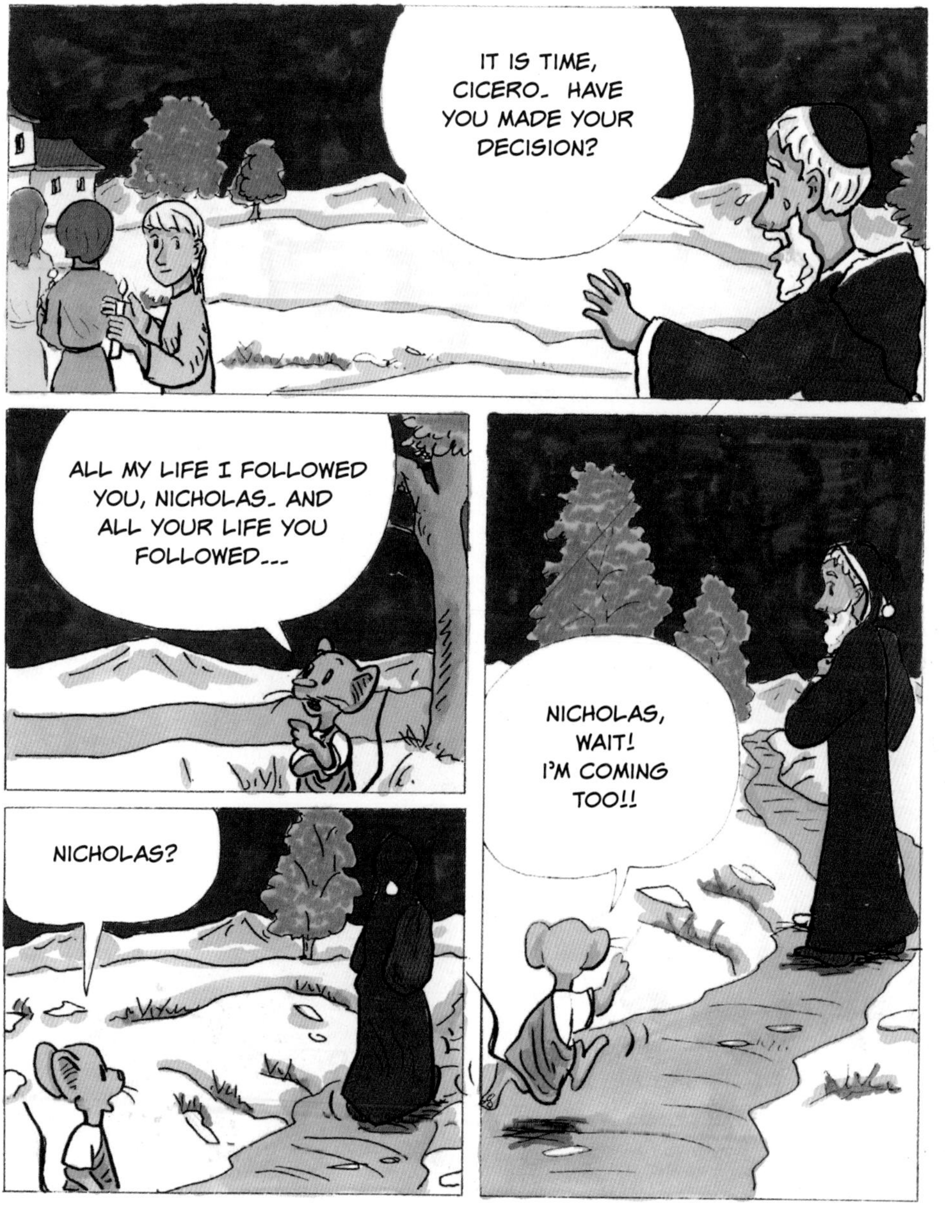
IT IS TIME, CICERO. HAVE YOU MADE YOUR DECISION?
ALL MY LIFE I FOLLOWED YOU, NICHOLAS. AND ALL YOUR LIFE YOU FOLLOWED...
NICHOLAS?
NICHOLAS, WAIT! I'M COMING TOO!!

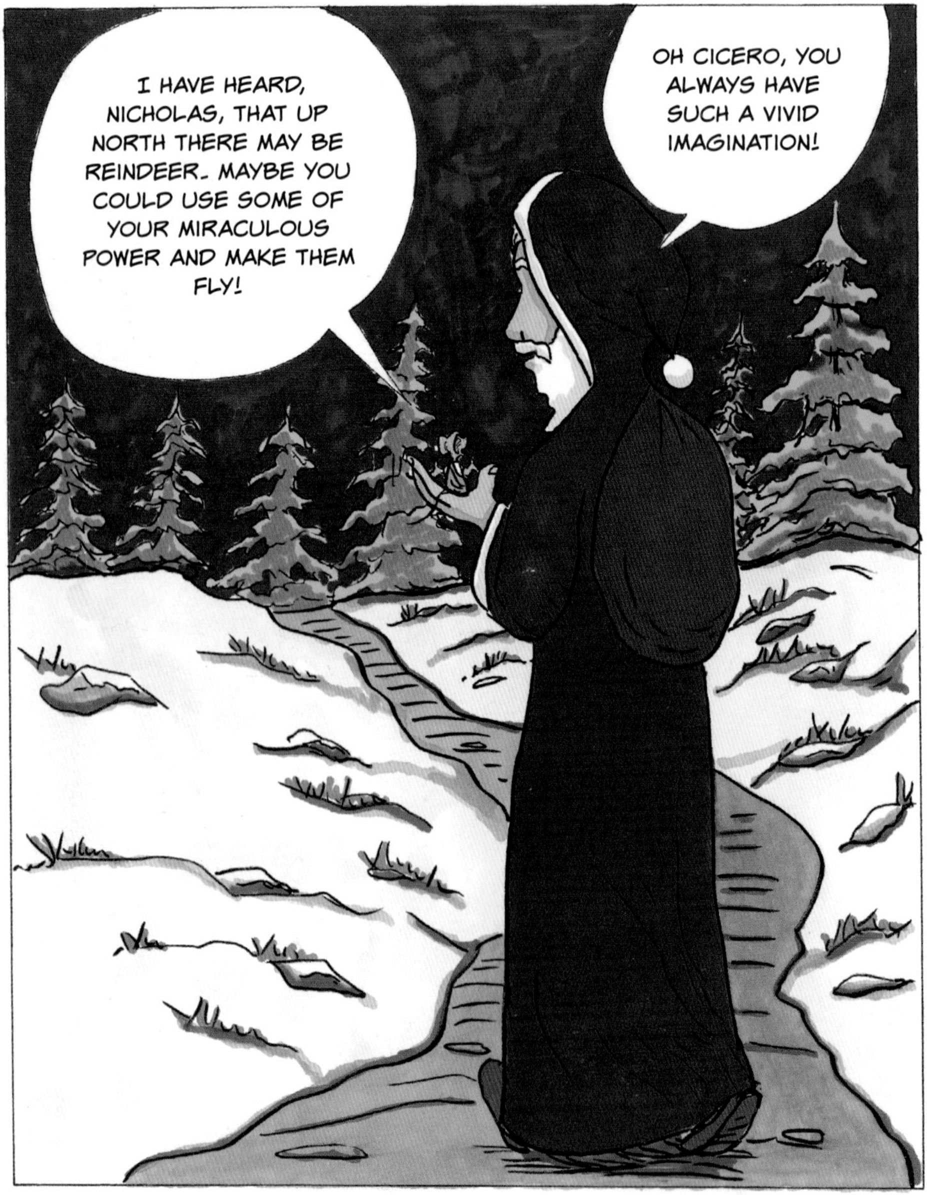
I HAVE HEARD, NICHOLAS, THAT UP NORTH THERE MAY BE REINDEER. MAYBE YOU COULD USE SOME OF YOUR MIRACULOUS POWER AND MAKE THEM FLY!
OH CICERO, YOU ALWAYS HAVE SUCH A VIVID IMAGINATION!

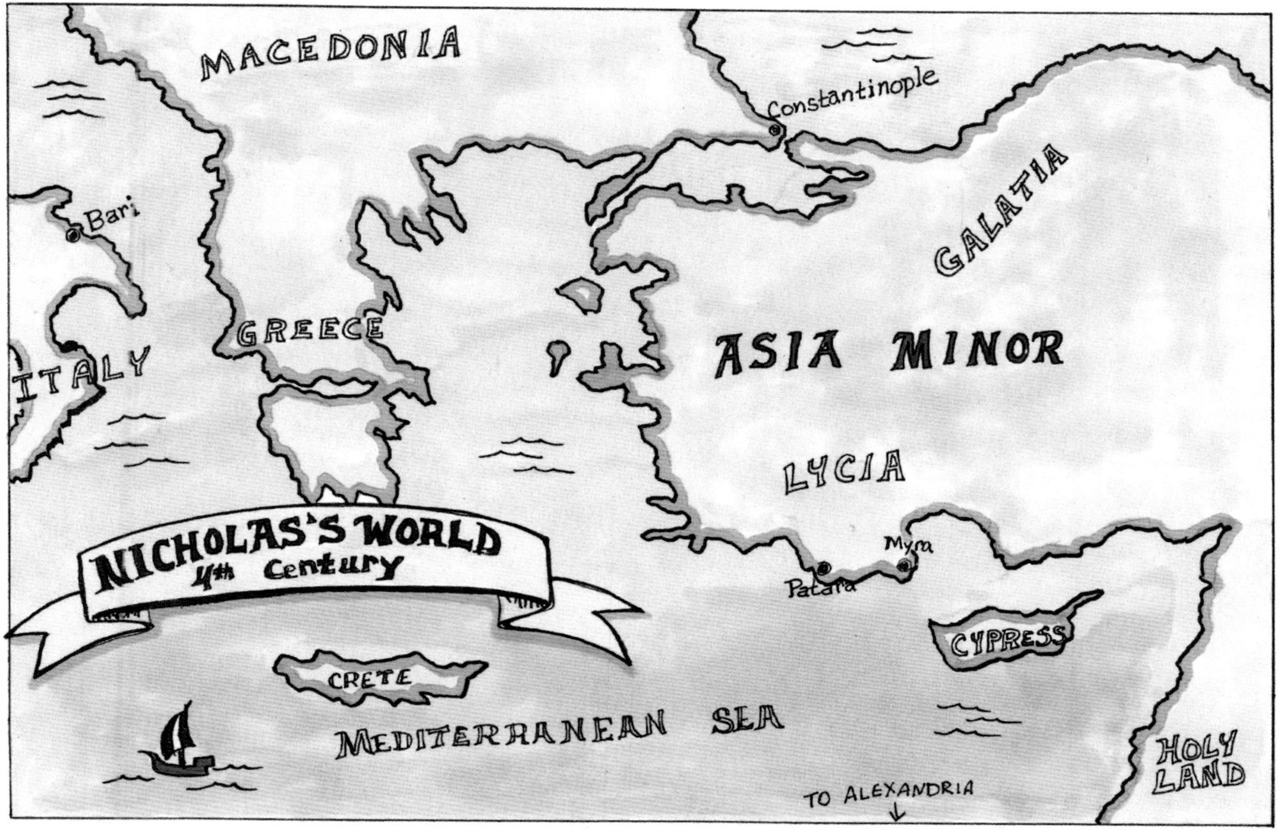
NICHOLAS'S WORLD
4th Century
MACEDONIA
Constantinople
GALATIA
Bari
ITALY
GREECE
ASIA MINOR
LYCIA
Patara
Myra
CYPRESS
CRETE
MEDITERRANEAN SEA
HOLY LAND
TO ALEXANDRIA

ABOUT PARACLETE PRESS

WHO WE ARE

Paraclete Press is a publisher of books, recordings, and DVDs on Christian spirituality. Our publishing represents a full expression of Christian belief and practice—from Catholic to Evangelical, from Protestant to Orthodox.

We are the publishing arm of the Community of Jesus, an ecumenical monastic community in the Benedictine tradition. As such, we are uniquely positioned in the marketplace without connection to a large corporation and with informal relationships to many branches and denominations of faith.

WHAT WE ARE DOING

Books Paraclete publishes books that show the richness and depth of what it means to be Christian. Although Benedictine spirituality is at the heart of all that we do, we publish books that reflect the Christian experience across many cultures, time periods, and houses of worship. We publish books that nourish the vibrant life of the church and its people—books about spiritual practice, formation, history, ideas, and customs.

We have several different series, including the best-selling Paraclete Essentials and Paraclete Giants series of classic texts in contemporary English; Voices from the Monastery—men and women monastics writing about living a spiritual life today; award-winning poetry; best-selling gift books for children on the occasions of baptism and first communion; and the Active Prayer Series that brings creativity and liveliness to any life of prayer.

Recordings From Gregorian chant to contemporary American choral works, our music recordings celebrate sacred choral music through the centuries. Paraclete distributes the recordings of the internationally acclaimed choir Gloriæ Dei Cantores, praised for their "rapt and fathomless spiritual intensity" by *American Record Guide*, and the Gloriæ Dei Cantores Schola, which specializes in the study and performance of Gregorian chant. Paraclete is also the exclusive North American distributor of the recordings of the Monastic Choir of St. Peter's Abbey in Solesmes, France, long considered to be a leading authority on Gregorian chant.

Videos Our videos offer spiritual help, healing, and biblical guidance for life issues: grief and loss, marriage, forgiveness, anger management, facing death, and spiritual formation.

Learn more about us at our website:
www.paracletepress.com, or call us toll-free at 1-800-451-5006.

SCAN
TO
READ
MORE

ALSO AVAILABLE FROM PARACLETE PRESS

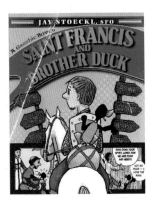

SAINT FRANCIS AND BROTHER DUCK
A Graphic Novel

Jay Stoeckl, OFS

See Saint Francis come to life as never before in this colorful graphic novel set in the hill-towns of Italy. Francis saves the life of an innocent duck, the only fictitious character in the story, and the two become each other's inspiration. As they grow in faith and friendship, Francis recognizes in Brother Duck everything that he desires in living the life of the gospel: humility, poverty, and a childlike imagination. Based on the real-life events of Francis of Assisi from his youthful desires to become a great knight to the call of God to become a Knight of Christ. Readers of all ages will enjoy the humor and ageless wisdom of this famous story, vividly retold, scene-by-scene.

ISBN: 978-1-61261-159-4 • 140 pages • $15.99, Paperback

Available from most booksellers or through Paraclete Press
www.paracletepress.com   1-800-451-5006